MW00896292

Two Souls, Forever One

By Cameron De Cessna
Copyright 2019

This book is a work of fiction. Names, characters, places, and incidents are the products of the author's imagination or are used fictitiously. Any resemblance to actual events, locales, or persons, living or dead, is entirely coincidental.

Two Souls, Forever One

By Cameron De Cessna
Copyright 2019

Chapter 1
Moving In

On Thursday, August 7, 1980, Christopher Walker backed a small U-Haul trailer, packed with much of his worldly goods, into his designated parking slot at Whisperwind Apartments in Jacksonville, Florida. He was driving his 1975, Buick Century station wagon. It, like the U-Haul, was packed to the roof with clothing, books, kitchenware, and pieces of furniture his parents had given him for his new home. Chris was twenty-two and had recently earned a Bachelor of Science in Education degree from the University of Florida. Although trained to teach science in a classroom setting if necessary, Chris's true career desire had been to work at a museum as a curator or museum instructor. His years of study and excellent grades at the university had paid off; he was about to embark on that very career, having landed a curator position at a major city museum.

During his last two years at university, he'd worked part-time as a student instructor for the Florida State Museum located on the university campus in Gainesville. His background and expertise teaching geology and astronomy for family groups and museum classes had earned the respect of the museum's administrators and educators. Unfortunately, there were no full-time museum positions available at the time he received his degree. Chris realized he might be forced to look elsewhere for employment even if it meant taking a teaching job at a local middle school or senior high until something opened up at a museum somewhere.

During the summer of 1980, after several months of futile searching for a science teaching job at local schools, Chris was pleased to hear of an opening at the Jacksonville Science Museum. His supervisor at the Florida State Museum had spotted an ad for a Physical Science

Curator in a professional journal and called Chris right away, suggesting he should interview for the job. With his supervisor's recommendation and after a successful interview, Chris had been offered the position. He would be paid as a Duval County teacher by the local school board as they were responsible for funding five teaching and curatorial positions at the institution. His pay would be roughly twenty-four thousand dollars per year for the twelve-month position and in 1980, which was an excellent starting salary for a newly graduated educator in a Florida city.

Chris had driven the ninety-odd miles from his family's home to Jacksonville a few days before and rented apartment 70-F located along the back side of the sprawling, three hundred unit complex. He preferred the rear location as it faced out upon the back acres of an elementary school's recreation yard. Numerous live oak trees and tall slash pines made the view nearly park-like from his perspective. An eight-foot-high chain link fence separated the apartment's perimeter road from the school property. His was a ground floor unit with a nice-sized kitchen, comfortable bedroom, bath and a large living room that opened via a sliding glass door onto a small, screen-enclosed, private patio. One of three swimming pools was nearby in the central portion of the apartment complex.

After uncoupling the trailer and parking his station wagon nearby, Chris started unloading his belongings after unlocking the apartment and starting the air conditioner. Rent was $210.00 a month, easily affordable on his new salary. Fortunately, he'd saved enough money over the past few months to cover beginning expenses. His parents, since he was an only child, had also pledged their support, if needed, until he could earn his first check.

This would be Chris's first time on his own and he looked forward to the freedom and challenge of independent living and his first full-time job. After spending nearly two hours unloading, he locked the apartment and towed the trailer to a nearby U-Haul dealership for drop off and a refund of his deposit. It was late afternoon, so he stopped at a McDonald's take-out window on the way back and picked up an early supper. This part of Jacksonville, known as San Jose, was a pleasant place to live with modern buildings, clean streets and beautifully tended parks and public spaces. His apartment was on Power's Avenue just a mile south of University Boulevard. The museum where he would be working was near the center of Jacksonville, on the south bank of the St. Johns River just eleven miles north of Chris's new home.

After returning from McDonald's and arriving back at his apartment he was hailed by a young couple as he unlocked his apartment door.

"New neighbor?" the young man asked as he smiled and then introduced his wife as Laurie and himself as Al Brock. "We live upstairs above your unit. Welcome to the neighborhood."

"Thanks, it's a pleasure to meet you. I'm Chris Walker." He extended his arm and shook hands with the smiling couple. "I just moved north from a small town near Gainesville."

"Where will you be working?" the man asked.

I'm the new Physical Science Curator at the Museum of Science."

Al said, "That sounds interesting. I'm an agent with Prudential Insurance and Laurie is a librarian at Wolfson High School, just north along Power's Avenue. We've lived here at Whisperwind for a year and a half and are pretty happy with the location."

"I looked around and these apartments seemed pretty nice for the price."

Laurie nodded and said, "It's quiet and safe. The management is getting ready to add a gatehouse soon and that'll make it even more secure." She glanced at Chris's left hand before asking, "Are you married or single?"

"Still single." Chris shrugged his shoulders resignedly, "I just graduated from the University of Florida a few months ago, in March and was lucky enough to learn of a museum position not too far from my family home."

"I would imagine museum work would be very interesting and fun," Laurie said with a smile.

"It's exactly what I'd hoped to do rather than teach in a classroom setting. I'm a certified teacher and actually work for Duval County Schools same as you, Mrs. Brock."

"Please feel free to use our first names, Chris." Al said, "We're Al and Laurie and hate formality. Again, welcome."

"Thanks." Chris raised the McDonald's bag and shook it a bit. "Well, I better get inside and eat a bite. Moving has me pretty hungry and I didn't feel like digging through the boxes this evening and fixing a meal. It was easier to visit the golden arches. I look forward to seeing you again and thanks for the welcome."

Chris went inside and spread out his meal on the small, circular dining room table that was provided as part of the limited furnishings with the unit. A loveseat sofa, two armchairs and an adjustable bed frame in the bedroom along with a chest of drawers were all that came as part of the deal. Chris had brought along his own set of queen-sized box springs and mattress as well as other odds and ends of furniture his parents had given him.

Chris smiled and shook his head a bit as he speculated on Laurie's question about whether he was married or single. *I'm definitely single and will no doubt stay that way for some time to come,* Chris thought with an audible sigh. *Marriage is nowhere in* my *future.*

As he ate in silence, beginning to feel slightly lonely and depressed, Chris reflected on his teen years and early adulthood. While seemingly outgoing and personable to others around him, he was, in reality, a very private and introverted young man who had suffered many years of quiet despair, shame, guilt, and unhappiness. Since the age of twelve, Chris realized he was different from his peers and by the time he was fourteen, he knew he wouldn't change. Chris was gay.

Junior and senior high school had been exceptionally difficult, for he was unable to adjust to and accept his sexual preference, or find others like himself with whom to socialize comfortably. He lived in constant fear that somehow his mom and dad would discover his shameful secret and stop loving him. He suffered nightmares occasionally in which he was discovered by his parents while kissing, or doing something even more shameful and intimate with another boy or man.

His only outlet had been fantasies and daydreams about falling in love with another teenager like himself, someone who he could be honest with and love intimately and completely. But the risk while living at home was simply too great and Chris was never able to take even a small step toward exploring his nature.

There were a few boys his age during his junior and senior high years that he felt might be gay, but he had no idea how to break the ice and make the first move toward friendship, let alone explore a more intimate relationship. Even the few times he'd been approached by another gay youth, he was too awkward and too much a coward to open up, act upon his urges and perhaps be himself for once.

He'd thought that perhaps when he started college he might feel more relaxed on campus and able to find same-sex companionship, but once again, as opportunities presented themselves, he backed away, burning one bridge after another that might have helped him navigate the labyrinth of his fears and insecurities. After each failed encounter with a possible gay companion, he berated himself for being such a coward and missing the very opportunity he was always seeking in his day and nighttime dreams. Daydreaming was such a safe and pleasant pastime. When it came to matters of the heart, Chris was his own worst enemy.

What am I so damned afraid of, he mused while sitting alone in his new apartment, picking at his meal in solitude and dissecting his shortcomings. *Why can't I find some way to be happy?* In every other aspect of his life, he was enjoying success. He'd graduated with honors, achieved his career goal and now looked forward to an exciting, challenging job in the very field he'd trained for. Here he sat in the first home of his own, but what was it worth if he was still terribly and completely alone with no one else with whom he might share his life and success. Even the thoughts of eating alone every night caused his meal to suddenly lose its flavor. His dinner suddenly tasted like nothing at all in his mouth. His chest heaved with a heartbreaking sob and tears began to flow down his cheeks.

He had felt depression and despair before, but somehow, here, on the eve of his success; it felt more painful than ever before. *This all has to end,* he told himself. *I can't stand it any longer. This pain has to stop, or I might as well give in and just die because I can't live this way.* His mind turned to the spiritual as he begged, *God! Please help me. Please end the loneliness, or go ahead and end me.*

He couldn't eat the rest of his meal and tossed the remainder of the Big Mac and now cold fries into the garbage disposal turned on the water tap and threw the switch. With a sigh, he went into the bathroom and started undressing. He was tired from the unpacking and rigors of moving and studied his reflection in the bathroom mirror as he removed his tee shirt, kicked off his shoes, stepped out of his jeans and removed his briefs and socks. Naked and exposed, he considered the young man looking back from the glass. He was not unattractive with light brown hair, hazel eyes and a slim, but healthy build. He had been told by his family and casual friends that he was handsome, but somehow never quite believed them, thinking they only said such things to be nice. Sexually he was generously endowed even though, for some reason, he doubted he might be appealing to another gay man.

Chris stepped into the bathtub and drew shut the glass-walled shower door. Adjusting the water temperature to a degree of heat that was barely tolerable, he threw the lever that diverted the flow to the shower head and stepped into the stinging, hot spray. The heat felt good and helped to relax his tight muscles and ease some of the emotional tension that had accumulated this afternoon. Even though it was barely six o'clock, he was considering an early bedtime. *I'm just tired from the move,* he thought. *I'll be all right tomorrow after a good night's sleep. I'll get over this and once I get to work at the museum, things will be better.* He knew, however, that he was only kidding himself. He'd been down this path a hundred times.

After the shower, he dried himself and padded naked into the bedroom where he located a box labeled linens. He opened it and made his bed with clean sheets and a light spread. He seldom slept in pajamas or anything besides briefs unless it was cold weather. Here, in his air-conditioned apartment, he simply crawled under the sheet and light spread while wearing nothing at all. He was alone and there was no one who might know or care otherwise, so he enjoyed the comfort and freedom of sleeping nude. Fatigue claimed him quickly and by seven, he was sound asleep.

It was sometime well after midnight when he awoke to find he was not alone in the bed. He was lying on his side and felt the warm touch of another's hand on his chest and the warmth of a body curled against his back. He was startled at first, but the hand was so comforting and reassuring. Whoever it was, slowly stroked his chest and snuggled even closer against him. He could feel the hardness of another man pressing between his thighs, moving occasionally and probing between his legs. The room was utterly dark and though he knew he should be frightened, he wasn't. The warmth and comfort of human contact somehow reassured and excited him. He could feel his body responding to the touch and he felt himself growing painfully hard and in need of release.

The arm, so lovingly draped over him, was gentle and comforting. There was love in that touch --- so much love. Whoever it was, was nuzzling against the back of his neck, kissing him occasionally and nibbling at his hair. His mysterious lover knew *exactly* what to do and how to touch him to give him maximum pleasure. He reached down and felt between his legs for the other's hardness and found it warm and wet and oh so satisfying.

Whatever is happening let it never end. Chris felt the other's hand moving downward along his lower chest, exploring his navel and ruffling through his pubic hair. It stroked him there momentarily before slowly moving up and over his wet, slippery hardness, squeezing and kneading his manhood until suddenly he could hold back no longer. His inner force gave way and he felt waves of unbelievable pleasure as again and again his body released its essence. He cried out, "Please, don't stop; don't stop!"

Chris awoke to the sound of his own pleading voice as his thoughts cleared and he realized what had happened. He was still grasping himself as the last spasm of his ejaculation ended. His hands were wet with his emission and the sheets fouled with the results of his vivid dream. Still somewhat confused, he groped for the nightstand and switched on a small lamp. He turned and looked behind himself, still half expecting to find his mysterious lover. It had been a dream of course. He closed his eyes and tears squeezed from beneath his lids.

He'd had wet dreams before, but never one in which he had actually masturbated in his sleep. This was new and rather frightening. The dream had been more vivid than anything he'd ever experienced. He had *felt* someone against him; *felt* the warmth and the movement and the *love*. Ashamed and angry with himself he tossed the top sheet to the side and saw that he had indeed ejaculated all over the clean bottom sheet.

"Shit!" he said aloud. Wiping his hands on the already soiled linens he sat up and rolled out of bed and began to strip the sheets before the moisture had a chance to soak through to the mattress pad beneath. Angry with himself, he rolled the sheets into a ball and flung them into one corner of the room as he thought, *I am so totally fucked up!* He pulled another set of clean sheets from the linen box and made the bed up once more. As he worked he found himself beginning to cry uncontrollably. *Why does it always have to be a dream? Why can't I find someone real to love me and allow me to love him? Why am I so damned afraid to let myself be who I am?* "I wish sometimes I'd never been born." These last few words were spoken aloud as he sat on the edge of the bed and cried for nearly ten minutes, burying his face in his hands.

Once under control, Chris slipped between the fresh sheets and soon fell asleep once more. This time his rest was unbroken and he awoke a few minutes after seven as indirect morning sunlight filtered through the bedroom window curtains. It was Friday, August 8, and he still had several days off before he was scheduled to begin his new job on Tuesday. That would give him plenty of time to unpack his belongings and set his new home in order.

First things first. After getting dressed, Chris gathered his soiled clothing including the sheets from the previous night and after digging through boxes until he located his laundry detergent, bleach, and fabric softener, he set off for the nearest of several communal laundry rooms. He had been issued a key to use for the machines provided for tenants. Unlike the coin-operated machines in Laundromats, these could only be started by a resident's laundry key. It was still early and no one else was using the room, so he loaded two machines with his whites and colored clothing. He added a measure of bleach to his sheets, towels, and underclothes all of which were white.

After starting the machines, he left the laundry and wandered through a breezeway toward the nearby swimming pool. This part of the apartment complex housed singles and married couples without children and therefore this pool was designated for adults only. The north end of the complex was the family section and provided a larger pool designed for children and was staffed during open hours by a lifeguard. None was assigned here. It was a little past eight o'clock and no one was using the pool. Chris walked closer and examined the water. The pool was spotlessly clean and he could smell the faint odor of chlorine and hear the thrum of the filtration system.

A dripping pool broom was fastened horizontally to one side of the decorative cement wall that enclosed the pool and patio area. It had obviously just been used to clean the pool, but there was no sign of the attendant. Chris thought about taking a swim while he waited for the laundry. He could still keep an eye on the laundry room door from the pool area while enjoying the water.

He checked on his laundry, returned to the apartment, changed into his swimming shorts and grabbed a large, fluffy green towel before heading back. Just as he entered the pool area from the laundry room side, another young man entered from a gate in the opposite side with a towel in hand. He was thin with straw-blond hair and was wearing glasses.

As he looked up and saw Chris, he stopped and fumbled a bit with his towel, wrapping it around himself as though shy and said, "Oh, sorry. I'll come back later if you want to swim. I don't mind. Sorry." He was turning to leave.

"Hey, it's okay. I don't mind. I'm just waiting for my wash to finish and decided to take a quick swim." He saw the fellow look around nervously as though trying to look anywhere else but at Chris. "Please don't leave on my account. It's a big pool and I doubt we'll get in

10

each other's way," Chris said with a smile.

"You sure? Some people like privacy when they swim and I want to make sure I'm not interrupting you."

"No, please stay. My name's Chris, Chris Walker. I just moved in yesterday --- apartment seventy around back, in building F."

The blond guy said, "Uh, thanks. I'm Walt. Walter Bower. Uh, it's nice to meet you. I live in number thirty-three, in building D. You sure I'm not messing up your privacy? If I am, I'll leave and come back later. Matter-of-fact, that would probably be better since I'm..."

"No, please don't leave on my account. Swim; enjoy yourself. I'll only be here a little while anyway. Hey, if *you* wanted privacy, *I'll* leave. I don't mind either. It's up to you. I don't want you to have to leave on my account. There's no need." Chris was observing how shy and reserved Walt seemed to be, first wrapping himself with his towel and being so quick to offer to leave. *Maybe he's as awkward around other people as I am. He seems kind of shy, but nice. Sooner or later I'm going to have to take some chances, make some new friends, Chris thought,* as he walked toward Walt and extended his hand.

"Come on, let's both enjoy the water. It's a pleasure to meet you." Walt smiled and shook Chris's hand gently. As he did so his towel slipped and fell to the ground. Both men bent instinctively to pick it up and knocked their heads painfully together.

"Ow, sorry," said Walt as he rubbed his forehead and grinned.

Chris had been first to the towel and handed it to the fellow as he massaged his own forehead and said, "I'm glad I ran into you, but I didn't intend to do it literally. Sorry. You okay?"

"I think so. You?"

"Yeah, I'm fine."

"Sorry. I'm kind of awkward and shy around other people," said Walt. "Always have been."

"I'm the same way, so don't feel bad. How long have you lived here at Whisperwind?"

"About six months. I'm a senior at the University of North Florida. It's a new college and they didn't have enough dorm rooms to go around, so my folks helped me get an apartment. I'm from De Land, Florida."

My folks live in a little town called Intercross, not far from Gainesville. I just graduated from the University of Florida and managed to get a job as a science curator at the Museum of Science downtown."

11

"Oh, I've been there. They have great laser shows at the planetarium; uh, they're called Cosmic Concerts."

"Sounds like fun."

"I love to go. They're opening a Moody Blues laser show next weekend and I plan on going. You like the Moody Blues?"

"Oh, for sure. One of my favorite songs by them is *Forever Autumn.* *Nights in White Satin* is a classic too. Hey, since I work there, I'll see about getting you a free pass."

"Wow. That would be super. The tickets are four bucks and with my budget, that's a lot, so I'd really appreciate a pass. Thanks. Uh, maybe we..." Walt looked awkward, stammered a bit and frowned.

"What were you about to say?" asked Chris.

"No. It's nothing --- never mind."

"Please, it's all right. What were you going to ask?"

"Uh, I doubt you'd want to, but I thought maybe you'd like to go along with me since you're a Moody Blues fan too. Sorry, it's forward of me and I imagine you're pretty busy just moving in and everything. You probably have a wife or girlfriend. That's why I stopped before asking. Sorry --- bad idea. Forget it."

Chris thought, *It's now or never. Gotta take the plunge and I don't mean in the pool. He just might be like me.* "Hey, it's a great idea, Walt. I'd love to go with you. I'm single, new in town and need to make some friends. No reason why you can't be the first."

Walt's eyes sparkled as he broke into a shy smile. "That's great. I've been in town nearly half a year and so far haven't made any friends. I'm sort of a hermit, I guess. I feel so out of place around other people my own age. How old are you, Chris?"

"I'm twenty-two, how about you?"

"Twenty-one, I just had a birthday a few weeks ago on July twentieth."

"You gotta be kidding. That's my birthday too. Wow, small world. See, we have something in common already. Who would have thought? I'm glad we met. I'm sort of a stay-at-home guy too. Never felt comfortable around others in school and even in college. I know how you feel."

"This is so cool," said Walt, this time breaking into a wide-eyed, boyish, goofy-looking grin that Chris found so nice. "Maybe we have even more in common. You wanna swim?"

"Let me check on my laundry and see if it's time to switch over to the driers. I'll just be a moment."

Walt again wrapped the towel around his middle and followed Chris into the laundry room and chatted as Chris moved the finished clothing to two driers and once again used his key to start the machines, setting them for fifty minutes.

"I guess you majored in science since you're a science curator at the museum."

"I have a Bachelor of Science in Education. Most museums favor a teaching degree in the curator's field, so I chose a split major in science and education. Most of my science work was in earth science, astronomy, and the physical sciences. You know --- chemistry and physics."

"Cool. I'm majoring in commercial art. I like to draw and have always had a knack for it."

"I paint a little with watercolors and oils occasionally, but my talent is pretty amateurish, I'm afraid," said Chris. He turned and smiled at Walt who seemed to be looking at his backside and legs. Walt's attention snapped back to Chris's face and he thought Walt blushed just a bit. "I'd like to see some of your work though, Walt if you'd care to share it with me."

"Yeah, sure. That would be super. No one's ever asked to see my work before."

"Let's go for a swim. The clothes will be dry in forty minutes or so." Both exited the laundry room and returned to the pool. Walt turned away as he removed his towel and laid it across a lounge chair. After taking off his glasses and placing them on his towel, he walked to the deep end of the pool and dove in. Chris followed soon after and joined Walt near the center of the pool where they treaded water a few feet apart. The water was warm but not too warm and felt refreshing as the young men began to swim back and forth, side by side, along the fifty-foot length of the pool. After six or seven laps, Chris stopped at the steps, sat down and waited for Walt to join him.

"Whew, that felt good," said Walt as he sat down a few feet away from Chris and folded his arms over his chest as though he was cold even though his chest was still underwater. He was obviously shy about his body and seemed awkward being this close to Chris. "I've been swimming the last two months trying to get myself in better shape. I'm so damned skinny and no matter how much I eat or exercise, I can't seem to put on any muscle or weight. My dad and mom both are thin too, so I suppose it's in my genes."

"Hey, you have nothing to be shy about. You look fine. You don't

13

have to be self-conscious around me." Chris smiled and added, "You seem kind of nervous, Walt. Relax. We're friends." Chris was now looking more closely at Walt's body as best he could through the shimmering water. Walt finally unclasped his arms and seemed to be a bit less tense and apprehensive. His skin was smooth and unblemished and Chris could see a bit of soft brown hair in the center of his chest and a hint of hair around his navel. Chris felt his body reacting and realized he was staring. He diverted his eyes and looked instead at Walt's face. Walt was smiling and looking back. As soon as their eyes met, they both blinked and looked elsewhere.

"Uh, I'm really looking forward to going to the laser show with you. Should we go on Friday night or Saturday?" asked Walt.

"Whichever's best for you; I have no plans for either night. It's your choice."

"Let's make it Friday. Eight, nine-thirty or eleven o'clock show?"

"You know the schedule better than I do and I work at the place," laughed Chris. "Of course, I haven't put in a single hour there yet. I start on Tuesday."

"I'm kind of a regular at the shows. I sometimes go every week. Guess they might think I'm obsessed or something." Walt shrugged his thin shoulders and his face broke into that cute, goofy grin. "I just like the artistic interplay of the music and lights. Their sound system is top notch and puts my little stereo to shame. Hey, I have some Moody Blues record albums if you ever want to borrow them."

"Thanks, so do I. You're welcome to my records too. If you want, after we swim and I finish the laundry, why don't you drop over and visit? You can look through my music and see if there's anything you'd like to listen to. I have some Alan Parsons Project, Pink Floyd, Tangerine Dream, that sort of stuff. I'm kind of into electronic and progressive rock instead of hard rock."

"I'm the same way. Wow, even more in common. Let's swim a few more laps. Maybe I'll actually grow a muscle somewhere, someday. One can only hope."

They swam for another twenty minutes stopping occasionally to rest and talk. Twice, Chris thought he saw Walt checking out his body, but he couldn't be sure. Something was telling him that his new friend might have more in common with him than a birthday, or his taste in music.

Chris was slightly aroused as they stepped from the pool and for the first time in his life he didn't try to hide it. He made sure to face Walt as he toweled off and was pleased to see that Walt was taking occasional glances at his shorts especially as he rubbed over his slight erection with the towel. He thought he could see a similar bulge in Walt's shorts as well even though Walt still tried his best to protect his modesty.

Soon it was time to separate, so Chris said, "Walt, give me about fifteen minutes to dry off, change clothes and fold my clothes. After that, come on over to my apartment, number seventy, building F. You can look through my records and we can talk some more. I've really enjoyed our time together this morning." He once again shook hands with Walt who smiled broadly and said he was glad to have met him.

Chris reflected as he walked toward the laundry room, *God, I hope he's gay. Maybe I've finally found someone I can open up to. He's good-looking, gentle-spoken and has the nicest smile. He seems kinda lonely and mixed up like me.*

Chapter 2
A Newfound Friend

It was a little more than a half hour before Chris heard a soft knock at his door. He'd unpacked a few more boxes and set aside two cartons containing his record collection for Walt to look through. He'd also set up his stereo equipment and speakers. He went to the door and peeked through the fisheye security lens and was pleased to see Walt outside. He opened the door and said, "Hey, Walt, come on in. Welcome to my collection of cardboard containers and confusion. Sorry for the mess, but I'll probably need another day or so to get everything unpacked and arranged in some sort of order."

"If you need some help, I'd be glad to volunteer." Walt was smiling as he entered, looking around at the array of boxes and belongings. He was wearing a long sleeve, blue-striped, western-style shirt and black denim jeans that fit him well. His shoes were black, penny loafers. Chris thought he looked pretty sharp. He had changed into light brown chinos with a short-sleeve, light green shirt and thought he caught Walt looking him over from time to time as he surveyed the living room. Chris had purposely worn the chinos since they were a bit tight and served to accent his physique and anatomy a bit more than most of his other clothing.

"Yeah, I'd love your company while unpacking. Would you like something to drink? Soda, beer, iced tea?"

"A soda sounds good. Coke, Sprite or whatever you have. I'm easy to please. Thanks for asking me over. I've really been kind of lost since I moved up from De Land. Even there I didn't go out much at all." Chris went to the refrigerator and pulled out two Cokes. He handed one to his new friend as he popped the top on the other, took a few sips and went back to unpacking a box of books.

Walt continued: "I'm an only child and pretty much stayed around the house with my folks. Dad was always getting after me to go out and meet gir...er, people and make some friends, but I just never was one to mix well." Walt sat down on one end of Chris's sofa and sipped at his soda.

Chris noticed Walt's near slip and felt even more excited about his prospects. "That's more we have in common. I'm an only kid too and stuck around the house a lot. I didn't live on campus during my college years since we were only thirty miles from the university."

"I would have preferred that too, but Stetson University, in Deland, is private and too darned expensive. I got financial help at UNF, so after community college, I had to move north."

"I commuted to Gainesville about thirty miles each day and preferred it that way since I wasn't into the college social scene. I was in no hurry to leave home." Chris had emptied the box of hardbacks and arranged them on his bookshelves. He tossed the box across the room to a growing pile of empties in one corner.

He continued speaking after sitting down on the sofa himself and looking at Walt. "Mom and Dad never pushed me to do otherwise and we all get along well. There's a lot of love in my family."

"That's like me. My folks and I are close too. I don't ever remember them having an argument or shouting at one another like the parents of some of my neighborhood friends did."

Chris added, "I was never rebellious as a teenager. I don't smoke or drink and I've never even thought about using drugs or marijuana. The beer I offered you a few minutes ago I keep in my fridge for when my dad comes to visit. He likes a cold Budweiser once in a while. I hardly ever drink the stuff."

"I'm the same way," said Walt. "Uh, do you, uh... Uh, never mind."

"What were you about to ask? You don't have to be shy, Walt. I won't bite."

"No. I was about to be nosy. I don't want to piss you off or embarrass you."

"It's okay, dude. Ask away. I do believe you're blushing," Chris said with a laugh. "You've got me curious. Now I'm gonna make you ask."

"What will you do if I don't?" asked Walt with a smile and a tilt of his head.

"Well, I don't exactly know. If we were better acquainted, I've been known to tickle a person until they give up information. I did it often to my cousin and he always turned into a basket case." Chris made a quick move with his hands toward Walt who yelped and leaned away raising his hands as though to fend off an attack. Chris laughed and said, "Go ahead now, ask, or I just might do it."

"Okay, but don't get upset for me being so nosy. I was gonna ask you if you do much dating?" Walt went silent and Chris saw that Walt's smile faded as he waited for an answer that would tell him a lot about Chris.

Chris was going to say, *once in a while*, his usual reply when others asked, but this time, he caught himself. *I'm not going to lie to this guy; I don't think I need to.* Instead, he said, "Maybe I'm weird, but I have to be honest, Walt. I've never been on a single date with a girl. Never had much interest in dating or socializing, going to parties or movies, that sort of thing."

"You won't feel awkward going to the Cosmic Concert with me this Friday, will you? I don't want to like force you to go, just to be nice."

"Heck no, I'm looking forward to it. I'm tired of being so reclusive."

"Me too, but I know what you mean about socializing. I've only gone on a date with a girl once and it was because a friend arranged it as a double date and I couldn't get out of it."

"Really?" Chris said with a chuckle.

"Yeah, I was only twelve anyway, so I doubt it counts as much of a date. She was about a foot taller than me; at least it seemed that way; she had pimples from hell and braces that were downright scary. She really needed them too."

"Gees --- that does sound creepy."

Walt chuckled as he went on, "We went to a real sappy romantic movie and during a love scene near the end of the film she leaned over and tried to kiss me and I backed off and sort of pushed her away. That was the end of that relationship. My friend teased the hell out of me for about a year. All I could see was all that shiny metal and pimples coming at me in a darkened theater and I panicked." Both young men were laughing as Walt sort of shivered and ended by saying, "Ugh!"

"I would have probably done the same thing at that age." He laughed and added, "I'd probably even do it now."

"Yeah, so would I." Both young men went silent and simply stared at one another. Chris saw a slight frown on Walt's face and at one point, he seemed about to say something more but chose not to.

Chris broke the uncomfortable silence by pointing out several cartons on an armchair nearby. "Uh, Walt, these two boxes are my record collection; you're welcome to borrow any you like."

While Chris began once more to unpack and put things away, Walt browsed through the hundred or so albums exclaiming occasionally when he found an especially interesting title.

Walt said, "I have a reel-to-reel, stereo tape deck, and a good quality turntable, so I may record a few of these. You have a great collection, Chris. Anything I have you're welcome to enjoy as well."

Chris smiled as he thought of the double meaning of that statement. He stepped over to where Walt was flipping through the last few records in the second box and almost without thinking, placed his hand on Walt's shoulder and said, "I'm glad someone else can enjoy the music. I'm really glad we met."

Walt jumped a bit at the touch, turned and smiled looking slightly surprised at where Chris's hand was resting. "Me too, you're uh, a heck of a nice guy and god knows I need a friend. Sometimes I get so damned depressed with no one to talk to. You're always welcome to come by my apartment too." He turned back to the records and said, "I've pulled out eight albums I'd like to borrow and record if that's okay."

"Sure. After you finish with those, come back for more," said Chris, as he gave Walt's shoulder a squeeze and stepped away hardly believing he had reached out the way he just did. The beautiful smile he got from Walt told him he hadn't done the wrong thing.

As the morning continued, Walt helped unpack kitchen items while Chris put them away in his pantry and cabinets. At noon, Chris suggested they go out for lunch. "It's on me for all your help. You like pizza?"

"Oh yeah, I know a great place too since you're new to town; they have a large, deep dish pizza with four ingredient choices for five bucks and that includes unlimited soda refills."

"Sounds good, we'll take my car since it's closer. You can ride shotgun and navigate."

Before long they were seated in a small pizzeria waiting for delivery of a large deep dish pizza with mushrooms, pepperoni, green peppers, and onions. Both were sipping root beers from frosted mugs as Walt chatted about his college classes. He was well into the second summer term which still had three more weeks before it ended.

Walt explained, "I went to Daytona Beach Community College for my first two years and got my associate of arts degree. It saved me a lot of money and I had to get through all the basic required subjects anyway."

"Yeah, I did the same. My folks and I moved north from Hollywood, Florida a couple of years ago; I attended Broward Community College in Fort Lauderdale for my associate of science degree. Once we moved north to Intercross, I had an easy commute to the university, so I did my last two years there and graduated last March."

Chris paused as their pizza arrived and each took a slice. Walt had been right, it was very good. After a few minutes of eating, Chris took a drink of soda before saying, "I'm glad I found the job I did because I wasn't looking forward to teaching in a school setting. Some kids are great, but there's so many who make it miserable for the serious students who want to learn. I'm not the kind who likes confrontation and dealing out discipline either."

"What duties will your new job include?" Walt asked.

"I'll be responsible for running the museum's new Science Theatre. I'll be presenting live Mr. Wizard type science shows for the public and visiting school students. I also have to maintain one exhibit hall on the second floor called the Science Mall. It has a load of hands-on exhibits that kids and visitors can interact with to help them learn science concepts."

"Oh yeah, I've been there. Sure they'll pay you for having so much fun? Think I can come to one of your shows?"

"You better; I'm counting on it. I'll see about getting you a permanent guest pass. As a curator, I should be able to do that. Maybe I can arrange an honorary membership to the whole museum."

Walt looked surprised. "You'd do that for me? That's really nice. I could go to all the planetarium shows then."

Chris smiled and said, "Hey, it's my pleasure. I was just thinking, Walt; since it's Friday, why should we wait until next week to go to a Cosmic Concert? Why don't we go this evening? I already have my staff ID card and a set of keys, so I won't have any problem getting you in as my guest. I'm really looking forward to it. Are they featuring the Moody Blues tonight?"

"No. This is the final weekend of a show featuring Manfred Mann's *Solar Fire* album. Are you familiar with it?"

"Not that particular album, but it sounds interesting. I like Manfred Mann, especially *Blinded by the Light*. Let's do the eight o'clock show, though, because I don't want to stay up too late. I have a full day of unpacking and arranging yet tomorrow. I really appreciated your help this morning. Having someone to talk with made the work go by a lot faster."

"You're welcome any time. I'm just glad to finally find a friend I can feel comfortable around. I'm a neurotic mess most of the time around other people my own age, but with you, I feel at ease."

"I kind of noticed how shy you were at first, even offering to leave the pool area so I wouldn't be disturbed." Walt looked shyly amused and nodded. Chris went on: "I'm glad I stopped you. It's been fun. I feel very much at ease around you too, Walt, more so than I've ever felt with anyone else for that matter. I think we're going to be good for each other."

"I think so too," said Walt, with a warm smile. This time he kept looking directly at Chris instead of glancing away as he often did.

After finishing the pizza they returned to Whisperwind and Walt continued to help Chris get his new home in order. By four o'clock, Chris suggested they take a break for the day and enjoy another swim before supper time and their upcoming visit to the planetarium. Chris had something else in mind he wanted to do to test Walt's interests. Walt left after saying he'd meet him at the pool in ten minutes. Chris went off to his bedroom and searched through his things until he found a rather snug fitting, brief-style swimsuit that he'd never worn before. It had been a gift from his aunt several years before and it was not the sort of suit he would have purchased or worn on his own. Now, for some reason, he wanted Walt to see him wearing it as it left very little to the imagination. His only fear was that he might not be able to easily disguise any spontaneous reaction he might have while daydreaming about his new friend.

Chris was somewhat surprised at himself. Somehow between seven this morning and now, he had started thinking in a whole new way. His self-disgust with his erotic dream and accident the previous night had perhaps prompted him to make a change in his life, especially after meeting Walt. *I'm pretty sure Walt might be gay. He's shy, introverted, has no interest in dating and sure seemed to be looking me over from time to time. Wait until he gets a look at my swimsuit.* Chris wanted to make sure Walt was facing him when he removed his towel before jumping in the pool. *Hope we have the place to ourselves.* That thought nearly made him change his mind and put on a more conservative suit, but he told himself, *No! I'm gonna be bold for a change and take a chance.*

Just as Chris reached the pool, two middle-aged women were gathering their things to leave. Walt showed up also wrapped in a beach towel and walked around to the side of the pool where Chris was moving two lounge chairs side by side for their things. Walt had removed his towel and was wearing the same suit he'd worn earlier. Chris made sure he was turned his way as he said, "Walt, I was thinking, since we're going to the museum this evening, we might as well have dinner together, that is if you have nothing else planned." As he finished speaking and before Walt could answer, Chris pulled off the towel and watched for Walt's reaction.

It was pretty obvious Walt was noticing because his eyes opened wider and went right to Chris's middle. He had been about to say something and a smile was forming on his face, but he stopped with his mouth open and stammered something that sounded like, "That um, uh, yeah --- supper's good --- yeah, supper." The poor guy averted his eyes as if Chris was naked. He nearly was. Chris laughed inwardly and was pleased to discover Walt was both attentive and shy about looking at him. It didn't take Walt long to dive into the pool. He surfaced along the side and was surprised to see Chris standing right above him getting ready to dive in as well. Again, Walt's eyes betrayed his interest and went right where it counted. He squinted too for better focus since he'd removed his glasses. Chris was now quite sure his new friend was more than likely gay.

They swam and talked for a half hour before Walt suggested they might want to get out and get dressed for supper and a show. Chris agreed and was the first to exit the pool. Instead of walking around to their chairs, he waited at the steps as Walt got out and gave his friend one more chance to take a few peeks. Walt didn't disappoint him. Walt was grinning as he walked past and said, "I enjoyed that. Sure beats swimming alone."

An hour later, after spending some time alone at their own apartments, they met at Walt's place. He showed Chris around his digs and pointed out two pieces of framed artwork. Chris was impressed and said so, "Damn, Walt, you really are very good. Sure your last name's not Disney?"

He chuckled before saying, "No, but thanks. These are two pieces I entered in an amateur contest last year in De Land; I won a few prizes for them."

He pointed out the painting on the left, the smaller of the two. "That one won third place." It was a watercolor of an elevated boardwalk winding through tropical plants and trees.

"It's beautiful." Chris moved right toward the larger of the two paintings;

"That one took first place for landscapes and best-of-show." It was a highly detailed, colored pencil rendering of a Florida river.

"That's the Saint John's River near my family's home in De Land.

It's not as wide down there as it is here in Jacksonville. I especially like doing natural settings or landscapes."

"It's fantastic. I'd sure call it first prize material. It must have taken patience to capture all the detail. I love landscapes and natural scenes myself. Chris patted Walt on the back and gave his shoulder a squeeze. Walt was blushing as Chris moved back to the smaller watercolor and asked, "Is this based upon a real location?"

"Uh huh, it's from a nature trail at Blue Springs State Park. It was one of my favorite places to go when I was growing up. There's a crystal clear spring there where the manatees swim right along with you in the winter when they migrate upstream. It's a beautiful spot."

"Looks like it. I'd like to go there sometime. Maybe someday we can go together. You ever do any camping, Walt?"

"No, I never have, but I'd like to someday."

Chris said, "Hey, next time I go to visit my folks, I'll bring back our pop-up camper trailer. I doubt they'll use it anyway since I've left the nest, so I might as well bring it up here. I'll have to make arrangements where to park it with the manager though. It's great to camp in. Think you'd like to try it out sometime?"

"Oh yeah, that would be super, especially since I've met you. I'm still kind of surprised at myself. You're so easy to be with."

"Thanks, I feel comfortable with you as well."

"Chris, you have no idea how screwed up I've been when it comes to socializing with other people. Somehow, you're different. It's like you and I are on the same wavelength or something."

"I know what you mean. I feel it too."

Walt was looking deep into Chris's eyes. "I'm usually shy or tongue-tied, but not with you. Everything seems right for a change. I'd love to go camping with you."

"I'll make sure and get the camper soon so we can start making plans for a short trip somewhere, maybe Blue Springs. When are your classes at the university?"

"Tuesdays, Wednesdays, Thursdays during the day and Wednesday evenings, this term. That frees me up for the weekends and Mondays, why?"

"Well, my days off are Sunday and Monday, so if we go camping it will have to be on those days. I'm too new at the job to ask for time off yet. Sounds like Sunday and Monday will work for us both. Hey, we better get going if we're going to get dinner and still catch the eight o'clock concert. My car or yours"

"We'll take mine this time since it's closer to my apartment. It's a little older than yours, a seventy-four Chevy Nova. Nothing fancy, but it gets me there."

"Great, let's go."

They decided on going Dutch at Denny's for dinner since both were on a tight budget. Chris would soon be doing better financially once his first paycheck came in. It was a little after seven when they finished and headed downtown toward the museum. It was located near Friendship Park along the south bank of the St. Johns River near the foot of the Main Street Bridge. The museum's doors were still locked and a few early patrons were already gathered on the steps. Chris saw there were a few staff members already inside preparing for visitors. The doors would open in a few minutes at seven-thirty. Chris had his keys so he led Walt to a side door marked **Staff Only** and opened it. Once inside, they walked to the front desk and Chris introduced himself to a young man working there.

"Hi, I'm Chris Walker, the new physical science curator and this is my friend, Walt Bower. We wanted to catch the eight o'clock Cosmic Concert. Walt here is a regular and tonight he's my guest if that's all right."

"Sure," said the young man with a smile. "I'm Dan Barber. We've heard there was a new curator on staff; welcome to the museum. I'm a part-time employee and volunteer. The upper floors are open and lit if you want to look around."

"Thanks, we will."

"We'll be opening the main doors in about ten minutes. I'll make sure two passes are held for you."

"Super. Thanks again, Dan. It was nice to meet you. Do you expect a crowd tonight?"

"We usually don't fill up for the eight o'clock show. The two later shows though will probably be a packed house tonight since its the last weekend for *Solar Fire*. It's a cool show. Hope you enjoy it. I think I've seen you here before, Walt."

"Oh yeah, I've been a fan for several months now. I met Chris at our apartment complex and we got to talking. Once I found out he's going to work here, I told him about the shows and here we are."

Chris and Walt climbed the central stairway to the second floor where Chris unlocked and showed Walt his new office and work area just opposite the elevator on the second floor. He'd spent two days looking the museum over a few weeks before when he'd interviewed for the job, so he sort of knew his way around. The room was somewhat cluttered and many of the shelves were bare. He would probably spend his first few days just getting settled in and making the place more workable. On one entire side of the room was a long row of wooden cabinets with wide, shallow drawers. Chris pulled one drawer open revealing a beautiful collection of sparkling mineral specimens of all varieties.

Walt said, "Oh wow! This is fantastic. I could spend hours looking through these drawers. I had a mineral and rock collection as a kid, but nothing like this."

"Hey, any time you want to come by, have the front desk call me. Once I have my schedule, you're welcome any time I'm free, or at work in here. You can browse to your heart's content."

"Thanks, Chris. That's very generous of you. I'll try not to make a nuisance of myself."

Chris showed Walt some of the other behind the scene areas of the museum including the new Science Theatre where he would soon be staging science shows. It was still under construction and had yet to be opened to the public. It smelled of new woodwork and fresh paint. His job was primarily for the purpose of staffing this new museum attraction.

They eventually worked their way back to the lobby and after picking up complimentary tickets, joined the line for the Cosmic Concert. Soon the doors opened and they took seats not far from the control console. Chris and Walt relaxed in the reclined seats and enjoyed the pre-show music which happened to be *Jupiter* from *The Planets,* by Gustav Holst.

Chris commented, "Seems kind of odd playing classical music before a rock music concert."

Walt chuckled and said, "Once you hear *Solar Fire*, you'll know why. Manfred Mann based the entire album on a light rock interpretation of Holst's suite, *The Planets.* This music, *Jupiter, the Bringer of Joy,* I believe, is one of the main themes; a song the Earth Band called, *I Bring Joy.*"

"Okay, I see the connection now. *Solar Fire, The Planets.* It's a clever approach."

Walt said, "I think they're about to start, *Jupiter* is ending and the lights are fading. Enjoy."

The concert was amazing and Chris was very impressed with both the effects and the way lasers and lights were combined to interpret the music. The show lasted about fifty minutes and included a few other Manfred Mann hits keeping with the outer space and planetary theme. The show ended with *Blinded by the Light* and did a pretty good job of doing just that using eye-searing strobes and other bright effects. In all, it was an enjoyable experience.

They returned home about nine-thirty. Walt drove by Chris's apartment to drop him off before heading for his own building. He parked, shut off the engine and stepped out of the car and walked around to the passenger side and extended his hand saying, "Chris, this has been a great day and evening. I'm sorry to see it end. I think meeting you has been one of the best things that's ever happened to me." They shook hands with gusto and both were openly smiling.

"Me too, Walt. You're one heck of a nice guy and a good friend. God knows, I've been needing one. I'm tired of the loneliness too and I think I've found someone who really understands me. We're two of a kind. Maybe next week we'll catch the Moody Blues concert; that or I'll pick up the camper and we'll take off for a state park somewhere. Good night, Walt, it's been fun. How about we get together tomorrow morning for a swim? Say nine o'clock?"

"Sure! I'll be there. Well, I better be going. It's been a long day. Take care and sleep well. I'll be thinking of you."

"Yeah, me too. Good night."

Just for a moment, Chris thought he saw Walt moving toward him as though to reach out for an embrace, but the young man stopped and turned before returning to his car. He started the engine and drove away. Chris watched until his car turned the corner and disappeared from sight. *Maybe I should have invited him in for a soda or a snack or something. Oh well. There'll be other opportunities. I think he wants more than simple friendship too. At least I sure hope he does. Time will tell.*

Chapter 3
Mutual Problems

Chris had provocative dreams that night, but no embarrassing accidents like the previous one. Instead, his dreams had a change of character. A certain blond-haired, blue-eyed, skinny, shy fellow popped in and out of his nocturnal fantasies. Chris awoke with a somewhat insistent and painful erection and lay in bed a few minutes more, day-dreaming further about his new friend.

After a late breakfast, Chris heard a soft knock at his door. He hadn't realized the time and looked to his clock, still un-hung and leaning against the kitchen baseboard; it was precisely nine o'clock. If it was Walt, he was certainly punctual as that was the exact time they'd agreed on for a swim. Chris went to the peephole and sure enough, it was Walt, looking about nervously and dressed for the pool. He opened the door and asked him in. Walt broke into a beautiful smile. He was dressed in his bathing shorts and a blue tee-shirt. His towel was thrown over his shoulder.

Chris apologized, "Sorry, I'm running a little late. I slept longer than expected and so I'll need a few minutes to get dressed for the pool. Have a seat. You can get a soda or something from the fridge if you'd like. I'll only be a few minutes."

"Take your time. I slept soundly last night and woke up with the sun. I'm not thirsty so I'll pass on the drink. Did you sleep well?"

"Sure did." Chris moved into his bedroom and closed the door halfway so he could still talk as he got dressed. "I had a dream and you were in it. I dreamt we were on a camping trip together and were hiking in the Smoky Mountains where I did some camping a few years ago."

"Maybe that's why my legs were aching when I woke up. Were we having fun?" Walt asked with a chuckle.

Chris laughed as he said, "Oh yeah! We were having a great time." Chris remembered one particularly vivid scene where they were both swimming nude in a clear forest pool. "We stopped for a swim in a pond along a mountain stream too and the view was fantastic." Of course, Chris wasn't thinking of mountain scenery.

"What were we wearing?" Walt asked with a chuckle almost as if he knew what Chris was thinking.

"Our swim shorts, I suppose. I don't really remember."

"I hope your dream was prophetic and we'll be able to go there someday. I can almost picture the scene. It might be a good subject for a drawing or painting."

"Yeah, it would. I've always enjoyed swimming in a lake or pond like that. There's a place in the national park, along the Little River, near Townsend Tennessee, I'd like to show you someday. It's a great place to swim; it's very secluded and beautiful."

"You know, Chris, there's something I've always wanted to do."

"What's that?" Chris asked as he stepped back into the living room wearing his brief-style bathing suit.

Walt's eyes once again scanned him and lingered once more where Chris thought they would. He hesitated a few seconds before saying, "I, uh... I always wanted to be somewhere where I could go skinny dipping. I've never told anyone else that, but it's kind of a fantasy of mine. Not that I'd do something like that in public. But, if I was out in the woods or far away from people, I'd like to try it."

"Sounds like fun. Maybe we can give it a try someday if we find a secluded spot. I wouldn't mind if it was just the two of us." Chris took a dining room chair and sat down directly in front of Walt.

Walt was still looking at Chris, but now seemed embarrassed and was fidgeting a bit. He glanced briefly at Chris's eyes and smiled as he said, "I can't believe I just told you that."

"What?"

"About the skinny dipping --- for some reason, I wanted to share that with someone I trust." Walt giggled and broke into his usual goofy grin before saying, "Chris, I really do trust you. I'm a little weird in some ways and I'm kind of tired of holding so much inside."

"It's okay; I'm not going to judge you. I carry around a load of baggage myself and I'd like to think I could share things like that with you if needed. I know we just met yesterday, but Walt, I feel good about our friendship. I enjoyed our date last night. I had a lot of fun just being with a friend --- talking and feeling free for a change."

"Yeah, me too; it *was* sort of like a date wasn't it. Everyone thinks of a date as a guy and a girl out together, but I guess two guys can go on a date and have fun if they want. Of course, it's for a different reason. Two guys are just out to have some fun, not romance or anything like that."

Chris smiled and said, "Sure; just for fun. Speaking of that, we're supposed to be swimming. You ready?"

Walt was looking introspective and finally said, "Uh, yeah. I'm ready. Let's go."

There was no one else at the pool when they arrived and after swimming ten or so laps, they rested on the steps for a while saying nothing. Both seemed deep in thought. No one else had entered the pool area as yet, so Chris decided to venture a few comments about his feelings. "Walt, we were talking before about us going out together and how much we enjoyed it. There's something I want to say and it's kind of hard for me to talk about."

"Hey, go right ahead. You can trust me."

Chris continued, "I know I can and that's why I don't mind talking about more personal things with you. If anything I say bothers you, please let me know 'cause it's some serious stuff I need to share with a friend and someone I trust. I'm only doing it because of that trust you just mentioned. Do you understand?"

"Sure," said Walt, as he gazed more intently at Chris's eyes and face. "You can talk about anything. I won't be bothered."

"Well, you know how you said our so-called date was just two guys having a fun night out and how with a guy and a girl it can take on a different meaning, right?" Walt nodded in agreement but was looking more intently at Chris. "Walt, there's something about me you need to understand because..."

Chris stopped speaking because two young couples he'd not met before were entering the pool area with towels and a cooler. They said hello and proceeded to set up their things at a small table with several deck chairs, not far away. After the guys returned the greeting, Walt turned to Chris and said, "What were you about to say?"

"Uh, let's discuss it later. It's kind of personal and now with all these other people around I'd be a bit uncomfortable talking. Like you, I'm still shy around other people; it's part of that baggage I told you I carry. Once we get back to my apartment, maybe we can speak more about it."

"Okay. I understand. Later. Let's take a few more laps and then get a little sun before we go back." They did just that and after basking in the sun for a half hour they found their way back to Chris's apartment.

After entering, Walt was looking around for somewhere to sit and said, "My swim suit's still a little damp. Maybe I should run home and change so I don't..."

Chris interrupted saying, "Hey, go ahead and sit down. You're not going to hurt a thing. Let me get us some iced tea. That okay with you?" Walt folded his towel in half and placed it on the sofa seat before he sat down on it.

"Sure. Tea sounds good. Uh, what was it you wanted to talk to me about at the pool when those people showed up? You seemed pretty serious. Anything I can do to help?"

"I don't know, Walt. Maybe," Chris said from the kitchen as he poured two glasses of iced tea. "I wanted to let you know that going to the concert with you was pretty special to me. Like you said, we've only known each other a day, but I trust you and feel comfortable around you. I hope to get to know you even better and would like us to spend more time with each other; if you'd like, that is."

"I would. It would be great."

Chris went on as he joined Walt in the living room, "Something inside is telling me you and I need that kind of friendship. I think we're both starving --- not for food, although we're both skinny." Walt chuckled and nodded his head in agreement. "Walt, I've been starved for friendship since I was about thirteen. I've never had a really close friend; the kind of friend I could trust completely and care deeply about as a true friend if you understand what I'm saying. I get the feeling you might be the same way. Am I right?" He took a seat in an easy chair opposite Walt.

Walt was looking strange. His hands were fidgeting and even shaking a bit. He rubbed at one eye with his left knuckles and sniffed and opened his mouth as if to speak, but sobbed instead and more tears began to flow from his bright blue eyes.

He managed to say, "Chris, I...I know what you mean. It *is* like I'm starving. I've been hoping to find someone I can trust completely as a close friend because up until now I've felt so damned alone!" He broke into even more sobs. Chris sensed his own control failing and felt tears gathering as he left his chair and sat beside Walt on the sofa.

"It's okay, buddy; it's okay." Chris put his left arm around Walt's shoulders and pulled him close. Walt leaned into the hug and buried his face against Chris's neck, throwing his left arm around his friend and sobbing with abandon.

"God! I'm so fucked up, Chris," Walt muttered, still with his face buried against Chris's neck and chest. "I'm crying like a damned schoolgirl. Thanks for putting up with me and my crazy emotions. It feels so darned good to be here with you right now. God, I've wanted to hug someone like this for so long."

Chris said, "I understand. I really do."

Walt sniffed and went on, "The loneliness has been eating me up like a damned cancer. You're right, I'm starved as hell. God, I'm glad we met. I don't want you to take this the wrong way, but Chris, I love having you as a friend. Somehow even after just a single day, something is telling me that we need each other. I was about at the breaking point a few days ago and was thinking about quitting school and going home just to end the loneliness; but not now." Walt started crying softly once more.

"It's okay, Walt, let it out, buddy." He held onto Walt as he broke down even more and sobbed with abandon for several minutes.

Finally, Walt was able to speak. "You're a life-saver, Chris. God, it feels good to be close to you. I hope you can understand what I'm feeling and not be embarrassed by a sentimental idiot like me. I just...," he started sobbing again, this time with relief.

"Easy, Walt, I've got you. I know what you're feeling because I'm feeling it too. It's so darned nice to hug you and feel you hugging me. It seems we've both been isolating ourselves too much from human contact." Walt finally looked up and faced Chris, his eyes scanning his companion's face seeing his tears and his understanding.

"I care about you, Walt. I really do." Chris pulled him tighter and for several minutes they sat together saying nothing, just holding each other and feeling the warmth and whatever was evolving between them.

Finally, Walt shifted and pulled away as he said, "God, I bet you wonder what kind of idiot you've made friends with. Twenty-four hours after we meet and I have a fuckin' nervous breakdown and lose it." Walt jerked away in panic. "Oh god! My nose just dripped on your chest. I'm so damned sorry. Jesus, I'm so fucked up. Let me wipe it off. Damn!"

"Hey, don't worry about it. What are friends for? Take it easy. It *snot* a problem; just let the matter drop." Walt sobbed and nearly choked with mixed emotions as he got the puns and had to laugh in spite of himself.

"Come here, Walt." Chris pulled him close again and this time whispered in his ear. "We're very close and special friends now and nothing is going to change that. We both need close friends right now to provide support for one another. I'm just as emotionally screwed up and starved for companionship as you are and Walt; that changes right now. We have each other and nothing else matters." Chris kissed

Walt's cheek gently and then buried his lips in his friend's soft blond hair. He felt Walt's hands stroking his back as the two simply held each other and shared the moment in silence.

Several minutes went by before the two separated. There seemed to be a new understanding between them as they smiled and looked more deeply into one another's eyes. Walt was the first to speak.

"Thanks, Chris. I'm sorry I lost it."

"I'm not," said Chris. "It was good for both of us. I feel so much better now that we've opened up more to each other. I hope I didn't freak you out by giving you a kiss on the cheek. I just thought you needed one along with our hug."

"It was nice. I was a bit surprised, but it really felt good to know you cared enough to do that. I didn't mind at all. Thanks. It's like you said; I've been starved for friendship. Thanks so much."

"It was my pleasure." Chris was suddenly at a loss for words. He wanted so much to go a step farther and admit his deepest secret, but all the years of hiding won out. The fear of rejection won out as well and he put off the moment of truth a bit longer by changing the subject. "Speaking of being starved, I'm pretty hungry after our emotional experience. I have some cold cuts, cheese, and some fresh onion rolls; sound good?"

"Oh yeah, you're right; I'm hungry too. Sorry again about dripping all over you. I was so embarrassed. Thanks for not being upset. Your puns were horrible, by the way, but at least you got me laughing. Criminy wiz, 'let the matter drop'."

"What's a little bodily fluid between two friends? It didn't bother me in the least. Walt, it felt really special holding you like I did. I've never held another person close like that and it felt good. The fact that neither one of us had a shirt on made it pretty unusual and I've got to confess something; I liked being close to you and feeling you rub my back the way you did. We connected and I think we needed to. I bet you've never been that close physically to someone else either. Am I right?"

Walt stared down at the ground for a few moments before answering. "Yeah, you're right. I've always felt odd if someone got too close or touched me, other than my parents when I was a kid. When you held me I felt safe and good for the first time in my adult life. There's something about you that makes me want to be close. I've had dreams about having a friend who I could hug like that, but never thought it could happen. Thanks again for being there for me today. I'll never forget it."

Chapter 4
Plans and Pranks

They worked side by side fixing lunch and took their plates outside to the small screened patio that opened off Chris's living room. It was shaded beneath an overhanging roof and a slight breeze blew through the screen making the August heat bearable. There was a small, round, wrought iron table with three patio chairs. They began their meal in silence exchanging smiles occasionally as their eyes met. Both were deep in thought as they enjoyed the sandwiches, chips and iced tea. Walt was the first to speak.

"Chris, if you want me to I'll stick around and give you a hand with unpacking this afternoon. I have nothing else to do and I really enjoy being with you. Please though, if you need to be alone, let me know. I don't want to make a nuisance of myself."

"No, I'd love to have your help and company. After this morning, I want you to feel free to come over whenever you want. I'm tired of being alone and I think you are too. Listen, I have an idea I'd like to run by you."

"Okay, I'm all ears."

"Tomorrow is Sunday. Do you have anything planned? Church or something you have to do?"

"Nope, I'm free. What do you have in mind?"

"Well, if we work together getting all my stuff unpacked today and maybe this evening, I thought about driving down to my parents' home tomorrow and picking up the camper. I have a hitch on my station wagon and there are a few other items I want to bring up from the house. There's some camping gear and that sort of thing since we talked about doing some camping. I'd like to invite you to come along. You can meet my folks and they can meet you. They're always asking me about making friends and I finally have one. How about it?"

"I'd love to go. I sort of know where you come from, but exactly where is Inter...?" Walt hesitated, trying to remember the name.

"Intercross. It's a little crossroads town a third of the way between Palatka and Gainesville. When we go back inside, I'll show you on a map. Their house is on a clay road about two miles off State Road 315 just north of the town. It's a pretty area with a lot of oak and pine woods, lakes, and best of all, quiet. I picked this rear apartment because of the trees and open space in the school's recreation yard. I'm not overly fond of cities, but that's where the work is."

Looking out beyond the screened patio, Walt agreed, "Yeah, it is a nice view. My patio looks out on more apartment buildings. I seldom use it. How far is it to your family home, Chris?"

"About ninety miles; an hour and a half drive south through Orange Park, Middleburg and a lot of pretty farming country in Clay County. While we're in Intercross, maybe we can take a swim at a private lake a friend of ours has a rental cabin on." Chris grinned and added, 'It would be a great place for skinny dipping if no one's renting the cabin. I swam there nude a couple of times."

"Were you swimming with anyone else?" Walt seemed a little alarmed at the idea, but Chris assured him he had been alone and it had been at night when he and his parents had rented the place while checking on their home's construction, years before.

"The guy was our contractor and told us we can swim there whenever we want. My folks have a pool also. We might even want to spend the night and drive back on Monday. If we do, will it interfere with your schedule?"

"No. As I've said, I lead a pretty boring life. Reading, listening to music and watching television is about it. All my current classes are Tuesday, Wednesday, Thursday and I go to Cosmic Concerts on the weekends. That's my ho-hum life in Jacksonville up until now."

"Well, I'm pleased to inform you that I'm going to do my best to liven up your boring life as I do the same to mine. Maybe we'll get sick of each other after a while, but I'm darned glad to have someone to talk to and share a meal with."

"Yeah, it's nice. The lunch was good. Let's get busy and get the rest of your stuff put away. The sooner we do it the better. Maybe we can get it all done before evening and relax before our trip tomorrow.

By working together, they were able to finish before five. Chris's apartment now looked more like a home. His books were neatly placed on two sets of shelving units he'd brought from home and the sofa and his two living room chairs were covered with colorful slip-covers his mom had given him. Photos of his parents and a few other relatives were placed on top of the shelves. A few paintings and a decorative mirror now hung on his living room wall. A centerpiece of silk flowers graced the dining room, as did a green linen tablecloth, two shiny brass candlesticks, and green candles.

Chris announced he was taking Walt out for a special meal this evening. "How do you like seafood?"

"I love it."

"Good. I'd like us to try a restaurant I saw not far from the museum along the riverfront. It was called Crawdaddy's. Ever been there?"

"No, I never have, but I've seen it. It's a wild looking place. They purposely built it to look like a collection of old river shacks and rusty tin buildings, but I've heard it has fantastic food and a great view of the river. I heard it's kind of pricy though."

"Hey, this is on me for all your help. Tell you what though; I am going to ask you if I can make a long distance call from your apartment this evening since my phone service won't be turned on until Monday or Tuesday. I have to call my folks and let them know we're coming for the trailer and might be staying overnight."

"Sure. If they're home, why don't you come over now and call? While we're there, I'll take a quick shower and get ready to go out."

Chris made the call and his parents were pleased to hear he had made a friend and said Walt would be welcome. His mom started planning a big meal as he made a wasted effort to ask her not to go to any special trouble. Moms would be moms; she was talking about a beef roast and that alone shut him up. Home cooking was never to be avoided, especially his mom's London broil. As he ended the conversation, he heard strange sounds coming from Walt's bedroom and bath. He could hear the shower running, but had to step closer to the bedroom door before he realized it was Walt singing as he showered. Chris had to grin as he heard a rather flat version of *I Know You're Out There Somewhere,* by the Moody Blues. Walt was exuberant in his delivery but lacked the right notes. His heart, however, was fully into the lyrics.

It was a selection from one of the albums he'd borrowed. Chris couldn't help himself as he went to Walt's stereo, located his *Legend of a Band* album and placed the LP on the turntable. He started it up, set the needle on the appropriate track and as the music started playing, he turned up the volume enough so Walt could hear it from the shower. Chris ran into the bedroom and waited. Walt's singing had stopped and he heard the water shut off shortly thereafter. A few moments later he saw the bathroom door open slightly and a squinting Walt appeared without his glasses and dripping wet. Chris was flattened against the bedroom wall to the left of the door hidden by a

36

tall chest of drawers.

Walt leaned out to listen. He called out, "Chris? That's kind of loud; the neighbors might get pissed."

Chris didn't answer. The loud music played on. Walt took two steps out of the bathroom with a towel wrapped around his middle and moved toward the door to the living room. Chris stepped quickly into the steamy bathroom and waited behind the still open door. He heard Walt calling for him from the living room to no avail. He heard the volume drop on the stereo and then Walt mumbled, "What the heck?" as he returned to the bedroom and re-entered the bath. Pushing the door shut and pulling off the towel to begin drying, Walt turned around just as Chris said, "Gotcha!"

Walt yelled, "Fuck!" and stumbled backward into the vanity and sink. "Jesus, Chris. I about had heart failure. Damn!" Walt was trying to wrap himself with the towel, but it wasn't cooperating. He was grinning at Chris while trying to cover his privates with the towel while saying, "Boy, I owe you one for that. My heart damn near gave up the ghost. Get out of here. Let me regain some of my dignity and get some clothes on. Get!"

"Hey, you're the guy who wanted to go skinny dipping." Chris laughed and left, but was thinking about what he'd just seen. Walt was as handsome and exciting looking without his clothing as he was wearing them. Chris was still laughing and teasing as he said from the bedroom, "I heard you singing and thought you might like some background music."

"I still owe you one," said Walt from the bathroom as he bent and peeking around the door frame.

Ten minutes later, Walt emerged from the bedroom dressed in black slacks and a white and red, pin-striped shirt. He was wearing a red tie and looked really sharp. He was shaking his head and grinning. "God, you about scared the crap out of me just now. Whatever made you pull that prank?"

"I don't know. I made it up as I went. You were singing the words about me being out there somewhere and I was, so I thought I'd pay you a surprise visit. There's one thing about me you might as well get used to; I like to tease and have fun with people I really care about. I can take it too if they like to play as well. I hope you're not angry." In an Elmer Fudd-like voice he added, "I'm so warry, warry sawwe I suppwized you naked in the baffwoom." And in his normal voice asked, "Am I forgiven? Can I have a forgiving hug? Pweeze?"

"Yeah, you're forgiven. Come here." Walt opened his arms much to Chris's surprise. He stepped close and the two embraced.

After parting with a laugh Chris said, "Boy, if I get a hug like that each time, I'll have to surprise you more often. That's the best part."

"Yeah," agreed Walt, "It is, isn't it. I really like you, Chris. You're so much fun to be around. You don't have to go to all the trouble of playing a joke though for a hug; I'm glad to oblige you anytime." He sort of laughed and smiled oddly.

"What?"

"Nothing, it's just that two days ago I would never have imagined myself saying that, but now... I've changed. I think I'm feeling things I've never felt before, being around you. What's going on?"

"I feel the same way, Walt. You're the best thing that's happened to me in quite a while." He stepped closer to his friend again and they embraced even more forcefully than before. "It's friendship, Walt, something we've both been needing desperately for a long time."

"Yeah, it feels great. You feel great. I could hang on to you the rest of the evening and wish I could." They separated, but each had a questioning look in their eyes as they drew apart. Their smiles were full of shy surprise at what they each were feeling. Chris's body had reacted and he wondered if Walt's was doing likewise. A quick glance at Walt's loose-fitting slacks told him nothing, but the shorts he was wearing hid little and for a moment he saw Walt glance downward and smile at what he saw there. Chris turned away before Walt could realize that he'd noticed him looking.

Supper at Crawdaddy's was wonderful even though a bit expensive. Chris didn't care. He was floating on a cloud the whole evening as he sat eating while enjoying his friend's handsome face and beautiful smile. After the meal, they walked along the St. Johns River watching a few boats as they cruised the wide waterway. Chris wanted to take Walt's hand and hold it or wrap one arm around his shoulder as they strolled, but others were out walking and Jacksonville society, in 1980, still wasn't ready to easily accept that.

"Thanks for dinner, Chris. It was very good. I love seafood anyway and that's probably the best I've ever tasted. What was that appetizer you ordered for us? I forget what you called it."

"Calamari, fried squid."

"Oh shit! Squid? I've never eaten squid before. Glad you didn't tell me. I probably wouldn't have tasted it, but I'm glad now that I did; it was good."

Chris went ahead and put one hand on Walt's shoulder and gave a quick rub as he said, "Glad you liked it. I figured it was best to keep it a secret until you had a chance to taste it."

"I'm really looking forward to tomorrow and our trip to your home. Maybe sometime soon we can make a trip to my house and you can meet my mom and dad. I think you'll like each other. My dad's a big football fan though and that's practically all he ever talks about. Personally, I hate the game and could never get into it. How about you?"

"I'm the same way, so I guess your dad and I won't be able to have much of a conversation about that."

"He's a Florida Gator fan, so just the fact you went to the University of Florida will make you all right in his view. He almost talked me into going there, but I wanted to go to a smaller university. Besides, I got a commercial art scholarship at UNF, so that helped make up my mind." Walt stopped and gazed out over the river at the reflected buildings and city lights twinkling and shimmering. "My dad's a diesel engine mechanic and doesn't make a whole lot of money, so they couldn't help out too much. I didn't want them to anyway. I'll feel better if I can do it on my own."

"I'm the same way. Dad retired early after working in road construction in South Florida, so he and Mom are financially comfortable and their home is completely paid for, but I wanted to make my own way. I got some help from a tuition scholarship and then I worked all through community college and at the university too. I'm debt free right now and glad of it."

They returned to Whisperwind a little before nine and Walt stepped into Chris's apartment for a few minutes before heading home.

"Thanks again for the great meal, Chris. I enjoyed being with you. What time should I show up tomorrow morning and what do I need to bring along?"

"Nine o'clock should be about right. Pack what you need for a night's stay. Bring along a swimsuit for the pool or the lake. You won't mind sharing my room at my parents' house, will you? The guest room where my mom does her sewing has to be re-carpeted according to Mom." He laughed before saying, "Their goofy tabby cat, Tom, knocked over an open bottle of fabric dye a few days ago and batted it all over the place. Mom said it ruined the light blue carpet.

She's talking seriously about trading in the cat for a stuffed animal and said to not be surprised when we see Tom because some of the dye splashed all over him too. Ever seen a half-green tabby?"

Walt laughed and said, "No, can't say I have. Sharing a room with you is no problem at all. It'll give us more time to talk and get to know each other even better. I have a sleeping bag I can bring if you'd feel better. I can sleep on the floor."

"No way. There's a big queen-sized bed in my room and I'm happy to share. I will warn you though that I sometimes wet the bed." Inwardly he thought of his accident a few nights before.

Walt blinked and looked puzzled. "Huh? You do?"

"Of course not, silly. I just wanted to see the look on your face. It was great."

"Damn --- You got me again. You and your pranks."

"Do I get another hug?"

"Oh, so that's the game. You're getting hooked on my affections. One hug and then good night --- just a hug. I'm not the kind of guy who goes any farther until at least the third date."

"Yeah? Well, tomorrow night might be pretty interesting since it will be our third time out together."

"Oh shit. I hadn't thought of that," said Walt. "We'll be sharing a bed too. Maybe I better take along that sleeping bag after all."

Chris reached out and the two friends shared a warm hug. Again it lasted a little longer than a casual embrace. Both seemed to enjoy what was happening in their friendship. "Good night, Walt," said Chris as they separated. "You're super."

"So are you. Good night."

Chapter 5
Breaking the Ice

They left the next morning shortly after nine-thirty in Chris's station wagon, crossing the St. Johns River on the nearly three-mile-long Buckman Bridge. After turning south in Orange Park along Blanding Boulevard, they gradually left behind the strip malls and usual urban clutter driving southwest into farm country. Before long they turned south along Florida Highway 315 and soon crossed the Putnam County line leaving Clay County behind. It wasn't much further before the land started changing to gently rolling hills, something unusual for Florida. Walt commented on it and Chris told him that this part of the state was at an elevation of over two-hundred feet above sea level; something rare in Florida, and was underlain with soft limestone, a landform that geologists called a karst formation.

"There're sinks and sinkholes all over the place around my home. I'll take you to see an especially impressive one called the Devil's Blue Hole, if we have time. There's a small sink beside our house. It's about eighty feet wide and twenty feet deep, kind of like a tree-filled crater."

Walt laughed and said, "Is it safe to walk in it? Could it collapse or something?"

"Well, wherever there're sinks there're caverns underneath too. Theoretically, it could happen, but it's been the same since at least 1909. I have a U.S. Geological Survey map issued that year and it shows our little sink exactly the same as it is now. I kind of wish it *would* cave in because I'd love to explore the caves underneath. I'm into spelunking."

"That's caving, right?" asked Walt. "Sounds kind of dangerous, but I guess it could be fun."

"Maybe we can go together someday in the future. I know the location of several caves in North Georgia we could visit. I'm a member of a caving club, or grotto, as they're called, and have two sets of gear. It would be fun."

"Sounds like it. I'm definitely interested."

"There's a great state park near the caves that we could camp in if we do go. I'd love to take you."

"Super. I need some diversity in my life."

"What kind of hobbies do you enjoy now?"

"I guess painting and drawing won't count too much longer as a hobby since I'm soon going to be doing it for a living. I like model railroading in HO scale. I wish I had room in the apartment, but it's a messy hobby with the wood and plaster and everything."

"That's something else we have in common. I have a model railroad at my parent's house. Speaking of which, our turn-off is just ahead on the right. It's clay roads from here on to the house so it might get a little bumpy. The recent rains have helped to pack the clay, but there're always ruts."

True to his prediction, the roads were like a washboard in some places and the Buick was rattling as they drove west for nearly two miles before taking a turn to the left and traveling south one more block. The labyrinth of wooded acres was part of a failed land development called Intercross Estates and was sectioned off into long, rectangular blocks each roughly a thousand by two hundred feet. A well-kept, concrete block home was ahead on the right and Chris pulled into an unpaved circular drive covered by soft pine straw.

Both young men stepped out and stretched a bit as they left the station wagon and headed for the home's front door. A dog was barking inside and was soon joined by a second.

Chris said, "Don't worry about the dogs. They're both friendly, but do their duty by barking. The big black one is Bear and the smaller, gray, ragged-looking poodle is Cindy. They're both good dogs and won't bite. There's also our temporarily green and gray tabby cat, Tom."

The front door opened before they could get to it and the two dogs ran out wiggling as they greeted Chris and Walt as well. Tails were wagging and Cindy nudged against Walt's legs for attention. Walt bent and scratched behind her ears and made friends. Bear came over for his share and was happy once he'd sniffed and been petted by the new guy. Chris's mom and dad had stepped onto the porch and each embraced their son. Greetings and introductions were made by Chris.

"I'm so glad, Chris has made a friend," said Amelia Walker. "We worry about him all alone and on his own for the first time in a big city. Please come inside. Just shove the dogs out of the way, Walt, and watch they don't trip you trying to get attention. We have a cat too somewhere."

"Chris was telling me about your green tabby. Sorry to hear he made a mess of your guest room."

"Would you like a free cat, Walt," said Chris Senior with a laugh. "Right now, I don't think he'd be missed. If you don't like the color you can dip him in some other shade of fabric dye." As they stepped inside, Amelia opened the door to the guest room just opposite the front door and pointed inside at the havoc the playful tabby had wrought.

"Oh wow," said Chris. "How could one cat and one bottle of dye go that far and do so much damage?" The light blue carpet was streaked everywhere with dark green splotches as well as several parts of two walls. From the nearby living room, Walt and Chris heard a low, 'merrow'.

"Ah, I hear the guilty boy now," said Chris, as he walked into the living room and picked up the cat; Its face and one flank were bright green. "You've been a bad boy, old fellah." The rest of the cat was the varied stripes of a normal gray tabby. The tip of his tail was green as well as two-thirds of his belly. He was a large cat weighing well over twenty pounds and lay upside down purring in Chris's arms. Walt could see he'd been neutered. He reached out and rubbed the cat's soft green belly and Tom closed his eyes in blissful satisfaction and purred all the louder.

"Hope you don't mind sharing a room with Chris, Walt. If you'd rather, we have a fold out sofa bed in the living room you're welcome to use," said Chris Senior.

"No, sir, Chris and I will be fine. We just met a few days ago, but Chris is one heck of a great guy. I'm glad to have him as a friend."

"You're still in college, right, Walt?" asked Amelia.

"Yes, ma'am, I still have one more year to go. We live in the same apartment complex and met at the pool. Seems we have a lot in common and both of us are starved for friendship and like a lot of the same things."

"Mom and Dad, guess what Walt's birthday is? Would you believe it's July twentieth, the same as mine? We're only a year apart in age."

"What an odd coincidence," said Amelia. "Chris, show Walt to your room so he can drop off his things and settle in. I'll start getting lunch ready for you guys. You better not tell me you ate some junk food on the way."

"Nope, we drove straight through."

"Good, I've got a mess of fresh fish breaded and ready for the deep fryer. Carl --- that's our down the road neighbor, Walt --- Carl brought us a string of bream and perch this morning. He and his wife, Doris were out on the St Johns yesterday and caught their limit and as usual, shared them with us. Do you like fish and hush puppies, Walt? Hope so, because that's what's on the menu."

"That will be great, Mrs. Walker. I love fried fish. Chris and I had seafood last night. I ate some squid for the first time and loved it. I had no idea what it was until I asked Chris later."

"Yeah, he tricked us into eating some of that in Gainesville once," said Chris's dad. "I'm glad he did too; it was good. It was kind of like fried shrimp, but even better tasting. Go ahead and get unpacked. I'll help Amelia set the table while you boys settle in. We're glad to have you, Walt. You're always welcome."

"Thanks, Mr. Walker. Thanks a lot. I feel very much at home already."

Walt stepped into and looked around Chris's former room, which was a large eighteen by fifteen foot, walnut-paneled room with a drop ceiling and an entire wall of books. A humongous queen-sized, four-poster bed was backed by a carved, cherry-wood headboard and a matching footboard. An antique, oak, corner cabinet stood in one corner filled with cut glass goblets and a variety of what-nots. An antique, wind-up Victrola graced another wall. A few oil paintings were tastefully hung on the paneled walls.

"Your room is beautiful, Chris. Bet you miss it."

"Sometimes, but it was time to leave the nest. That, and like now, I can always come back."

"Your folks are great. I know you miss them and they miss you. I saw a few tears in your mom's eyes after she hugged you."

"Yeah, I'm lucky to have such great parents. They've been married thirty-one years. I kind of came along late in their marriage. You can park your bag here on the desk if you want. I'll put my stuff over here on the dresser."

"Thanks. I think I saw the sink you were telling me about as we pulled into the driveway. It's just right of the garage, right?"

"Yeah. Come on, I'll take you on a quick tour while the fish start frying."

Chris walked Walt around the property pointing out a number of fruit trees, a nicely-tended garden and eventually led him down a flight of concrete steps he and his dad had added to one side of the sink. In the bottom was a cleared area with an iron barbecue grill mounted on an iron post.

"This is nice down here. The whole place is wonderful. It's so quiet and comfortable. The air is fresh and the only sounds are the birds and a few cicadas. I love it."

"Thanks, so do I. I miss it too, but that's life. Gotta go where the work is."

They returned to the house and entered via the side patio door. Inside was a thirty-foot long swimming pool surrounded by white urn planters and a small statue of an angelic-looking little boy balancing a platter and vase of plants on his head.

Lunch was great as the fish were fresh-caught and had never been frozen which always robs most of the flavor from fish. After eating, Chris suggested they go for a swim in the pool and before long they were swimming and diving in the warm, clear water. Chris's folks sat nearby and watched the young men enjoy themselves.

Amelia told them that supper would be light after the fried fish and that tomorrow's lunch would be the promised roast beef dinner. Chris took Walt for a ride after lunch showing him some of the local points of interest. One stop was at the large sinkhole Chris had described to his friend earlier.

After parking along a hardtop road about five miles from his home, Chris led Walt westward into the woods along a dirt track that showed extensive use by vehicles. The sand was white, dry and sugar-like, however, and there was one place where it looked as though someone may have gotten their car stuck. Just beyond was an open space in the trees and several tall live oaks bent outward over an enormous opening in the ground. The sinkhole was about ninety feet across; eighty feet below was a pool of greenish-tinted water. A knotted rope hung from one of the overhanging live oak trees. No one else was around, but Chris told Walt that on the weekends there were often a group of local teens swinging and diving into the pool below.

Walt replied, "That's not for me. I get the creeps if I have to walk near a cliff or along the roof of a building. I have a slight fear of heights."

After their return and another swim in the pool, supper was a variety of cold cuts, fresh sliced tomatoes from the garden and sliced cheeses on warm, homemade bread. Walt said he was in love with Amelia's baking and ate two large sandwiches to prove it.

After supper, the two friends went for a long walk along the clay roads west of the house. There were miles of sectioned-off properties that, as yet, had neither been sold nor settled on. The lots were choked with blackjack oaks, scrub pines, and three-foot-high, wild rosemary bushes. Walt asked about a number of wide, large holes here and there along the way.

"Those are gopher tortoise burrows," he explained. "They're an endangered species, but not around here. You have to be careful as you walk because their burrows sometimes give way under your feet and you can twist or break an ankle in one of those things. Rattlesnakes share the holes with the tortoises too, so you don't want to reach down there."

At one point, Walt surprised Chris by reaching out and placing one hand between Chris's shoulders as they walked along. It was a spontaneous gesture and felt nice. Chris turned and smiled and said, "It's so nice to be here with you."

"Chris, you don't mind my hand on your back do you? I felt like reaching out just now. I'm so happy and content and simply wanted to share a touch."

"I don't mind at all."

"Chris, you are so different from anyone I've ever known. I'm thinking things and feeling things I've never dared think before. Please tell me if I do anything that seems too odd or forward. I haven't crossed any lines have I?"

"No, I'm feeling the same way. I have to tell you something and I hope you're ready to hear it. I've never had the courage to talk about this with another person, but I feel that with you it won't matter."

They had stopped along the side of the clay road about four block ends from Chris's house. The sun was going down and the light was fading into shades of orange and red.

"Walt, as I told you, I've never been one to date or socialize with girls or even other guys for that matter. I think you and I might have something even more special in common than a birthday." He hesitated a moment as he thought, *Here goes.* "Walt, I'm attracted to guys rather than girls. Do you know what I'm trying to say?"

"Yeah, and it doesn't matter." Chris nodded and smiled. "I'm the same way and my god, Chris, I think I'm falling in love with you."

"I don't have to think about it; there's no question about it, I love you. Walt, you are so handsome and wonderful. Everything about you is absolutely perfect. The last few days have been the best days of my life. Meeting you and learning about you has made me feel things I've never felt before. Walt, please come here; I want to hold you and never let go."

The two young men stepped close and as they did their eyes sparkled with warmth and budding love. Each was exploring unknown territory. As they came together in a warm embrace, their lips parted and Chris turned his head slightly to the right as Walt did the same; their lips met and merged in their first kiss.

Never before had either man felt such powerful emotions like those they shared during those magical moments. Their deep and intense kiss went on and on as each fell even more under the spell of first love. Walt felt Chris's body press against his and felt the warm hardness of his lover's excitement. His own manhood was throbbing as he too pressed against his lover for the first time. Both had dreamed of a moment like this for many years wondering when or if they would ever experience something this wonderful and with who it might be.

Walt's hands dropped toward the base of Chris's back where he reached beneath his companion's shirt and ran his hand up along his smooth back and spine, counting every wonderful vertebra and basking in the warmth of this wonderful man's life force. His fingers explored Chris's warm skin as he felt Chris's hand reach between them and run up and over his belly, chest and sensitive breasts. Their kiss finally ended as both stepped apart breathless, gazing into each other's eyes.

"Oh my god, Chris, I love you so much! This is a dream come true. I never thought it could happen to me. Don't ever stop loving me; I couldn't bear it. Please promise me you won't."

"I won't, Walt. I feel half crazy right now; I want to run around like a little kid and shout out to everyone how much I love you. God, you feel good against me. I'm so damned excited and hard I can barely stand it. I want to make love to you tonight. I'd do it right here if we could. I hope you want the same thing because I can hardly wait to be alone with you and show you how I feel. Can I touch you?"

"God, yes! Just be careful. I'm about ready to explode down there. Go easy. My god, it's so hard it hurts."

Chris fumbled with Walt's zipper and the top clasp of his jeans as Walt ran his fingers through Chris's light brown hair. Chris looked down as Walt's snow white briefs appeared as his jeans fell open. He gently pulled down his friend's jeans and saw the shape of his sex and the wetness around its tip. He touched the wetness lightly and felt Walt jump with the sensation and harden even more against his hand.

Walt leaned forward and kissed Chris repeatedly while he fought for control as Chris carefully explored his secret places.

Walt gasped, "Oh my god, Chris; that feels wonderful. Careful, I'm about to burst." Chris gently pulled Walt's briefs downward until his moist and throbbing penis was freed and exposed to the red light of the setting sun. His light brown, fluffy puff of pubic hair graced his slim and long penis. He was circumcised and the firm, smooth head of his sex was wet with moisture and more was emerging from its opening. Chris had dreamed of a moment like this for years and now was finally able to bend and kiss away the wetness. Walt's emission was warm, slippery and slightly salty. As Chris's lips and tongue caressed him, Walt gasped and pushed forward into his willing mouth. Chris felt Walt's need, but he didn't want him to come too early, so he pulled away before he spoke.

"You are so beautiful, Walt. I can hardly wait until we can be together tonight. God, I wish it was now." Chris pulled Walt's briefs back into place before saying, "Please, touch me now like I did you. I want to feel your hands around me. I want to feel your lips there too if you want to do that."

Walt kissed Chris deeply as soon as he stood back up. As he did so, Chris unsnapped his trousers and lowered his zipper as Walt pushed his warm fingers under the band of his briefs and played in his dark pubic hair. His touch was electric and Chris moaned with pleasure as he kissed Walt's forehead, eyes, nose, and lips. Walt pulled down Chris's briefs and his erection hardened even more as Walt then bent and kissed him there, sucking away the flowing liquid and playing his fingers over his tight and sensitive scrotum. Chris too was circumcised. Walt cupped his sex and squeezed gently to milk more warm fluid from his lover so he could suck it away. It was all Chris could do to maintain control as he ran his fingers through Walt's golden hair.

Finally, Walt's attentions were becoming more than he could handle. Chris gasped and asked him to stop although he wished more than anything for him to keep doing what he was doing. "I love you so much, Walt. Just hug me close for now. If you do anything more down there I'm going to explode and I want our first time together to be special when we're in my bed. God, you feel so good against me." They had once again embraced and Chris's penis, still out of his briefs pushed into Walt's front as they kissed long and deeply.

Finally gaining some level of control, they stepped apart and adjusted their clothing before returning to the house. For most of the way walking back, as it was growing dark and no one was around, they held hands as they strolled slowly toward Chris's home occasionally kissing or nuzzling in one another's soft hair.

"Your folks have no idea about you being gay, do they?" asked Walt.

"No. I've always been too chicken to bring up the topic. They may have suspicions since I never dated, or even pretended to like girls. Probably deep down they might wonder, maybe more so now that I've brought home a very handsome young man for them to meet."

"Think they'll ask you about it privately? I sure don't want to cause you any problems."

"No, they'll not say anything. Besides, I'm not a little boy under their roof any longer. And you're just a new friend as far as they know. Don't let it worry you. I love you and you love me and that's all that matters now."

"What about their religious views? Will this cause any friction?"

"I don't think so. We're Episcopal and our church is probably the most liberal of all Protestant faiths when it comes to gay issues. The national board of bishops is talking about ordaining gay priests pretty soon. Mom and Dad have both said they favor that."

"Wow. That's pretty good then."

"Yeah, Mom and Dad will be fine. Don't let it concern you. I'll probably come clean with them in the near future, now that I've found you."

The house was in sight, so they kissed deeply one more time before walking the remainder of the way. As they returned through the patio's screen door, the two dogs came out of the house to greet them wiggling once more for attention.

"Have a nice walk, fellows?" asked Chris's dad as they stepped into the living room.

Walt answered, "Oh, yes sir, Mr. Walker. I'll never forget it. We've been enjoying nature and the quiet. Chris showed me some things I've never seen before, but certainly wanted to." Walt grinned at Chris who rolled his eyes and smiled back.

"Good. I'm glad you enjoyed a walk in the woods. A lot of young people today just don't seem to appreciate nature and its hidden beauty. Chris always has and I'm glad to see he's found a friend who can appreciate it the same way he does. I think you guys will be good for one another. You're welcome to visit whenever you like."

"Thanks. I look forward to it. Chris and I sure appreciate the use of the camper. I've never gone camping and Chris is making plans for us to do that in the next few weeks."

"With Chris gone, Amelia and I won't be doing any camping, so we're giving it to him. Remind me tomorrow morning, Chris, and we'll dig out the title. Your name's already on it and the registration, so all you'll have to do is let your auto insurance company know, so it's covered."

The evening wore on as both Chris and Walt waited with anticipation for bedtime to finally arrive. A little after ten, Chris's parents announced they were heading off to bed.

"You boys are welcome to sit up and watch television or whatever as long as you want," said Amelia as she and her husband turned off the kitchen lights and went about the house making sure everything was fine before retiring.

Chris said, "Thanks, Mother, but we're both going to go to bed soon too. It's been a long day and we're both sorta tired."

"Thanks again for everything, Mr. and Mrs. Walker. Good night."

Once his parents' bedroom door closed, Chris smiled at Walt sitting beside him on the sofa and switched off the television with the remote control. Walt skooched closer and ran his left arm behind his companion's back and gave him a hug. Chris leaned over and kissed Walt's cheek. For a while they just sat together in the darkened room and listened to the night sounds through the open window at their backs. A whip-poor-will called a few times and they heard soft chittering sounds that Chris said were flying squirrels gliding from tree to tree as they did their nocturnal foraging.

"This is so nice," said Walt as he nuzzled against Chris's hair and nibbled at his right ear.

"What? The night sounds, or my ear?"

"Both, silly. What a day this has been. I don't want it to end," said Walt as he hugged Chris even more tightly. I'm feeling so many things right now that my mind is overloaded. I never thought three days ago that my life could change so much for the better. I thank God for guiding you my way, Chris. I'm one lucky and happy guy."

"Me too. Just feeling you touching and loving me has made me feel complete for the first time since I was a kid. All those years of teenaged confusion and self-hatred about being gay are over now. I've found the man I want to love."

"Me too," said Walt. "It all happened so fast too. My mind can

50

hardly wrap itself around it all."

"The best is still ahead," added Chris. "If those few minutes on the way back from our walk this evening are any indication of what's about to happen in my room, I'm going to be the happiest guy in the world. We're about to take a big step, Partner. Are you ready, Walt?"

"Yeah, more than ready. I like the sound of that word you just used too: partner. That sums it up so well. We're two parts of something pretty special. I can hardly wait to be with you completely. By the looks of our shorts we both are *hardly* able to wait."

"Looks that way."

Walt giggled as he reached over and squeezed Chris's erection. "Damn, I've always wanted to do that to another guy and now I can. I love you, and I'm ready to show just how much. Let's not wait another second."

Chapter 6
Fulfillment

Once inside, Chris closed and locked the bedroom door. He turned to Walt and hugged him close kissing him long and intensely. He ran his hand down over Walt's warm back and found the waistband of his shorts and slid his hand inside and down cupping and squeezing Walt's thin but firm left cheek. Walt did the same but explored between Chris's cheeks running his fingers along and into his warm and slightly moist cleft. Chris did the same and probed until he found Walt's warm and tight opening. He touched him there gently as Walt did the same to him. Their lips parted and they looked into each other's eyes and chuckled.

Chris teased, "I bet you've always wanted to do that to some guy too, right?"

"I confess; guilty as charged. I'm sorry my butt's so skinny and narrow. I like yours better. It's nice and soft and warm and tonight it's mine to explore and get to know better."

"Walt, you have nothing to be ashamed about. I like skinny guys with nice tight cheeks. Believe me, you are exactly what I like in a guy. From the moment I saw you at the pool the other morning, my mind was undressing you."

"Yeah, you even sneaked into my bathroom and got a free peek yesterday when you scared the crap out of me. I saw you looking and was secretly excited to see you do it. I had my suspicions by then already. When you showed up in that hide-nothing, bathing suit, I was doing some hard thinking too and I do mean hard. You really look good in those. I wish you'd brought them along."

"Well, I considered it, but with my folks around I thought it best not to. Right now, you get to see everything anyway. The bathing suit would be a distraction. Let me help you out of your clothing. I really want to see every last beautiful part of you."

Each helped the other remove their clothing until they both stood naked, aroused and beautiful. Their bodies came together and they kissed while pressing closely and forcefully. As they kissed and nuzzled at one another, their hands found all of their secret places stroking, exploring and squeezing until they both were breathless and damp with desire. Chris finally pulled away, went to the bed and threw back the cover and top sheet. He pulled open a dresser drawer, took out two fluffy beach towels and spread them over the bed where they would soon lay together and make love.

Walt watched as his lover moved about. *His body is so beautiful,* he thought as he saw Chris prepare a place for them to join for the first time. As he finished, Chris turned and held out his hand in invitation. Walt smiled and took it. Chris led him to the left side of the bed.

Walt sat down while Chris walked to the wall and switched off the overhead lights. Leaving on a small table lamp, he sat down on the right side of the bed, smiled at Walt and stretched out. Walt joined him and the two rolled together and hugged, pressing their aroused bodies as close as possible. Walt felt Chris take him in hand and guide him between his warm thighs. He did the same with Chris's erection and felt him harden and sigh with satisfaction. Chris's right arm and hand moved over his butt and pulled them even more tightly together. For a time they simply laid closely together, moving slightly as their bodies became more and more aroused. They kissed and felt each other's wetness below as fluid poured from their openings, lubricating and helping to stimulate their erections.

Within a few minutes, Chris said, "If we do this another minute, I'm going to lose it. God, it feels so good. Walt, I want to ask you before I do this, but one of my dreams is to make love orally. Will that cause a problem or make you feel uncomfortable?"

"Oh no. That's what I want for both of us anyway. Please do it to me now. I can't wait much longer. I want your mouth on me so much. I'm so ready."

Chris pulled out and both men laid flat on the bed caressing one another's chests and pubic mounds. Walt played with Chris's navel probing into its depths with one finger as Chris played with Walt's breasts. Chris sat up, leaned close and kissed the center of his partner's chest feeling the light fluffy brown hair growing there. He moved downward and pulled at the hair around Walt's navel with his lips. Walt giggled and said it tickled.

Chris nuzzled in Walt's soft brown pubic hair teasing with his tongue and lips, as he drew in the exciting manly scent of Walt's hair and played with his moist and dripping penis. From time to time he took Walt in his mouth and sucked as he moved up and down along his shaft. Walt was jumping as though having a seizure and soon had to say stop as his body nearly lost the battle for control. More clear mucus flowed as his body arched and he nearly came. Chris remained very still until he felt Walt relax.

"God, that was close. I'm afraid I can't take much more, Chris. Please do it to me so I can do it to you. I want to feel it come inside your mouth. I want you to taste me and love me so much."

"Okay, Walt. I do love you." Chris pulled Walt's thin legs apart and laid down between them. He kissed and nibbled at Walt's large, tight scrotum and nuzzled around the base of his six-inch long penis. With his left hand, he collected some mucus from his own penis and pushed beneath his partner and wet Walt's opening. With one finger he pushed inside just a bit as he nibbled at his companion's sack and the base of his penis. Walt was gasping and shivering with pleasure and saying, "Oh god," over and over through clenched teeth.

With one finger inside Walt, Chris held his manhood firmly, bending it downward with his left hand and taking its pulsing warmth into his mouth. He played over the warm and slippery head with his tongue until Walt gasped for him to stop, but instead, he thrust down and over his friend's hardness sucking tightly and moving his finger inside his rear opening. Walt was tensing and his thin knees were rising from the bed and gripping Chris's sides as Walt drew back and drew back and finally exploded with a series of uncontrollable shudders.

"Oh my god! uh, uh, uh ...Oh Chris, don't stop. It's wonderful. I love you so much!" Walt was sobbing and grasping at Chris's head, pulling at his hair with one hand and stroking his cheek with the other. Walt's warm, delicious semen was filling Chris's mouth and he nearly came spontaneously himself with the intensity of emotions as he felt his partner's essence bursting into his mouth. It tasted so good --- salty and sweet at the same time. He could smell and taste it's earthy scent as he swallowed. As the orgasm finally ended, Chris pulled away, squeezed out the last glistening white drops and rubbed Walt's semen over his lips and beneath his nose. The scent was overwhelmingly exotic and sexy. *God, I love this guy,* he thought as he stroked his partner's pubic area and nuzzled his once-secret places.

After a few minutes of cuddling and recovery for Walt, it was Chris's turn and Walt was not about to disappoint him. As shy and reserved as Walt had seemed during their first few days together and now that all his secrets were revealed to the young man with whom he'd fallen in love, Walt became like a wild animal. Chris was amazed as his new lover drove him nearly mad with his love-making.

For someone completely inexperienced in actual sexual expression, but who had lived in a world of sexual fantasy and imaginary lovers, Walt seemed to know every possible way to give Chris pleasure.

For nearly fifteen minutes of amazing foreplay, he brought Chris to the very brink of release, time after time until the poor fellow was practically begging Walt to end it. Using his hands, lips, tongue, penis and even his feet, he teased, tickled and gradually drove his very appreciative partner half mad with pleasure. He could be kissing Chris's face, caressing his chest with his right hand, stroking his pubic area with his left hand and tickling the bottom of Chris's feet with his toes; all at the same time. He was everywhere. When he finally chose to center his attention on Chris's sexual parts his technique was amazingly expert. He seemed to know exactly how to take Chris to the very edge of orgasm, hold him there indefinitely and then stop just before the moment of no return. Chris was almost frustrated with the suspense and anticipation and finally begged Walt to end it.

When that magical moment finally came, Chris had to restrain himself from crying out as he experienced the most powerful and satisfying climax he'd ever felt. It went on and on and filled Walt's hungry mouth to near its limit. As Chris's pleasure ended, Walt crawled up and over him and kissed him deeply, sharing Chris's own semen back and forth between their mouths as Walt thrust his penis between Chris's legs and came again there.

Finally sated, Walt collapsed on Chris's chest and sobbed with the emotional release saying over and over how much he loved Chris as Chris held Walt close and covered his face with kisses and nuzzled against Walt's sweaty hair and face.

They were both so sweaty, sticky and spent after their love-making that they decided to quietly take a quick dip in the swimming pool. It was still not quite midnight and if they were quiet, it shouldn't awaken Chris's folks. A window air conditioner in their bedroom would probably mask any sounds they might make. They wore shorts but nothing else and once they were in the water and felt that they would not be observed, they slipped out of the suits and occasionally embraced and coupled orally underwater. Both were able to reach orgasm fairly quickly and held the semen in their mouth long enough to share it between them as they had done after Chris's climax in the bedroom.

After leaving the pool, returning to the bedroom and gently drying one another, Chris and Walt laid in each other's arms kissing and cuddling leisurely until sleep finally took them. Both dreamed of one another and their first intimate and magical night together.

The next morning they slept in until nearly ten o'clock after awakening at sunrise and making love once more. Their coupling this time was more relaxed and Walt didn't lose himself in the moment and nearly devour Chris like he'd done the night before. It was as if his first encounter had released all the years of sexual cravings and desire in one magnificent act. Chris commented on it after they awoke again at ten.

"My god, Walt! What the hell happened last night? I never expected you to do the things you did to me. I'm not complaining, mind you." Walt was grinning shyly and blushing which made it even more amusing.

"I don't know. I totally lost it, Chris. All those years waiting and wishing for someone wonderful like you and then to finally find myself there and able to do whatever I'd always dreamed of doing, I just sort of lost my mind. God, it was great."

"Yeah, especially for me. Wow! I thought I was being eaten by a sex-crazed cannibal. I think you either licked, sucked, bit or tickled every square inch of my body sometime during that attack upon my virginity. Will I always have that to look forward to?"

"Maybe something like it. I doubt I could ever repeat everything I did. I wasn't myself. I simply had to do everything I could think of for you before the dream ended. I was actually afraid that it was all a dream for a little while. I'm weird. What can I say? I love you so much, Chris, that it almost hurts."

"It was wonderful. You're wonderful. Well, let's get up and find something to eat. I'm starved and half afraid you'll turn cannibal on me again and eat something that won't grow back. My dick's kind of messed up now anyway. I think you might have sucked a little too hard, or maybe chewed on it at some point. The tip's kind of purple, see." Indeed the head of his penis was a bright reddish purple, resembling a ripe plum.

"Oh, damn. I'm so sorry. I'll try not to get so carried away next time. I hope it's not sore because I sure didn't want to hurt you."

"No, it's okay. It's kind of like a hicky I suppose, only a little farther down than the average one. It's something to remember you by this week when I'm alone and missing you."

"I have to warn you then, Chris. I don't intend for you to be alone

56

very much from now on. If you end up missing anything it's gonna be privacy. I found the guy I want to love forever and I'm a tenacious son of a gun. Think you're ready for that?"

"Oh yeah, so very ready. Come here. Breakfast can wait a few more minutes. I wanna eat you."

"Ooo, speaking of sex-starved cannibals..."

Chapter 7
New Arrangements & Worries at Work

The rest of the visit to Chris's home was most enjoyable. The promised beef roast was out-of-this-world according to Walt and Chris both, much to Amelia's delight. She packed some leftovers for their supper that evening after their return to Jacksonville. Around two o'clock, Chris and Walt hooked the Coleman camper to the hitch of his Buick wagon and a half hour later pulled away from the house as the Walker's waved goodbye and wished their son and his new friend well, asking that they come back soon for a visit. Chris's mom said they were planning a visit to Jacksonville in a few weeks.

The return trip north was pleasant and they arrived safely around five. Chris would have to ask the management about parking space for the camper in the next few days. They warmed the leftovers from the roast beef dinner and each sipped at a glass of red wine. Walt was gazing in silence at Chris from across the small, four-person dining table. Chris had lit the two green candles which up until now had always been simply for decoration. It just seemed right to do so.

Chris smiled and said, "A penny for your thoughts, Walt. Something's on your mind, I can tell."

Walt blinked and seemed to wake up from a trance. "Sorry. Yeah, I was kinda out there. I've just been considering all that's changed in my life and I suppose in yours too. My whole perspective has done a one-eighty." He reached across the table with one hand and Chris took it automatically in his and squeezed. "See, a simple thing as that. Two days ago I would never do that and you would have probably looked at me like I was an idiot if I had. That's what love has done to us, Chris. It's wonderful. We're so connected."

"Yeah, I'm holding your hand. We're connected," teased Chris with a smile. He saw Walt frown a bit and added, "Just kidding. I know what you mean and it is pretty wonderful. I love you, dude. I've fallen completely and hope it never ends." He gave Walt's hand another squeeze before letting go, coming around the table and bending over his lover and hugging him from behind and kissing the top of his head. "I love everything about you from the top of your head to your little toes. Last night changed me too. Every time I look at you I want to touch you to make sure you're real and still here."

"It feels so good to be touched too. As I told you before, I was always leery of being touched by anyone. Now, with you, I find myself craving it."

"Listen, Walt, there's something I want to talk about." Chris pulled up the chair beside Walt's seat, sat down, took both of Walt's hands in his and looked into his beautiful blue eyes. "If this is too soon for me to ask this, let me know, okay? After last night and all we are feeling, I want to ask you if you want to start staying with me here for a while to see if we're not just hooked on a feeling, but really are falling in love. Call it a trial period. If you need some space, or I do, we can always separate for a night or two, but I'd really like to try living together for a while. What do you think?"

"That's what I was thinking of asking you when I spaced out a few minutes ago. See, great minds think alike."

"Yeah, and horny gay guys think of having sex every night with their best buddy and having someone to snuggle with, kiss and talk to. So, do you want to try it out for a while and see what happens?"

"You bet," said Walt, leaning forward for a kiss that he got without any complaint. "If this does work out between us, and I have a good feeling it will, do you think we might eventually make it a permanent thing? One of the reasons I ask is that my lease comes up for renewal next month and if we do decide to be together, that would be a good time to make the move permanently. It will give us a month to try out our relationship before I have to let the management know."

Chris added, "If we do, maybe I can get them to change my lease over to a larger apartment with two bedrooms. That will give the appearance that we are just splitting expenses and not bring too much attention to our lifestyle. It's mainly for our parent's sake. Personally, if we do stick together, I'm thinking about telling my folks about it, but I'm not saying you have to do the same with yours. You know better how they might react and that will be your decision. Also, if our folks come to visit, we can let them have one of the rooms and we can bite the bullet and double up, or so it would seem."

Walt laughed and said, "My folks might be more of a challenge than yours. I can see your folks don't question your judgment. My mom would probably be okay, but my dad's a different story. He loves me and I love him, but he's kind of the macho type." Walt rolled his eyes as he went on, "As I told you his world revolves around diesel engines, football, and baseball. He's a television addict and frustrates

Mom sometimes because of it. I could see how much your folks are in tune with one another. Dad and Mom love each other a lot, but Dad's not the type to show it openly. I saw your folks holding hands on the patio as they watched us swim. There's still so much romance in their lives. It was nice to see. They're great people."

"Thanks. So, if you're comfortable with it, we'll give co-habitation a try. I sure like the idea of having you right beside me every night where I can reach out and love you and have you love me. Just please promise me something. If you are going to go wild once in a while like you did last night, let me know in advance so I can take some vitamins or energy bars to help me keep up. God, Walt, I thought I was wrestling with a damned lion."

Walt started laughing and Chris kissed him again. "Sorry, Chris, that's what happens when a twenty-one-year-old, sex-starved man suddenly gets to do everything he's wanted to do since he was thirteen. I had a ball."

"Yeah, two of them and I have the teeth marks to prove it."

"What? I bit your balls?" Walt started giggling. "You didn't tell me about that. I don't even remember what all I was doing. Sorry."

"I'm just kidding. It was more like softly chewing, not biting and I kinda liked it. So, why don't we go to your place and pack up a few things you might need for the next night or two. I have to go to work in the morning and you have classes, so the weekend is nearly over. We have to remember August eighth and tenth, by the way."

"Why is that?" asked Walt.

"Well, if this works out --- and I'm pretty sure it will --- those dates will be our anniversary. We met on the eighth and made love on the tenth. They certainly are important dates to me."

"Yeah, I agree. See, I told you I always wait for the third date before I nearly savage my boyfriends."

"I think you meant to say, boy*friend*, as we were both blushing virgins before the tenth." They shared a laugh, a hug, and a kiss before setting off to pack Walt's things for their first few days together.

That evening they retired at nine. Perhaps it would be more accurate to say they got into bed at nine. For the next hour and a half they were hardly sleeping, but after another memorable session of exploring their bodies and senses, they fell asleep in one another's arms, tired and satisfied. Their love-making was slower and gentler this time and both felt their relationship was off to a healthy start.

Sometime during the night Chris awoke and experienced a moment of déjà vu as he once more felt a warm presence behind him, a firm penis tucked between his thighs and a loving arm draped across his side and chest. This time it wasn't a teasing dream, however, and he thanked the fates that he'd found, and was now loved by, his wonderful companion.

The next morning, when Chris's alarm went off at six, both felt well-rested and ready to assume the normal routine of their lives. Walt's first class wasn't until nine, so he had a little more leeway in preparing for the day. Chris had gone off to take a shower and was pleasantly surprised when he was joined by Walt who helped wash his back and generally made an ordinary shower extraordinary. They both wanted to make love but knew that there wasn't enough time to get that involved. Chris had to be at work by eight, so after the shower, they ate breakfast and talked about their daily plans.

Walt had European Art History from nine to eleven-thirty and Advanced Airbrush class and lab from one until four that afternoon. He would be home by four-thirty.

Chris said he had a half-hour-long staff meeting first thing at eight. That was a regularly scheduled event for administrative and curatorial staff on alternate Tuesdays. The museum was always closed to the public on Mondays and its normal week for the public ran from Tuesdays through Sundays. He would spend most of his first week just getting his office in order and begin production work for his first Science Theatre show.

At breakfast, Walt asked, "Have they told you what the show has to be about, or is it up to you?"

"It's completely up to me, apparently. When I was hired, I asked Richard Pike, the senior science curator about it and he said the theatre was entirely mine to run. He's a nice guy and I don't see him as putting down on me like some supervisors might. Treats me like an equal, even though I'm the new guy. I think he's gay, by the way."

"Oh really?" said Walt with just a touch of concern in his voice. "How do you know?"

"Don't worry, Walt. No need for concern. Richard is thirty-five and his companion was helping him do some carpentry work on the day of my interview. When Richard showed me around, the day of my interview, Carl, that's his buddy's name, shook my hand and introduced himself as Richard's roommate. He's sort of feminine and rested his hand on Richard's arm as if to say, 'he's mine'. I was kind of glad to see two gay guys were working at the museum. It made me feel less worried my nature might cause problems down the line. You have no need to be jealous. Carl's nice, but I really don't feel attracted to real feminine guys."

"Oh, I'm not jealous. I trust you. I was just surprised you knew Richard was gay being so new to the job."

"Yeah, don't you worry one bit, I've found the man I want to be with and he's everything I could possibly hope for."

"Good. I feel the same way."

Chris said, "This evening we'll need to go shopping. I didn't pack too many fresh food items or meat, so think about some stuff you like; I'll do the same and we'll come up with a grocery list before we go out. Eating out is nice, but gets expensive. Besides, I'm a pretty good cook, if I do say so myself. Mom taught me a lot. How about you, do you like to cook?"

"Yeah, I'm not too bad at it. My specialty is Italian-American dishes; ravioli, lasagna, noodles Alfredo, chef salads, stuff like that. I have about fifteen pounds of ground beef and some chicken breasts in my freezer I'll bring over. I have some vegetables for salads and cooking also."

"Good," said Chris. "My specialty is eating Italian-American food. My cooking tends toward bread-making, roasts, seafood, soups, stews, and vegetable dishes."

"Sounds like we'll be eating pretty well."

Chris left for work at seven-thirty and gave Walt an extra key to his apartment. Walt did the same for him and after Chris left, Walt went to his apartment to gather his books and school materials before leaving for the university.

Chris's first day went well and he was surprised, at the beginning of the staff meeting once he was introduced to everyone, when the museum director, Mrs. Wilkinson, handed him a check for two-hundred dollars as a welcoming gift from the museum staff fund. He thanked her and the other staff, saying it would help a lot until he could collect his first paycheck in two weeks from the school board.

The rest of Chris's day was spent setting up his office and work area. Richard showed him a storage room where extra office furniture and cabinets were kept and told him to request whatever he needed;

support staff would move it to his office, or the theatre. By the end of the day, his office and work area looked well-organized and serviceable. Since the fall school term had not yet started, there were a number of junior museum helpers around the place to act as guides and aids to the curators.

One thirteen-year-old boy, Sebastian Selkirk, introduced himself and offered to help Chris in any way he could. He turned out to be a great helper. Sebastian was from Liverpool, England, and was extremely bright and polite. He took directions well and stuck to whatever task Chris gave him. His mom, Libby Selkirk, was a part-time staff member who taught classes in crafts and pottery-making in one of the museum's many classrooms.

Libby was pleased that Sebastian had found a niche as she put it while talking with Chris at the end of the workday. She hugged her smiling son close and said, "Seb's been saying he wanted to get involved in the new Science Theatre once it opened, so I believe he went looking for you as soon as he heard you'd joined the staff this morning. If he makes a nuisance of himself, just send him off, or let me know." She hugged her tall and somewhat shy son again as he blushed from the attention.

"I'm glad to have the help, Libby. Sebastian's a bright fellow and I'll make sure he has an active role in our theatre shows. I'll need an on-stage assistant for the Saturday public shows, Seb, so be prepared. Tomorrow we'll start planning the first production. I've decided on a show about static electricity --- something rather shocking for the good people of Jacksonville."

Sebastian smiled and said, "Thanks, Mr. Walker. I'd love to help."

Walt was already home when Chris arrived and greeted him with a hug and kiss as soon as he was in the door.

"Wow! That was nice to come home to. I didn't even get a chance to yell out, Honey, I'm home. I feel like... well, like we're a family. I love you, Walt."

"I love you too. We are a family as far as I'm concerned. How was your day?"

"It was great. Look what Ms. Wilkinson and the museum gave me, or I should say us. I'll get my pronouns sorted out eventually. It's a welcome check for two hundred bucks. That's gonna help until my first check comes in two weeks. My pay will be about eight hundred and fifty every two weeks. We should be able to do *very well* on that.

I'm thinking about setting aside so much each check toward a down payment for a home someday."

"Wow. That would sure be nice."

"Once I'm sure of the job and feel comfortable here, I'd like to put the money into something more permanent than rent payments."

"That's a good idea. If we do go in together for one apartment, I'll contribute all I can. I don't have much, but I'll sure do what I can."

"I know you will. I'm not concerned. Let's give it a try, one step at a time, and see what happens. I have a good feeling about us."

"Me too."

The next two weeks went very well for the new companions. On Friday of their first week together, they went to the new Moody Blues Cosmic Concert and both were very pleased with the show.

On days when he had no classes, Walt tagged along with Chris to the museum and helped him with producing the new show. Chris needed several charts and diagrams drawn that would later be photographed and rear screen projected in the theatre to help teach about static electricity.

Chris commandeered an old drafting table from the storage room and some art supplies from the art classroom and set them up for Walt in one part of the preparation area in the rear of the Science Theatre. Walt got right to work and before long had created exactly what Chris needed. The planetarium's technician converted them to 35mm slides for projection.

The planetarium curator, Phil Trace, saw Walt's work and asked if he would be interested in working part-time to create some graphics for him; Walt was more than happy to do it and earn the extra money.

During the few weeks before public school opened, Sebastian became Chris's shadow and was truly an asset. He had a number of skills that made him helpful and best of all was a self-starter. When he saw something that needed doing, even if it was only to dust shelves, Seb pitched in and did it without being asked. Once he met Walt, he made friends with him as well. As the month of August drew near an end, Sebastian was groaning about school starting.

He jokingly asked, "Chris, since you're a Duval County teacher, can't you have me assigned here as your student instead of my having to go to school?"

"Sorry, Seb, you gotta go through school and eventually college the same way I did. I'm sure going to miss your help though. You can come on weekends. I'm planning on you being my on-stage assistant for the Saturday shows and I'm sure Richard will welcome your assistance on Sundays. You're still my main helper, no matter what. I mean it; your help this month has been a godsend and I'm gonna miss you." Chris was surprised to see tears appearing in the sensitive teen's eyes as he contemplated his days at the museum being cut back to once or twice a week. "Hey, Seb; it's okay, buddy."

"I'm sorry. I'm going to miss you so much. I wish I lived closer to you and could come over and visit you once in a while during the week." Sebastian lived on the north side of the St. Johns River and his home was nearly sixteen miles from Chris and Walt's apartment. Unfortunately, their lifestyle precluded having a thirteen-year-old over on a regular basis. No one at the museum yet knew his and Walt's true relationship, or that they were for all practical purposes a couple sharing an apartment.

"Tell you what, Walt and I plan to do some camping this fall from time to time. Maybe one of these weekends we can invite you along if it's okay with your folks. That would be fun. Richard has told me he may like to switch out a few Saturdays with me so he can take off occasionally. He could present the theatre show and I'd have a Saturday off. In return, I'd work a Sunday for him at a later date. I won't forget you."

"Is Walt your best friend, Chris?"

"He sure is. We live in the same apartment building and hang out a lot during our off time." Chris saw how he would have to tread lightly here. He had picked up a couple of times on Seb's symptoms of hero worship and maybe something even more. Sebastian seemed the type of young fellow that just might lean in the same direction as Walt and himself. If so, both would have to be very careful.

"You're nearly fourteen, so you'll be starting eighth grade this year, right?" asked Chris.

"No, I'll be in ninth grade at Stanton Prep, the science and math magnet school. I was skipped a grade a year ago."

"Wow! I knew you were smart. That's super. I've heard Stanton has quite a reputation even though it's only been in operation for a year or two. I'm impressed. I hear it's hard to get in and that they only take the cream of the crop. No wonder I have the best and smartest assistant curator in the museum."

Sebastian was blushing and looking a bit bashful as Chris stepped close and ruffled the boy's jet black hair. He was surprised when

Sebastian threw his arms around him and hugged him tightly, looking up into Chris's eyes with adoration. *I gotta be real careful here,* he thought as he hugged him back briefly and then stepped away.

That evening he told Walt what had happened and how he thought Sebastian might be developing a crush on him. "I think he might be gay, Hon and I don't want either of us to do the wrong thing, nor do I want to over-encourage him. You aren't jealous are you?" Chris was grinning as he said it.

"Of course not; I think it's kind of sweet. If I was a thirteen-year-old gay boy, I sure would be in love with you."

"Don't even joke about it, Walt. I don't want Seb hurt; I especially don't want our privacy invaded, or my morality brought into question. If Seb starts to get too overly-friendly, I'll have to have a talk with him and maybe stop having him around so much. I'm a school teacher and you know how rumors can start and blow up into a major mess for teachers and students in a situation like this."

"Sorry, I didn't mean to make light of it, but you are one heck of a likable guy and if Seb is gay, he's probably trying to figure himself out the same way we did when we were that age. Hey, I had a crush on several teachers in junior and senior high. It happens."

"Yeah, I did too and that's what makes me nervous. I was too shy to act on it, but Seb threw his arms around me today and gave me a more than friendly hug. He's not as shy as we were. English boys have a tendency to be more open about things like this from what I've heard."

"Yeah, England threw out all the Puritans with their conservative ideas about sex a long time ago and we got stuck with them over here in America. Too many of them ran for office too."

"True. I'm still going to tread very carefully around the boy just in case. I'll limit how much time I spend alone with him. Once school starts he'll only be coming in on Saturdays and you'll most likely be there too, so that'll help. It's only six days before school starts, so he'll have less contact with me after that."

Nothing drastic happened with Sebastian over the last week of the month. On Friday, August twenty-ninth, Richard was passing through the Science Mall exhibit area as Chris was making minor repairs to a pedal-powered generator the kids loved to wear out and asked Chris to come by his office after he finished with the machine.

A bit later, Chris knocked and then opened the door to Richard's office. Richard was on the phone but motioned for him to come in and have a seat. He did so and soon Rich hung up and smiled.

"Hey, Chris, thanks for coming by. I wanted to say that your work so far for your first few weeks here has made a good impression on both me and Mrs. Wilkinson. You're doing great and it looks like the theatre is about to open for business. She would like to put out a news release announcing the opening show for the third weekend of September. Is that a realistic date for you, or do you need more time?"

Chris said, "Thanks for your support and confidence. The third weekend sounds fine. I'll write up a blurb about the show for you and her to edit as you choose for the release. I'm calling the show *The Spark Factory* if that's cool with you."

"Good choice."

"I'm thinking about doing the show in makeup as Michael Faraday. Few of our patrons would know what he really looked like. I thought about Ben Franklin, but I'm too young to look that old and everyone has certain expectations of what he looks like."

"That sounds great. I was wondering about the mutton chop whiskers you've been growing. Since I'll be doing Sunday shows, I might need to grow a pair myself or else use crepe hair makeup. We'll get some pictures of you in costume for the release."

"I might need a purchase order for a makeup kit and some other supplies I'll need now and in the future. I'm going to visit some thrift shops for some old clothing I can have sewn into a costume for the late eighteen hundreds. My mom said she'll help with the costume if necessary."

The makeup kit will be no problem. I'll call the bookkeeper and have you put on the authorized purchaser list for our account with Norcosco Theatre supplies, out of Atlanta. Call them and get what you need, but if it's over three hundred dollars, let me know as I'll have to approve that with the boss. As for the costume, my friend, come with me. Boy, do I have a surprise for you. We're about the same size too, so whatever costume we come up with should serve us both."

Richard led Chris to the third floor of the building and asked him to step behind a diorama display of Seminole Indians. Out of sight of visitors, was a door set in the wall of the exhibit room completely hidden by the display. Richard said, "If I haven't disoriented you completely, you'll realize the space beyond this door would be high above the planetarium dome. Most big museums have an attic and storage area. This is ours." Richard was grinning and obviously enjoying acting so mysteriously.

He continued: "We have a lady who works in here; her name is Nelda. She seldom comes out or mingles with the staff and public. She's a sweet soul, but somewhat eccentric and reclusive. She's the museum's conservator and it's her job to mind and maintain the collections that are not on display. Wait till you see this place. She's the only one who knows exactly what all we have in here."

"You're kidding."

"Nope, she's our living inventory. You ask for it and if we have it, she'll take you right to it. Let's see --- I want you to tell her you need an eighteenth-century morning suit, for a gentleman of your proportions. Tell her in exactly those words for if you stammer and are inexact in what you ask for, she will bend your ear for at least an hour telling you all about the importance of knowing exactly what you want." Richard was smiling as he repeated, *"An eighteenth century morning suit, for a gentleman of my proportions.* Got it?"

"I think so, *An eighteenth-century morning suit, for a gentleman of my proportions."*

"Okay, here we go. Richard inserted a key in the lock, without turning it and knocked exactly five times and waited. He whispered, "It's key thirty. You have one on your ring for the next time you visit," Richard whispered. "Don't forget the secret knock too."

From inside they heard a high pitched female voice, "Please feel free to enter." Richard was lip-syncing her words as she said them, grinning all the while. He turned the key and opened the door. Inside was a large, and somewhat amazing room. Chris estimated it was somewhere in the range of seventy feet square. There was row after row of shelves, cabinets, wooden crates and baskets stretching throughout the dimly lit room. A middle-aged lady in what could only be described as a granny dress appeared at the end of the hallway just ahead of them.

Richard spoke, "Ms. Nelda, it is my sincere pleasure to introduce our new Physical Science Curator, Mr. Christopher Walker, who answers to Chris. He has need of your unique talents and services." Richard motioned for Chris to follow him as they approached the smiling lady.

"It's a pleasure to make your acquaintance, young sir. How might I help you?"

"Madam, I have need of an eighteenth-century morning suit, for a gentleman of my proportions."

"Very good; you know exactly what you want. I appreciate that, young man and allow me to bid you welcome to the museum and its archives. Please follow me if you will." She turned and stepped back the way she had come, turning to the left at the end of the passage. Richard and Chris caught up and followed her through the labyrinth of shelves until she stopped in front of the fifth tall wardrobe cabinet in a row of perhaps a dozen. It was unmarked in any way. She opened the double doors of the cabinet and then turned to Chris, looked him over carefully from head to toe, then reached into the cabinet where about thirty men's suits hung on wooden hangers, each covered with clear plastic laundry bags like those used by dry cleaners only longer. She selected three outfits and removed them from the rack and handed them to Chris.

"Any one of these three will serve your needs. Please follow me and we will fill out the necessary forms for you to take temporary possession of, and responsibility for, the garments."

She closed the wardrobe and set off toward her office at a sprightly clip. Richard and Chris had to step lively to keep up. Once at her enormous, carved, teak desk, she pulled three forms from a pigeonhole cabinet behind and began to fill them out using an antique fountain pen that she dipped in a silver, antique inkwell. Before long, she turned the forms toward Chris and asked that he sign them.

Chris wanted so badly to say, *'Shall I use ink or blood, Madam?'* but signed them in silence. Once finished, he said, "I shall take exceptional care of these precious items Ma'am and will return them clean and unblemished once they are no longer needed. That should be sometime shortly before Christmas as I will be using them in the Science Theatre for a new show in which I shall portray the scientist, Michael Faraday. Thank you for your kindness and expertise. I am gratefully in your debt."

"I like this young man very much, Mr. Pike. He knows what he wants and he knows how to treat a lady. Have a good day, gentlemen." With that, she returned to her desk and began working on an old book she was re-binding. Richard led Chris to the door and they left the archive room.

"Whew!" said Chris with obvious relief. "My god, it was like I'd stepped back into the eighteenth century. Where did the museum find her?"

Richard shrugged his shoulders. "No one really knows. She's been with the museum since it started in an old Victorian house on the other side of the river. Some of us joke that she's actually a ghost that came along with the collections." Richard laughed as he led Chris toward the third-floor elevator doors. "Only Mrs. Wilkinson knows her exact history. I have to compliment you. You picked up right away and made it through the gauntlet without a hitch. The last newbe I brought up here asked her one question too many and it took him nearly three hours to escape the room. In fact, I had to come back and rescue him."

"I've never seen her before around the museum."

"And you normally won't. She uses the emergency fire stairway along the side of the planetarium tower to come and go as she wants. She's here before most of the staff in the morning and is often the last to leave. We've had a separate security system installed on the safety stairwell just for her use. She'll attend mandatory, full staff meetings and the museum's Christmas party in December. Outside the archive room she's a different person altogether, laughing and acting pretty much normal, but in there, she's all about business and propriety." Richard paused to press the call button for the lift and as they waited for the elevator doors to open he added, "Museums have mysteries, Chris and she's one of ours. Take good care of those suits."

"What if they don't fit? Should I take them back?"

"Oh, they'll fit. Depend on it. In the inside pockets will be a handwritten history of the item you can read. Everything she knows about each suit will be there. If we ever lose Nelda, it'll take the museum five years to figure out the collections and catalog them the modern way." The stainless steel doors opened and they stepped into the elevator car. Richard pressed the button for the second floor as he told Chris, "We've made suggestions about using one of these new desktop computers to catalog everything and she just glares at whoever is making the suggestion until he or she gives in and changes the subject."

"I bet she can glare too. She's nice, but kind of scary at the same time," chuckled Chris.

"We nearly lost our accreditation a few years back when some anal retentive dickhead from the Association of American Museums found we didn't have a complete *type*-written inventory of our collections. Mrs. Wilkinson made a few calls and mentioned Nelda's name a few times." Richard paused for effect as the elevator arrived and opened on the second floor.

"The Director of the Smithsonian Institution in Washington, no less, called back and chatted with the guy from the AAM and suddenly we got our accreditation. Another unsolved mystery about our Ms. Nelda."

"That's amazing. I'm not sure if I'm half-scared or looking forward to my next encounter with her." Both laughed.

They had returned to the door of Richard's office by that time and Chris thought the discussion was over, but Richard asked him in and said, "Uh, Chris, I have something else I'd like to chat about if you don't mind. It's not exactly work-related, it's on a personal note, but I want to talk about it anyway if it's okay with you. If what I have to say bothers you at any time please tell me and I'll leave it alone."

Chris was a little puzzled, but said, "No, it's fine. Let's talk."

After sitting down, Richard opened a small refrigerator near his desk and offered Chris a choice of canned sodas. Chris opted for a root beer and Richard passed one over. After popping the opening, Richard sipped at a Coke and then said, "Unless you're particularly dense, which I know you're not, you've probably figured out that my roommate and I are more than roommates. We're gay, No great surprise."

"Hey, I have no problems with that, if that's what you wanted to discuss. I think it's great. Carl's a hell of a nice guy. I'm glad for you."

"Thought you might be. If I may, I'd like to ask if you and your friend Walt are of a similar nature? If I'm wrong, or out of line for asking, please let me know and that will be that. I'm not your enemy."

"No, Richard, it's fine. Walt and I are a couple and are very much in love. He's great. We met the day I moved in and over the past few weeks we've gone from friends to a whole lot more. We're sharing my apartment and he's decided not to renew his lease and move in permanently."

"That's wonderful. I'm glad for you both. The reason I'm asking is that from time to time Carl and I would like to invite you guys over to our place for dinner or a show or something. Maybe it would help you feel more comfortable and at home if you two have a few gay friends to socialize with. Neither one of us are into partner swapping, nor do we have any other agenda beyond friendship."

"Richard, I appreciate it. I'll let Walt know and I think he'll agree with me that we'd love to get to know you guys better. We're the same way, very much exclusive. Heck, we were both introverted virgins until three days after we met and it's been a fantastic couple of weeks so far. He really completes me and for the first time in my life, I'm not so damned depressed and lonely. That was one big concern about taking this job, as I was worried I might be discovered and could lose my position. Seeing you and Carl together made me feel a lot less concerned."

"Good. I'll tell Carl and maybe soon we can get together for dinner. Carl works as an assistant chef at one of Jacksonville's top restaurants, so you're in for a treat."

"We'd be happy to come over. As soon as we're more domestically settled, we'll have you guys over, or take you out for dinner some night. We're going to ask our apartment manager if we can move into a two bedroom unit so we'll have a place for our parents to stay when they visit and to cover up our lifestyle until we both can let our folks know our sexual preference."

"Carl and I have both been through that and are glad we finally came out to our folks. I'm thirty-two and my folks have known since I was twenty. Carl's been out with his mom for over eight years now. His dad died when he was younger, so it's just his mom who knows. She loves me like a second son now and fusses over me like a hen all the time." Richard smiled and extended his hand across the desk and as Chris responded said, "Chris, I'm glad we talked."

"Me too, and thanks for your acceptance." Chris was about to leave, but hesitated and said, "Oh, Richard, there's something else that Walt and I were discussing recently and I want your advice about it. This deals with both subjects: lifestyle and work. You know Sebastian, my junior curator helper?" Richard nodded and grinned.

"Bet I know what this is about. I've seen him following you around with doe eyes. Listen, he fixated on me for a while too at the beginning of the summer. Have a talk with his mom, Libby. She's a liberated lady and so is his dad. She knows Seb's gay and in that stage when he's looking for a hero to worship." Richard came around the desk and was walking with Chris toward his office door.

"She already knows he's fascinated with you. She mentioned it last week and said it was adorable. Welcome to the pedestal, Mr. Hero. Talk with her and then she'll probably have a meeting with you and Sebastian and it'll all work out. She's not concerned you'll take advantage of him and neither is her husband, Nigel. Hell, Nigel's bisexual anyway, but is loyal to Libby."

"You're kidding. I noticed he was rather flamboyant."

72

"They're a very liberated English family and you will come to love them the same way I do. Not that I would ever do it, but she told me once that if I thought Seb needed an introduction to sex, she had no problem if I was his teacher. She said better me than some stranger who could hurt him. I told her I could never cross that line, but if he needed someone to talk to, I'd help him out, but only with her or Nigel's permission at the time."

"You're kidding me? She actually said that?"

"Yep, Libby and Nigel are unique parents and love that boy no matter what he is. He's going to turn out okay without all the fears, guilt and hang-ups that most of us grew up with." He smiled and patted Chris on the back. "Talk to her. It takes a bit of courage at first, but you'll feel better afterward. If you want I can call her in advance and set up a time for the two of you to talk."

"Not just yet, Richard. Let me talk this over with Walt first. Whew! I'm glad I brought it up with you. I was worried about his attentions. He hugged me recently and I didn't quite know how to handle it. He's such a sweet kid and sharp as a tack. I told him he could go camping with Walt and me sometime but only meant it as a gesture. I'm still not sure it would be a good idea."

"Ask Libby. She'll probably tell you to go ahead and take him along. I know exactly what she'll say. She'll tell you that if you and Walt want to let him see you hugging or kissing it will do him good to see what happiness two gay guys can share. As I said, she's one of a kind."

Chapter 8
Lifestyle Discussions & Camping Plans

Over the next few weeks, Chris and Walt had many things to discuss besides Sebastian. After talking to the apartment management, Chris was permitted to transfer his lease to a two bedroom unit in the next building along the back of the complex. It was an upstairs unit whose slightly larger screened balcony looked out on an even denser copse of trees near the very far corner of the school playground. Parking space was available also for the camper in a gated lot nearby. The larger apartment gave them an additional two hundred square feet and the rent was somewhat less than they were paying for two separate single bedroom apartments. Doing this saved them roughly a hundred twenty dollars a month --- a welcome sum.

The week after they made their move to the new unit, they decided to go camping at Blue Springs State Park near Orange City, Florida. It would be just the two of them and they were able to arrange their schedules so both had Saturday through Monday off allowing two nights at the campground. It was in late September and the weather was still warm and comfortable --- not too hot and not too chilly. They enjoyed walking the nature trails, swimming in the crystal clear spring beside the manatees who were just beginning to make their way to the headspring for the winter months. The park rules were to look, but not touch or otherwise disturb the docile creatures.

The constant temperature of the water in the crystalline spring made it possible for manatees to survive the winter. Even though Florida was sub-tropical, the cold Atlantic Ocean waters and inland waterways became too cold for the warm-blooded mammals and their young. Manatees along the Florida coasts commonly sought out the warmer springs and warm water outflows of power plants along coastal rivers. Their greatest danger during those times was mankind and his propeller-driven pleasure boats.

Chris and Walt's evenings there were filled with quiet love-making as they relaxed far away from the city and enjoyed the sights and sounds of Florida's natural environment. So far, their relationship was stable and satisfying for both.

Chris met Walt's family the week before they went camping and got along very well with his mom, Linda, and his dad, Steve. Walt had been right; simply because Chris had graduated from the University of Florida, his dad warmed to him even after Chris admitted he was no football fan. He told Mr. Bower he had attended several basketball games while at the university and that helped to make him a true Gator. Conversation with Walt's dad was able to turn to other subjects after that. Walt grinned as Chris handled the sports subject so well.

His dad did ask a few uncomfortable questions about Chris's social life and if he had a female romantic interest since moving to Jacksonville. Chris evaded the question and talked about his time-consuming duties at the museum and thus turned the conversation aside with his typical verbal skill. Walt, sitting nearby, rolled his eyes and smiled. Eventually, this topic would have to be dealt with as Mr. Bower made a few comments about how he worried about Walt's lack of social contacts with the opposite sex.

After returning from their camping trip, Walt and Chris discussed the topic of Sebastian, for the boy often called, asking when they were going to take him camping. On Saturdays, he followed them around the museum like a puppy still clearly enamored with not only Chris but Walt as well.

"So," asked Chris one evening just after talking with Seb on the phone with his typical request about camping. "What should we do about my exuberant young apprentice? I think I should have that talk with his mom. I confess it's kind of scary to talk with a parent about the topic. Richard told me Libby has already figured you and me out. Probably most of the staff has too. No one seems to care and that's good. It's common in museums I suppose, having so many artistic and creative people working there."

Walt agreed and said, "I think talking to Libby and maybe Nigel too would be best. Let's see what they say and take it from there. He's a sweet kid and I don't want him to be confused. He needs to know that we like him, but that's as far as it can go. Once he knows we're gay and he can come to us for advice about the subject, maybe he'll be less apt to expect anything more. He's living on imagination right now and we need to bring him down to earth."

"What he needs is another boy about his age with similar interests to interact with," said Chris. "I don't think he's as shy as the two of us were at his age. That's what screwed us up and kept us so lonely for so many years. He seems more apt to focus on older guys instead of his peers."

Walt said, "Yeah, I like older guys too, especially if they're a-year-older."

Chris leaned over and gave Walt a quick kiss. "I'm sure glad you came into my life even if it was a little late, you sure were worth the wait, Hon." They were sitting side by side on the sofa and began nuzzling, kissing and touching here and there --- mostly there. Soon they left the sofa and went off and shared a shower before retiring to their bedroom for their usual nightly activities.

Libby knocked at Chris's office door the following Tuesday morning at ten. Chris had asked her at the weekly staff meeting if he could speak to her about Sebastian. Richard had already let her know Chris might soon need to discuss the boy with her.

Chris began the conversation. "Uh, thanks for coming by, Libby. This is somewhat of an awkward topic I need to discuss with you. It's about Sebastian and..."

"I'm sure I know exactly what this is about, Chris," said Libby with a giggle. "All he talks about is Chris this and Chris that, with a Walt or two thrown in. He went through the same thing with Richard last June. He's fallen madly in love with you and Walt. He's been a hopeless romantic since he was ten or so and simply adores gay young men like you fellows. Don't give it a worry. Nigel and I trust you completely. Just the fact you've asked to talk tells me that. Richard told me you'd probably soon discuss it."

"Yes, well it's made me rather uncomfortable, Libby and I don't want to hurt Seb's feelings, or make him feel I don't want him around, or not like him. He's a very sensitive and brilliant boy. What should I do?"

"Nigel and I believe he simply wants love and attention from you and Walt, not necessarily sex. We've already discussed things with him about his preferences, so he knows we're happy with him no matter what he chooses to do in life. He sees you and Walt as a loving couple and that's a wonderful thing for him to see." She smiled and gave Chris's arm a pat. "Society is so harsh in its perception of homosexual and bisexual people. Nigel, before he met me, visited both sides of the street, as it were. He was with a young man in Liverpool for nearly three years before he met me and we hit it off. Seb knows that, by-the-way, and is not affected by his father's past sexual explorations. We want our boy to explore every aspect of life, but of course, we don't want him hurt."

"You are one amazing lady, Libby. Walt and I are still both discussing coming out to our folks, especially now that we share a closet if you get my meaning."

"Oh, Chris, do it. If your parents love you and you have no reason to believe they don't, by all means, clear the air and you'll feel so much better and so will they. They've probably got it figured out anyway, especially if they've seen you and Walt together. Your eyes, when you look at one another, told me within minutes of how much love you share. You two make a beautiful couple."

Chris smiled and nodded. "Thanks, Libby, we're very happy."

"I know Seb has been driving you nearly to bedlam asking about a camping holiday. You have our permission to take him along. Let him see you both being yourselves, natural and loving with one another. That's a lesson he needs to learn so he'll be better prepared someday to feel the joy you both feel. I know you fellows are not going to take advantage of him even though he'd probably love every minute of it." Libby laughed and said, "I see you blushing, dear. Don't feel bothered hugging and kissing him when he shows affection for you. He wants and needs that. That's a part of life and as a gay child, he needs to feel loved and accepted by good role models like you and Walt. It needn't lead to sex." She leaned a bit closer and half whispered, "Once he's a bit older, if it happens to lead to more intimate contacts, Nigel and I won't be angry if you and Walt do make love to him. He'd be learning from two fine examples."

"Dear God, Libby! We have no intention of doing anything like that. He's only thirteen for heaven's sake. Neither Walt nor I want to go to prison." Chris shook his head and smiled. "I understand about an occasional hug and letting him see Walt and me sharing affection, but nothing as bold as what you suggested."

Libby feigned a sigh and said, "Oh your poor repressed Americans. I understand though. Please take him along camping if for no other reason than to shut him up for a while. That's all we hear at home. He said something about a cave or something. Is that where you plan to go?"

"Oh, Walt and I have considered doing that just after Christmas, but that's a much longer trip into the Georgia Mountains. We'll take Seb along if you'd like when the time comes. Our next trip will be to Ichetucknee Springs not far from Lake City. We'll take him with us on that trip."

"Oh, good, will he need anything special for the outing?"

Chris thought for a moment before saying, "He'll need to rent a wetsuit since we'll be floating several miles down a chilly spring run. He'll need a good face mask and a snorkel too. We're planning that trip for next weekend from Saturday until Monday. Will it be all right for him to miss a day of school on Monday?"

"Of course, he'll learn more with you fellows than he'd learn during a week in a stuffy classroom. I'll make arrangements with his teachers. He can write a report or something about the trip."

"You're a heck of a great mom, Libby. Sebastian is one very lucky boy to have you and Nigel. I only hope his time with us will help him better adjust to his nature. We won't do anything to harm that boy, we love him too."

"Listen, Chris, I know next to nothing about wet masks and snorkel suits, or whatever. Let me write you a check and have you and Walt take care of whatever he needs. I'll include a bit more for expenses, gas and food and what not." She scratched away at her checkbook even as Chris told her the wetsuit rental and cost of a mask would be less than thirty dollars. She handed him a check for two hundred dollars and he immediately reacted.

"Oh, good lord, Libby! This is too much! The whole trip won't cost us this much for gas, food, and everything. Please, I can't take this it's too..."

"Nonsense, Nigel and I are doing very well with his advertising firm and he told me to do this. This will also help with the winter trip to the cave and I'm sure you'll need some special equipment for that. We insist and won't hear no, understand. Just be good friends and teachers for our boy."

Chris reluctantly took the check with the understanding he would use it to buy the extra equipment Seb would need for the caving trip in December. Libby gave him a hug and a quick kiss on the cheek before leaving his office.

Sebastian called every night throughout the remainder of that week asking each day if there was anything else he needed to pack. Once Seb was home from school on Friday afternoon, Chris and Walt crossed the Saint Johns River into the Riverside District of the city and picked him up to visit a dive shop and rent their wetsuits. Sebastian chatted non-stop in the car about the upcoming trip until Chris finally had to say, "Sebastian! Chill, buddy! You're going to burst a blood vessel or something."

Sebastian was grinning and said, "Sorry. I'm just excited. This will be my first camping trip ever and I'm so glad you've decided to let me go along with you. I love you both so much and have been dreaming of going with you. Sorry, I'm so excited. I'm gay too you know, like you guys and to actually be going with you is like a dream come true for me. I hope you don't mind me talking about you being gay. Mom told me I should feel free to talk with you if the subject came up and I thought maybe I'd better be the one to bring it up since you both might be shy about it and..."

Walt was giggling as Chris was trying to drive and keep from choking from laughter himself. Chris was finally forced to shout, "**SEBASTIAN! CHILL!** You're going to use up all the oxygen in the car." He glanced at the bubbly kid and couldn't help but feel a surge of love for the boy. "My god, son, take it easy. What has gotten into you? You're never this wild at the museum. Did you get hold of some kind of speed pill or something?" Seb was sitting between them in the front seat of Chris's Buick grinning, so Walt pulled him against him and started tickling the boy's ribs and belly. Sebastian started giggling.

Walt then rapped on Seb's head while saying, "Chris, where's the off switch on this crazy lad? Maybe his folks put the wrong set of batteries in him this evening and he's running on too much voltage. He's like that pink, battery bunny on TV." Seb was still giggling and now couldn't stop. He was trying to say something but was laughing too hard to get it out.

Finally, he managed to say. "Oh Chris, please pull in at a petrol station or something. I gotta pee."

"I knew you were full of something tonight, Seb."

Luckily, they were near a Shell station so Chris turned in. Seb climbed over Walt, ran from the station wagon as soon as it stopped and tore around the side of the station.

A few moments later he came running back around with a panicked look and yelled, "I need a bloody key"

Chris and Walt were in stitches by now as the poor kid ran into the station and practically tore the key off the wall to the surprise of the attendant. He once more sped around the side and after a few minutes returned at a normal pace looking much relieved. He returned the key to the attendant and rejoined Walt and Chris.

"I almost made it, but not quite," he said as he pointed to a small wet spot on the front of his jeans. Leaked a *wee* bit before I could get my wanker out. Whew, don't make me laugh so hard like that; I almost soiled the seat covers. How far is it to the dive shop? Are we nearly there?"

Walt and Chris looked at one another and burst out laughing once more. Before pulling out they both gave the boy a hug and a kiss on the cheek. He beamed at the attention.

At the dive shop, they each selected rental wetsuits and bought a dive mask and snorkel for the boy. Sebastian had recently been fitted with contact lenses as had Walt, so they didn't need prescription masks. Chris and Walt both already had masks and snorkels. While there, Chris bought three large inner tubes similar to those used in truck tires, but these were made especially for swimming or diving and had the diver's red and white symbol painted on their sides. They would be the best alternative to float down the Ichetucknee River if they became tired floating in their wetsuits.

Once they returned to Sebastian's house, he begged them and his parents to let him go home with Chris and Walt since the next day they would be going on their trip anyway. He said he was all packed, so they agreed it did make more sense. Seb was ecstatic and ran off to get his gear which amounted to three enormous duffle bags of *camping supplies*. After assuring him that he would not need a hiking rack, backpack, or a web belt complete with canteen, compass, hunting knife and several other official boy scouts labeled items, they reduced his load to a more sensible and manageable single duffle bag.

Nigel laughed and said, "I told you so, Daniel Boon. You're floating down a river, Seb, not hiking the bloody Appalachian Trail."

"Seb grinned and said, "Well, I didn't know, Dad, and it's better to be prepared. They taught us that in the Boy Scouts." Nigel just laughed and gave his boy a kiss and hug.

"Take good care of each other, fellows. Maybe Libby and I will have a few days of peace now that he's off with you down the river. We were about to tie a gag on him."

It was close to nine o'clock when they finally reached Whisperwind Apartments. Seb had never been there and followed Chris and Walt to their unit. Once inside, they showed Seb to the guest room and told him to stow his camping equipment there until morning.

Chris said, "Sebastian, we'll let you take a shower first tonight, especially since you wet your pants today." He was grinning at the boy and holding his nose. "There are towels and soap in the bathroom.

Walt and I will take our showers later before we go to bed. Hop to it now and get your bath. We'll be right out here if you need anything."

Soon they heard the sound of the shower. Apparently, Seb had left the bathroom door open as they could easily hear the water running. Walt looked at Chris and said, "Jesus, he's been hyper all evening. You'd think we were taking him on a trip to the moon, he's so excited. Didn't he say he was in the Boy Scouts? You'd think he'd have gone camping sometime with them."

"Yeah, it does seem odd. Maybe he wasn't in the scouts long enough to do anything like that. We'll ask him when he comes out. He's such a sweet kid. It should be fun for all of us this weekend. Sometimes I think that the worst thing about being gay is not being able to have kids. Some states allow gay parents to adopt, but I don't think Florida is one of them. Maybe someday, when we're older, we might be able to do something like that. I'd love to have a child, how about you?"

"Never thought about it until now, but since you brought it up, I think it would be great especially once both of us are working and may soon have a home of our own." Walt snuggled closer to Chris and kissed him before saying, "It would probably be best to get an older child rather than an infant. With both of us working, that would make more sense."

"Yeah, maybe a five or six-year-old."

Walt added, "There're so many kids without homes. I recently read in a magazine how a lot of foreign children are available for adoption; it would be nice to give one a home in America."

"You never know, partner. If the child is as crazy as Seb was tonight, however, we might have to consider sedatives." Chris laughed.

Just about that time, Sebastian appeared in the living room with a towel wrapped around his middle and a smile on his face. "I heard that last part. Sorry I was so excited earlier. I have been so anxious to be with you guys and kind of lost control."

Walt teased, "Of your behavior, or your bladder?"

"Both, it seems. Sorry, I piddled a widdle. I couldn't stop laughing. No harm done. I washed out my underwear in the shower and hung them up to dry. I'll toss them in the wash once I get home."

Seb glanced around the room before saying, "You guys have a nice home. It's clean and neat."

"Thanks," said Chris.

"I kind of expected it to be maybe a little messier, like my room."

Sebastian went back to the guest room and returned with a pair of pajamas and proceeded right there to remove the towel, finish drying his hair and get dressed. Chris and Walt were both surprised at his lack of shyness as he faced them and started asking questions about where the water comes from in a spring. He was well-matured for a thirteen-year-old with a full growth of black pubic hair. He, like most boys born in England and Europe, was uncircumcised. He pulled on his PJs without underwear.

Chris was explaining the Floridan Aquifer and how it fed numerous springs around the state and as soon as Seb was dressed he came over to the sofa where they were sitting and squeezed in between the two saying, "I love you guys. Thanks for taking me along this time. Can I have a hug before bedtime?"

Walt said, "You sure can. We love you too. I know how much Chris appreciates all of your help at the Science Theatre. I've learned what a fine young man you are too from the times I've worked with Chris and you at the museum. Come here, buddy." Walt gave Seb a warm and sincere hug and a quick kiss on his forehead. Sebastian wiggled with pleasure before turning to Chris for the same. Chris didn't disappoint him and gave him a hug and a kiss on the end of his nose.

"I wish I was twenty-one," said Sebastian with a mischievous grin.

"Why is that?" asked Chris.

"Because I'd steal you away from Walt, or maybe steal Walt away from you. Maybe even all three of us could, uh, you know." Seb had an impish look on his cute face as he wiggled his eyebrows at each of them. Walt laughed outright while Chris just shook his head and smiled.

"I hope I can find a boyfriend someday as nice as you guys." They both laughed and Walt ruffled Seb's still damp black hair.

"You will," said Walt. "You're so lucky, Seb, to have parents who you can be honest with about your sexuality. Both of us still haven't gotten brave enough to tell our moms and dads, but we're planning on doing it soon. We don't want to hide anymore now that we have one another. We want our families to love us both and appreciate how very happy we are."

Chris said, "Well, I think we all need to go to bed. Tomorrow is a busy day and we'll be getting an early start."

"What time do we need to get up?" asked the boy.

"Oh, about three in the morning should do," said Walt with a straight face.

"Three? Why so early?" He was looking back and forth between them with wide eyes.

Chris set him straight, "Walt's just kidding. I'll set the alarm for about six. We'll eat breakfast and get rolling by seven or so. The camper is already packed and our other gear and your stuff can go in the station wagon. Off to bed, big guy. Come on, you're not too old to be tucked in are you?"

"Not by you guys. Heck, I might even have a bad dream tonight and need one of you to sleep with me." Seb grinned and wiggled his eyebrows again in a come-hither look. "I wouldn't mind at all snuggling with someone."

"I bet you wouldn't, you little stinker," said Walt. "I'm not sure either one of us would be safe sharing a bed with a horny, gay, thirteen-year-old." Seb snickered and gave Walt another hug before getting up and heading to the guest bedroom. They followed him in and waited until he jumped into bed and smiled, waiting like a ten-year-old to be tucked in.

Chris walked over and said, "Walt, exactly how do you tuck in a thirteen-year-old?"

Walt said, "Well, like this. You tuck him in here," and he poked Seb in the side with one finger, "Then you tuck him here," as he poked Seb in the belly. By now Sebastian was laughing as he was very ticklish.

Chris joined in saying, "Oh okay, I can do that," as he joined in the tickling. "How long do we have to do this, Walt?"

"Until he laughs so hard he pees his pants."

"He did that already today. Does that count?"

"Stop it, pleeeease! I really do have to go now. Stop!"

After a few seconds more they let him up and sure enough, Sebastian threw the covers to the side and ran for the bathroom. They heard the sound of him peeing as he said from the open bathroom, "I owe you guys one for doing that. I'll get my revenge before the weekend's over."

He returned looking wary, but they let him approach and this time did tuck him in with a hug and a brief kiss on the cheek. His last words, as they turned off the light and said goodnight were, "I love you guys. I'm moving in next week." They closed the door except for a few inches and returned to the living room.

Chris flopped on the sofa beside Walt and gave him a side hug and a kiss before saying, "That was fun. He's one super kid. Maybe someday you and I *can* adopt a child. If he or she is anything like Seb, we'd be two happy and lucky guys. I enjoyed tucking him in as much as he did. Felt good to hear him laugh and say he loved us."

"I know. I'm glad we're taking him along."

Chapter 9
Down the Ichetucknee

Sebastian was a sound sleeper and it took several attempts to rouse him. He blinked and looked confused as Chris bent over him and gently shook his shoulder until he finally looked around and determined where he was. He reached up for a hug once he realized Chris was the one trying to rouse him. Chris obliged him and soon, Seb was up and dressed in black gym shorts and a black tee shirt with a *Dark Side of the Moon,* Pink Floyd prism and spectrum logo on its front. He was wearing white canvas deck shoes with white athletic socks as he made his appearance at the breakfast table where Chris and Walt were already eating cereal and sipping coffee.

"You look quite sharp, Seb. What do you want to drink, buddy?" asked Walt. Orange juice, milk, coffee?"

"Coffee. I like it with lots of sugar and milk. I like frosted flakes too." A large box was already on the table. "Could I have some toast, please?"

"Sure, help yourself. Bread's in the breadbox and the toaster is on the kitchen counter. It's set for lightly browned," said Chris.

Seb set about fixing some and poured himself a cup of coffee from the Mr. Coffee machine. He soon joined them at the table with his coffee and toast, poured himself a bowl of cereal and began to eat. He'd found a jar of homemade blackberry preserves in the fridge and commented on how good it tasted.

"My mom canned that and gave me about twelve jars," said Chris. "They have a berry patch on their land. If you like it, I'll give you a jar to take home with you at the end of the weekend."

"That's great. It's really good. I kind of like all the crunchy little seeds."

They were on the road as planned by seven o'clock driving west on Interstate Ten. It was Chris's plan to take I-10 as far as Lake City and from there follow a number of back roads to the state park located southwest of the city.

Although there was plenty of room in the back seat, Sebastian insisted on sitting between Walt and Chris. Fortunately there was an extra seat belt in the front; otherwise, Seb would have had to settle for the back.

The journey was uneventful and upon arriving at the state park around eleven, they paid for a campsite for two nights and drove to the camping area where they located a nice spot well-enclosed by trees, not far from the shower and restrooms. After backing the camper trailer into the site, Chris got out of the station wagon and stretched while Walt and Sebastian walked around the campsite, picked up a few bits of trash and brushed live oak leaves off the aluminum picnic table. Being October, some of the trees were showing slight changes of color, especially the broadleaf oaks. The predominant live oaks were evergreen, but in fall shed their old leaves as new ones immediately replaced them. The area was covered by the small, curved, brown leaves and numerous acorns that also fell during that time of year.

There was a clean and fresh scent to the air and Seb seemed charged with excitement as he went about exploring the area. Chris soon reined him in. Everyone pitched in and helped to set up the camper. Sebastian had never seen it erected and was fascinated with how everything fell into place to create a comfortable, enclosed environment with two double beds, a four-person table, a sink, and a two-burner gas stove. Below the two benches that flanked the table were large storage compartments and beneath the sink and stove were a sizable pantry, water tank, and waste water container. An aluminum screen door even fit into one side fastened to the canvas with strong zippers and snaps.

Seb asked, "What about a toilet?"

Walt told him it was either one of two choices; the comfort station, or the nightjar, a one-gallon plastic mayonnaise jar for urinating at night. Seb wrinkled his nose at the second choice.

Chris teased and said, "The youngest camper gets to clean the jar every morning, or whenever it needs it." More nose wrinkling on Seb's part. "Hey, Seb, we're not camping at the Hilton." After the camper was readied, it was time for lunch, so Walt and Chris started setting out what would be needed to make some cold cut and cheese sandwiches along with potato chips, cookies, and soft drinks. Soon they were eating while enjoying the quiet of the woods. No other campers were near their site so far, but the day was young. By evening, the campground, which had about thirty sites, might be full, although fall often was not a busy time in Florida parks.

Chris told the others that after their lunch settled, they would spend the first afternoon floating down the upper section of the Ichetucknee River, a trip of about two miles. The park ran a bus back from several take-out locations every fifteen minutes to return tube riders to the main spring and camping area. The last bus ran at seven o'clock.

After lunch was cleaned up, all three visited the restroom and then returned to the camper, closed the privacy curtains and changed into their bathing suits. The wetsuits would be donned later near the headspring. The water temperature of the spring and river was consistently seventy-five degrees. That normally was not terribly uncomfortable for short-term swimming, but floating down the river for several hours could cause discomfort and severe chilling. The wetsuits retained body heat and since they would not be wearing a weight belt, the suit made them more buoyant and able to float easily on the surface while peering below through their dive masks. Breathing was accomplished by using a snorkel. The water of the Ichetucknee was unbelievably pure and clear as were most of Florida's many springs. On a sunny day, one could normally see a hundred feet ahead through the crystal-like water.

The three hiked along a well-tended nature trail that ran for about a quarter mile from the campground to the area around the headspring. There was a station supplying compressed air for inflating inner tubes, so they filled the three they'd brought along. The tube would provide floatation if they chose to float upon the water for a stretch of the river. A short line was tied to each that could be clipped to their wet suit to keep the tube handy as they floated along with the constant two miles per hour current.

After arriving at the headspring itself, they looked down on a bowl-shaped area of shallow, clear, blue water about forty feet in diameter. A number of small children, teens and adults splashed there enjoying the clear cool water. At one end of the depression was a six by two foot wide opening where water flowed from the ground at a constant rate thus creating the river. At the opposite end of the headspring, the water flowed westward and became the Ichetucknee River. Tubers, canoeists and divers entered the river just past this area from a wooden dock and launching platform.

Chris recommended they get started so they moved along to the launching dock. It was deserted when they arrived, so they helped one another into their wetsuits and swim fins. Sebastian and Walt were both wearing their contact lenses so they could see well underwater through their masks. The Ichetucknee was less than ten feet wide at this point and no more than four feet deep. Waving eelgrass covered the bottom and signs were posted asking divers and swimmers not to walk on it as it was a natural aid in preventing stream bed erosion. There were rocky outcrops of limestone here and there as well as sandy sections of the bottom to give one a place to stand until ready to launch downriver.

Once they were ready, all three pushed off from the dock and stretched out with their arms pointing forward and let the current carry them along down the river. The water was only four to six feet deep this close to the river's beginning and there were only a few idle fish going about their business, occasionally watching the three as they passed overhead. The tubes bobbed along beside and behind them on short tethers. After floating about two hundred feet down the river, Chris motioned for them to surface. They continued to float along while he asked if everyone was doing okay.

Sebastian was grinning and said, "This is so amazing. With my arms stretched out in front of me, I feel like Superman flying over the bottom of the river. It's so cool to see the fish and all the things on the bottom. The river is so clean!"

Chris said, "That's why it's very important to preserve places like this, Seb. Florida is blessed with hundreds of clean, fresh-water springs. I just hope they last. The water that feeds these springs comes from rainwater percolating down through the limestone in about ten or so Florida counties in this area. Unfortunately, there has been so much development and large cattle ranches added in recent years that now there's concern about pollutants leaching into the water from those sources. It won't take much to ruin all this. Chemical fertilizer, cattle poop, and city wastewater can all poison the aquifer so badly it might never recover. Enjoy it while you can."

They continued once again to float and look downward as the river grew wider and deeper as it was joined by other small streams from other springs causing it to gradually grow in volume. The current sped up slightly and the bottom was often as deep as twenty feet below as they seemed to fly over it. Old logs, partially preserved by the cold water lay crisscrossed over one another in some places.

Seb reached out and tapped both Walt and Chris pointing toward a moving brown shape as it swam over and around some of the logs. It was an otter doing its best to catch a small fish that kept darting in and around the logs. Before they could see if the otter was successful, however, the current swept them out of sight of the agile hunter.

An hour later, they passed beneath a cable stretched ten feet above the river bearing a sign indicating the first take-out location was coming up on the left side of the stream. They started making their way in that direction as the river here was nearly eighty feet wide, but still crystal clear. The current was doing its best to keep them near mid-stream, but with a little effort they moved left and were able to touch the rocky bottom near the exit point. They stepped out of the stream into the warm, mid-afternoon sun. Removing their swim fins, but leaving their wetsuits and dive slippers on, they walked toward a marked trail leading to the bus stop for a return to the camping area and headspring.

Chris suggested they leave the bottom half of their wetsuits on but remove the tops as they were getting rather hot and uncomfortable in the warm sunlight. Within ten minutes the shuttle bus appeared and after a short trip, they got off at the campground shuttle station. The bus continued on with other passengers toward the headspring station. After walking to their campsite, they removed the bottom of their wet-suits and washed themselves and their suits using a short hose Chris normally used to connect the camper's sink to the water tap at the site.

All three were refreshed, but a bit tired after their two-hour float down the Ichetucknee. Sebastian was still excited and went on chattering about some of the things he had seen along the river. Walt and Chris were pleased the boy had enjoyed his first float trip so much. The next day they planned to repeat the same leg of the journey, but then continue on to the second exit site, another four miles downriver.

They let Seb start and tend a charcoal fire in a raised hibachi-like barbecue grill after thoroughly scrubbing its grill with steel wool and dish soap. Walt blended together ground beef, chopped onions, green peppers, and steak sauce to form six large hamburger patties; two for each of them. Soon the meat was sizzling on the grill teasing everyone's appetite with its delicious scent. Within fifteen minutes they were enjoying the burgers served on toasted buns and served with cold potato salad, corn chips, and soft drinks. Chris said they would have dessert later after he made a trip to the nearby camp store for some ice cream.

From time to time, when there were no other campers in sight, Chris or Walt would give one another a hug or a careful kiss as they went about their camping duties. They wanted Sebastian to see the close relationship they shared as Libby had suggested they do. It seemed strange at first, but they saw her wisdom in what Seb needed to see and experience. Sebastian smiled each time he saw them showing affection and usually came close for a hug himself. The two young men by now felt comfortable and enjoyed having the boy around. Walt whispered to his companion at one point, "I'm sure now it would be nice someday to have a child of our own. It makes me feel good to have him around; makes me feel less different and alien from the rest of the world."

"Me too, he's a swell kid. Thank God his folks understand and accept him so well. Imagine how different he would be if they weren't so liberal-minded."

"Yeah, he'd be like we were growing up, lonely, shy and somewhat lost. Look at him," said Walt. "He sees us talking about him and I bet within a few seconds he'll get up and join us wanting a hug or a hair ruffle."

"That's no bet, Walt." Sure enough, Sebastian smiled and came over and leaned against Chris who gave him a hug while Walt ruffled his fluffy black hair.

"Thanks again for bringing me along. I love you guys so much. The river was beautiful and I think this is the most fun I've had ever."

"That's good, Seb. We were just saying how glad we are that you're with us. Before it gets dark, if you want, we can walk the nature trail that leads to Blue Bottom Spring. It's one of the three large springs that feed the main river. Would you like that?" asked Chris.

"Sure. How far is it?"

"Only about a quarter mile trail, one way. We should be able to walk it in a half hour and be back in time to buy some ice cream to enjoy before nightfall."

They walked the trail to the large, deep spring which featured an elevated boardwalk that allowed one to walk out over a part of the spring and peer down into a gaping hole from which the water flowed constantly. Blue Bottom Spring was the main source of the Ichetucknee's water but was not the first spring along the way and, therefore, was not officially the headspring. After returning to the campsite and visiting the camp store along the way, the three entered the camper as a few mosquitoes were beginning to gather and bite as the sun went down.

Chapter 10
Bedtime Stories

Once inside, they sat at the small table and enjoyed their ice cream while discussing some of the things they'd seen that day. By eight-thirty it was fully dark outside, so Walt closed a few of the privacy curtains that faced toward other campsites and suggested they get ready for bed. Chris pulled linens from the storage lockers and he and Seb made the two double beds as Walt cleaned up the few dishes remaining from their dessert. As the campsite was equipped with electrical outlets, they were able to use the interior lights built into the camper. An outlet was also available if they needed to plug in an electric fan. The temperature was pleasant and Chris said he doubted they would need the fan once they settled in. A light sheet for each bed should be sufficient for comfort.

Once the beds were made, they changed into their sleepwear. Chris and Walt wore only shorts and tee-shirts while Seb chose to wear only his briefs and a tee-shirt. He asked, "Which bed are you guys going to use?"

Walt said they would take the one on the side where the table had been erected and later removed once they were through eating. Seb then sat on the edge of the other bed and talked as Walt and Chris crawled up on their side and sat, Indian style, listening to the boy.

Sebastian said, "I'm not very sleepy yet. Is it okay for us to talk a little until we get sleepy?"

Walt answered, "Sure; neither of us is ready for sleep just yet either."

"Uh, guys, would it be okay for me to come over and sit with you on your side until it's time to go to sleep?

Chris smiled at Walt and said, "Sure, Seb. Come on over."

The boy grinned and practically flew across the camper and jumped into bed between the two. They grabbed him and began tickling him from both sides until he was breathless. Afterward, he snuggled first against Chris and then Walt and said, "This is so great. Thanks again for bringing me. You guys are like a second set of parents to me. I really do love you both and hope you love me." It seemed Seb craved occasional reassurance of their feelings for him.

Walt smiled and said, "We do Seb. We were saying earlier that we wish someday to find a way to have a kid, especially if he, or she, for that matter, was as nice as you."

"How could you guys have a kid?" Sebastian said with wrinkled brow.

Chris said, "Well, we thought that maybe someday we might be able to adopt a boy or girl. Not a baby, but an older child who might be in need of a home. We can't do it right now as we are both still getting used to each other. We're making sure we're compatible and really want to be together for the rest of our lives. The decision to have a family is a very important one that we especially have to be careful making. Being gay makes the whole process of building a family much more difficult."

"Please ask for a gay boy my age and then I'll have a boyfriend too. We can all be one big, happy, gay family."

"Well, that would be nice if it worked out that way, but I don't think the adoption people would be too pleased with us if we asked for a gay teenager."

"Yeah, I guess that's true," said the boy with a sigh. "It's a shame so many people simply can't understand that gay people are people too."

Walt added, "Right now in Florida, gay people are not allowed to adopt kids. Some states allow it, but there aren't many that do. Gay couples have no legal rights at all. If Chris had to go to a hospital for some reason, I couldn't even visit him in an emergency room, or intensive care unit. Only immediate family can do that. Even though we consider each other immediate family now, the law doesn't. Maybe someday things will change."

"That's terribly unfair and downright rotten," said Sebastian with a frown.

"If we wanted to adopt, it would have to be done by only one of us and we could not let the authorities know we're a gay couple, or the adoption might be terminated and we could even go to jail," added Chris.

"That's so wrong," said Sebastian as he frowned and shook his head. "I sure hope the laws can be changed. I'd like to adopt some kids too someday with my boyfriend if I ever find one."

"Oh you will," said Walt. "Trust me. You are one very special young man with a beautiful personality. You've accepted your nature and have your family's support and love. You have no idea how fortunate you are, Seb."

Sebastian sat quietly for a few moments before saying, "Would you guys mind if I ask you a real personal question?"

Walt said, "Well, that would depend upon how personal it is. Neither one of us mind answering your questions, but some might not be too appropriate for us to discuss with a gay teenager."

Chris asked, "What was it you wanted to ask about, Seb?"

"I've kind of been wondering how each of you first discovered that you were different, that you were gay? Hope that's not too personal."

Walt ruffled Seb's soft black hair and said, "No, that's a fine question. I don't mind sharing that with you and I doubt Chris will either. Am I right, Chris?"

"Yeah, I'm fine with that. I had just turned twelve; it was during the last few months of sixth grade. All my friends were talking about an end of the year dance that was being organized for my elementary school and I was in a panic."

"How come?" asked Seb.

"They were all talking about what girl they were going to invite to the dance and talking about how they looked and I was simply lost. I didn't know any girl well enough to ask her out. I was so darned shy, Seb, not only around girls but around boys too. I only had about three close friends who I played with and most of them were shy and kind of awkward too."

Walt added, "I was the same way. A total square with no idea about what my body was about to throw at me. At twelve, I still hadn't started growing any body hair yet, but I was beginning to take an interest in boys' bodies. I loved going to De Leon Springs north of De Land and watch the older boys in their bathing suits. I didn't know why, but I really liked watching them dive and swim and... Well, I'll tell you more of my story later. Sorry I interrupted, Chris."

Chris laughed and said, "It's okay. Let's see, I was telling about my three friends. Looking back, I think one of them may have been gay too, but at the time I had no idea about homosexuality or anything. I was wondering why I was starting to grow hair in places it had never grown before and why my penis seemed to get hard all the time. Seems like it was happening several times an hour during those years."

Sebastian giggled, "Mine started doing that when I was twelve too. It still does see." He pointed toward his briefs and indeed there was evidence of an erection.

Walt threw a loose fold of the blanket over Seb's front and said, "Down boy. There will be no exhibitions of horniness this evening, or we change the subject right now."

"Sorry. The subject is interesting and *it* has a mind of its own. You know what I mean." Sebastian grinned with his usual mischievous look.

Walt said, "Chris, once again we apologize. Please continue."

"Uh, where was I?"

Seb said with a grin, "You were getting hard every couple of minutes."

Chris gave him a withering look and said, "Yeah. I started wondering why it only happened when I was thinking about my friends who of course were all boys. Two of them talked about girls from time to time, but one didn't. His name was Jeff. He was always really quiet and was always smiling at me. Whenever we did anything like play a game, or go to a movie, he always wanted to sit by me or play on my side. I liked him too because he and I got along very well. I'd sometimes get in arguments with the other two boys, but never with Jeff."

Sebastian said, "Did you ever kiss him, or want to kiss him?"

Chris started to frown and say no, but hesitated, "You know, I was about to say no, but I have to be honest with you, Seb. Looking back, I remember a time when I really did want to kiss him." Chris laughed and shook his head. "I'd almost forgotten about it, but your question brought back the memory."

"Cool. Tell us about it," prompted Sebastian.

"Okay. We'd seen an old vampire movie at a theatre in North Miami; that's where I was living then. The four of us had gone to the theatre on a Saturday afternoon and after supper, we got together and decided to play vampires."

Sebastian said, "I've never heard of that game."

"We just made it up. It was sort of like hide and seek and the idea was for one person to be the vampire and hunt for the other three who would hide somewhere in one of two adjacent backyards. One was my yard and the other was Jacob's, another of the boys. We'd played for a while and it was my turn to be the vampire, so I covered my eyes and counted to fifty while my buddies hid. At fifty, I started looking. I found Jacob first and I wrestled with him on the ground. The object was that if we could hold the person down and act like we were biting their neck, they became a vampire and could go on the hunt too. If they got loose and got away, they could hide again."

Seb, looking interested said, "Cool. Sounds like fun. So what happened?"

"Well, I wrestled Jacob down, acted like I was biting him and made him a vampire. He took off then trying to find either Jeff or Glen, my third friend. Pretty soon I heard him yell out that he had found Glen, but he'd gotten away. Just about that time, I saw a sneaker sticking out from behind a clump of bushes and knew it was Jeff trying to hide. I crept up to the bushes and pounced right on top of him."

"What happened, did you bite him and make him a vampire?" It was easy to tell that Sebastian was into the story and anxious now.

"Well, he'd been on his hands and knees, so he kind of got flattened to the ground when I jumped on him. I had him pinned and was about to act like I was biting his neck when he said, 'I surrender, Master. Make me a vampire with your deadly kiss and I shall join you for all eternity.' Jeff was a natural actor and really got into the part."

"Did you kiss him?" asked Walt, who by now was just as involved as Sebastian.

"Not exactly."

Both Walt and Seb said, "Aw."

"Wait now, the story's not over. The fat lady hasn't sung yet."

Seb said, "Fat lady? What's a fat lady have to do with it? Did she catch you two in the bushes?"

Walt laughed and said "I'll explain it later, Seb. Forget the obese female."

"Huh?"

Chris said, "Shut up, both of you, so I can finish. Gees! Anyway, I had Jeff pinned down, but I relaxed just enough and he rolled over on his back and was facing me. I held his shoulders down and was kneeling over him with my hips over his middle to keep his legs from rising. He was smiling up at me saying, 'Take me, Master. Make me your slave forever. Give me the eternal kiss.' We'd seen one of those campy, melodramatic horror movies, and Jeff was hamming it up. Of course in the film, it was always a young woman the vampire was after."

"Did you get a hard-on?" asked Sebastian. "You know, squatting over his privates and him saying those things. It's got me hard just listening and wishing it had been me underneath you."

"Criminy, Seb. You do have it bad."

Walt snickered and asked, "Well, Chris; did you?"

"What?"

"Get hard?"

"Okay, okay. Yeah, I did. It was kind of a sexy moment for me. I went along with the melodrama and told him I would give him the eternal kiss. I let go of his shoulders but continued to hold him down with my body. He was smiling at me in kind of a funny way and something told me to kiss him and not on the neck."

"Did you?" asked both of his listeners.

"I sure wanted to; I unbuttoned the top two buttons of his shirt to expose his chest and neck, bent over him and put my lips to his neck."

"Cool," said Sebastian in a low whisper.

"I pulled him close and started to nibble at his neck with my teeth even though I wanted to kiss him. He was saying, 'Master, I am yours forever.' over and over. I just kept nipping at his neck and was slowly moving up over his neck toward his chin and planned eventually to nibble at his lips." Chris stopped.

After a pregnant silence, both Walt and Seb said, "Well? --- What happened?"

"He started yelling and rolling around begging me to get off him and let him up."

"Was he freaking out because of what you were trying to do," asked Walt. "Did he realize you were really trying to kiss him?"

Chris laughed and said, "No, he'd just discovered he had rolled over on a nest of red ants and they were starting to give him their own kind of nibble. He bucked me off yelling 'Ants! Oh god!' and stripped off his shirt. I helped brush off about a hundred red ants that were all over his back and sides. Some had even gotten down the back of his pants and were stinging his behind."

Sebastian said, "Did he pull off his pants and let you help get the ants out of his crack? Bet that was fun. I'd have liked doing that."

"No, he reached inside and brushed them off as best he could. He went running home after that and later said he had about forty stings in total. I got a few myself. He said his mom put salve on him to ease the pain."

Sebastian was looking disappointed. "That story has a rotten ending. Just when you were about to kiss him, and it seemed like he wanted you to, the bloody ants had to start stinging."

"Yeah, it was always my luck. I didn't get to kiss a boy again for nearly ten years."

Sebastian asked, "Ten years? Who'd you kiss that time?"

"This guy right here and I'm going to do it again right now because this time the story has a happy ending." With that, he leaned over Seb and gave Walt a warm kiss on his mouth. "Mmmm, it's so much better without the *bloody* ants." Everyone had a good laugh.

"So," said Sebastian, "Did you ever do anything else with Jeff? It sounds to me like he might have enjoyed that kiss."

"No, unfortunately, he moved away a few weeks after that --- somewhere in the Midwest. But, after that, I started having a lot of daydreams and nighttime dreams about him and other boys. I began to realize that I was different and out of place. That was in the seventies and people didn't talk about being gay very much back then."

"Did you ever ask your folks about it?"

"I was too afraid and ashamed, Seb. I had no idea what being gay was all about. I had no frame of reference. That's where you've been so lucky. Your parents saw the signs in you and talked about it when you were young and helped you see you weren't abnormal. That's the way I looked at myself for the next ten years. I believed I was abnormal and would never find happiness. I imagine Walt's experiences were pretty much the same."

Walt nodded in agreement and said, "Sebastian, I withdrew into a fantasy world to escape the reality of who I was. As Chris said, it all came from shame. Chris said his body started changing when he was about twelve and in sixth grade. I was a little late in my growth and didn't start growing pubic hair until I was nearly fourteen. Trouble is, my interests were already on boys and men. From the time I was six or seven; my heroes were always boys or young men."

Seb asked, "What, like in movies, or TV shows?"

"Yeah and in real life too. My interests weren't what you might expect either, I wasn't focused on strong, hero types, or the kind of boys who played football and baseball."

"How about superheroes like Superman, Green Lantern or Flash?" Sebastian queried. "I kind of like their outfits with the tight pants and you know."

"Well, yeah, I kind of liked that too, but for the most part, I was attracted to quiet and very intelligent boys my age as well as older teenagers and young men. I had one history teacher in seventh grade who I especially liked. He was very smart and was willing to spend time talking to me if I stayed after class. He was my last teacher of the day and I often would hang around the school and help him clean the room or put things away just to spend time with him. He'd traveled a lot and knew so much about the world."

"Was he gay, do you think," asked Chris. "Did he ever give you that impression?"

"No, not that I could tell for sure. He wasn't married and was only about twenty-three or so. The thing I liked about him the most was that he was willing to talk to a shy, curious and very lonely boy who wanted a friend so badly." Walt sniffed and had to stop for a moment.

"You okay, Walt?" asked Chris.

"Yeah, I'm fine. He was my first crush, I guess and I was going through so much emotional stress about that time that I didn't understand. My mind was maturing, but my body wasn't keeping up. I was having erections and strange day and night dreams that made me ashamed all the time. Like you, Chris, I had no one I could talk to, or get advice from."

"I wish we could have been there for you then," said Sebastian as he gave Walt a hug. "I sure would have loved you and talked to you if I had known you."

"Thanks, Seb. You're a treasure. Yeah, I was really mixed up for a while. All the other boys could talk about their girlfriends openly, but I could only pretend and act like I fit in. I used my artistic interests and talent to start drawing some of my fantasies. I had a secret sketchbook, one that if my folks had ever found it, I would have been in trouble. I made drawings of some of the boys at school that were very realistic. They were some very good-quality colored pencil and charcoal sketches, only trouble is they were all nudes and most were pretty aroused and very provocative. I had a talent for drawing and used it to satisfy myself."

"Do you still have it?" asked Sebastian with obvious interest.

"Have what? Talent?"

"No. The sketchbook. I'd like to see it."

"I bet you would, you little porn addict." Walt smiled and said, "Sorry to disappoint you, but I finally got rid of it when I was about seventeen. I was afraid someone would find it and my secret would be exposed."

"You can draw me sometime if you want. I won't mind posing."

"Behave yourself, Seb," said Walt. "I gave that up a long time ago. It was making me hate myself too much when I'd draw some boy or man and then use the drawing to masturbate with." Walt became very quiet and a few tears appeared at the corners of his eyes.

He finally said, "You know it's one of the worse things ever when a person starts hating himself and that was what I was doing. I hated that my penis got hard when I looked at the other boys, or thought about hugging or kissing Mr. Andrews, the teacher I liked so much. I drew him doing all sorts of things with me and if those drawings had been found, he would probably have been arrested. I was in most of my drawings too." Walt sobbed again and had to stop.

Chris asked Seb to change places with him so he could sit beside Walt and hold him close for a few minutes. "Looks like you might have needed this talk tonight, Walt. You still have a lot to get over, Hon."

"I'm so sorry, my questions have made you feel bad, Walt," said Sebastian who slid off the end of the camper bed and crawled back on Walt's other side. "I didn't mean to do that."

Walt was smiling as Seb held him from one side and Chris from the other. "No, guys, it's okay. I think Chris is right. I still have a lot to get over. Those were hard times for a teenager who had no idea who or what he really was. I simply had no one I could go to and get answers, so I withdrew more and more into myself. I became even shyer and awkward around people."

"Even at school?" asked Sebastian.

"Oh, yeah, middle school and senior high were terrible. I was the target of every damned bully at both schools. I wish I had a dollar for every wedgie, arm punch or queer call I got in junior high."

"Didn't you have any friends at all, Walt?" asked the boy.

"I had a few. They were like me, outcasts --- the type of boy nobody else wanted around. One boy, Thomas Cavendish, suffered from epilepsy and had to take all kinds of medications to keep from having seizures. He kept it a secret for a while, but after his first seizure in the lunchroom, he was marked for abuse. Another was a boy from India, Rani Chopra. He was very intelligent and wore glasses about a half inch thick. He was definitely bully-bait and an outcast." Walt sobbed and sniffed several times. "Even with all their social baggage, I felt lucky to have both as friends. Neither one was gay though. Rani talked all the time about girls and kept being rejected by every girl he tried to talk to. Thomas brought a Playboy magazine to school one day to keep in his locker and share with us. He and Rani poured over it every chance they got until Thomas got caught with it and had to serve detention. Needless to say, it did nothing for me. I had to pretend to be excited by the photos. Oh, and in high school, I had a few crushes on some of my other teachers, but couldn't do anything about that."

"So, Walt, you never had a boyfriend until you met Chris?" asked Sebastian.

"Yeah, he's my first and I hope my last because I never want to lose him. For the first time in my life, I feel at peace and complete when I'm around this guy." He gave Chris a kiss and then nuzzled in his hair as Chris held him close.

Sebastian giggled and said, "I see you still have a thing for teachers, Walt."

Walt said, "I guess you're right. I never made that connection until now. Yeah, I finally landed me a teacher and boy, am I glad of it." He gave Chris another kiss before saying, "I have another boyfriend now too. This one's not for having sex with though. This boyfriend is for talking to, hugging once in a while, tickling until he pees himself and sharing my life stories with. I'm lucky to have him and he's you, Seb." Walt gave the boy a hug and a kiss on the forehead.

Sebastian smiled and said, "I want to be your boyfriend and Chris's boyfriend forever too. I love you guys so much. I'm happy you found one another. I hope I'm so lucky."

"Me too," said Walt. "Tell you what; sometime in the next few weeks, I'll do a colored pencil portrait of you and maybe one of all three of us, but I'll make sure everyone is properly clothed."

"Okay," said Seb. "I'd like that."

Chris reminded them it was nearly ten o'clock and that they had another busy day on the river the next morning. Sebastian went to his bed on the other side of the camper and once he was settled in, Chris turned off the lights after giving the boy a good night hug and kiss. Walt and Chris refrained from making love due to Seb's presence but still cuddled as they drifted off to sleep.

The rest of that weekend was one they would all remember for some time to come. Sebastian became an important part of Chris and Walt's relationship and more and more they talked of a future when they might adopt a child of their own.

Chapter 11
Coming Out

The remainder of October and most of November passed without any notable events for Walt and Chris. Both sets of their parents visited during late October and having the extra room was a convenience. They discovered, however, that maintaining the illusion that the extra room was Walt's was a real pain as they had to move many of his belongings into the room before the parents visited. That included most of his clothes and many of his personal effects. Both were realizing that it was going to be troublesome to keep the appearance of separate bedrooms going. Finally, they had a long talk about the big question, *when would they come out to their folks?* It was just after a visit from Chris's mom and dad.

They were getting ready for bed after moving most of Walt's clothing and effects back to their common room when Chris said, "You know something? This is going to get pretty old, Walt. I'm beginning to think my folks might be guessing the truth anyway."

"Why is that? I didn't pick up on anything while they were here."

"It really happened the last time we went to their house. Remember how my mom told you the guest room was ready for use again after being refurbished and you said it was no use to mess it up and that you and I could bunk together like the first visit?"

"Yeah, I tried to make it sound like I was just trying to make things easier for her. Was I wrong?"

"No, Walt," Chris said with a chuckle. "What you missed was the little smile that played over her face as you said it. Think about how quick she agreed with you too. She whispered something to my dad right after you said it and he smiled too and kind of shook his head as if to say, 'Oh well'."

"Oops."

"Dude, I think they know already and I think it's going to be okay. I need to come clean and tell them. I'm tired of lying to my parents. They love and trust me; they sure like you and I just think it's time."

"You're positive about this?"

"Yeah, it's time."

"Once done, it's done. I agree though; just the few times I've been around your folks, I see how much they love and trust you and I couldn't be treated better than they've treated me so far. They probably realize something is not quite kosher."

"Yeah, they know."

"So when do we make it official?" Walt asked as they both climbed into bed and snuggled close beside each other.

Chris studied for a while and said, "Let's do it next weekend. It's still several weeks until Thanksgiving and I don't want to do it on the holiday. We can go for a visit and spring the news the first evening we're there. It's going to be scary for me, but with you by my side, it won't be half as bad. I just want to get it over with. As Sebastian said, it's not going to change the way they love me. And one reason I'm ready to do this is so they can love you more since you're my family now too."

"Thanks, you have no idea how much it means whenever you refer to us as a family. Uh, how are you going to bring up the subject?"

"Yeah, well, there's that. I just can't say: Great meal, Mom; by the way, I'm gay, Walt and I are in love and we're enjoying sex every night. Please pass the peas, Dad." Chris chuckled, "I don't want either of them to have a heart attack."

Walt laughed and said, "I don't think it'll come as such a surprise. I believe they know what's going on anyway. Turning down the guest room was a giveaway. Whichever way you decide to tell them, I'll be right beside you ready to run away as fast as I can and let you explain everything to them."

"You'd better not. I'm going to need all the shared courage I can get. I think I'll ask them to sit down with us because I want to discuss some things about my future. That will work as a line to get things started."

"I believe it's going to be a lot easier with your folks compared to mine. Mom will probably be okay with it; maybe she even knows now, but Dad... well, that's the big unknown. He's so much into sports and macho stuff. Everything is a competition with him." Walt laughed and said, "He got me to sign up for Little League when I was ten or eleven and my god, was that ever a disaster. I didn't have glasses yet and about the only thing I could catch was a cold."

"Yeah, my folks asked me about Little League, but at least when I said I wasn't interested, they didn't push it."

"Try-outs were awful; I think Dad made a sizable contribution to the uniform fund and that's what it took to get me on the team."

Chris chuckled and said, "What position did you play?"

"Mostly left bench," said Walt with a laugh. "Suffered a few injuries --- splinters mostly," he said, shaking his head and laughing. "Chris, I was a walking disaster for the team. After four months of pure torture for the coach and the other kids, I retired permanently from baseball. I think the whole time I only got maybe two or three hits that I could run on."

"How did your dad take it?"

"He was pretty good actually. He never made fun of me and came to every game he could. He thanked me for trying and let me quit when I asked, without making me feel like a failure. He started taking me bowling and thank god, by then I had glasses, liked the game and we really enjoyed our time together."

"Hey, that's something else we can start doing together. I like to bowl too and Powers Lanes isn't far from the apartment. You know as I think about it, why don't we suggest to your dad, next time we go to De Land, the three of us go bowling. It'll help put him in a good mood and afterward, once we get back to your home, maybe it will be a good time to get the big secret off your chest. You know I'll be right there to help get you through it."

"That's a good idea. You know one of the ideas I've been toying with is to talk to my folks separately --- Mom first. I think doing it that way might be better because she might have some insight as to how Dad's going to take it."

"Whatever you feel is best." Chris paused in thought while stroking Walt's chest and belly. "I think we'll both be so relieved once we get this over with. I'm ashamed sometimes that Sebastian is so much at ease about his sexuality around Libby and Nigel and here we are still sneaking around and making our own lives more difficult. I'll give Mom and Dad a call in the morning and let them know we'll be driving down this weekend. Right now though I have something else I want to do."

"What's that?"

"Dim the light and I'll show you."

The following Saturday afternoon, after work at the museum, Chris and Walt drove south to Intercross and arrived in time for dinner with Chris's folks at six-thirty. As usual, the dogs and even Tom --- who was back to his normal coloration by then --- greeted the two with exuberance. Exuberance for Tom was three rubs against their legs as soon as they entered the house. Walt picked him up and he began to purr like a fuzzy electric motor.

"You know, Chris, I think we should get a cat. They're allowed in the apartments and they're such clean animals."

Chris's dad said, "That would be good for you guys. Just don't leave any dye bottles around."

Mrs. Walker said, "You know, boys, our neighbor, Jane, has four kittens right now that are just weaned. I'm sure she'd love to give you one. Every one of them is gray like the mama cat. There's one with just a little black fur on the tip of her tail; she's always the first to come to me if I reach into their box. It's a female and when you find one like that who's so friendly, they usually make a fine pet."

Chris said, "Sounds good to me. If Walt wants, we can go tomorrow and take a look at the kitten. I think though, that once she's a little older, we might want to have her spayed so we won't have suitors showing up at ungodly hours singing for her attention." Everyone laughed and agreed that was probably best for an apartment cat.

Mrs. Walker said, "Well, I'm sure you fellows are ready for supper. Come on and sit down and I'll have it on the table in a few minutes. Hope you like lasagna and garlic bread."

Walt said, "Oh gosh, yeah. I love it. I knew I smelled something Italian cooking. Smells great."

Mrs. Walker continued, "We were kind of surprised you decided to come down this weekend since we'd just visited you last week. We're glad you did though. Walt, you're family too, you know and we sure enjoy having you. We're glad for Chris knowing he has a close friend and isn't all alone up there in the big city. Cities are full of people, but can often be the loneliest places to live."

"Has everything been going fine with work and school, fellows?" asked Chris Senior.

"Oh, yeah, Dad, I'm putting the final touches on my next show. It'll open right after Thanksgiving."

"Does it have a Christmas or holiday theme?" asked Amelia, as she carried a hot pan of lasagna to the table and went back for more food. Walt was helping carry bowls and a basket of steaming garlic bread to the table where Chris Junior and Chris Senior were already seated.

"Sort of, it was hard coming up with a science show that could tie into the holidays, but I managed. The last show, *The Spark Factory*, was about static electricity, so for the holidays, I put together a show about light. Hanukah is the Festival of Lights for Jewish folks and light has always been a Christian theme this time of year, so I'll be doing a show using prisms, lasers, lenses, mirrors and what not, to teach about light."

"Are you doing this one in costume?" asked his father.

"Uh huh, I'm dressing as Sir Isaac Newton, who did some of the first work with prisms and the spectrum. I bought this fantastic big prism from a scientific supply company. It's four inches on a side and throws a beautiful spectrum across the entire theatre wall where I'll be mounting a white screen. I'm using a thousand watt, quartz-iodine, and focused lamp assembly for a light source. I hope you can come to see the show."

"We plan to," replied his mom. "Well, dig in guys. Hope you like the lasagna."

Everyone ate with gusto and exchanged small talk about Walt's college classes, his plans for a commercial art career and Chris's plans for future theatre offerings. As the meal neared its conclusion and everyone was enjoying their dessert of orange sherbet, Chris said, "Uh, Mother and Daddy, right after we finish dessert, Walt and I want to talk with both of you about something concerning our future."

"Sounds ominous, fellows, is everything okay?"

"Everything's great, Mr. Walker," said Walt. "We just want to share some special news with you."

After Chris and Walt helped clean up the table and load the dishwasher, it was time for everyone to have a seat and talk. Chris looked at Walt who gave him a smile and a thumbs-up sign when no one was looking. He and Walt sat side by side on the sofa while Amelia and Chris Senior took seats in two comfortable armchairs across from them.

"So, boys, what's up?" asked Chris's dad.

Chris took a deep breath, gave Walt one more look and said, "Mother and Dad, there's something I should have talked with you about a long time ago I suppose, but I just didn't know how to do it. It's a difficult subject and I... Well, I had to think about it a lot before I could say anything." Chris felt tears gathering in his eyes and sniffed once before trying to go on.

"It's okay, Chris, I'm right here to help if you need it," said Walt. Chris Senior and Amelia were looking back and forth between the youths and at each other with confused expressions.

"You know, I've always been kind of a loner, never going out much and being pretty much content to stay home with you and all. I'm different than most guys I suppose and well... I never much wanted to go out on dates or hang out with girls. Walt's kind of the same way and we have an awful lot in common." Chris was breaking down and sniffling a lot now and a few tears were coursing down his cheeks. He couldn't look at his folks but gave a quick glance at Walt.

Chris's mom came to his rescue after smiling at Chris Senior. She came over and sat beside her son on the couch and gave him a side hug. "I think I know what this is all about, and if I'm right, you and Walt have nothing to be ashamed of, or worry about. Your daddy and I love you both."

"Thanks, Mother. I'm sorry I'm so messed up; I never wanted to make you or Daddy ashamed of me..."

"Honey, relax. You and Walt are in love aren't you?" She looked over at Walt and reached out for his hand too. Mr. Walker came close and knelt in front of his son taking his hands.

Chris Senior said, "We've sort of understood what was happening ever since Walt first visited, but we wanted you fellows to tell us when you were ready. Maybe we should have talked with you more about these things while you were growing up, but we were kind of chicken ourselves and didn't want to make a mistake and embarrass you and us both. Son, since you were about sixteen, we sort of had it in the back of our minds that you might like boys instead of girls. We still love you and now we love Walt too."

Chris was crying now with relief as was Walt. Chris Senior reached out and took Walt's hand as well and squeezed it.

Mrs. Walker said, "I'm so happy for you both. I'm sure it hasn't been easy for either one of you growing up and wondering why you were different from most fellows. I often wondered if there was something we did wrong as parents, but I've done a lot of reading on the subject lately and most experts are saying that being homosexual, or gay, as it's now called, is something you're born with. It's probably genetic. You're still our boy and we love you with all our heart. Now we have Walt to love too."

"Thanks, Mrs. Walker. It means a lot to me to hear you say that. I love Chris so much. I've never had someone I've felt this close to. He completes me and makes me feel like a whole person for the first time in my life."

"Do your parents know, Walt?" asked Chris's dad.

"Not yet, but they soon will. We plan to have a talk with them next weekend. I hope things will go just as well as they did this evening.

You are such wonderful parents. I love you too."

Chris was getting himself together and whispered, "Thanks for loving us, Mother and Dad. I was afraid to talk about this, but now I'm so relieved it's all out in the open. Walt and I were meant for one another and it looks like we're going to be partners for a long time to come. We've never had an argument or felt any reason to distrust each other. We want to live together for the rest of our lives."

"We already knew you fellows were sleeping with one another, you know. Your mother found that out last week when we visited." Chris Senior was grinning and both Walt and Chris looked at him with a puzzled expression.

Mrs. Walker said, "You fellows slipped up with the bed in your guest room. The time before last, when we visited, I put fresh sheets on the bed the morning we left. Do you know how I could never get you to use boxed hospital corners on your sheets when you make a bed? Well, the sheets still had the boxed corners I made the bed with on our last visit. I knew the bed hadn't been used by anyone else."

Chris was smiling and shaking his head.

"At least now we don't have to keep moving my stuff around every time you come for a visit," said Walt. "We thought we were getting away with it, but I guess moms are a lot smarter than their sons and boyfriends. I never could master boxed sheet corners either. When you lifted the bed-spread you literally *uncovered* our secret." Everyone enjoyed a laugh.

"Well, now we can all be more at ease and comfortable," said Chris Senior. "I'm happy for both of you. Don't feel awkward if you guys want to hug or kiss around us. I'm sure there have been times you've wanted to and couldn't. It won't bother us in the least. Like we've said, we've sort of been expecting this, so it's no great surprise."

"Thanks, Dad. That means so much to me; or to us, I should say." With that, he pulled Walt close and kissed him with feeling.

The rest of the visit went very well. On Sunday, they went to see the neighbor woman about a kitten and came back with the friendly female with the black tip on her tail. After some consideration, they settled on naming her, Tipsy.

Monday evening found them driving back to Jacksonville; Tipsy was curled up asleep in Walt's lap as they crossed the Buckman Bridge over the St. Johns River. It was about eight o'clock and the sun had set an hour before. Walt started a cassette tape in the car's player and they were listening to the Largo movement, from Dvorak's *New World Symphony*. They had discovered another common love --- that of classical music. Walt had a fairly extensive collection of albums and tapes and now their travel was often marked by the gentle strains of music such as what was playing.

"It's been a great weekend, Walt," said Chris. "I hope next weekend goes as well. I'm sure it will. Does your dad like to drink a few beers when he goes bowling?"

Walt laughed and said, "Yeah, he usually has one."

"Maybe we should make sure he has about three or four before we spring the news."

"Oh, hell no," said Walt with a chuckle. "He'll listen, but then forget and I'd have to tell him all over again later."

The following weekend was the one just before Thanksgiving and if all went well, Chris's family proposed that both families might want to get together for a joint Thanksgiving meal at their home in Intercross. It would be a way for both families to meet each other and get in better touch with their sons' lives. Walt thanked the Walkers but said it would depend a lot on how things went during the meeting with his parents.

On Saturday afternoon, Walt and Chris arrived at the Bower home in De Land and enjoyed dinner with the family. As planned, Walt wanted to talk first with his mother before springing the news on his dad. His father seemed in a good mood and didn't once discuss football during, or after the meal. Once supper was cleaned up, Chris joined Mr. Bower in the living room where they started watching a movie on television. Walt made the excuse that he would help his mom clean up the kitchen after dinner and went off with her. After they finished, he asked to speak to her alone on their screened patio.

"Thanks, Mom. There's something I want to discuss with you privately. At some point, I'll call Chris out here too. Dad's watching a movie and what I have to say I'd rather talk to you about first before I talk with Dad." His mom was looking partly amused, as well as curious.

"It must be something pretty serious. Is everything okay? Are you having problems making ends meet? I know how expensive everything is."

"No Mom, it's not money. I'm doing fine with money especially since Chris and I are sharing rent on one apartment instead of two."

"Oh, I bet I know what's happening. Are you and Chris not getting along as well as expected and now you're stuck with a shared lease? Well, if you need..."

"No, Mom. It's not that. Just listen and I'll try to tell you what's really going on. Chris and I are getting along very well. In fact, what I have to say might explain how very well we're getting along." Walt hesitated and gathered his courage.

"Go ahead, honey. Whatever is troubling you, we can work it out. Relax and tell me. Are you crying, sweetheart?" She'd noticed the few tears gathering at the corners of Walt's eyes.

"Yeah, a little, Mom. This is just hard for me to talk about; please just give me time and be patient with me." He took a deep breath and finally resumed, "Mom, ever since I was about twelve, I discovered that I'm different from most boys. I was always too shy to talk to girls and never really felt like doing it anyway. Mom, I hope what I'm about to say isn't going to hurt you, because that's something I'd never want to do. Mom --- I'm a --- oh, Mom, I'm gay. I like guys. I like Chris, or rather I love Chris and he loves me. Please don't hate me or hate him. I'm so sorry..."

She reached out and brushed a few strands of hair from Walt's brow. "Oh, sweetheart, there's no way in the world I could hate you. I sort of thought several times while you were growing up that you might be gay. I wish I'd had the courage to talk with you about it, but I never could find a way to discuss it. I still love you and you'll always be my boy." She took Walt's hand and asked, "So you and Chris have fallen in love?"

"Yeah, Mom; I love him so much. He's the most wonderful person I've ever known."

"Honey, I'm glad for you. You've always seemed to be so lost and lonely. I'm glad you have Chris. He's such a gentle young man, intelligent like you and so clean-cut and polite. Do you think it's just a temporary thing, or are you guys really serious about each other?"

Oh, Mom, he's everything I've always been looking for. He fills in all the gaps in my life and for the first time, I don't fear the future. I was almost ready to quit school and come home I was so damned lonely, but then I met him and found he was just as lonely and mixed up as I was. He and I both have never been involved with anyone else. There really is such a thing as love at first sight. After three days, we knew we were right for each other."

"Love at first sight is *very* real. It was that way for your dad and I.

I'm so glad for you." She scooted closer on the patio sofa and held Walt, brushing her fingers through his golden hair and kissing away some of his tears.

"Thanks, Mom. I want to go get Chris now and see if you want to ask him anything. Also, we both want to talk to you about how Dad is going to handle this. He's my main concern. I had a feeling that you would understand, but I'm not sure how Dad will react."

"Go get Chris, sweetheart and we'll talk. I don't think you have a thing to worry about with your daddy."

A few minutes later, Walt returned with Chris in tow. Mrs. Bower greeted him with a hug and kiss. "I'm so glad for you boys. Welcome to the family, Chris."

"Thanks, Mrs. Bower, for accepting us and your kind welcome. I want to make a promise to you right now. I promise I will never willingly hurt or bring harm to Walt. He's my other half now and I love him more than life itself."

"Please call me Linda or even Mom."

"Thanks, I will. Uh, I think Walt and I are most concerned about how our bombshell might affect Mr. Bower. I sure don't want to bring discord or unhappiness to your family."

"I think things will work out all right. Please, have a seat and let me explain something to both of you. It's my turn to reveal a family secret." Walt looked confused as he turned toward his mom and asked."

"Family secret?"

"Your dad has had prior experience in dealing with this subject."

"My god, Mom; Dad's gay?"

"Good heavens no, silly! You're living proof of that. You know your Uncle Tim who lives up in Atlanta?" Walt nodded. "Well, Tim's gay and your daddy was always the one he was closest to in their family. Your dad's older brother, your Uncle Victor, never had much to do with Tim, but your daddy and his sister, your Aunt Veronica loved the hell out of Tim. You've never had much of a chance to meet him. Maybe soon we should get you two together as he used to love visiting and playing with you years ago when you were a toddler."

"Wow, I have a gay uncle. That's so cool. So dad's okay with him?"

"Yes, and he's often compared you to your Uncle Tim. You even look a little like him. I think your dad might already suspect you to be gay. The last time you visited with Chris, he and I talked and he was speculating about whether you and Uncle Tim might have a lot in common. Your dad even said, and I quote, 'If Walt's like Tim, I wish he'd let us know, so we don't have to keep pussy-footing around. He seems mighty attached to Chris and maybe those two are more than meets the eye.'"

"Well, I'll be darned. I never would have thought that Dad would see through us that easily."

"He's your father, Walt and loves you more than you might realize. You know how he is --- Mr. Macho, who can never let anyone see what he's really feeling. Ever notice when a sad movie is on television, he always has to go to the bathroom or work on something in the garage during the sad parts. He's never been able to make it all the way through that Christmas movie, *It's a Wonderful Life.* He's a big softy, but don't let on you know it. Let him keep his pride."

"I won't let on." Walt chuckled as he said, "This is so amazing. After all these years, I'm just learning about what my father is really like."

"Yes, and you're about to reveal *your* true nature to him, aren't you? Walt, your Uncle Tim has a lot in common with your dad, but he's more open about his feelings. He cries openly at the drop of a hat in a sad movie or while he's reading one of his romance novels. He's not ashamed to show his feelings." She giggled and stroked Walt's hair. "His partner, Ricky, teases him something awful about it, but I've seen him get emotional too. You guys really need to go visit those two. It will thrill Tim to death that he's not the only gay man in the family. We went for a visit last year and that's when we finally met Ricky. Your dad and Tim did a lot of catching up. They still love each other so much, so don't you worry about your Dad. He'll probably be relieved and proud of himself for having figured it out already. That man lives and breathes to love you and me both. He just has a hard time showing it and that's okay. It's who he is and we love him anyway, don't we?"

"We were going to ask him to go bowling tomorrow night and get him a few beers and then tell him," said Chris with a chuckle.

Mrs. Bower said, "I think you ought to talk to him first and then after you spring the news, take him bowling without the beers. He'll feel better bonding with you two if he knows in advance. Ask him more about Tim and he'll warm right up. He really does love Tim and he'll love the two of you guys even more."

The next day after breakfast, Walt asked if he and Chris could have a talk with Mr. Bower. Soon they were seated in the back yard under a gazebo Walt and his father had built together a few years before.

"What's up fellows? Is this something you don't want your mom to hear, Walt?"

"No Dad. We had a talk with her last night already and now it's your turn. I'd like to ask you more about Uncle Tim. I can just barely remember him."

Steve Bower looked somewhat at a loss and frowned a bit before saying, "Why the sudden interest in Tim? You barely know him. Your mother and I visited him in Atlanta recently and we're thinking of going up to see him this winter, maybe after New Year."

"You love Tim, don't you Dad?"

"Well sure. I wish I could get to see him more often, but he's a busy man and so are we so we just don't get time together as much as we'd like. I get along better with him than I do with Vick; that's my older brother, Chris. Vick's always been such a stuffed shirt and is too damned conservative for my tastes. Dear God, he's a Republican, you know. Oh, uh, sorry, Chris, if you happen to be a Republican, but uh..."

"It's okay, Mr. Bower," Chris said with an inward smile. "I'm a Democrat just like my folks."

"Oh, it's great you have good sensible parents. I made a mistake once and voted for Nixon and I swear I'll never vote Republican again. He and his gang of crooks almost pulled this country apart. Never again. I sure hated to see Carter lose this last election. Now we're stuck with a damned movie star of all things. Sorry, I'm off the subject. What about Tim?"

Walt was grinning at Chris by now and said, "Mom told me about Uncle Tim, Dad. He's gay."

"Oh, uh, she told you did she? Well, yeah, he is, but let me tell you, he's a real gem of a guy. What he does and who he is doesn't matter a damned bit to me. He's my brother and I love him no matter what."

"So, you accept him just the way he is, right?"

"Yep, and I hope you do too if you ever meet him. I'll not have you judging him at all. God made him that way and that's that."

"It makes Chris and me really happy to hear you say that, Dad, because Chris and I are exactly like Uncle Tim and his buddy Rick." Walt just stared at his dad who got a blank look on his face and then opened his mouth as though to speak and then closed it.

After a few moments, however, he was able to get started, "You guys are like Tim? You and Chris are uh, like partners and everything?"

"Yep, we love each other and share a bedroom and everything."

"Well, you know I was telling your mother once I thought you might be like Tim."

"Yeah, that's what she said when we talked to her. You okay with Chris and me, Dad?"

"Uh, yeah, I'm fine with it. Kind of wondered why you never went out on dates. Sort of figured you and Tim might have that in common. You even look like he did when he was about twenty. He's skinny and wears glasses."

Mr. Bower sniffed twice and said, "Listen, Walt, you're my son, and nothing would ever make me stop loving you. Chris, I think you're one hell of a nice fellah too. You're smart, well-mannered and a Democrat, to boot. Shows you have good sense. I'm glad you guys get along well. You're welcome here anytime. Chris, we'd like to think of you now as part of the family, that is if you fellahs are planning to stick together for a while. It'll be good for Walt. He needs someone to be with. I suppose I have to give up on having grandkids, but what the hell."

Chris said, "Thanks, Mr. Bower. It means so much to both of us. Like I told Walt's mom, I'll never willingly hurt Walt, or bring him harm. I love him too much and feel like he's a part of me now. As far as the grandkids go, well, we've talked about maybe adopting a child someday. Some gay people are doing that now."

"Oh, now that's an idea. That would be great."

"Florida is still against it, but there are other more liberal states where it's allowed and we could adopt in one state and then still live in Florida. It's just that Florida won't let us adopt a child here. So don't give up hope yet."

"It's those damned Republicans in the Legislature. They've taken over the state with their old fashioned ideas and all that Moral Majority crap and that Bryant woman shooting her mouth off about gay folks. Bob Graham has tried, but it's an up-hill battle to get anything done with those idiots in the legislature bucking him all the time. Florida won't be right until those bastards are long gone." Walt's dad saw his son beginning to grin and halted. "Sorry; I'm off the subject. I think you two adopting a kid would be super. When do you think you'll be ready?"

Chris smiled and said, "We want to make sure we have a stable relationship before we take on a child. We have a cat though, so you have a grandcat."

Mr. Bower said, "A grandcat?" He laughed and said, "Damn! Now I've heard it all. You're crazy, Chris, but I like you, son. Put it there." He extended his hand, but after taking it, Chris pulled him into a hug and was pleased that Mr. Bower hugged him right back with a big smile and a pat on the back.

Walt gave his dad a long and very warm hug as well and as they parted, both had tears in their eyes although Mr. Bower started complaining about the bright sunlight and pollen giving his allergies a rough time.

Chapter 12
Winter Vacation

Thanksgiving was a complete success as both families became better acquainted over a traditional turkey dinner at the Walker home in Intercross. Christmas dinner was planned for the Bower home in De Land. The love shared by Chris and Walt now served to unite the two families and help them better adjust to and understand their sons' nature and relationship.

For Walt, the weeks after Thanksgiving were spent in study and preparation for his fall term finals while Chris worked on a new Science Theatre show about minerals, rocks, and fossils for mid-January through March of the coming year, 1981. Chris hadn't yet selected a title for the program.

As Christmas drew near, Chris and Walt began to make plans for a vacation trip for the week and a half following Christmas. They secretly discussed their plans with Libby and Nigel for they planned to take Sebastian along as they did some caving, mineral and fossil collecting while winter camping. His parents, of course, gave their permission, but Walt and Chris planned to torture the poor boy by talking about the trip but not inviting him until the last minute. In fact, his Christmas gift from the two would be a set of caving gear including a helmet, lamp, boots, and other accouterments necessary for the unusual sport. His parents planned some of his holiday gifts around the camping theme as well and sought advice from Chris and Walt as to what he might need.

Christmas dinner was celebrated by both sets of parents and their sons on December twenty-fourth instead of the twenty-fifth at the Bower home in De Land. This would allow Walt and Chris to make ready for their trip more easily on Christmas day and drop by the Selkirk home to give Seb his gifts and finally tell him he was included in their plans. Chris's parents would take custody of Tipsy for the duration of the vacation trip, so they wouldn't have to worry about putting her in a kennel. Tipsy was also scheduled for minor surgery with an Intercross veterinarian while they were gone on their winter trip.

The joint family celebration on Christmas Eve at the Bower family home was a joyous affair and the two families grew even closer. The Bowers had asked Walt and Chris to come a few days before Christmas and spend time with them and upon their arrival; Walt was surprised to find that his uncle Tim and his companion, Ricky, had flown down for a weeklong visit. Walt and Chris had planned on stopping to see Tim in Atlanta while traveling north but had been disappointed to find out from Tim that he and Ricky wouldn't be there. Now Walt knew why and was able to spend even more time with Tim. Walt, as well as Chris, enjoyed a few days getting to know Walt's gay uncle and his partner better. They drove back to Jacksonville late on Christmas Eve.

On Christmas morning, they packed the camper and the Buick Century station wagon. Just after one o'clock, they set off in Walt's car to have dinner with the Selkirks and spring their surprise on Sebastian. Libby had called to say the poor boy was heartbroken thinking they were going without him.

The look of unbridled joy on Sebastian's face as they sprung the news and then watched him open his gifts made their Christmas. The sensitive boy broke down and cried as he hugged them and thanked them for taking him along. His mom and dad gave him a few more packages of hiking boots, a rock hammer, warm clothing and a few other items for the trip.

As Sebastian ran off to pack for the trip, Nigel and Libby gave an envelope to Walt and Chris telling them that inside was a registered power of attorney document to act as Sebastian's guardians in the event of an accident or medical emergency. In addition, there was a check for five hundred dollars to assist with trip expenses and serve as their Christmas gift. When Walt and Chris fussed about the size of the gift they hushed them saying it was the least they could do for being Sebastian's American uncles. Nigel owned and managed the largest billboard advertising agency in Jacksonville and the family was financially comfortable.

Libby said, "Listen, we love you every bit as much as Seb does and want to help out as best we can. You're very much members of our family now and if something happened to Nigel and me, you two would be our first choice to become Seb's adoptive parents."

"Wow," said Walt. "That's something for you to have that much confidence in us. Thank you."

Nigel went on to say, "We both have close relatives, but none we feel would serve as role models and parental figures for Seb, especially considering his sexual nature. Chris and Walt, you may as well know that Libby and I have made just such arrangements in our will in the event of some accident in which we either would be killed or disabled."

"My god, Nigel," said Chris. "That's... I don't quite know what to say. Uh, I hope that never happens, but in case it did, we would do everything in our power to justify your trust. Wow. That's a lot to take in."

"You have my word too," said Walt. "God forbid it would ever happen, but we'd make sure Seb had a good loving home. You've only known us a few months. Are you sure we would be your choice?"

"Without a doubt, you fellows would be best for our son," said Libby. "My sister is a wonderful person, but she's a flighty, silly idiot when it comes to being a mother figure. She wouldn't know how to begin to raise a boy like Seb. She lives in Manchester, England and the pollution alone would stunt Seb's growth. Nigel's two brothers are older and are both involved more with their business careers in Liverpool than with their own families. No, you both already love Seb and know his needs better than anyone, so, you're our choice. Now, if you feel uncomfortable with the idea, we can certainly change things. Think about it and let us know. We're both in excellent health and are certainly not planning on having an accident or whatever. It's only a precaution we feel all parents should take as responsible adults."

Chris spoke for them both, "It's an honor to be your choice and we accept the responsibility. Thanks for having that kind of trust in us."

Nigel said, "Good. That's settled then. We feel better knowing you're willing. Neither of us has told Sebastian about it and would prefer it stays that way. No need to cause him concern."

About that time Sebastian returned from his room once again dragging along twice the number of bags and clothing he would need, but Walt and Chris said nothing. They had plenty of room in the camper and station wagon, so if it made Seb happy to over-pack, so be it.

After once more wishing Nigel and Libby a Merry Christmas and Happy New Year in advance; the three left for Walt and Chris's apartment. As usual, Seb was chattering with excitement and could hardly be contained.

After arriving at the apartment, they packed a number of things in the Buick and a roof-top carrier so they could get an earlier start in the morning. Afterward, they enjoyed a bowl of ice cream while Walt and Chris reviewed a map of Georgia with Sebastian, showing him where their first day's travel would take them. It was their plan to travel north-westward from Jacksonville toward Cordele, Georgia then take Interstate Seventy-five north through Atlanta. Another fifty miles beyond the city, they would leave the Interstate and travel north-westward along secondary roads to Dade County, Georgia, located in the northwestern-most corner of the state where it bordered Alabama and Tennessee.

"What's in Dade County?" asked Sebastian of Chris.

"Caves and mountains. Lots of caves and mountains."

"Cool. Will we be camping in a cave?"

"No," laughed Walt as he ruffled Seb's dark hair. "We'll be staying at a campground in a State Park. I believe it's called Cloudland Canyon. Right, Chris?"

"Yep, it's a beautiful place located on one part of Lookout Mountain. See, it's marked right here near the town of Trenton, Georgia. There's a wide gap or cleft in the mountains and the park sort of wraps around both sides of the chasm. The canyon is about a thousand feet deep below the rim and has beautiful rock formations, waterfalls, and dense forests."

"Sounds wonderful," said Seb.

"We'll be staying on the western rim of the canyon where the campsites are big and isolated, so we won't have to be right up against another camper or tent. That's where I camped the last time I went caving. Since it's winter, there won't be many trees with their leaves like there are in summer, so it might not be as pretty as I remember it. You guys are going to love it though."

"I love you, guys. Thanks again for taking me along," said Seb as he leaned between them and gave them a hug.

"Well, I think we all need to hit the sack pretty soon. We have a very busy day of driving and sight-seeing ahead of us tomorrow."

"I'm not very sleepy yet," said Sebastian. "I hope I can get to sleep. I'm kind of excited. Think I could snuggle with you guys for a little while until I get sleepy?"

Walt grinned at Chris who smiled too and said, "Okay, just a little while though. Walt and I will share the driving, but we have nearly four hundred miles to cover tomorrow, so we'll need our sleep."

"Are you guys, uh, gonna do it tonight?"

"Do what?" said Walt.

"You know... Make love."

Chris said, "Oh, for heaven's sake, Seb. Is that all you think about? Walt, what are we going to do with this silly, horny, English child?"

"You could let me watch," said Seb with an impish grin. "As part of my education, you know. You're a teacher, Chris and I'm a very enthusiastic and curious student. I always get good grades and will do any homework you guys assign me after the lesson."

"I have no idea what we should do, Chris. Castration comes to mind. It might save us a lot of trouble in the future. You grab hold of him and I'll get that new set of knives Mom and Dad gave us for Christmas."

Chris grabbed the wiggling boy and lifted him completely off the floor and carried him squealing into their bedroom. Once there he tossed him on the bed and held him down while Walt unlaced his shoes and pulled them off. Next Walt pulled off his socks and tickled his feet. Seb began laughing hysterically.

"Hold his legs and hips, Walt, while I get his sweater and sweatshirt off. Keep tickling him. He's laughing so hard he can't fight back. Good. I got his shirts off. Now you hold his chest down and I'll pull off his pants. Careful, he might bite. I think he's wanted one of us to pull down his pants for a while anyway. Now's our big chance."

Sebastian was laughing so hard he could hardly get his breath, but finally managed to say as Chris got hold of his belt, "Oh, god! Please stop. I'll pee my pants. I have to go real bad. Please!"

Chris unhooked the belt, unzipped Seb's pants and pulled Seb's corduroy trousers off leaving him only in his underwear. Indeed he had wet himself just a bit, so they finally let him up.

"I'll get you guys for that," Seb wailed as he took off for the bathroom. A few moments later they hear the splatter of urine in the toilet as both laughed and continued to tease him verbally. He appeared at their bedroom door a few moments later and said, "That's unfair. You ganged up on me. Made me wet myself a bit too."

"What are you going to do about it?" asked Walt. "You never seem to be able to hold your water. We might have to take him back to his mummy, Chris."

"That or pick up some Pampers in the morning. Didn't think we'd need any of those. I thought most kids stopped wetting their pants at about three. Maybe he's..."

Chris never finished because Seb growled and charged them in the bed and started tickling them as best he could as the three rolled, laughed and romped for several minutes until they heard someone pounding on the wall from the apartment next door. All three stopped and looked guilty.

Walt said, "Oops, guess we got carried away. It's time to get some sleep anyway. Put on some pajamas, Seb, if you're going to snuggle with us for a little while. We have to get dressed for bed too."

Once Walt and Chris changed into their pajamas and climbed into bed, Seb snuggled in between them after Chris dimmed the bedroom lights. After chatting for a while they all began to yawn and get sleepy. Chris kept suggesting Seb go to his room, but he kept asking for another five minutes and another five minutes until...

Chris and Walt awoke to the sound of the alarm at five-thirty. Seb was sound asleep as Chris and Walt opened their eyes and saw the boy still asleep between them. Walt smiled and leaned over Seb and gave Chris a quick kiss. They both gave the boy a kiss on each cheek as he stirred and opened his eyes.

"Hi," he said as he smiled and looked at each of them. "I love you guys."

"We love you too, Seb. Guess you managed to sleep with us after all," said Walt.

"Yeah, it was fun."

Chris grinned and said, "Today's the big day. We have to get going. We have the largest state, area wise, east of the Mississippi to cross today the long way, from corner to corner. Who's hungry for a quick breakfast?" Everyone was.

By eight they were on the road driving north out of Jacksonville on U.S. 1 and a little before nine they'd crossed the Saint Marys River into Georgia near Folkston, heading northwest through the pine-covered, coastal flatlands of Southeast Georgia. West of the highway, as they drove toward the town of Waycross, was the Okefenokee Swamp. As one small town after another passed behind, Walt handed each a cup of hot coffee from a thermos. Already well-laced with milk and sugar, since they all liked it that way, it hit the spot along with some homemade brownies Libby had given them for the road.

Seb was looking through a faux-leather case of tape cassettes that held some of Walt and Chris's favorite music. He finally chose one labeled, *The Other Side of Life,* one of several Moody Blues tapes. He inserted it into the player, started to re-wind it and asked, "I've heard you guys talking about the Moody Blues. I think the planetarium had a Cosmic Concert of their music too. Is it like most blues music?"

Chris laughed and said, "It's not blues music at all, Seb. The Moody Blues are a British progressive rock band. I'm surprised you've never heard of them, coming from England yourself."

Sebastian started the tape at its beginning. The first cut, *Your Wildest Dreams* started playing and Seb, listening to the weird, electronic sounding intro, said, "Sounds pretty good --- kind of spacey." The rhythm picked up and soon the lead singer started the first verse.

Walt, as usual, was singing along slightly off-key as the song continued. Seb was grinning and said, "I like this kind of music. I think I saw another of their albums in here too."

Chris said, "Yeah, there's several; both of us love their music. At home, we have about nine of their records and I think we have three of their tapes in the box here. Glad you like them too. Just don't play it too loud; I need to hear in case someone blows a horn or something. Walt's really into it and always likes to sing along."

Sebastian leaned over and whispered, "I think I'd rather hear them sing. Walt's a little flat."

"Yeah, but don't tell him, he's having too much fun." Walt's head was wagging up and down with the beat as he looked out the passenger side window and continued to sing along.

By the time Seb had played all three Moody Blues tapes, they'd reached Interstate 75. It was time to stop for lunch, so Chris pulled into a Burger King at the Cordele exit where they ate a Whopper, fries and a shake before returning to the road, this time with Walt driving. By one o'clock they passed Macon and continued along I-75 north toward Atlanta. After passing through the busy city and continuing on for another fifty miles or so, they left the Interstate at the Calhoun exit and took a series of secondary roads northwest through the foothills of the Appalachians.

It was nearly four o'clock when they reached the entrance of Cloudland Canyon State Park and arranged for a campsite for two days. Driving through the park along the western side of the canyon, they reached the campground and found a level and well-kept, pull-through site. Within a half hour, they'd opened and erected the camper trailer. Walt set about getting things ready for a supper of grilled hot dogs, beans and potato salad with cold canned fruit for dessert.

Because it was winter, the temperature at this altitude was dropping quickly and all were wearing sweaters and heavy jeans. By six-thirty, the sun was about to set, so the three walked a short distance from their campsite to the canyon rim and watched the sun setting over the far end of the canyon. Sebastian was standing between them as he said, "This is so beautiful. Tomorrow evening, I want to see if we can take some pictures of the sunset from here. Are we going to be able to hike down into the canyon while we're here?"

"Maybe," said Chris as they walked back to the camper. "Tomorrow morning though, we're going caving. If all goes well, we'll be able to explore two caves I'm familiar with. If we do any hiking, we'll probably do it the day after tomorrow. We have plenty of time and if we need to, we can pay for a third night at our campsite."

"Have you ever hiked into the canyon?" asked Walt.

"No, but I'd like to eventually. There are supposed to be several small waterfalls along the way. Going down will be an easy walk, but coming up will be a bit tiring. The park brochure suggests the walk takes about four hours down and back."

After reaching the camper they made up the beds and got ready to head to the comfort station for a hot shower. The restrooms were no more than five hundred feet away and they were pleased to find they had the place to themselves. Winter was not a busy time at Cloudland Canyon and they'd seen only a few other campers, RV's and tents around the campgrounds. The shower room was a wall of four shower heads with no separating partitions for privacy. Two rows of wooden benches were nearby for towels and clothing.

All three striped and were glad to get under the hot water as the air was fairly cold that evening, somewhere in the mid-forties. Chris and Walt couldn't help but notice that Sebastian was sneaking a few looks at them as they bathed and was having a slight reaction. He did nothing to hide it, nor did he make any comments. Soon they dried off and got dressed quickly and returned to the camper. Once inside, Walt pulled out a small electric heater from one of the storage compartments, set it on the floor and plugged it in. Within a few minutes, it had removed the chill from the interior. All of the windows were equipped with clear plastic that zipped around to close them from the cold air. Chris told them to leave the window covers open just a little on each window for fresh air, but for the most part, the camper was sealed against the cold wind.

Chris set up the table while suggesting they have some hot cocoa and talk about the next day's caving trip. "I want to review a few simple safety rules you both need to know before you enter a cave. I'm a member of the Dogwood City Grotto, a local caving club and later, once you both explore two caves, you guys can join too. I'll sign as your sponsor. There's a caver check-in registry at the Trenton fire and police station and we'll be letting them know where we're going and when we plan to come back. It's really important to do that in case of an emergency. The caves we're going to explore are very safe, but we'll still go by the rules."

"Is it against the law to go caving without letting the police know?" asked Walt as he tended a pot of water on the gas stove for cocoa.

"No, but if you don't and then need to be rescued, there's a hell of a big fine and you have to pay for the rescue services."

"Ooo, I bet that would cost a lot, too," said Walt.

"I'm sure it would. The fire company has a special team trained in cave rescues. We're going to check in at the fire station before and after each cave."

"What other rules do we need to know about?" asked Sebastian.

"First, we do no harm to the cave. No taking rock specimens, or breaking off a stalactite souvenir. We carry out everything we take in. That includes our own wastes. We'll need to use the bathroom before we enter or else poop or pee in a plastic bag if we don't."

"Ooo," said Sebastian. "That's gross."

"Caves are very delicate ecosystems, Seb. Our wastes can affect the balance of nature and cause harm to the very specialized wildlife in the cave."

"Wildlife?" asked Walt with some degree of concern.

"That's the second rule. We don't bother the native wildlife. Bats, insects, cave fish and a few amphibians like salamanders and newts call it home."

Walt said, "Oh, that's not so bad. When you said wildlife I was thinking bears, cougars, and snakes. A few little bats won't be so bad."

"If you see any bats clinging to the walls or ceilings, don't disturb them. It's the beginning of winter and they're hibernating. They only have enough energy to see them through until spring and if we cause them to fly around to get away from us, they burn up some of that energy and might die before they can leave in the spring and get food."

"Wow," said Seb. "The bats won't fly around and bite us will they?"

"No. They're harmless. The ones that live in these caves are the species *myotis lucifugus*, or little brown bats. They're docile, insect-eaters and won't bother us at all. It's not like in the movies. They don't get tangled in people's hair, suck blood, or bite unless you touch or hurt them. Their echolocation is so good they can fly through an utterly dark cave filled with stalactites and columns at thirty miles an hour and never hit a thing."

"Wow," marveled Seb.

"What's the third rule?" asked Walt.

"It has to do with you guys as individuals. Caving is a very special sport and isn't for everyone. If at any time either of you feels uncomfortable being underground, squeezing through tight places, or if you're bothered by deep holes or ledges, let me know. I don't want either of you to do something that frightens or disturbs you. Don't be ashamed to tell me what you're feeling. Accidents happen when people push themselves past their limits. The two caves we'll visit are not dangerous and there are only a few tight squeezes and a few shallow holes or ledges. Nearly all our movement through the caves will be horizontal, with no repelling or rope climbing necessary."

"Any more rules, Chris?" asked Walt. "Everything you've said so far makes good sense."

"Those are the main ones. As we go along, I'll tell you more. Right now, I'm tired from a long day of driving. After we have our cocoa we need to get some sleep."

Within a half hour, they had enjoyed their hot drink and all were sound asleep.

Chapter 13
Underground Adventures

The next morning was cold --- extremely cold. Walt and Chris both awoke shortly after six as Walt's travel alarm went off with a clatter. Seb slept on like one of the dead; Walt and Chris heard him gently snoring, so they took advantage of the situation and spent a half hour making love quietly and enjoying the solitude and quiet. Afterward, they got up and dressed in warm clothing and started boiling water for coffee. Walt stepped over to Sebastian's bed and looked at the boy who was still soundly asleep. His lips were moving a bit as though speaking as he dreamed of something. A carefree smile was on his handsome young face. Walt brushed his fingers through the boy's soft black hair and felt a warm surge of protective love such as a parent might feel for his own child.

Sebastian's eyes fluttered open and he stretched as he looked up at Walt and smiled. He raised his arms for a hug and got one. Chris had come close by now and got one too.

"Hi," said Seb. "What time is it?"

"Nearly seven. You ready for breakfast?" asked Walt. Seb nodded and threw the covers to the side.

"I gotta go to the bathroom first. Brrr, it's cold!"

"Wait until you step outside," said Chris. "I think it's close to freezing. Get dressed in your caving clothes before you go out. I've laid out some old jeans and warm shirts for caving, Seb. Soon as you get your boots on you can step out and find a bush to water. We'll hit the comfort station later."

As soon as Seb dressed, he stepped out and immediately said, "Whew! You're right, it's frigid." A few minutes later he returned and joined his friends at the table and started sipping hot coffee and munching on a sticky bun Chris had placed before him.

Within an hour, they'd packed their caving gear in the Buick, locked up the camper and gotten underway. After leaving the state park, they descended a winding mountain road with crazy hairpin turns that had Seb gripping his seat until they finally reached the valley below and drove into the small town of Trenton, Georgia. Their first stop was at the fire station near the town's center where they spoke to one of the firemen who registered their names and noted their plans for the day's caving.

Chris showed his membership card for the Dogwood City Grotto and was pleased to find that the fireman was also a member. He introduced himself as Bill Ward and praised the three for doing things the right way. Chris told him they would be exploring Howard's Waterfall Cave first and would check back in once they successfully exited the cave later in the day. Bill knew the cave and went on to tell them that a search would not be triggered unless they failed to report back after five hours of their intended exit time of around noon.

After registering, Chris drove north out of town until he spotted a paved service road winding off to the left. After following it for less than three hundred feet he pulled off along the right side of the road into a gravel-strewn clearing. About fifty feet to the right was a gentle hillside covered with heavy woods. Between them and the hillside was a thick growth of high weeds and brush. Chris invited them to get out and look around.

"How far do we have to hike to get to the cave?" asked Walt.

"Thirty or forty feet," laughed Chris.

Seb asked, "It's that close? I can't see it." He was looking up along the tree-covered hillside.

"Let's get our gear on and I'll let you show us the way, Sebastian. Put on your helmets, knee pads, backpacks, and be sure to check your lamps." They had already prepared the backpacks the night before to include food, water in canteens, first aid supplies (just in case of an accident), a forty-foot long coil of rope (also for emergency), candles, extra batteries, etcetera. Walt was carrying a camera loaded with color slide film and a strobe flash unit. It was carefully wrapped in a bubble-wrap bag to avoid damage if it banged against the cavern ceiling or walls as they explored.

Once they were decked out looking like three miners or explorers, Sebastian asked, "You said I get to lead the way, Chris. I have no idea which way to go."

"Okay, I'll give you a clue. Caves are a constant temperature year round. Caves in this part of Georgia are usually fifty-seven degrees. It's just a little above freezing out here right now, so it's warmer in the cave. Caves are also fairly damp and most importantly, they breathe."

"They breathe? Like, inhale and exhale, breathe? How come?"

"Remember your basic science: Warm air rises and cold air falls.

The air in the cave is warmer than the outside air, so which way would you expect the air to be moving near a cave entrance, Seb?"

"Uh, the air should be flowing into the cave if the cave goes up into the hill. If it goes down deeper into the ground, the air would be flowing out. Can you tell me which?"

"You are one smart fellow to ask that because it makes all the difference. This cave mostly goes deeper from here," said Chris as Walt gave the boy a pat on the back. "Now consider that the air in the cave is warmer and very damp. What should you look for?"

Seb thought for a few moments and then smiled as he said. "Vapor. Fog."

"Give the boy Grand Prize! Excellent. Now, go look for the cave."

Sebastian walked over toward the bushes and grassy area and looked about for less than a minute before saying, "Over here! There's a patch of fog over here and I can smell something too. Smells damp --- like a wet rock."

Walt laughed and said softly, "That's one smart kid, Chris. Look at him. He's having a ball." Seb was pushing through the brush and had found a narrow trail leading downward into a slight depression not easily seen from the road. The depression continued off to the right along a dry stream bed.

"Here it is guys! Here it is! I found it!" Seb was pointing to a low shelf of rock protruding outward over a dark opening from where the fog was forming slowly, mixing with and fading away in the cold air.

Once all three had climbed down to the opening located in a depression about six feet lower than the surface, they readied to enter the cave. Because the opening was only three feet in height, they would have to crawl into it over a collection of broken rock fragments that had washed out of the cave over the years. All were glad for their knee pads and canvas gloves as they crawled inside for twenty or so feet before they could stand up in the first cavern chamber.

"Wow! This is so cool," said Sebastian as he stood up and looked around the thirty by twenty-foot chamber using his helmet light to peer upward at stalactites and other cavern formations around the room. Another passageway led from the room to their left that would lead them deeper into the cave. Chris now took the lead and guided them farther along through a series of passages and chambers showing them the best way to navigate a number of difficult rock formations which sometimes seemed at first to block their way. After a half hour of walking, crawling and wiggling through a few tight places, Chris invited them to sit down on a flat rock surface in one large chamber as he wanted to show them something.

"Okay, guys. This is a bit of a test for you both, as new spelunkers. We're going to turn off our lights and sit very quietly for a little while. I want to see how you handle utter darkness and complete silence. Probably neither one of you has ever been somewhere like this and experienced total sensory loss. It can be pretty creepy at first and a few people have a tendency to panic. I want to make sure you guys can handle it. Seb and Walt take off your helmets and turn off your headlamps." They did so. "Okay; now I'm going to do the same."

As Chris switched off his lamp, complete and utter darkness enveloped them.

"Hold your hands in front of your eyes and try to see them. You can't. That's utter darkness.

"Cool," said Sebastian. "It's like being blind, I guess."

"That's right. Everybody okay so far?"

Walt and Seb said they were fine.

"Next, I want everyone to be very quiet for several minutes. You might be able to hear your own heart beating or the pulse in your neck, but little else. This room is very dry and dust is everywhere, so it absorbs sound completely. There's no water dripping in here either, so you won't even hear that. Now I'll shut up so you can experience true silence."

For the next few minutes, it was completely quiet until Chris again spoke saying, "Did either of you hear your heartbeat?"

Sebastian said, "I think I might have. I could hear the air whistling in my nose because I'm a little stopped up, but that was it."

Walt who was sitting beside the boy laughed and said, "I could hear your nose too and wondered what it was. It was creepy, like a faint whistle every time you breathed."

Chris leaned over in the darkness from Walt's other side, felt for Walt's face and gave him a kiss.

"Either there's an amorous bat in here or my boyfriend is taking advantage of me, Seb. Something or somebody just gave me a kiss." He felt Seb do the same from the other side and laughed. "Wow, I'm having a great time in the dark, fellows. Do it again." Walt leaned back quickly, however, so as Chris and Seb leaned out to kiss his cheeks in the dark, they missed him and connected with one another's lips.

"What the..." said Chris as Sebastian giggled and said, "I don't think that was Walt I just snogged." Chris switched on the headlamp on his helmet resting in his lap and saw how Walt had leaned backward and tricked them. All three shared a laugh.

Chris suggested they eat a snack before leaving the quiet room; he opened a pouch on his backpack and passed around some Snicker bars. As they munched on the candy, Chris used his lamp and pointed out a cluster of three small bats clinging to the ceiling not far away. Up until now, they hadn't seen any of the flying mammals. He moved the light away slightly, so as not to disturb their sleep.

"I thought they'd be bigger," said Walt. They're only about the size of a mouse."

"Those are the little brown bats I told you about. That's the only kind I've ever run across in caves around here."

Over the next hour, they delved deeper into the cave and finally reached the last chamber that could be accessed. There was more cavern beyond, but there was no way to squeeze into the small opening that led farther. Their lights showed it opened into another large room, but there was no possible way, without breaking rocks and damaging the cave, that the rest of the cave could be explored.

On the way back, Chris led them along a different path at one point to a second entrance to the cave. This one ended in a very large and high chamber where piles of boulders led upward along the far wall to a large opening where sunlight could be seen.

"When it rains," said Chris, water pours down over those rocks and permeates into the ground along the cavern passages. That's why the place is called Howard's Waterfall Cave."

"I was wondering," said Walt. I've been looking for a waterfall and so far haven't seen any running water anywhere. I was going to ask, but now I see how it would be quite a waterfall if it were to rain. I really wouldn't want to be in here when it did. We might get washed out."

"Let's start climbing over the rocks because that's our way out," said Chris. "In the springtime is when you have to worry about rain and washouts. Winter's safe as it's the dry season around here."

After reaching the exit they found themselves at the end of a dry stream-bed and followed it a short distance. After about a thousand paces, Chris had them leave the dry stream and led them through a stand of winter-bare sweet gum trees that brought them out on the same road where the Buick was parked. It was not far away on the opposite side of the road they had crossed under while exploring.

They were muddy and hungry and enjoyed lunch at a local fast food place with outdoor tables. It was called the Highland Drive-in and was decorated with a Scottish theme. All three enjoyed a heaping plate of fish, hushpuppies and a butterscotch milkshake.

The rest of the day was spent exploring another local cavern known as Hurricane Cave near the town of Rising Fawn, Georgia. After each cave, the trio reported in at the Trenton fire station. By four o'clock, they returned to Cloudland Canyon State Park, tired, dirty and very hungry. Showers came first due to the mud and sweat that had accumulated due to the day's explorations. Coin-operated washers and dryers were nearby and they dropped all of their muddy and sweaty clothing in for washing while they used the showers.

By the time they returned to the camper, fixed their meal of grilled cheeseburgers, baked beans and ice cream from the camp store, it was dark. They recovered their caving clothes from the driers in the laundry room. Everyone dressed in warm flannel pajamas as the air was again very cold outside. The small space heater kept the camper comfortable. Seb once again wanted to sit with Walt and Chris in their bed while they talked about their day and plans for the next week.

Sebastian couldn't stop chattering about all he had experienced while caving. In talking, he did clear up one mystery; he had joined the Boy Scouts for a short time in Savannah, Georgia where they had lived briefly after moving to the United States, but wasn't in the troop long enough to go on a major hike or outing. After moving to Jacksonville, he became involved with the museum and never signed up with a local troop.

Seb had picked up a number of interesting-looking rocks from near the entrance to Howard's Cave and was looking them over and asking Chris what they were. Chris identified some schist, chert and limestone rocks as well as a few quartz minerals common to the area. Many of the rocks he said were leaverite. The boy seemed impressed until he noticed that so many of the leaverite specimens were totally un-alike. He finally asked, "What *is* leaverite?"

Chris said with a completely straight face, "Those rocks are called leaverite because they're worthless. When you find one, you should *leave-er-rite* where you found it."

Seb looked confused for only a second until Walt chuckled and he got the pun. "You should have told me when I was picking them up. That's mean. *Leaverite*. Gees."

Chris ruffled his hair and said, "You were having fun and besides, now you have some common rocks to study so you'll know what to leave behind next time. Most of them, by the way, are various forms of limestone, quartz minerals and feldspars, all very common rocks in this part of Georgia."

Chris had allowed Sebastian to take one small souvenir from the cave, a short, thin stalactite, as it was already broken off from the ceiling and lying along the path in Hurricane Cave. The boy treasured it like it was made of gold and vowed to start a rock and mineral collection using it as the first specimen.

Chris explained how he was planning to collect a number of rock, mineral and fossil samples along the way as they explored the southern Appalachians during the next few days of their trip. "I want to have lots of samples to use as prizes during the upcoming earth science show. Kids especially stay more focused if there is a chance of winning a prize for the right answer, or other hands-on participation during a show or lesson."

Walt agreed and added, "Will we be going anywhere where we might visit a rock shop?"

"I can plan for it if you like. I want to take us up through Tennessee and Kentucky over the next few days and on the way back we'll take a more easterly route so we can go through Franklin, North Carolina where there are pay-per-bucket, do-it-yourself, ruby and sapphire mines and four or five rock shops in the town itself. We'll do some mining and visit the shops there. Did you have something special in mind you wanted to look for, Walt?"

"Well, you know how much I enjoy going through those mineral cabinets in your office. I'm like Sebastian and think I'd like to start a small collection. I want to see if I can pick up some good quality pieces and maybe find a nice display cabinet too. I've set aside about seventy-five dollars just for minerals for the trip and figured we'd find some for free and then I can also buy some in a shop."

Sebastian asked, "What's planned for tomorrow?"

"Well, you guys were asking about hiking the canyon, so if you want we can do that. There're other options as well. One is to drive up to Chattanooga and then travel east along U.S. Highway Sixty-four. Near the town of Parkland, Tennessee is a road cut where piles of black shale have been exposed. In the shale are cubic crystals of iron pyrite or fool's gold. I've been to the site and there's no doubt you'll find museum quality specimens there."

"Oh, that would be cool to do," said Sebastian. "What about you

Walt?"

"Sounds like fun. Tomorrow's weather report said it was going to be cold again, so climbing into the canyon around waterfalls might be pretty chilly. Not much sun will reach into the woods in that canyon. Maybe we can come back to Cloudland Canyon next summer when it's warm and explore the canyon more thoroughly."

"I've been here in summer and with all the trees covered by their leaves, it's much prettier then anyway," added Chris.

"Then I vote for the pyrite," said Walt. How big are the crystals?"

"They range in size from a half inch to two inches square and are fairly easy to remove from the shale which is relatively soft. The best way is to collect the shale with the crystal in it and take it back home where we'll be able to carefully remove the crystals with dental tools. It takes a while to do it right and not scratch or ruin the crystals."

"What else lies in that direction?" asked Walt.

"Well, along the same road is an ancient streambed exposed in a road cut just east of Cleveland, Tennessee that has fossil trilobites, little crab-like critters that lived back during the Devonian Period. That was long before the dinosaurs came along."

"Anything else along the way?" asked Walt.

"Yeah, in Murphy, North Carolina, there's a talc mine. It's famous for having some of the purest talc in the world. The owner lives near the mine and I've met him in the past. He's very open-minded about helping out geology students by allowing them to visit the mine and take specimens. His idea of a nice specimen, by-the-way is often a chunk of talc about a foot or two in width. It's beautiful stuff either pale translucent white or pale green. We'll stop in and see if he's able to let us visit. Last time I was here, the mine was closed as he operates it only a few months a year and still makes money. His name is Don Hitchcock and the Hitchcock Mine sells exclusively to Avon and Revlon for their powder products. I imagine he does very well."

"Cool," said Seb. "Where will we camp if we go that way?".

"We can find another state park in North Carolina. There're lots of nice parks in the area including Great Smoky Mountain National Park."

The votes were unanimous for moving on to the fossil and mineral sites the next day. By then it was nearing nine o'clock, so everyone turned in for the night. Seb, as usual, wanted to snuggle for a little while, but finally and reluctantly moved over to his side of the camper. Once Chris and Walt heard him snoring softly, they made love and were soon sound asleep themselves.

Chapter 14
Rock Hounds and Puppy Love

The next morning, after eating breakfast and breaking camp, they left Cloudland Canyon State Park and once more descended the twisty mountain road into Trenton, Georgia. From there, with Chris driving, they headed north on Interstate 59 and soon crossed into Tennessee and skirted around Chattanooga on its Interstate bypass. They left the city behind heading east along U.S. 64.

Just past the town of Cleveland, Tennessee, Chris started watching the left side of the highway for a particular landmark he was familiar with.

"When I was in college, I took a one-week course called Geology of the Southeastern United States. I and about fifteen other geology students were led all through the southeast by our professor, Doctor Pierce. We traveled by bus and made a lot of stops along the way where Dr. Pierce knew fossil and mineral specimens were easy to locate. I'm looking for one of them now. You guys can help."

"How?" asked Sebastian

"We just passed mile marker 36. Watch for a road cut on the left that has a band of rounded rocks shaped like a big wide U across it. It's an old stream bed that was covered up during the Devonian period but exposed in cross section when they cut the road through the hillside. In the shale that was laid down as mud, just above the rounded rocks, there are trilobite fossils. If you carefully pry apart the layers of soft shale you'll find them. They vary from a half inch long up to three inches long and are very well-preserved. Last time I was here I found about twenty in an hour."

"Wow," said Walt. "That's a lot for such a short time. Think there's still some left behind for us?"

"I'm sure of it. Keep an eye out, it can't be much farther." Chris had been going as slowly as possible without blocking traffic.

It was Sebastian who spotted the road cut first and said, "Chris! Is that it?" He was pointing ahead to the left and sure enough, his sharp eyes had spotted the curving line of rounded stones exposed in cross-section, which was once the bottom of a stream or small river.

Chris guided the Buick past the formation and told Seb he'd been correct and found it. "I'm going to go on past and then turn around as soon as I can find a spot that's safe; then we'll drive back and park along the road cut. There's enough shoulder for us to park safely." He did so and soon they cruised to a stop along the formation.

"You'll need your rock hammers, a couple of plastic bags, a small paint brush, a set of dental tools and a screwdriver. There's several of each in the collecting kit."

"Why do we need a screwdriver?" asked Seb.

"It'll help you split the layers of shale. Shale is a rock that was made in layers when mud settled a long time ago. It's turned to rock, but still splits along the layers. As the mud formed, dead creatures got trapped in the mud and now have become hard fossils. Their bodies rotted away leaving an empty space like a mold. Calcium carbonate --- that's limestone --- or some other mineral, crystallized inside the empty space over time and made the harder fossil casting. The specimens are relatively hard while the shale around them is very soft. You can use the brushes and dental tools to work them away from the shale."

They gathered their tools and approached the rock face. Chris showed them how to carefully pry out a chunk of the soft shale. The piece he removed was about a foot square in width and length and about three inches thick. Its many layers were easily visible along the sides of the rather flat specimen. Chris showed them how to use the screwdriver to split off layer after layer of the rock. Between the layers of the third section, he teased apart was a beautifully preserved specimen of a trilobite. It was dark gray limestone, an inch and a half long and a little under an inch in width. Somewhat resembling a horseshoe crab, it was obviously a primitive life form that had swarmed in the seas and streams over three hundred million years in the past.

All three set to work splitting shale. Walt won the honor that morning for the largest specimen found. About a half hour, after they started splitting shale and looking, Walt let out a yell and at first Chris though he had been hurt. His subsequent yelps, however, were those of joy. He showed his fellow searchers a beautiful three and a half inch long trilobite in excellent condition. After carefully removing the harder, gray, limestone fossil from the softer yellow shale, he carefully wrapped it in tissue, bagged and tagged it and placed it in the station wagon.

Sebastian found the most, however, discovering over forty

specimens by the time they moved on just before eleven. Chris took a number of photos of his companions at work as they searched the shale layers for fossils. He planned to project the color slides as part of his rock and mineral presentation to show visitors how fossil hunters did their thing.

They stopped at a roadside table just after noon for lunch. A few miles farther along Route 64 was the site where Chris had told them they would find pyrite crystals. It was a road cut along the banks of Lake Ocoee, a Tennessee Valley Authority, or TVA, man-made lake, created as part of the flood control and rural electrification act passed during Franklin D. Roosevelt's administration that put many men to work and helped end the Great Depression of the 1930s.

There, searching among the piles of black shale gathered at the base of the cut, they each found at least twenty, high-quality, cubic crystals of the shiny mineral, iron pyrite that most people know as fool's gold. It only slightly resembles the precious metal and its only value is to mineral collectors. These extremely fine specimens were composed of chemically pure, natural crystals of iron sulfide.

After leaving the pyrite site, Chris drove eastward into North Carolina and soon they arrived at the town of Murphy. Not far from the center of town, Chris drove along a gravel road until they came to a private drive leading up to a beautifully constructed log home on a wooded hill. They were in luck and Mr. Don Hitchcock, the mine owner Chris had described earlier was home and welcomed them saying he remembered Chris from his travels with his college class several years before. As expected, he gave them permission to visit the nearby mine which was closed for the season.

After leading them to the mine in his jeep, Mr. Hitchcock told them to take whatever specimens they wished from a pile of scrap beside the main mine building and crusher. Everyone was able to collect a number of fine specimens and several *Pocket Pieces* --- a term Chris used to describe extremely large samples --- of the beautiful, pale green and white mineral.

By three, they'd driven on to Cherokee, North Carolina, where the southern entrance to Great Smoky Mountain National Park was located. It was Chris's plan to camp in the national park at the Smokemont Campground. By five they entered the park, drove a short distance to the well-kept and scenic campground, paid their nightly fee and set up the camper. By seven, it was starting to get cold as well as very dark, due to the surrounding mountains, as they prepared their evening meal of grilled hot dogs, baked potatoes, cheese curls and cold canned peaches for dessert. After a full day, digging and climbing over rocks searching for specimens, the meal seemed extra special and all ate like the healthy young men they were.

There were no shower facilities at the campground, so it was necessary for each to take a sponge bath in either the restroom sinks or in the camper. All were pretty dirty and sweaty from the day's activities, and chose to boil water on the camper's gas stove and bathe in the camper. By spreading a waterproof tarp on the floor, each was able to use hot water to sponge off, one at a time. All of the camper's windows were curtained for privacy and by now, none of them were shy about being nude in front of the others. Seb especially seemed to be enjoying the bath, or perhaps it would be more appropriate to say in watching his companions bathing.

The temperature that night was cold, but not terribly so. The thermometer in the camper was designed to show inside as well as outside temperature and reported thirty-eight degrees outdoors and sixty-four within. Using the gas stove to heat the bath water had contributed to the warmth.

Walt had pulled a muscle earlier in the day while climbing over a pile of slate at the pyrite site and was complaining of pain in his right shoulder and side. Chris offered to give him a back rub with analgesic balm, so Walt stretched out, face down across the bed in just his pajama bottoms while Chris massaged his aching muscles. Sebastian offered to help too. Walt grinned knowingly at Chris and told the boy he could massage his left shoulder, so the boy climbed on the bed beside him and followed Chris's example and rubbed more liniment into Walt's muscles. Soon Walt was purring with satisfaction from the attention.

By the time they finished, the camper positively reeked with the scent of wintergreen to the point that their eyes were watering, so they had to open a few curtains and windows for fresh air. Chris had brought along a small electric space heater and since the campsite featured electrical hookups he took advantage of the power outlet and heater to warm the interior.

By ten, it was time for them to get some sleep as the next day they planned to explore some of the features of the national park. Being early winter, there was a slight chance of snow in higher elevations. Chris hoped that wouldn't happen as he had no chains or gear for winter driving.

As they made the two beds with two layers each of blankets, Seb asked to snuggle between them for a few minutes before going off to his bed. They both enjoyed the boy's presence and Walt thanked him for helping massage his shoulder.

After Seb went off to his bed, where they soon heard him snoring lightly, Chris and Walt slipped out of their pajamas and held each other close as they talked.

"I'm so happy, Chris. Being here with you is very special to me. The last six months of my life has been worth all the lonely years as a teenager. Knowing you're within reach and that you totally love me makes my life so meaningful."

"Thanks, Hon. Believe me, I feel the same. Having Sebastian along too is pretty special. He is one beautiful soul, so free and accepting of who he is. Sometimes I find myself feeling like a father when he's around."

"Yeah, me too. It was a hell of a surprise when Nigel and Libby told us about the will. For them to have that kind of trust in us is unbelievably nice. I hope and pray it never happens, but if they were ever to meet with tragedy, Sebastian wouldn't lack for love. Next to you, Walt, and our parents, he's the next most important person in my life. I'd do anything to protect that boy. He teases a lot about his sexuality and I'm sure, deep down, he'd like nothing more than to join us when we make love, but he still knows and respects the limits."

"Yeah, I was watching him as he rubbed your back this evening. He was doing it because he loves you. He had on only briefs and *did not* get an erection. I was really proud of him. I sure hope he finds someone as wonderful as you, Walt, to love him and treat him right someday. I've become so protective of him that if he did find a boyfriend who hurt him, I'd probably get in trouble myself for what I might do. Seb's very much like our son now. He has four loving parents; not just Libby and Nigel."

Walt said, "I feel the same. He's so different. Most young teens are starting to become rebellious and rude. Not Sebastian. That's what being raised in a loving and free-thinking home can do. Nigel and Libby have never tried to control the boy and mold him into what they want him to be."

"Our folks didn't either," Chris added, "Most of our problems came from the world and times we grew up in. Being gay during our teen years we had to be so hush-hush and secretive; always hiding our true selves."

Walt said, "We both felt shame and couldn't go to our parents for advice and help because of it."

"In reality, they would have accepted us, but society had taught us that being gay was shameful and we thought they might stop loving us," said Chris as he pulled Walt even closer and kissed his warm and soft neck. "God I love you. I want to crawl right inside you sometimes and be closer than ever. Don't ever leave me, Walt. It would kill me."

"It would take an act of God to do it, Hon. I know what you're saying. Feeling your warm body against mine, your hardness between my thighs and the scent of your hair and skin is like nothing else in the world. You *are* my world now and I want to love you." Walt pulled away from their embrace, tossed the blanket to the side and moved downward as Chris rolled flat on his back and spread his legs for Walt who snuggled there kissing his thighs and nuzzling at his warm and excited secret places.

Chris was humming with pleasure as Walt's warm, insistent mouth enveloped his sex sliding tightly down and over its wet and swollen tip. Chris's lower body moved up and down in the bed slightly as Walt took him deeply, moving with the rhythm of their heartbeats. Within a few minutes, Walt was forced to stop as Chris gasped he was about to come. Walt spent several minutes kissing and nibbling at his scrotum to allow his partner a reprieve before he once again carried him close to the point of ecstasy.

Chris was running his hands through Walt's soft hair, over his cheeks, and along his back as their lovemaking progressed to the magic moment when Chris asked Walt to stop and Walt refused, tightening his lips and surrounding Chris's throbbing shaft with his left hand. Chris sucked in air between his teeth as his knees rose slightly from the bed and his loins pounded with a powerful flood of warm semen.

Walt felt the forceful surge of his lover's fluid burst into his mouth, warm, vital and delicious. He nearly came spontaneously himself as he shared Chris's passion. As soon as the flow ended and he felt Chris relax, Walt crawled up beside his partner urging him to take his place between his own legs as he could hardly wait. Walt held Chris's life fluid within his mouth as Chris kissed, sucked and fondled him below, gradually bringing him to the crowning pinnacle of delight he had just visited himself. After several teasing journeys along the climb to the peak, Chris carried Walt to the summit and over.

Walt moaned softly and clutched at Chris's shoulders and neck as resounding waves of utter joy pounded through his secret parts filling his lover's hungry mouth with warm and living seed. After the tide ebbed, Chris crawled up and over him as Walt and Chris's lips met and they shared the warm fluids of their love in a long and passionate kiss.

Only a small glimmer of light from a distant fixture at a nearby restroom served to illuminate the camper, but it was sufficient to silhouette the two young lovers as they spent their passion. Sebastian had awakened a little after Walt and Chris had finished talking and moved on to making love. Due to what they perceived as near darkness, they had thrown the blankets to the side as they met each other's needs. Sebastian lay spellbound, on his side of the camper, watching a shadow play of their coupling.

As he realized what they were doing, Sebastian rolled on his back with his head turned, still watching his friends as they moved and made love to one another. He slipped out of his pajamas and briefs, tossed his covers aside and began to touch and stroke himself. Within seconds he was wet with excitement and retracted his foreskin to better enjoy the sensation of touch as his mind made him a part of Walt and Chris's actions.

He saw Walt's silhouetted face in profile sliding up and down over Chris's erection and had to contain himself and carefully control his own sensations as he danced around the edge of pleasure. He wanted to make it last until perhaps he could see Chris reach his climax. He wanted to crest at the same time. As he saw Chris's knees raise from the bed and his hands clutch at Walt's hair and neck, he squeezed himself tightly and moved ever so slowly as Chris's body gave up the battle and writhed in ecstasy.

Sebastian's simultaneous orgasm was, without a doubt, the most powerful he had ever experienced and his semen splattered against his neck, something it had never done before. Over and over his young loins expelled the warm seed. The boy nearly passed out from the intensity of the climax. After both he and Chris relaxed as their orgasms came to an end, he watched in shadow as Walt finished and reversed positions with his companion.

Sebastian felt the many pools of warm semen spewed across his smooth and hairless chest. He gathered it with his fingers and brought it to his nose, smelling the earthy, male scent he'd learned to relish.

His heart was racing and he felt himself harden again as he saw Chris giving pleasure to Walt. Even though for a few seconds his flesh felt irritated, he started stroking himself using some of his remaining semen as a lubricant and soon began the climb to climax.

As Walt approached the eruptive moment, so did Sebastian. He felt, again, like he had before, that he was a part of their love, as though Chris's mouth was around him instead of his own hand. Walt's chest was arching from the bed slightly and Seb even heard him whisper a warning of his climax as Chris refused him and took him all the way. As he heard Walt sob with pleasure, he again felt his inner sexual organs surge with another memorable ejaculation. He was pleasantly amazed that he could again produce so much semen. He had done two in a row before, but the second always took longer and produced only a little semen. Not this time, however.

Watching Walt and Chris had stimulated the boy to new heights of sexual bliss. What he saw this evening would serve for some time as a memorable vision to better his nightly pleasure. Now Chris and Walt kissed and he watched as they clutched at one another and exchanged their fluids through a long and wet kiss.

It was a new and exciting sensual experience especially as he imagined himself to be a part of what was happening a few feet away. He fantasized about what Walt and Chris might taste like, either sharing with their mouths or directly from the source. He wanted so much to share his fluid with them, allowing them to drink from his fountain and become a third partner in their deep and special love.

Chapter 15
Mountain Confessions

It was reasonably cold the next morning when Walt was the first to awaken, step to the door and quietly open it and peek out. There was an impressive accumulation of ice crystals on their picnic table, the ground and nearby tree branches. At first, Walt thought it might have snowed, but it was only heavy frost. He stepped out and looked around at the white wonderland. The ice crystals crunched beneath the loafers he had slipped on before leaving the camper. It was still half dark as dawn came later in the depths of the mountains. He'd looked at his watch just before leaving the camper and found it was six-forty. He saw no other campers or tents nearby so he stepped behind a nearby boulder to empty his bladder.

As he peed, he felt the chill of a slight breeze and shivered as he expelled the last few drops. Going back inside he saw that Chris was still sleeping soundly as was Sebastian. The boy was partly uncovered, so Walt stepped over and was about to tuck him in when he saw that Seb was naked and all curled up from being cold. The space heater had kept the interior relatively warm, but not that warm. Seb's bare behind was sticking out from beneath the covers and Walt grinned and shook his head as he tried to figure out why Seb had slept naked on such a cold night.

Walt gently raised the blanket from Seb and tried to free it so he could cover the boy's rear, but he was clutching it so fiercely that the motion was enough to awaken him and he suddenly rolled over on his belly dragging the covers even farther off his body.

Sebastian mumbled, "Ooo --- it's cold." He turned his head and looked up at Walt who was grinning and staring at his exposed posterior. "Oh, bloody hell. Sorry, Walt." Sebastian rolled over on his back and tried to free the blanket to cover himself, but that only revealed his prominent erection. He giggled and managed to cover himself. "Sorry."

"Why in the world are you sleeping naked, Seb? Are you crazy?" whispered Walt. "It's in the forties in here and well below freezing outside. Where are your pajamas?"

"Uh, they're under here somewhere." Seb started digging around near his feet and soon retrieved them and struggled to don them under the covers. "Bloody hell --- I got them backward." More struggling ensued.

Walt chuckled and turned away to give him some degree of privacy and whispered so as not to awaken Chris, "What in the world would possess you to sleep in the buff, Kiddo?" Sebastian started giggling and said, "I have to pee. I'll tell you after I go."

"Careful, it's icy outside. Put on some shoes. Step outside and go behind the big rock beyond the picnic table. That's what I did. It'll save us having to service the nightjar. It's too far to the restroom in this cold anyway. Better pull on a sweater or a coat. I didn't and wished I had."

Seb did so, stepped out and within a few minutes rushed back inside saying, "Whoa! It must be about three degrees out there."

Chris was still sleeping soundly as Seb returned, so Walt motioned for Seb to be as quiet as possible. Walt had just started heating some water on the gas stove for coffee and whispered to Sebastian, "We'll let him sleep as long as he wants."

"I like to watch him sleep," said Sebastian. "He's really a beautiful person. So are you, Walt." The boy leaned close and got the hug he expected from his friend. "Sorry I was starkers when I woke up this morning."

"Yeah, what was that all about?" whispered Walt with a laugh.

"Well, you know how it is sometimes. I, uh, woke up last night and, uh, felt the urge to uh, well, you know, so I pulled off my pajamas and did it and, uh, I guess I fell asleep afterward and you know the rest."

"Yeah, I know. I get sleepy afterward myself. Takes a lot out of you," Walt snickered as did the boy. "Your secret is safe with me." Walt got up to check on the water, but it hadn't yet come to a boil. He sat back down with Seb on the edge of the boy's bed. He noticed the boy was introspective and very quiet and was leaning against him. He heard the boy sniff and saw a tear at the corner of his eye.

"Sebastian, are you all right? A bit homesick maybe?"

"Oh no. I love being here with you guys. I just... I don't know. Sometimes I think I love you guys too much. I just wish I was older."

"Why older? Being nearly fourteen is one of the greatest times of your life. You'll realize that someday when you're old and decrepit like Chris and me."

"You're not old. You're about twenty-two right?"

"Twenty-one actually. Chris is twenty-two. Did you know we have the same birthday? July twentieth."

"You do? Wow, that's cool. Mine's March twenty-sixth."

"So why the tears just now? Is there something else bothering you?"

Sebastian hesitated a little too long before saying, "No, I..."

"Talk to me, son. Chris and I love you and we're both here when you need us. If something is bothering you, I want to help. When you're sad, I'm sad and I'm sure Chris would be if he was awake."

"I feel ashamed of something that happened last night."

"Masturbation is nothing to be ashamed of, Kiddo."

"It wasn't that."

"Okay, was it about me finding you naked this morning?"

"No, but kind of, I suppose. I hope you won't be angry with me. I sort of saw something last night and well I..."

"Did you wake up just after Chris and I went to bed?"

"Yeah"

"Uh huh. Did you maybe hear us loving one another? Was that it?"

"Yeah. When I realized what was happening, I should have turned away and thought about something else, but I didn't. I could see your silhouettes from the restroom light behind you and well... Walt, I'm so sorry, but I watched. It was so beautiful seeing you both loving one another. Please forgive me. I won't ever do it again."

The boy was crying for real now and Walt hugged him close and rocked him back and forth as he kissed his hair.

"So, you kinda slipped off your pajamas and joined in on your own, right?"

"Oh yes, I'm so sorry, Walt. I feel positively filthy now."

"It's okay. I would have probably done the same thing if I had seen two men loving each other when I was your age. Is there anything you want to ask me about what you saw? Was there anything that bothered or confused you?"

"No. It was beautiful. I always wondered what guys like us do. I'd heard about certain things but never knew for sure until last night. You guys used your mouth."

"Uh huh. Did that bother you, or gross you out?"

"No. It made me get harder and made me wish I was there with you. I'm sorry. It's wrong to think things like that."

"No, Sebastian. It's human. You are a normal gay teenager discovering yourself. You saw us loving one another and that's all right. Think about kids who see people they love hurting each another. What do those children learn? I'll tell you. They learn to hurt the people they love. What you saw happen between Chris and me was something very good and wonderful."

Sebastian sniffed and nodded.

"I love that guy over there more than life itself. I've only known him a short time now, but Sebastian, I would give my life for him, I love him so much. I love you too and would do the same. My love for you, Sebastian --- and Chris would say the same --- is like a parent's love for a child. We consider you a part of our family now."

"Thanks, Walt. I love you guys so much too. Sometimes though, love is so confusing. Part of me loves you like family, but part of me wants to love your bodies and be with you when you have sex. Please don't hold that against me. I know it can't happen, but I wish it could."

"Thank you for being honest, Sebastian. We will never hold honesty against you. We love you too much for that. Chris and I can't have children like a straight couple, but we have you now and that's very special to us. Hey, look over there, Sleeping Beauty is stirring. Go give him a kiss. He'd like that."

Sebastian did and was rewarded by a warm hug and kiss from Chris. "What brought that on, buddy? Sure is a nice way to be greeted in the morning. Now I want one from Walt."

Walt joined them and gave Chris a warm and intimate kiss. As Chris sat up along the side of the bed, he was flanked by Walt and Sebastian and all joined in a group hug.

"Somebody tell me what all the loving and hugging is all about. Not that I'm complaining, 'cause it sure is nice to have such a super greeting in the morning."

Sebastian said, "Walt and I have just had a very important discussion about love and I wanted to show you what I've learned. Do I pass?"

"Oh yes, with an A-plus. Hey, I hate to change a great subject, but I have to go in the worst way. How cold is it outside?"

Walt consulted the thermometer and reported, "Twenty-two degrees. It's fifty-eight in here. Be prepared for a shock. We used the big rock beyond the picnic table. It's too damned cold to run to the comfort station just yet. Put on a coat or sweater and watch out for ice. The ground's frozen."

The water was boiling now and by the time Chris returned, Seb had set up the folding table and Walt was pouring coffee for everyone. Milk and sugar were on the table and Walt was digging out some bowls and cereal along with several sweet rolls they had bought the day before. Soon all were eating their breakfast and making plans for the day's explorations in the national park.

Despite the cold, the three had a wonderful day experiencing the park in winter. Chris had been to the Smokies before, but never in winter. The traffic jams of summer were absent and the views of the mountains in the clear cold air were breathtaking. The higher peaks were covered in snow and as they crossed the North Carolina, Tennessee border along the crest of the Smokies, at Newfound Gap, snow flurries were flying. It was Walt's first time ever seeing snow.

The access road to Clingman's Dome, the highest point in the park, was closed during winter months, so they were not able to visit the lookout tower located there 6,643 feet above sea level. After descending into Tennessee they drove north along U.S. 441 as it meandered through the park, stopping at a number of scenic overlooks and points of interest. They walked a one-mile trail to Laurel Falls just west of the Gatlinburg visitor center. They were the only hikers using the trail that day and met no one else either going or returning. Icicles had formed overnight along various ledges the water slipped over, giving an exotic and fantastic look to the falls.

Sebastian was in heaven, taking pictures, asking questions about the mountains and hearing Chris's stories about the early settlers who first discovered and settled the isolated coves and hollows among the mountains. Chris had visited this area many times before with his family while growing up and was very familiar with the natural and social history of the Smokies.

By three o'clock, Chris suggested they leave the park and find a campground somewhere outside the western park gate at Townsend, Tennessee. After driving a winding road that followed the wildly meandering Little River, they left the park and soon located a beautiful campsite in a private campground just beyond the park's northwestern boundaries in Townsend. The Little River they had been following that afternoon ran directly behind the site, so the sound of the stream tumbling over rocks would serve to lull them to sleep after evening fell.

Walt spoke privately with Chris about what Sebastian had seen the night before and assured him no harm had been done. Chris agreed that what Seb had witnessed was probably good for him as an example of two gay men in love. It was not what they would have chosen him to see, but as it had already happened, they felt he had

146

suffered no harm.

Chapter 16
Moon Bows & Country Cousins

The last day of 1980 found the three travelers on the back roads of Tennessee heading north toward Corbin, Kentucky. Chris chose to take back roads simply for their scenic value rather than travel the Interstate highways. He wanted Walt and Sebastian to see Eastern Tennessee, which was the more mountainous and most beautiful part of the state in his opinion.

Their intended destination was twofold. Chris wanted to camp that night in Cumberland Falls State Park, in Kentucky, where one of the most spectacular waterfalls east of the Mississippi River was located. The falls were high as well as wide as the Cumberland River pounded over a seventy-foot escarpment. The falls were unique for another reason too, for it and Niagara were the only two waterfalls in the United States, oriented in just the right way, to exhibit a rare sight on clear nights of a full moon. A vivid moonbow would appear if conditions were just right. They would be arriving on the second night of the full moon and there was a chance they might be able to enjoy the rare sight.

Also near the city of Corbin, Kentucky, not far away from the falls, Walt's Aunt, Henna Fallon, lived with her two children. Henna was his mother's younger sister by four years and her only sibling. Walt's mom had suggested that if they were in the area it might be nice to pay his aunt and two cousins a visit, as they were having a difficult time. Henna's husband had been killed in a coal mining accident less than a year before and she and her kids had been having a rough time emotionally ever since.

Walt had last seen his aunt four or five years earlier when she and her family had made a trip to Florida on vacation. He remembered joining them as they visited Disney World in Orlando and Daytona Beach. She had two children, a girl, Sally, who would now be about seventeen or eighteen and a boy, Arthur Jr., who would be about twelve or thirteen.

Corbin was located in a rather depressed part of Kentucky where the economy was based almost entirely on coal mining. Recent environmental legislation had closed hundreds of strip mines in the area that had scarred and poisoned the land, making it unusable for much else. Henna's husband, Arthur senior, had been crushed beneath a rock slide along one face of an open mine pit. It took seven days just to dig out the bodies of Arthur and his fellow workers for proper burial.

Walt's mom and dad had offered several times since the tragedy to help the family if they wanted to move south to De Land, but Henna was a mountain girl and stubborn about leaving the area, or accepting charity. Walt remembered the children as shy, gangly, youngsters who looked upon the wonders of Disney World as though they had been transported to another planet. Neither, up to the time of their Florida visit, had ever been outside of Eastern Kentucky. Walt, then in his senior year of high school, had taken both children swimming at De Leon Springs and the beach at Daytona. Walt's present concern was about his lifestyle and how his aunt might perceive him if ever his and Chris's relationship came to light.

Walt warned Sebastian to be very careful about what was said during the visit. Henna was a staunch, Born Again Christian and much to his dad's chagrin, a Republican. He had no idea what his young cousins might be like after the four years since he'd seen them. Sebastian said he would be extra careful, but started asking a lot of questions about young Arthur, especially since they were about the same age.

"Don't get any ideas, Seb," warned Chris with a laugh, as they discussed the upcoming visit while traveling north. "We're only going to visit for New Year's dinner on the first and then we'll be returning to our campsite." Chris planned to stay two nights at the state park near the falls. Walt had called ahead to let his aunt Henna know they would be in the area and she had invited them for the holiday meal, quite pleased to have family pay a visit.

They reached Cumberland Falls around four and paid for a campsite for two nights. The weather had improved and the afternoon temperature was in the mid-seventies. There was no bad weather predicted, so they might be lucky enough to see the famous moonbow if the sky was clear enough to allow the full moon to shine across the mists that formed above the falling water. After setting up, Walt suggested they eat dinner at a beautiful log restaurant and lodge in the park and then visit the nearby falls. That would save them the trouble of preparing a meal and give them plenty of time to see the falls in daylight as well as moonlight later.

After a fantastic meal, the three companions walked to the nearby falls, an awe-inspiring work of nature. The two hundred foot wide cataract plummeted seventy or so feet creating a whirling cloud of fine mist around the plunge-pool at its base. Even from where they stood along a viewing rail, the mist reached them feeling cool and wetting their skin after only a few moments. It was this constant cloud of fine spray that helped form the moonbow. Because it was late afternoon, the sun's rays were not angled properly to create a proper rainbow. Early morning sun, however, coming from the east, did that nearly every day. The moon, rising in the east was able to do the same thing when full and bright enough to create the optical wonder.

According to a sign near the viewing area, the moon was scheduled to rise high enough that night at eight thirty, so they had nearly an hour to wait. There was a short trail descending toward the base of the falls, so they walked along it, but as they got close to the falls, the spray was so intense and cold they realized they would end up soaked to the skin, so they turned back. Sebastian laughed and said they should have brought along wetsuits as they'd used at Ichetucknee Springs.

It was well after dark when they returned to the viewing site where a few other people had gathered to watch for the moonbow. The glow of the rising moon could be seen off in the trees to the southeast by eight fifteen and everyone waited for the magical moment when moonlight would break above the trees and illuminate the falls. At eight thirty-eight, a cloud obscured the eastern sky and everyone groaned with dismay. But at eight forty-five, the cloud moved away, the rays of the bright full moon illuminated the rolling mist and the great bow of soft colors arched across the waterfall touching the Cumberland River with its magic. A collective sigh from the twenty or so visitors broke the stillness.

Walt had brought along a folding tripod and was taking time exposures of the moonbow. A few foolish tourists were using flash cameras in an attempt to capture the moment until a park ranger told them they were wasting their film and disturbing others with the flash. The dim but distinct moonbow could only be captured using a time exposure. The ranger described how people might take such a photo and provided several park-owned tripods for their use.

By nine, Walt, Chris, and Sebastian walked back to their campsite and settled in for the night. Since they need not get up so early the next morning, they played several games of Clue Sebastian had packed along, sipped warm cocoa and munched on cookies. At eleven thirty, they dressed for bed and, as usual, Sebastian insisted on snuggling between Chris and Walt before retiring to his own nest on the opposite side of the camper.

"What time will we be going to your aunt's house, Walt?" asked the boy.

"Well, Aunt Henna said the meal will be at about two, so I suppose we'll drive to their house around ten or eleven so we'll have time for me to visit with her and the kids. It's been four or five years since I last saw them. I think Sally is either finished high school or about to graduate this spring. Arthur's probably in middle school."

"Is he nice? I mean is he friendly?"

Walt grinned at Chris who was biting his lips and smiling too. "Well, Sebastian, I have to be honest with you, when I saw him last he was a rather nasty-looking customer. I've never seen such a miserable nine-year-old. It's probably from growing up as a hunchback. With that, the warts, buck teeth, and his crossed eyes, he's had a rough life."

"Aw, Walt, quit it. You're teasing. What's he *really* like?"

"Don't you want to know about his sister too? She's really good looking. I would think a teenage boy like you would be interested in such a pretty young lady."

Sebastian was trying his best to glare at Walt but soon had to give in and laugh. "You know I'm not into girls. I just wondered what Arthur might look like. He's your relative and I wondered if he's as handsome as you."

"Oh, here we go, Chris. He's flattering me to get info about my innocent young cousin. What should we do with him, partner?"

"As I've said before, castration comes to mind. That or put him in a chastity belt while we visit your family. Poor Arthur might be in danger from this hormone-charged sex fiend."

"Guys! I'm just curious. He's my age and maybe we can be friends. I need friends just like you guys need friends. It doesn't matter if he's gay or not. Quit teasing."

Walt hugged the boy and said, "Okay, buddy. Tell you what; I have a photo of Arthur in my wallet. Hand me my jeans and I'll show you."

Seb rushed over to one of the storage bins and pulled out Walt's blue jeans. Walt took them and extricated his wallet from one back pocket. He leafed through it until he found two posed school photos, one of Sally and one of Arthur, each taken a year before. Sebastian took one quick glance at Sally's photo and a much more intense scrutiny of Arthur. Chris and Walt both noticed and grinned.

The photo showed a thin-faced, blond-haired, blue-eyed boy of twelve with a nice smile and wearing wire-rimmed glasses. He was dressed in a light blue dress shirt with a dark blue, striped tie. He had high cheekbones and full lips slightly parted that exposed his straight white teeth.

"So what do you think, Seb?"

"Gosh, he's really handsome. Great looks run in your family, Walt. Think he might be gay?"

"Well, why don't you ask him first thing tomorrow when you meet him," teased Chris. "I'm sure that will make a great first impression. If he is, you're in luck. If he's not, well, I have a first aid kit to help with your busted nose."

"I'm just talking. I won't ask him such a thing the first time we meet. Gees."

Chris ruffled the boy's hair until he got a smile. "I'm just teasing, kiddo. You know how much we love you when we tease like this. Ask Walt about how I like to tease him and pull pranks. Tell him about when we first met, Walt; the time I sneaked into your bathroom and scared you while you were naked." Seb's eyes lit up at the mention of naked.

Of course, Sebastian begged to hear the story, but Walt told him to wait until bedtime and reminded everyone it was nearly midnight. They all watched the clock as the last few minutes of 1980 ticked by and as the small digital clock indicated twelve they all embraced and wished one another a happy new year.

After celebrating 1981's beginning, Walt told Seb to get in bed and cover up and he'd tell him the story about being surprised in the shower. As Seb readied for bed, Walt whispered for him to be sure and keep his pajama pants on this time. Seb giggled, as he slid under the covers. After the story, he settled down and finally went to sleep. Walt and Chris pulled the privacy curtain closed on their side before making love briefly and drifting off to sleep themselves.

The next morning Sebastian was the first to rise and decided to surprise the others by preparing breakfast. He put water on to boil, scrambled six eggs along with a bit of butter, onion powder, cheese, bacon bits, and parsley flakes. He was just about to pour the egg mixture into a hot skillet when Walt and Chris woke up, pulled aside the privacy curtain and saw a grinning Sebastian at work at the two burner stove. He'd set up the table and laid out paper plates, utensils and a loaf of dark rye bread to go with the eggs.

"Well, would you look at this, Walt," said Chris as he swung his legs over the side of the bed and stood up.

Walt did the same and said, "Sebastian, I'm so proud of you. What a nice surprise. We nearly had breakfast in bed, Chris. Are we lucky to have this fine young man as our best buddy or what?" Sebastian was beaming as both gave him warm hugs and a kiss on the cheek as they slipped on their shoes and prepared to make a quick trip to the nearby comfort station. When they returned, the food was ready and all sat down to enjoy Seb's cooking.

The eggs were delicious and Walt asked, "Where did you learn to cook so well, Seb? These eggs are great. I taste the onion, cheese and bacon bits. They're really good." Chris seconded the compliment.

"Thanks, guys. Mom's been showing me how to cook lately and I thought I'd surprise you this morning. I almost used some of the sausages in the ice chest, but I didn't want to do it without asking first."

"Oh, anytime, Seb. You don't have to ask. What's in the food chest is for all of us," said Chris.

"So --- are you ready to meet my aunt and cousins today, Seb?"

"Uh huh. I'm looking forward to it. How far away are they from here?"

"Not too far, about eighteen or twenty miles northeast of the falls. They live on this side of Corbin, so we won't have to drive all the way to the town. They have a home in the country near the mines where my uncle worked before he was killed in the accident." Walt had already explained what happened to Arthur senior to Seb who had been sad to hear what happened to the family.

"Do they live on a farm?"

"No, I haven't been to their house since I was about ten; it's a two-story brick home on several acres. I think there's a horse ranch just left of their property. A small stream forms one border and the other side is thick woods running back to the nearby mountains."

"Cool. Maybe Arthur can show me around."

"I'm sure he'd be glad to." Walt smiled at Chris as Sebastian went about clearing the table. Chris and Walt helped with the clean up too and soon all were ready to head for the comfort station to get a shower before their trip to Walt's relatives.

By nine-thirty, all were bathed and dressed for the day. Chris unhooked the camper trailer from the station wagon. They left the locked camper at its site and headed toward Corbin.

Walt was navigating as Chris drove. He had a hand-drawn map his mom had given them and had no trouble locating the place. It was in a relatively flat area between two low mountain ridges. On one ridge to the left of the road, they could see the entire top of the mountain had been sliced away by strip mining. It was bare and ugly. They turned right off the highway and drove through an open gate along a gravel road leading up to the modest-sized, two-story home. Walt said it looked like his relatives had about five or six acres. As they approached the house, the front door opened and a middle-aged, heavy-set woman appeared followed by an older teenage girl and a tall, thin boy. All of them waved and Chris tooted the horn in reply.

The car had no sooner stopped when Sebastian opened the car door and hopped out. He waited for Walt and Chris but was smiling and looking at the people on the porch, especially at young Arthur who was smiling back, his head slightly inclined downward as though somewhat shy. Walt led them to the porch and introduced his companions to his family after giving each of them a hug. Sebastian shook hands with Walt's Aunt and thanked her for her hospitality and wished her a happy new year. He next greeted Sally who complimented Sebastian on his manners and then he turned to Arthur and extended his hand to the boy who smiled and took it.

Arthur spoke softly and said, "Happy new year. I'm glad to meet you. Are you from England? Your accent sounds English."

"Uh huh, I was born in Liverpool, but we moved to America when I was seven. I still have a bit of accent, but my folks and I are U.S. citizens now. You have a nice place to live. It's really pretty here."

"Thanks. I'm glad you like it. Come on inside. I'll get us a Nehi. You like orange or grape?"

"Grape sounds wonderful, thanks." The two boys went inside as Walt talked with his aunt and Sally. Chris watched with pleasure as the two boys easily made friends. Seb looked back at him as he went inside with a wide smile on his face. Chris gave him a wink.

Once inside, Walt and Chris talked with Henna and Sally in the living room. Henna, from time to time, left the room to check on a ham she had baking in the oven. Sally was telling Walt how she would be completing high school in June at the church school she attended in Corbin. She announced proudly she was planning to join the ministry and would be enrolling in a Church of Christ seminary as soon as school was over. It was located in Cleveland, Tennessee and she had qualified for a full scholarship.

Even though Chris knew of Walt's feelings about fundamentalist churches, he listened as Walt politely showed his support and congratulated the girl. Henna was ecstatic about Sally's plans and went on to say she hoped Arthur would choose to do the Lord's work someday too. Again, Walt smiled and said that would be nice. He gave Chris a look from time to time that said it all.

While the adults chatted, the boys went outdoors for a brief tour of the place. Arthur was a soft-spoken, shy boy around the adults, but seemed to hit it off with Sebastian right away. After grabbing a grape Nehi soda for each of them from the refrigerator, Arthur led Seb out the back door and downhill to the stream that ran along the eastern border of their land. He showed him a crude rock dam he'd built along the stream to create a shallow clear pool. It was flanked by three weeping willow trees --- now bare of leaves until spring --- and standing thickets of leaf-bare greenbrier vines.

"This place is great in the summer for swimming. It's too cold now or we could go skinny dipping."

"That would be cool," said Sebastian with a chuckle.

"I sometimes fish here too 'cause there's lots of brookies in the stream."

"Brookies?" asked Seb.

"Brook trout. They're small and have a lot of little bones, but boy are they good eat'n." The boy's accent was definitely Eastern Kentucky. Sebastian loved it. He couldn't take his eyes off the lad.

"Chris and Walt took me to a beautiful clear river in Florida; the Ichetucknee. It was cold too and we had to rent wetsuits in order to float five miles down the river. We would have gotten too cold otherwise. Wish we had two of those suits right now. I'd love to go swimming with you, Arthur."

"You can call me Art or Arty; all my friends do. Wish you lived closer so we could go swimming this summer. Maybe Walt can bring you back to see us then too. How old are you?"

"I'm thirteen. I'll be fourteen on March twenty-sixth."

"You're shit'n me! Criminy, I was born the same day and I'll be fourteen then too. That's somethin'! We'll have to send each other a birthday card." ˙

"Neat. Walt and Chris have the same birthday too; July twentieth;

Walt is one year younger than Chris though. That's such a strange coincidence. Maybe we were fated to meet since we were born the same day. Wait until I tell Chris and Walt."

"You wanna be blood brothers?"

"What do you mean? Does that mean to prick your finger with a pin or needle and share blood?"

"Uh huh. Since we're born the same day I think it would be cool. I don't have a needle, but I have a knife. We could use that. We'll go up to the garage and use some alcohol to sterilize it first. It hurts a little, but not much if you do it quick."

"I'm not so sure about a knife. Sure we can't get a needle from your house?"

"I suppose we could. I know where Sally keeps her sewing stuff. I'll try to get a needle from her. Come on, I'll race you to the back porch." He took off with a very happy English boy following along beside. They both touched the porch at nearly the same time and Arty declared the race a tie.

Arthur went inside and told Seb to wait on the back porch. A few minutes later he emerged smiling with two needles shining between his fingers. "One for each of us. I poured a little rubbin' alcohol on 'em in the bathroom, so they should be pretty clean. Let's go to the garage loft. I have a hideout there we can use."

Arty led his new buddy to an old wooden outbuilding that somewhat resembled a garage although there wasn't enough room inside for a car. The place was piled high with an assortment of old rusting farm equipment, tools, odds and ends of wood, some power tools and stacks of old magazines and seed catalogs.

Arty said, "Come on over here. There's a ladder we can use to go up to the loft."

The boy reached up and pulled a knotted cord releasing a spring-loaded attic stairway that squeaked, unfolded and led upward into darkness. As soon as Arty made it to the top, he must have thrown a switch because a light came on somewhere above. Sebastian followed him up the stairs. Once there, Sebastian looked around at a high ceilinged attic where a number of cardboard and wooden boxes, as well as various pieces of old furniture, were strewn about haphazardly on the floorboards. Arty led him off toward one end where he saw an old sofa, two wooden chairs, and stacks of old National Geographic and Life magazines. A second light bulb lit that end of the attic.

"Welcome to my hideout. Only my best friends are allowed to come

156

here."

"I'm honored," said Seb. "Thank you. What do we have to do now to become blood brothers?"

"Well, we each have to promise to be friends forever and ever and never betray one another. Then we stick each other's finger and hold the two bloody fingers together for five minutes; then we're blood brothers."

"That's all there is to it? Cool. Let's do it."

Using the two needles, each boy took the necessary oath, pricked the other's thumb, squeezed up a drop of blood and held them together for what they judged was five minutes before letting go and shaking hands. During the solemn ceremony, they chatted.

"Do you like living in America better than England?"

"Oh yes. Liverpool was rather dirty and stinky from shipyards and factories. England's nice out in the countryside, but I was only able to go there once in a while on holiday. I like Jacksonville. It's still a little stinky too with a paper mill and chemical plants, but I have more to do now. I'm a volunteer junior curator at the museum where Chris works. Walt goes there and helps out too."

"What do you, Walt and Chris do at the museum?"

"Chris runs the Science Theatre and I help him to present the weekend shows. He and I demonstrate science experiments to people who are visiting. He dresses up in costumes and makeup to make him look like famous scientists like Michael Faraday and Isaac Newton. He's very smart and a fabulous teacher. He and Walt are my best friends."

"Do you have a girlfriend?" Arty asked.

"No. I have too many other interests just now," said Sebastian. "How about you?"

"I don't either. I'm pretty busy now being the man of the house. I have a lot of chores around here to help Mom with."

"I was sorry to hear about your father, Arty. Walt told me what happened. I'm sure you miss him."

"Thanks. It was pretty bad at first, but I'm getting used to it. I still have bad days when I wish I had him around to talk with about things."

"My dad and mom are great. My dad owns an outdoor advertising company; they make and put up billboards and large signs. Mom works a few days a week at the museum too and leads school children around the exhibits. That's how I met Chris and then met Walt, his best friend."

"Walt's in college, isn't he?"

"Uh huh. He'll soon be finished his bachelor's degree in art. He plans to become a commercial artist. Don't tell him, but my dad already has a great job lined up for him at his advertising company. Walt's artwork is really good."

"I won't tell. That's mighty nice of your dad. Thank him for me and my family when you get home."

"I will. You're a really nice guy too, Arty. I wish you lived closer so we could see each other more often. I don't really have any friends my own age that I get along with. The kids at school are into sports and girls and all manner of things that I find rather droll."

"Droll? What's that mean exactly?"

Sebastian giggled and said, "It means boring, silly and a waste of time. Sports and especially girls are droll, at least as far as I'm concerned."

"I feel the same way. I enjoy other things better myself."

"That's why I like to be with Chris and Walt. They love me as much as my parents do. They take me places and include me in a lot of fun things they do. I go over to their apartment as often as I can."

"They live in the same apartment?" asked Arthur.

Sebastian realized he may have slipped a bit there so he said, "Yes, they have a two bedroom apartment and share the costs that way. It helps Walt a lot since he's still at university and isn't working yet. Chris makes pretty good money as a teacher assigned to the museum, but since they're friends, he's happy to let Walt live in the second room to save them both money."

"Oh, okay. That makes sense." Sebastian relaxed and told himself he had to be more careful. Arty might seem like a country boy, but he was pretty sharp-minded."

"Do you like school?" asked Sebastian.

"Yep, especially history and science. I'd love to visit the theatre where you work with Chris. Does he let you do experiments with the science things there?"

"Oh yes. But I have to always tell him what I plan to do. He has stuff there that could blow up if you used them the wrong way."

"Cool." Arty smiled at Sebastian for a few seconds in silence and then continued, "You have any brothers or sisters?"

"Nope, I'm an only child. I'm glad in many ways. I wouldn't mind having a younger brother, but not a sister. Oh, I don't mean to say anything bad about you since you have a sister. She's quite nice. It's just me. I never seem to know how to talk to girls. The ones at my school are like aliens or something."

"I know what you mean," agreed Art. "I'm the same way. Some of them always want to talk with me and one even tried to get me to make out with her, but that's just wrong."

Seb was a bit surprised at what Arty had said so he asked, "Is it because of your religious beliefs that you preferred not to kiss the girl when she asked?"

"Oh no, I'm not as religious as Mom and Sally, but don't tell them so. I'm more like Daddy. He went along with it but he and I often talked and we both thought that some of the things our pastor was saying was a little too odd. No, I didn't want to kiss the girl because I didn't love her."

"What do you mean? Maybe she loved *you*."

"Maybe, but I couldn't kiss her back. I think people should only kiss if they both love one another. At least kisses on the lips like she wanted me to do."

"Is there a girl that maybe you care enough about to want to kiss now?" asked Seb, hoping for a certain negative answer.

He got it when Art said, "Nope. I guess I'm just not old enough to want to fall in love with girls. So far I have too many other things on my mind and stuff to do."

"I can understand that. I'm the same way. Girls are simply a waste of my time right now."

Arty looked out a small attic window and said, "We better see if it's time to eat. I didn't tell Mom where we'd be, although she'd probably figure it out. Maybe we can go for a walk in the woods and talk some more after we eat."

"Sure. I'd like that. I wish I could spend a few days with you, but we have to start back for Jacksonville in the morning. We're staying at Cumberland Falls in a camper."

"It's nice there."

"Oh, yes. We got to see the moonbow last night and that was super cool."

"Yeah, I've seen it a couple of times. Daddy used to take us to the falls once in a while. Maybe this summer I can talk Mom into visiting Walt in Jacksonville and seeing my aunt and uncle in De Land. They're Walt's parents."

"I hope you can. I'd love to see you again. Especially since we have the same birthday and we're blood brothers. I want your address so I can write to you once in a while. Mom and Dad will let me call you too."

"I might not be able to call you back often as our bills get pretty high sometimes and the phone company charges a lot for long distance calls."

"That's okay. I'll call and we can talk."

The boys left the loft and ambled back to the house. The meal was about fifteen minutes from being served, so Arty showed Seb his bedroom. It was upstairs and the first room on the left. There were a number of well-built and nicely painted model planes hanging from the ceiling. A large model of an aircraft carrier stood on a display shelf above Arty's desk. The room was a bit cluttered and there were a few soiled clothes on the floor beside the bed.

"Sorry, my room's a little messy. Mom gave me heck about it and I straightened up some before you got here. I was just about finished when I heard your car arrive."

"That's okay. My room's the same way. My mom gets after me too."

"Hey, feel free to look around. I have to use the bathroom; I'll be right back." Arthur left the room and turned left down the hall. Seb heard the bathroom door close. He walked over beside the bed and looked down at the soiled clothing. He had the sudden urge to do something completely crazy but hesitated. After weighing the matter in his mind he thought, *Why not? It'll only take a moment.* He reached down and picked up a pair of Arty's briefs and shook them out. He raised them to his face and nuzzled their front with his nose and lips. He could smell a slight scent and felt himself getting painfully hard. He had a crazy urge to tuck them into his pocket or stuff them down his own pants to take with him when he heard the toilet flush next door. He took one last sniff and kissed them before returning them to the pile near his feet.

Sebastian was shaking a bit with both excitement and a touch of guilt when Arty returned smiling. Seb was pretending to look more closely at the ship model.

He said, "The Saratoga is stationed at Mayport, near Jacksonville. I've seen it and taken a tour. This is the Enterprise, isn't it?"

"Yeah, it was the last gift I ever got from Daddy. I'm going to keep it forever." Arty reached out and ran his fingers over the side of the three-foot-long model and as he did, he started crying. "I miss him so much."

Sebastian stepped close and put his arm around Arty's shoulder and hugged him as he said, "I'm so sorry he died. I wish I could have met him." Arty smiled through his tears as he turned and hugged Sebastian back.

"Thanks. You're the first friend who ever said that and cared enough to hug me. I'm really glad now that we're blood brothers. You're mighty nice, Sebastian. Thanks."

"It's my pleasure." Seb gave him one more hug before letting go. He could feel his erection returning as he looked at the boy's tear-filled eyes. He reached out and brushed his fingers through his friend's soft blond hair a few times. Arty smiled and didn't turn away from the touch as most boys would. Both boys just looked intently at the other for a few seconds before stepping apart.

Arthur said, "Thanks. We better go downstairs and get ready to eat." Seb's mind was whirling as he considered the way Arty had reacted to his advances. Most boys would have either shied away or gotten angry. *Maybe,* thought Sebastian. *Maybe he's exactly like me.*

All through the meal Sebastian kept glancing at Arthur and was pleased to see that each time he did, the boy always broke into a smile. They were seated nearly opposite one another at the table.

Chapter 17
Birds and Bees

After a dessert of homemade apple cake with cherry vanilla ice cream, the boys went off to spend more time together. Sally took on the task of clean up assisted by Chris when Henna asked to speak with Walt alone. She apologized for seeming rude but explained that she needed to talk with Walt concerning some family business. After hearing of Henna's religious views, Chris wondered if she was about to question Walt about their friendship. Walt was privately expecting the same.

That was not the case, however; as Walt soon discovered. He and his aunt sat down on the front porch swing and after a few moments of small talk about her sister in De Land, Henna brought up the real subject of her need to talk.

"Walt, I'm sorry I had to ask for some private time with you, but I need your advice about something. I'm concerned about my son. Arthur has been having a rough time of things since his daddy was killed. We all have for that matter, but that boy was close to his daddy and I worry that he's holding back his grief too much sometimes. He's at that age when a boy needs a father or a trusted man in his life. He'll be fourteen in March and you know all the things that happen to a boy that age; the changes and all. It's hard for me to talk to him about those things and he's too shy to bring them up."

"Would you like me to talk with him, Henna? I'd be more than happy to stand in for Arthur since he's not with us now."

"Oh, would you? That would mean so much to me. He's been having trouble making friends and has gotten into some trouble at school. Some bully was picking on him and he finally had enough of his crap and hauled off and punched him in the nose. I was proud of him for standing up to the boy, but at the same time, I don't want him to grow up mean. He's a sensitive boy, quiet and happy to be in quiet places like his daddy was. He spends hours in the woods and loves it there. God knows I miss Arthur senior and every day I see more of him in that boy."

"He's a fine young man. Whatever I can do, Aunt Henna, you know I'll do it. He seems to be having an easy time making friends with

Sebastian."

"I know and it's good to see. What an amazing coincidence they were born the same day. You said your friend, Chris and you share a birthday too but are off by a year. That's so odd."

"I'll take some time before we leave this afternoon and have a talk with Arty. I'll see if he has any bird and bee questions that might need answering. He's going to be one handsome man someday like his dad. You're doing a fine job raising him too, Henna. I'm sure it hasn't been easy. Sally is so sweet and dedicated to her goals. I hope she finds what she's looking for at the seminary."

"Thanks, Walt. You're a sweetheart. Sometimes I feel so tired and run down from all the work and responsibility. The last few months have been especially bad. Arthur's death pension from Peabody Coal and the settlement from the insurance company finally came through and have given us a comfortable nest egg, so financially we're doing well. The mortgage on the land and house has been paid off and I'm putting as much aside as I can for Arty's college fund. I think he'll be smart enough to make it there."

"I'm sure he will and if need be, I'll do what I can for him when that time comes."

"I sure wish we lived closer. You would be good for Arty. His new buddy, Sebastian would too."

"Why don't you plan on driving down this summer and visiting with Mom and Dad for a week or two? It would be good for you all. We'd love to have you. Mom's been saying how much she'd like for you to visit."

"Oh maybe, we'll see. It's hard to just leave the place for a couple of weeks."

"Think about this as well. If you can't make it, how about sending Arty down to Jacksonville for a few weeks after school's out? He could hang out at the museum with Chris, Sebastian and me on the days I'm free. The change would be good for him."

"That might be a good idea. I could drive him down, visit with Sis and your dad for a few days and leave Arty with you for a couple of weeks. He could take a bus or train home. He's old enough to handle that."

"I'll pay for a plane ticket back to Lexington and you can pick him up there. It's safer than a bus. Bus stations and fourteen-year-old boys are not a safe combination nowadays. The airlines take very good care of young travelers."

"I suppose that's true. Let's plan on it, but don't tell Arty just yet in case things change. He's had enough disappointment for a while. You're a saint, Walt. Thanks for being such a good nephew. We love you."

They returned to the house just as Chris and Sally finished the dishes and joined them in the living room. Chris was describing his job to Sally as they came in. Walt explained to the others how he needed to have a chat with Arty at Henna's request and went off to find the two boys. As he stepped out onto the back porch, he saw the boys just about to enter the woods along the right side of the property. Walt put two fingers to his teeth and gave a long and very loud whistle. A few seconds later the sound reached the boys and they turned. Walt motioned them to come back and they did so at a trot.

As they reached the porch, Sebastian said almost breathlessly, "It's not time to go, is it? Please say we can have some more time. Arty was going to show me the woods."

"No, you'll have time. Henna asked me to talk with Arty about something in private. Will you mind if I have a few minutes alone with him, Seb?"

"No. That's okay. I'm glad we don't have to go right away. Arty, you can show me the woods right after you and Walt talk. I have to use the bathroom anyway. I was planning on watering one of the trees in the woods when you whistled. I never knew you could whistle like that, Walt. You have to teach me."

Seb went indoors as Walt gave his cousin a hair ruffle and asked him to take a walk with him. Arty was looking curious as to why Walt had been asked to chat with him."

"Is there anything wrong, Walt?"

"Nope, your mom thought that maybe you might have a few questions about things that you would normally ask your dad, you know, the birds and the bees. She wants me to step in for your daddy for that kind of thing and I told her I would be happy to do it."

"Wow. That's kind of a surprise. Uh, I really don't know what to ask. We learned a little about those things in health class last year."

"Well, I can tell you're growing tall. Any questions about changes your body has been making that you don't quite understand?"

"I don't think so. What kind of changes?"

"Well, how about hair? I'm sure by now you have been growing hair around your privates and maybe under your arms. How about we start there? When did you start growing pubic hair?" Walt felt a little odd asking but knew it was a necessity for a boy Arty's age.

"Uh, I started growing hair down there last year when I was about twelve and a half. I kinda wish it was dark, but it's like my head and real blond. You can hardly see it from a distance."

Walt laughed and patted the boy's back. "A true blond, huh? That's cool. Often happens that way. Don't let it bother you."

Arty grinned and asked, "Are you a true blond, Walt?"

Walt laughed and said, "No, just my head. My armpits and elsewhere are brown. How about underarms? Getting hair there yet?"

"Nothing yet, least I don't think so. Take a look, Walt." The boy pulled up his flannel shirt and undershirt so Walt could see his armpits.

"There's just a little fuzz starting there. Won't be long, Arty. Are you using deodorant yet?"

"Yeah, Mom got me some roll on. I use it every day."

"Good grooming is important if you want to make friends and keep them. How about girls? You have a girlfriend yet?"

Art looked toward the ground as he answered, "Nope. Not yet. I don't have much time for that right now. Maybe once I'm in the last few years of high school."

Walt considered that statement from his own perspective and remembered he'd used the same excuse. Maybe Arty was having some sexual identity issues. He'd have to tread very carefully along that path.

Walt asked, "Do you like looking at girls? Does it affect you whenever you think about them and the way they look?"

"Not too much, maybe sometimes."

"Okay. Do you know about masturbation?"

Arty looked a little surprised, but answered, "Uh, yeah. Did Mom want you to ask me about that?"

"No," Walt chuckled. "Being a guy though and having been thirteen myself; I know that sometimes boys feel ashamed when they play with themselves. I want to assure you that it's perfectly normal to do it. How old were you when you discovered how that happens?"

"It was last month, just before Christmas. I woke up hard one morning and was kind of wet. I didn't know what was going on. I thought I had some kind of infection." The boy giggled. "When I wiped myself off, it felt funny and I got harder. Then I started rubbing myself with the wet stuff and all of the sudden it happened. A whole bunch of sperm came out and it felt real good."

"I'm proud of you for speaking with me about this. You never need to be shy about this subject with me. If you need to talk to me, have your mom give me a call. She'll give us privacy to talk on the phone. I'm officially your male role model now, according to your mom, so please keep in touch. How often do you get the urge to masturbate, if I may ask?"

Arty grinned sheepishly and said, "Pretty much every night. Is that too much? It won't hurt me later will it?"

"No, those tales about making you go blind, or growing hair on the palm of your hand are just part of a bad joke." Both shared a laugh.

"What do you think about when you do it? It's important for me to know how you think and what's on your mind. Nothing you say will ever reach your mom's ears unless you tell me to discuss it with her."

"Well, I mostly just look at myself down there as I do it." Arty hesitated and Walt sensed there was more to come so he waited for the boy to continue. "Maybe this is weird, but sometimes I wish I had a twin brother and we could do it to each other. Is it wrong to think that way?"

"No, Arty. Whatever makes you happy. It's your body and your special time to enjoy yourself. Everyone is different and we all have our own interpretation of what turns us on. Do you ever think about a girl doing it to you, or about touching a girl while you do it?"

"No. Sometimes that bothers me, 'cause all my friends talk about girls all the time. Maybe as I get older I'll be more interested in them."

"If you have secrets or concerns, please trust me. As you grow older, I'll share some of my own views about things with you. I had a lot of trouble adjusting to sexual issues when I was your age, so I'm happy to help."

"Okay, Walt. Thanks."

"Mind if I ask a few more questions, Arty?"

"No. I'm glad to talk to someone about it."

"Okay. Again, if I ask you something that's too personal, let me know. I don't want to embarrass you or make you feel uncomfortable. You said you don't ever think about girls when you masturbate. Do you ever think about other boys other than having a twin?"

Arthur just looked at Walt in silence and shook his head no, but the corners of his eyes begin to fill with tears. Walt ruffled the boy's hair and pulled him into a hug. "Arthur, if you do have thoughts like that and want to talk about it, I'm right here for you. I won't judge you or love you any less. Some boys occasionally do have those thoughts and it's okay."

"No, I don't, but if I ever do, I'll talk to you about it. Is that all you want to ask me today?"

Walt could see the doors of communication were closing rapidly so he said, "Yeah, but always remember, Arty, I'm ready to listen when you need me. Don't hesitate. Call me or write a letter. I'll answer you and respect your privacy. I will never judge you or think anything bad about you no matter what you tell me. I love you, son, and always will, no matter what."

"Thanks, Walt. I love you too. Maybe I can visit you in Florida someday."

"Count on it. Why don't you go and find Sebastian? I'm glad you guys have made friends. He's very special to me too and I think you two have a lot in common besides your birthday."

"I really like him, Walt. He's so different from the kids around here. In my room earlier, I was feeling bad as I talked about Daddy and cried a little. I felt a little embarrassed for crying, but Sebastian gave me a hug. It kind of surprised me."

"How did that make you feel, son?"

"It felt good. None of my friends at school ever did that when the accident happened. I sure wish Sebastian lived closer, 'cause I'd like him to be my best friend. Please stay as long as you can this afternoon so I can spend more time with him."

"Okay, kiddo." Walt gave the boy a hug and a kiss on his forehead. "Go find Seb. Have fun. Enjoy being a teenager." Arty ran off in the direction of the house to locate Seb. Walt stood for a few minutes beneath an apple tree, bare of its leaves due to winter and contemplated his young cousin. The signs were all there. Walt had a feeling their conversation wasn't over concerning Arty's interests. The boy was burdened with guilt and shame. That had to change before he got much older. Now, more than ever, Walt felt it would be good for Arthur to visit during the coming summer.

Chapter 18
Sharing Secrets

Sebastian had been watching from a kitchen window as Walt talked with Arthur. He felt just a twinge of jealousy as Walt ruffled the boy's hair but quickly chastised himself as he reasoned that Arty was Walt's cousin and now that the boy's dad had died, Walt was more important to the boy as a male role model. He had wondered what was going on when Arthur raised his shirt and for some reason showed Walt his bare chest. Arty was turned away so Sebastian couldn't see what he was showing Walt.

Chris came up behind him and rested his hands on Sebastian's shoulders and kissed the top of his head. "Feeling a little left out, kiddo? Walt's just trying to help Arty out. He's been through some rough times lately."

"I know. I'm glad Walt's able to help him. I felt a little funny at first, but I understand. Walt is like you, Chris. He's full of love and has plenty to go around for all of us."

"God, son, I love you so much for saying that. You are one very special young man. Someday, some lucky guy is going to team up with you and boy will he be landing a prize."

About this time Arty was heading for the house, so Sebastian stepped out to meet him on the back porch. Together they went off toward the woods beyond Arthur's property.

Walt joined his partner on the porch as well and shared his thoughts about Arthur. "Chris, I think maybe those theories about homosexuality running in families might be true. Arty's sure showing some of the signs. He's hiding it well, but I can sense he's ashamed and very afraid. I suggested to Henna that she bring him down for a visit this summer and maybe let him stay with us a week or so. Hope that's okay with you."

"Sure, that won't bother me in the least. I'm sure Sebastian wouldn't complain either."

"Maybe we can help him out. I'm sure a lot of his guilt comes from his mom's religious views. Arthur senior was not as hooked on that stuff as Henna is. It's a shame Arty lost him the way he did."

"Yeah, it's a tough thing for a boy to deal with at that age."

"I'll do whatever I can to help the kid out. If he is gay, he's going to have a rocky road to travel around here. This part of Kentucky is the buckle on the Bible Belt."

Once they reached the woods, Arthur led Sebastian along a well-used trail that gradually led them up-hill past massive outcroppings of dark, hard shale and very old hardwood trees. Arty was pointing out various plants and trees sharing what his dad had taught him about the natural things that grew in the area. They finally came to an open meadow with a gentle slope where Arthur sat down on a flat rock and talked to his new friend.

"I call this rock my thinking place. Daddy and I used to come here sometimes and just talk."

Sebastian didn't say anything, but simply gazed at his new friend. The bright sunlight was highlighting his soft blond hair as a gentle breeze ruffled it occasionally. Sebastian thought Arthur the most beautiful boy he'd ever seen and wanted more than anything to reach out and touch him.

Arty finally said, "You're so lucky to live close to Walt. He's a really nice person and is my favorite cousin. I have a few cousins on my Daddy's side of the family, but they're older than me and don't live around here. Daddy's brothers don't have much to do with us since he died. I think Walt really cares about me. He invited me to come see him in Florida sometime; maybe this summer."

"Oh, Arty, that would be wonderful. You and I could spend loads of time together then. I'd like to get to know you better. I really don't have many friends my own age."

"Me neither. The kids at school live all through the hollow, but none of 'em live close that I'd want to get to know anyhow. I had to hit one boy a few months ago who's my age. He was trying to bully and make fun of me all the time, so when he pushed me one time too many I hit him in the nose."

"Wow! Did he bleed?"

"You bet he did. Cried like a girl too. He's one of those who can dish it out, but can't take it. That's the first time I ever hit anyone. For some reason, I just got tired of being called names and being laughed at."

"I know what you mean. I had some of that in elementary school because I got good grades and because of my accent. Once I got to middle school, I'd learned to fit in better and now I go to a science magnet school due to good grades; the kids there are much more concerned with learning than with silly stuff like sports and girls."

"I have good grades too. I wish they had a school like that around here. Mom says I should plan on going to college after high school. I got advanced a grade last year and I'm in ninth instead of eighth. That's one reason I was getting picked on. I'm a year younger than the other kids."

"I'm in ninth too," said Sebastian. "I was able to skip seventh grade after taking a stack of tests. The school I go to is called Stanton Prep and it starts with seventh grade and runs to twelfth."

"What time will you guys be leaving? I wish we had more time together."

"I imagine we'll leave before dark. I wish we had a week. It's just my luck; I find a good friend and he lives about a zillion miles away. Believe me, though; I'm going to write and call. I'm allowed to make long distance calls, so I'll call you as often as I can. We just can't talk for a long time and run up too big of a bill. We can write too. That only costs a stamp. I have a typewriter, do you?"

"Mom has an electric one I can use, but I haven't learned to type yet. Maybe I'll start learning."

"We better head back in case Chris and Walt do decide to leave earlier. We can hang out in your room or garage hideout until it's time to go."

"Yeah, at least we'll have that much time together. I have some things to ask you and tell you too. Walt and I talked about some personal stuff and I want to know from you if you think he'll tell my mom about some secrets I told him."

"That depends, I would guess. If he thinks it's something that could hurt you or cause you to get into trouble, he might, but otherwise, I'd trust him or Chris for that matter with my secrets. He's your cousin and I'm pretty sure he'd never do you that way."

They started walking back through the woods toward Art's home. Sebastian continued: "I love Walt and Chris both like extra dads. I even overheard something that I wasn't supposed to hear and I'd like to tell you."

"I won't give away anything you tell me. We're blood brothers and that means a lot when it comes to secrets."

"That's good."

"What was it you overheard?"

"Mom and Dad were talking to Chris and Walt and I was supposed to be in my room packing for this trip. I was just about to step into the room where they were talking when I heard Dad say that he and my mom had made arrangements in their will, so if something happens to them, Walt and Chris would be my new parents."

"Wow! But they're two guys." Sebastian realized that once again he had slipped a bit and had to backpedal.

"Well, they would be my guardians, not my parents. It just means that they would share in the responsibility of raising me. If something did happen to my folks, I'd sure feel sad, but my first choice would be to live with Chris and Walt. I love them and they love me. We've all said it to one another."

"Yeah, Walt told me today that since Daddy's gone, he loves me and wanted me to know that I can ask him questions I might have only asked Daddy." Arty giggled a bit and said, "Walt asked me if I needed to ask any questions about the birds and the bees. You know, sex."

"Did he? That's good. He's answered questions for me on that subject and I'll tell you, he and Chris can be trusted to give you honest information and won't make fun of you for asking."

"Yeah, I think you're right."

Sebastian grinned and asked, "Did you ask him anything?"

"Not too much. He asked me if I knew certain things and I told him I knew a little bit. I'll tell you more once we get in the loft. Come on, we're almost there. Race you to the garage."

"Gees, you're always racing me without warning," Seb panted as he tried to catch up with his blond-haired friend. This time Arty won the race easily with a twenty-foot lead.

"Darn, you're used to running up-hill," Sebastian said as he clutched his sides and tried to catch his breath. "Florida's flat and I don't live around big yards like this to practice in. Let's go to the loft."

The boys once again climbed the stairway and were soon sitting side by side on the old sofa.

"So what did you and Walt talk about concerning sex?" Sebastian was anxious to learn what Arty knew about his favorite subject.

"Well, he asked if I had hair down below, over my privates." He looked at Seb before going on.

"So, do you?" said Sebastian with a grin.

"Yeah, I started getting it when I was about twelve and a half. Uh, do you?"

"Yeah, a lot, I started getting thick, black hair down there when I was eleven or so."

"It's black? Mine's the same color as my hair. It's blond." He said it as though ashamed of the color.

"Wow, I've never seen any boy with blond hair down there. All the boys I've seen in the shower at school had either brown or black hair. Oh, there was one red-head too. His pubic hair was bright orange." Both boys laughed.

"I bet blond hair down there looks cool. What else did Walt ask you?"

Arthur looked a little surprised at what Seb had said about blond pubic hair looking cool, but continued: "Well, Walt asked me about armpit hair and I'm only just getting a little there. It's blond too, you wanna see? I showed it to Walt."

"Sure. I'd like to if you don't mind." That explained what the shirt being raised was all about.

Once again, as he had for Walt, Arty raised his flannel and tee shirts and showed Seb his armpits. Seb saw only a tiny bit of hair in the dim attic light."

"Do you have hair there yet?" asked Arthur.

"Yeah, it's black too," said Seb with a smile.

"Can I see?"

"Sure." Sebastian stood proudly and pulled up his shirts exposing his ample growth of hair there.

"Wow! You have a lot and it's real dark black. It's cool looking."

"You can feel it if you want," Sebastian said that before thinking and immediately wished that he hadn't. He watched for Arty's reaction and was happy to see him smile.

"You don't mind?"

"Nope. We're blood brothers."

Arty reached out and gently felt the hair, letting it run through his fingers. "It's soft. Thanks for letting me do that. I feel kind of silly in a way, but since we're blood brothers, I think it's all right for us to do things like that."

"Of course, I trust you completely," said Sebastian as he smiled and thought to himself, *Wow. He liked it. Maybe he's gay too. That would be wonderful.*

Sebastian went on: "So what else did you and Walt talk about? Mind answering?"

"No, I guess not. He asked me if I knew about masturbation and I

172

told him I did. You know what that is, don't you?"

"Uh huh, I learned how that happens about two years ago."

"Wow! Two years ago? I just found out about it right before Christmas."

"It's pretty neat, isn't it?"

"Yeah, does it feel real good for you?" Arthur's face was a bit flushed as he waited for Seb's answer.

"Oh yeah, it's about the best thing in the world. How about you? Do you do it often?"

"Uh, yeah, pretty often. I've always been scared someone would catch me doing it and I'd get in trouble. Walt told me today that it's okay and what I do with my body is my business."

"That's true. I do it just about every night. My dad told me it was nothing to be ashamed of, but to do it when I'm by myself and never in public."

"In public? Who'd do it in public?"

Dad said there are some weird people who get a thrill by exposing themselves without asking another person if it's all right to do it in front of them. It's against the law too."

"I bet it is. Hope nobody ever does that to me."

Sebastian was very excited by now due to their discussion and wanted to ask Arthur one last thing to see if he was willing to go a little farther. He finally got up the courage and asked, "Would you like to see my pubic hair?"

Arthur looked very surprised and was about to say no, but something made him say, "I wouldn't mind if you wanted to show me. It's no different than looking at our underarm hair, I suppose. I'd like to see it if it's okay with you."

"Sure." Sebastian unhooked his belt and lowered his jeans and briefs enough to expose his ample supply of pubic hair.

Arty leaned forward and said, "Wow! You have a lot and it's just as black as the hair on your head. Thanks for showing me."

"Can I see yours now?" asked Sebastian. "I won't tell anyone we did this."

"Okay, I guess it's all right. Other boys have seen me naked in the shower and all I'm showing you is my hair." He undid his belt and did the same as Seb had done by lowering his pants and underwear just enough to let his new friend see his small puff of golden blond hair.

"That's so neat. It really looks nice, all blond like that. The hair is straight and soft looking. Mine is getting kind of curly and thicker now. Is yours soft?" Sebastian immediately thought Arty might think he was talking about his penis so he corrected himself. "What I meant to say is your hair down there soft. I didn't mean your uh..."

Art laughed and said, "I know. I knew you meant the hair. Yeah, it's pretty soft." He stared at Sebastian while still holding his jeans open and surprised himself as he whispered, "Uh, I don't mind if you feel it. We're blood brothers," he said as if that gave permission for a number of new experiences today.

Seb smiled and whispered back, "Thanks, I'd like to very much." He brushed his fingertips over the soft strands of Arthur's hair. "It really is soft." Sebastian was staring intently at Art as he said, "If you want to touch mine, you can."

"Okay," Arty said in a near whisper as he looked on with amazement as Seb opened his pants once again so his friend could touch the hair. Sebastian made sure this time to pull his briefs open just enough so that Arty could glimpse the base of his penis. Just as Arty gently ran his fingers through Sebastian's ample hair and smiled, they heard Walt calling them from somewhere outside. Both zipped up in a hurry with guilty looks on their faces.

"Looks like you have to go, Sebastian. I've only known you for one afternoon, but I'm going to miss you a lot."

"Me too. I swear, I'll write and call when I can. I like you so much. Would it be okay if I give you a hug up here before we go downstairs? That way no one can say anything about it."

"Sure. I'd like that. I want to hug you goodbye too." Arty had tears in his eyes and so did Seb as they clutched at one another and held on for nearly a half minute. Finally, they heard Walt just outside calling again and reluctantly broke their embrace and separated. Arty wiped a few tears from his eyes as did Sebastian.

Sebastian called out, "We're coming, Walt. Give us a minute."

They soon exited the garage and Walt was waiting for them both just outside the door. "Sorry, fellows but we have to go. I'm glad you boys had a chance to get to know each other. Whenever you visit Florida, Arthur, I'll make sure Sebastian is able to come over and spend more time with you. Sorry, we don't have more time today."

Within fifteen minutes, the three were ready to leave. Walt gave his aunt and two cousins each a warm hug and kiss. Chris shook hands with Sally and Arty, but Henna insisted on a hug and said, "Chris, you are welcome to come back for a visit anytime and that goes for you too, Sebastian. You're a fine young gentleman. I only wish you lived closer because I think you'd make a fine friend for Arthur."

"Thank you, Ms. Henna. I plan to write to Arty and, if it's all right with you, I'd like to give him a call occasionally."

"Anytime you want, Sebastian. I'll let Arty give you a call too, once in a while. Did you fellows exchange numbers and addresses?" The boys assured her that they had.

Seb gave Henna, Sally, and Arthur a hug. Arty got the longest and fiercest hug of all and Sebastian managed to whisper in Arty's ear just before they pulled apart, "I love you, Blood Brother." He also managed to give Arty a brief kiss on the neck as well. Arty was smiling and looked pleasantly surprised as Seb smiled at him just afterward.

"Me too," Arty said. "I hope I can see you again this summer. They flung themselves together again and Arty managed a soft kiss beside Seb's ear this time as he too whispered, "I love you very much too, Sebastian. Please don't forget me."

"I won't. Not ever," whispered Seb as he left his new friend and quickly got in the station wagon.

Henna whispered to Walt and Chris, "That's so sweet. It's good to see two boys show affection. Most are too silly and stubborn to show how they feel. Arthur senior was always one to show his feelings too; that's one of the reasons I loved him so much." Henna had tears in her eyes by now. "Give my compliments to Sebastian's parents; they've raised a fine young man."

Sebastian was bawling like a small child as Walt drove through the gate at his Aunt Henna's place. Chris crawled over the seat back and joined the heartbroken boy in an effort to comfort him.

"Wow, buddy. You must have really connected with Arty. We'll make sure you get to see him this summer. If Walt tells me it's okay, I tell you a secret. You know what I'm talking about, right, Walt?"

Walt glanced back using the rearview mirror and nodded to his lover. "You mean Henna's plans for a visit?"

"Uh huh."

"Yeah, go ahead and tell him, but remember Seb, when you call Arthur, you have to keep this a secret in case things don't work out. I don't want him hurt or disappointed."

"I promise," sobbed the young teen as he wiped his eyes and nose with a clean handkerchief Chris had given him.

Chris continued: "Henna told Walt that this summer, probably as soon as school lets out, she's going to drive south to visit her sister, that's Walt's mom and his dad in De Land. She also plans to allow Arthur to stay with Walt and I for two to four weeks. You've fallen in love with him haven't you?"

"Oh yes, Chris. I think he's gay too. He just told me he loves me. He said he doesn't have a girlfriend and isn't interested in girls either. We're blood brothers too. We each pricked our fingers and held them together for five minutes and promised to always be honest and truthful and loyal to each other."

"Wow. You guys pricked your fingers. That's pretty special, as long as you didn't finger your pricks." Chris was grinning and hugging Seb close as the boy got the joke, but gave him a hurt look. "Sorry. That was sort of out of line --- just trying to cheer you up."

"I know, but I'm very serious about this. There was something about Arthur the moment we first started talking. He just seems right to me. He told me about what he and Walt talked about and everything he said seemed to show that he and I might be alike. I really think he's gay. I hope he is because I could fall in love with him."

"Sounds like that might have already happened," said Walt from the driver's seat. "Chris, after talking with Arty, I think Seb might be right. He was giving me all the usual excuses for not having an active girl interest. Heterosexual boys can't tell you enough about their girlfriends. It's hard to get them to shut up once you bring up the subject. Gay boys always have a list of valid reasons why they don't have a girl. You might remember that Seb for the future, whenever someone asks you."

"Okay, I will."

"When I asked Arty if he ever had sexual thoughts about boys, he shook his head no, but his eyes were filling with tears. He acted like he didn't want to talk any more after that, but I think he did. Next time I see him, or even if I call, I'm going to press the issue. He's feeling shame and guilt and I, rather we, need to help him get past that and face reality. Once he accepts himself, he'll be so much better off"

Chris then said, "What about Henna and her beliefs? Sally is about to study to become a fundamentalist minister, or pastor, or whatever they're called. I doubt either of them will be as accepting as Nigel and Libby are with our boy here."

"Yeah, I know. That's the monkey wrench in the works. Sooner or later, though, they might *have* to address the subject. That will have to be up to Arthur for the most part. The main issue will be to get *him* to accept who and what he is. If he is gay, and as I said, I'm pretty sure he is, he'll have to deal with his family.

Sebastian said, "I'm so glad to hear he's going to come down this summer. He's so nice, guys and handsome too. We have the same birthday and everything. He has blond hair like you Walt only it's lighter. He's got blond hair everywhere." Seb stopped, realizing what he'd said.

"Whoa, partner." laughed Chris. "Exactly how did you discover that piece of information?"

"Uh, he told me."

"It just came up in conversation?"

"Well, yeah. He was telling me about his conversation with Walt. He said Walt asked him about pubic hair. You did, right, Walt?"

"Yeah, I did."

"That's when he told me he grew pubic hair when he was twelve and it's blond."

Walt said, "Well if he was willing to tell you that, he's probably gay. I can't see a heterosexual boy volunteering that sort of info to another boy he just met a few hours before. Did he ask about yours?"

"Uh huh. And I told him mine's black."

Chris asked with a grin, looking Sebastian directly in the eyes, "Anything else, Seb?"

Sebastian thought for several seconds in silence and then said with a grin. "He showed me."

"Showed you what?" asked Chris and Walt at nearly the same time.

"His blond pubic hair. He let me touch it too. He's gay, isn't he? A straight boy would never do that, would he?"

"Damn, you work fast," laughed Walt. "Did you show him yours and let him have a feel?"

Sebastian giggled and said, "Uh huh. It was fun."

"I bet it was," said Chris. "Yeah, he's gay. No doubt about it. Looks like you might have landed your first boyfriend, Sebastian. No wonder you guys were crying as we left."

"He was crying too?" asked Sebastian. "I had to get in the car and look away. He was crying too?"

"Yep," said Walt. "He was wiping his eyes with his shirt sleeve and sniffling. As soon as we pulled out, he ran back in the house."

Chris asked, "Did you guys do anything else? Was my joke about pricking your finger on target?"

"No. But I wish it was," giggled Sebastian. "I sure would have liked to have seen more. Walt, have you ever seen him naked?"

"Yeah. I helped my mom change his diaper once when he was about a-year-old. I was about ten or so when they visited us in De Land that time. Why?"

"How big was it?" asked Seb with a grin.

Walt laughed and said, "He was only a-year-old, Seb, for heaven's sake. Maybe it was an inch long at the most. I'm sure he's grown a bit since then. You'll have something else to look forward to this summer. Maybe I'll buy you guys a tape measure for your birthdays. Criminy."

Chris said, "Sebastian, for now, you need to relax. Summer will roll around soon and then you guys can maybe get to be even closer friends. I see a bulge in your britches, so maybe we need to change the subject before you have to change your undies."

Chapter 19
Winter and Spring - A Vow and a Ring

The return to Jacksonville after the winter vacation trip was uneventful and all three resumed their lives. Walt had two more terms at Jacksonville University to complete before earning his bachelor degree in commercial art. His class load was fairly heavy during the winter term which would run from January through mid-March. His final spring term would be no less demanding.

Chris's public science theatre program dealing with rocks, minerals, and fossils was very popular especially with young visitors; everyone under sixteen received a mineral, rock or fossil specimen from a grab bag, before leaving the theatre. The three had spent the last few days of their journey homeward collecting specimens at several well-known sites throughout North Carolina, Tennessee, and Georgia. As promised, they were able to visit the ruby mines near Franklin North Carolina and spend some time and money in the various rock shops in the town. The rear end of the station wagon was dipping a little low with the weight of the materials by the time they reached Whisperwind Apartments on Powers Avenue.

Sebastian could barely wait to get home so he could call Arthur. In fact, at one campsite in Central Georgia, Sebastian turned up missing from their site prompting Walt and Chris to go searching for him, not without a certain degree of panic. They found him feeding quarters into a pay phone beside the camp store chatting merrily away on a long distance call with Arthur. Upon their arrival, he ended the conversation with a short-lived smile. Both Chris and Walt gave him hell for wandering off, whereupon he said, "I left a note on the picnic table. You guys were busy washing and separating rock specimens at the restroom, so I left a note."

Upon their arrival at their site, they discovered that Seb had indeed left a note. It was a small scrap of paper held down by a Coleman Lantern standing on the table. Only a few inches of it was visible. It said simply:

Went to store to make a call
Love Seb

"Arty was surprised to hear from me so soon. He said he's going to start bugging his mom about going to Florida as soon as school starts back up."

Walt asked, "So, you didn't tell him that she's planning to do it anyway did you?"

"No. I told you I wouldn't and I keep my promises. Gees, you guys have to start trusting me. I'm sorry you were worried about me being gone, but I'll always leave a note or let you know somehow."

Sebastian moped around a bit until Chris and Walt sat him down and explained that they trusted him, but because they were responsible for him and loved him so much, finding him missing had caused them to panic.

Walt put it best, "How would you feel if we didn't care enough to worry? You're like our son, Sebastian. You're a part of our family, not just some kid we pal around with. The thought that someone might have snatched you, or harmed you, made us half-sick with concern. Turn it around, kiddo. How would you have felt if you'd come back from the phone and not been able to find us?"

That put things in a whole new light for Seb, so he agreed he could have done a little better job of letting them know and promised to always do so in the future.

Winter gave way to spring and the bond between Chris and Walt grew ever stronger. Their partnership seemed destined to be a long term thing as neither faced any type of domestic crisis during the first nine months of their relationship. Chris was beginning to discuss with Walt the possibility of buying a home in the area as he was very pleased with his job. Mrs. Wilkinson and the rest of the museum administration were extremely complimentary of his work so far. Attendance at the Science Theatre was growing for it had become a major feature of the museum's offerings.

At a full and formal staff meeting in early March, Mrs. Wilkinson announced that a major donation and matching fund grant, totaling sixteen million dollars, had come their way. The museum was about to expand its floor space by over four hundred percent by adding on a new, three-story building beside the existing structure. It would include a new and much larger planetarium, a new science theatre, where science shows, as well as plays and other events, could be presented. The four hundred seat auditorium, designed to look like a Victorian period, science lecture hall, would have full theatre lighting, a state-of-the-art sound system and funding for a larger stock of demonstration equipment. The target date for opening was two years away and initial construction would begin in a month.

Chris was informed, in a separate meeting with Mrs. Wilkinson, he would be promoted from Physical Science Curator to Science Director and his salary from the school system would be changed from a teaching position to an administrative standing. Basically, he would soon be paid the same as a school dean or vice principal with the opportunity for advancement to principal level in the years to come if he earned a master degree.

The new planetarium would have a sixty-foot diameter dome instead of the existing forty-foot diameter hemispheric screen. Mr. Trace would be promoted in the same way that Chris had been. Richard Pike was to become the Assistant Museum Director and take more of an active part in the general administration of the facility.

These staffing changes would be taking place in advance of the completion of the new building so the new directors could be a part of the planning and implementation of the institution's growth.

On a sad note, Mrs. Wilkinson announced that six months after the completion and grand opening of the new addition, she would be retiring as would Ms. Nelda, the secretive and odd lady who minded the stored collections. Chris was informed that six to nine months before the new science theatre opened he would be able to hire a full-time Physical Science Curator to assist him with the theatre's operation and would oversee a new Life Sciences Curator position as well. He would also be allocated funds for a part-time staffer to help present shows on weekends and some school days.

Chris could hardly wait for Walt to arrive home from classes that afternoon. He'd made reservations at Crawdaddy's Restaurant for a private room for him, Walt and the Selkirks, Libby, Nigel and of course Sebastian. He told Walt only that he had some big news to share and wanted to celebrate in style with him and their closest friends. Walt's curiosity was intense as Chris kept him in suspense until they arrived at the restaurant and were joined by their friends. Once they settled into a private, third story room overlooking the wide Saint Johns River and ordered their meal, Chris asked a waiter to please serve everyone champagne. Seb received sparkling grape juice.

Libby, being a museum employee knew, of course, what was coming. She and Chris had planned the dinner party and decided that even Nigel would not know the news until their dinner announcement and celebration. Libby had been promoted to Conservator of

Collections and would be gradually replacing Ms. Nelda who would soon be retiring and had reluctantly agreed to begin computerization of the museum's vast inventory of artifacts and items. The two would be working closely together over a two year period to accomplish the task.

Once everyone was served champagne and had ordered their meals, Chris stood, tapped his glass and shared the good news with everyone. A few mouths stood agape as he finished his presentation. He'd brought along copies of the architectural drawings of the new building additions all senior staff had been given and passed them around the room. One was a drawing of the interior of the new Science Theatre. He turned the floor over to Libby who announced her own promotion after which everyone applauded once more.

Just before the food arrived, Nigel tapped his glass and asked to speak to everyone.

"My friends, all of this good news is stupendous. I was going to wait a bit until college terms were over to make an announcement of my own, but considering all that has happened; I'm going to share my good news tonight as well. I am proud to announce that I will be offering a senior position to a new graphic artist and designer of my acquaintance who just happens to be earning his bachelor degree in June. Walt, of course, you are free to decline, but I will be utterly crushed and never forgive you if you do. I heard you once say that you were concerned about finding a job after graduation due to the stiff competition in the commercial art world. My friend, I need the best artists and designers in the city for my company and if you accept my offer this evening I will have one. What do you say, Walter?"

Walt was looking pale as he nodded and managed to finally make a few words leave his lips. "Oh, Nigel, I... I don't know what to say. I was thinking about asking you after graduation, but... "Walt was shedding a few tears by now and choked a bit before going on.

Nigel said, "It's exceptionally easy, Walt, just say yes."

"Oh yes. Thank you so very much. I will do my very best for Selkirk Promotions. Thank you."

"Wonderful. That's all settled. I'll tell you more of what I have in mind for you later. I'm venturing into a whole new aspect of advertising and feel you will be the best man to be at the helm."

"Thanks once again. I'm speechless."

"Good. We've all talked far too long," said Nigel. "The food is arriving and I am absolutely famished."

The rest of the evening was magical as everyone shared in the exciting future for both families.

Once Walt and Chris returned to their apartment, Chris suggested they take a shower together before partaking in their favorite pastime of making love.

Later, as they lay nude beside one another and before they did much, Chris said, "Hon, I want to talk about something very serious before we do what we most like to do. These past months have been the best of my life because of you and your love. I wish we could be like straight couples and get married because if we could, I'd be kneeling right now and offering you a ring. As a matter of fact, I'm going to do that anyway."

Chris got up from the bed, still completely naked and opened the drawer of his nightstand and took out a small box. Walt sat up on the edge of the bed, wide-eyed as Chris knelt before him, opened a small, velvet-covered box, and took out a beautiful gold ring set with a dark red stone surrounded by a dozen or so diamonds.

"Oh my god!" said Walt as Chris took his hand and held the ring out.

"Will, you, Walter Allen Bower, consent to be my life partner, my lifelong friend and my trusted soul-mate as long as we both shall live?"

"Oh, Chris, of course, I will. I love you so very much. You're my living treasure and like you often say, my other half. Yes, yes, a thousand times yes!"

Chris slipped the ring over Walt's finger and gently kissed him. As their lips finally parted he whispered, "Robert Browning put it so well when he wrote, 'Grow old along with me! The best is yet to be, the last of life, for which the first was made.'"

Walt nodded and said, "I hope our lives are very long and filled with the wonder and joy I'm feeling tonight. You've made me so happy, Chris."

Walt was beginning to cry but managed to say, "Oh, I wish I had a ring to give you. As soon as I can afford one I'm going to..."

"No need, I wanted us both to have similar rings and that is exactly what I purchased." Chris reached into the nightstand drawer once more and handed Walt a nearly identical ring. Its center stone was blue. He held out his hand for Walt to put the ring on his finger. Walt kissed him and did so.

Chris then eased his lover back on the bed and made love to him with all the fervor of their very first time together. Both would remember the night for some time to come.

The next morning, which was Saturday, Chris was awakened by Walt's kisses and looked up into his sky blue eyes. Walt had been crying again.

"What's wrong, Walt? Are you okay?"

"Oh, I'm more than okay. Why didn't you tell me there was an inscription inside the ring? It's beautiful."

"I wanted you to discover it on your own. Read it."

Walt swallowed and wiped his eyes before sharing the words out loud:

Walter & Christopher
Two Souls, Forever One

"I wish so much we could be married, Walt. Maybe someday it will happen for gay men and women. Maybe the world will become a little less mean and oppressive to people like us. If it ever happens, I want to be your husband and I want you to be mine."

"I will. In fact, as far as I'm concerned, I am now. I love you more than life itself."

"Thanks, Walt. I feel the same way. God, you're wonderful. I love you with all my heart." Once again they coupled and shared their bodies, their souls and their love.

Chapter 20
Nest Building

Sebastian and Arthur, though several hundred miles apart, celebrated their shared fourteenth birthday on March twenty-sixth. Both boys had been exchanging letters and phone calls throughout January, February, and March. Arthur called Sebastian on their birthday pleased to announce that his mom had decided to visit her sister and brother-in-law in De Land for a few days in early June. He was even more excited to tell Sebastian that she would be allowing him to remain a month with his cousin Walt in Jacksonville after she returned to Eastern Kentucky.

Sebastian, of course, already knew, but feigned surprise and told his friend he could hardly wait to see him. They started making plans of what they would see and do during Arty's visit to Jacksonville. Arty had sent Sebastian a number of photos of himself and his family; Sebastian displayed them in frames on his desk and chest of drawers. He sent pictures to Arty as well and hoped he was as pleased as he was to have them.

Sebastian especially favored a photo of Arthur wearing a bathing suit that had been taken the summer before at Lake Cumberland, Kentucky. Seb was sorry that Arty's suit was of the gym shorts variety and revealed so little, but Art's beautiful chest and golden hair filled Seb's heart with longing and pride that Art was his beloved friend. Sebastian sent Arthur several photos he'd asked Chris to take of him at the apartment pool while wearing a form-fitting, light blue Speedo. When Walt and Chris teased him about it, he said in all sincerity, "You have to use the right bait if you want to land a prize fish."

In early April, Chris and Walt discussed their future and decided it was time to start house hunting. He and Walt took their time reviewing real estate ads and flyers making a few visits to prospective homes in the Southside and Mandarin area of Duval County. By the last few weeks of April, they had narrowed their search down to three homes that especially drew their attention. They were looking for a three bedroom two bath house, somewhere in the forty to fifty thousand dollar range.

Many new homes of that size in suburban Duval County were far beyond their means, even with Chris and Walt's future job prospects and advancements. They were looking for an older home in a semi-rural location with mature trees and a large lot. The home at the top of their list was a twenty-five-year-old, ranch style, brick home on two and a half acres of land slightly north of the town of Mandarin, Florida. Living there would mean a longer commute for both men, but the price, sixty-three thousand, the large backward sloping lot and the home's location on a small, cypress-lined creek that ran into the Saint Johns River a half mile away, made it perfect for their tastes and needs.

The home had been well cared for over the years by a couple now in their mid-seventies and had become more than they could tend to at their advancing age; both were moving to an elder-care condo in Neptune Beach. It was a Sale-by-Owner listing and therefore was more open to negotiation. After discussing the home extensively, Chris made an offer of fifty-nine thousand with a six thousand dollar down payment and the couple accepted. Chris's bank had already approved him for a loan under those conditions, so financing went quickly. The couple asked for two weeks to make their move, so on Sunday, May third, Walt and Chris started moving their things into the house.

Chris had to secure the loan in his name alone even though Walt would be sharing in the costs. So that Walt's interests would be properly covered in the event of Chris's death, Chris set up a living trust agreement naming each of them as the other's immediate heir. They had already done that with their bank accounts and other assets. The title of the house was issued in both of their names as co-owners and both prepared Power of Attorney documents that allowed them to make legal and medical decisions for one another if an emergency occurred.

The house was centered on two and a half acres, separated from other nearby homes by mature hedges and plantings that blocked access as well as the view. The living room was spacious and featured a brick planter separating it from a skylight-lit and spacious dining room. The kitchen was a bit smaller than they'd hoped for, but the size of all the other rooms in the house and the fact it included a screened patio and swimming pool made up for it. The master bedroom opened out on the pool area via a sliding glass door. Two smaller bedrooms opened off the living room on the opposite side of the house from the master bedroom. Another moderate-sized room had been furnished as a library or study and could easily be used, if necessary as a fourth bedroom.

Because the former owners were moving to a furnished condo, much of their furniture was included with the purchase. Other than new mattresses and box springs for the bed frames, little needed to be bought right away. They would soon need a new riding lawnmower, as the one left by the former owners was old and nearly worn out. Included with the house was a sixteen-foot, fiberglass boat with a small outboard engine that could be used to traverse the creek and access the Saint Johns River a half mile away. A small dock was located along the creek.

Chris's parents gave them new linens, towels, pillows as well as a number of power tools including a power drill, a circular saw, a sander, and a weed eater. Walt's family gave them a new riding lawnmower as a house-warming gift. Chris's mom, Amelia, told them she would sew a complete set of matching sofa and chair covers to protect their furniture during casual use and several new sets of drapes for their bedrooms as the existing sets were somewhat faded. The living room draperies and carpet throughout the home were fairly new and would serve for some time to come.

Sebastian spent his weekends with Walt and Chris who hired him to handle most of their lawn care. Their land featured a number of mature citrus trees including several varieties of oranges, two types of grapefruits, a tangerine and a lime tree. In addition, there was an arbor hanging full with soon-to-ripen scuppernong and muscadine grapes. Two pear trees and three pecan trees that would bear nuts in the early fall were in the rear yard of the property too. The front yard was graced with several islands of mature azalea bushes that would blaze with bloom every March, several large dogwoods, two magnolias, and several enormous old live oaks, hung with beard-like, Spanish moss.

A small kitchen garden was located in one section of the rear yard and Walt, who enjoyed gardening, took it on as his project. There were tomato, onion, cabbage and a number of other root vegetables already planted and ready to harvest and enjoy in early summer.

As May drew to a close, Walt was entrenched in his final term's class work preparing for his final exams and could spend very little time at the museum helping out as he usually did. Chris was very busy creating a new summer science theatre show about atomic energy and its early history. He'd called the show *Eve of the Atom* to Walt's groans about the terrible play on words. All three, especially Sebastian, were anticipating the arrival of Henna and Arthur during the second week of June. Walt had sent his aunt a map to help her locate their new home. From there, she could continue on to De Land and his parent's home for the first part of their visit. Sally would not be coming along as she would be entering the seminary immediately after high school graduation.

Sebastian had asked if he could stay at Chris and Walt's new house during the time of Arthur's visit after Henna returned to Kentucky. His parents were consulted and of course had no objection except to tell Walt and Chris that if Walt needed time alone with his cousin, he should let Sebastian know and send him home for a few days. Walt said it would be fine for the boy to stay. He and Chris had already told Libby and Nigel privately that they believed Arty might be gay and discussed the ramifications of that with Seb's parents.

Walt asked the big question almost immediately, "What if it turns out that Arty is gay and he and Sebastian hit it off. How far should we allow them to go?"

Libby grinned and said, "As far as they want. This is Sebastian's time to make the discoveries that all young people have to make. With him and young Arthur we don't have to worry about pregnancy, do we?"

Nigel agreed and said, "The decision will be completely up to you really, as Arthur will be in your care. How would his mother react if she found out those two were experimenting?"

"Not well, I'm afraid. She's a strict fundamentalist and a member of the Church of Christ; they're pretty set in their ways about homosexuality. That worries me for Arty's sake. If he is gay, and I'm pretty sure he is, he's going to have a rough time of it eventually. That's one of the things I want to discuss with him while he's here."

"Does his mother have any idea about you and Chris?" asked Libby

Walt answered, "Not a clue as far as we know. If she did, I doubt Arty would be staying with us."

"That could be a sticky wicket, fellows," added Nigel. "Be careful."

"We plan to. Chris and I have discussed it at length and our main reason for allowing him to visit is to give him a chance to discuss his preference with others who won't condemn and then shun him. I don't think his mom would stop loving him, but, she might drown him with guilt."

Chris joined in. "Walt and I both feel he at least has to know that Walt is one relative who won't reject him if something does happen and his mom reacts badly."

"We'll give Sebastian some guidelines to follow too, so he doesn't overstep his boundaries and cause Arthur and you any grief," said Libby. "You know how he is sometimes. The exuberance overrides the common sense. Keep a leash on him."

"Will do, Libby," said Chris. "It's so nice to have close friends like you and Nigel who know us, love us and accept us. You're not just friends, to us you're family."

"We feel the very same way, Love," said Libby.

On Saturday, June sixth, both the Walker and the Bower family attended Walt's graduation from the University of North Florida. Also in attendance were the Selkirks.

On Thursday, June ninth, since public school had ended for summer vacation, Sebastian was staying the night in anticipation of Arty's arrival the next day. Henna had decided to make the trip in two days rather than one so she would not be so tired from driving. They would arrive at Walt and Chris's home around noon and after a meal with them, would travel the additional hundred fifty miles south to De Land to stay with Walt's folks.

Arthur would be going along with his mother for that part of their visit. On the way back to Kentucky, Henna would drop Arty off with Chris and Walt for a month's stay in Jacksonville with his cousin. From there, she would continue on home alone.

Sebastian helped to give the house a thorough cleaning, tended to the pool and mowed the lawn to make sure everything was looking sharp. He was certainly not a lazy young man and didn't need to be told what to do. He accepted the fact that he was just as much a part of this family as he was his own. By evening, when Chris arrived home from the museum, he had little to do before Henna and Arty's visit, for Walt and Seb had already done it.

Walt would be starting work at Nigel's firm in early July which allowed him nearly a month to relax, gather his thoughts and prepare for his budding career. Nigel had still not told him exactly what his new job would entail, but he was looking forward to the challenge.

That evening, Sebastian asked as usual to snuggle with his friends before going off to his room to sleep. Everyone had gone for a swim in the pool before getting dressed for bed. Once he wriggled in between Walt and Chris he said, "Guys, I need some advice. We've all talked about how we think Arthur is gay like us. If it turns out he is, how should I let him know I'm interested in being his boyfriend?"

Walt said, "Remember, neither one of us were brave enough to show our feelings to anyone when we were your age. We had to go through introverted, gay boys' hell until we were past twenty. Chris is my first boyfriend and I'm his. You'll just have to find your own way. From what you told us, you didn't have any trouble breaking the ice back in January. Hell, you guys were playing with each other's pubic hair within an hour or two. I think Arty will be as anxious to experiment as you."

"Yes, but there's something that bothers me; I just don't want to rush right to the touch and feel part. I want Arthur to know that I have deep feelings for him. I know I only met him for those few hours that one day, but something inside of me keeps telling me that he's special and that I want him to know that I ...well, that I truly love him." Seb looked from one to the other as they smiled at the boy.

Chris was the first to speak. "Sebastian, you never cease to amaze me, son. What you've just said is so very mature and good. You've already learned that sex is more than a few minutes of groping, rubbing, grunting and having an orgasm. Most boys your age are so hooked on the orgasm part; it takes them many years to realize what you already seem to know. Sex is best when it's a product of love. Some guys never learn that, gay and straight alike."

Walt pulled the boy close and added, "God, son, I sure love you. If Arty is gay and you two guys do fall in love, boy is he in for a treat. As I talk with him I'm going to do all I can to make sure he knows that sex is more than a few minutes of pleasure."

"You know, Seb," said Chris. "There is one thing that you need to keep in mind. You guys are only fourteen. He's going to be here a month and then he'll be going home to Kentucky. It will probably be a long time before you and he can see one another again. If you do fall in love, how will he handle that? How will *you* handle that?"

"I know. That worries me too. I'm going to miss him so much. I did after meeting him that one day in January. I sure wish his mom would move to Florida."

Walt said, "I doubt that'll happen, Seb. She's so used to Eastern Kentucky. It's funny how some people get tied so completely to a place, but she's one of them. She grew up there. My mom, on the other hand, was happy to leave once she met my dad. He was working for a trucking company doing diesel engine repairs and had been sent to one of the trucking firm's service facilities for a six month period. It was in Corbin and that's where he met my mom. They had a few dates and before they knew it, they'd fallen in love. When he had to go back to his homeplace in Ocala, he asked her to marry him and she said yes. Leaving Kentucky didn't bother her in the least as she's always been one to adapt to nearly anything."

"How long were they married before you were born, Walt?"

"Well, mom got pregnant within six months after their marriage, but she lost that baby due to a miscarriage after four months. I would have had an older sister if she'd lived. It was nearly a year before they got lucky again and that time I made it into the world, but Mom had to have an operation for me to do it."

"You were a Cesarean baby?"

"Yep, and after me, Mom couldn't have another child, so I ended up being an only, like Chris and you."

"So you don't think your aunt Henna will ever leave Kentucky?"

"No, Seb. She's a mountain girl. She's very different from my mom. Now that Sally is in seminary, she'll stay for sure as their church is sponsoring Sally and my aunt would feel an obligation to stay around there. Everyone hopes that Sally will come back and be the pastor of their church after four years of study.

"So Arthur's stuck there too. Shit! Sorry, that just slipped out."

"It's okay. You have reason to be frustrated," said Chris. "I know it won't help for me to repeat this old quote but here goes, 'Absence makes the heart grow fonder'. If Arty and you do fall in love, your love might have to be tested by old Father Time. There're four years between fourteen and eighteen. Arthur and even you may meet new friends and develop relationships with them. Your love for him might be what's known as puppy love, or your first crush."

"You guys were my first crush. But now I know the difference. I love you guys in a different way. I still have nighttime dreams about making love to you though, but I'm smart enough to tell you about it and not get my hopes up."

"Good for you. We're both glad to hear you say that," added Chris as they both gave the boy a good night hug and kiss before sending him off to bed.

Chapter 21
Reunion

Shortly before noon the next day, Walt and Sebastian heard a car horn beep as Henna's Chevy van turned in along their drive. Sebastian nearly tore the front door from its hinges as he crowded past Walt and ran out to meet their guests. Henna waved as she stepped out of the vehicle and started toward the house. She looked tired and road-weary as Walt embraced her on the porch. Arthur too had rushed from the van and ran toward Sebastian, but at the last moment stopped, looked awkward for a few seconds and then offered his hand for a shake.

Sebastian had no intention of merely shaking his hand. Seb threw his arms around the surprised boy and gave him a bear hug that caused Arty to grunt from its intensity. He grinned and returned the hug.

"Hi, Sebastian, I've really been looking forward to seeing you. Let me give Walt a hug too." He turned to his cousin who was, along with everyone else, watching with amusement the reunion between the two boys. Sebastian had tears in his eyes and still had one hand on Arty's shoulder.

Walt hugged the boy as did Chris who had come home early from work for the occasion and had just stepped out of the house. Arty seemed pleased at the warm reception, but quickly returned to Seb's side and threw one arm around his shoulders.

"Walt and Chris, you fellows have a beautiful place here," said Henna as Walt led them inside followed lastly by Chris. "Whew, I'm glad that drive is over. This afternoon though, we still have to drive on south to De Land. I just need a few hours and I'll feel more rested. The last few months have been stressful and tiring. I suppose I needed a vacation."

Walt said, "I'm glad you finally came to that conclusion. Henna, you have to take it easy sometimes."

She went on: "Since I lost Arthur, I've had so much more to do to keep the place up. With Sally going off to seminary now, it'll be even harder. Arty has been a great help. He's the man of the family now and pulls his weight very well."

192

"I'm proud of you, Arthur," said Walt. "I had every confidence that you would step into your daddy's shoes and take on more responsibility. You're a fine young man." Arty was blushing.

Chris said, "Well, please have a seat and rest a bit before lunch. We hope you like Italian food as today we're having homemade ricotta and sausage-filled Ravioli with fried eggplant, tossed salad and raspberry gelato for dessert. All cooked, by the way, by Walt who is an absolute master when it comes to Italian cuisine."

Walt added, "Seb helped too."

Chris said, "When you come back, on your way north, Henna, I'll be the chef. My specialty is meats, soups, vegetables, and seafood. I'm thinking seafood."

Henna laughed and said, "How do you fellows stay so slim with such a menu. We both dearly love Italian and seafood."

Walt excused himself and stepped away to check on the meal. Sebastian was busy setting the table with Arty's help. Chris and Henna talked about the house and the location.

Arthur stepped close to Sebastian as he helped set knives, forks, and spoons in their places beside the china. "I sure have missed you, Seb. I've never had a friend like you before. I don't know what it is, but you're so different from anyone my age I've ever met. I'm always so darned awkward around other guys my age and with girls, forget it. I never know what to say to them. When I do say something, most of them make fun of me."

Seb asked, "Is there any particular girl you especially like to talk to, you know someone that might be a girlfriend?"

"No. I haven't really wanted to have a girlfriend yet. I'm weird, I suppose. The other boys are crazy about them. It's all they talk about." He whispered, "Tits, boobs, pussies, first base, second base --- I just don't get it yet, how about you?"

Sebastian looked at his friend wondering if he shouldn't just tell him where his real interest was but decided against it. "I'm the same way. The girls at my school are so stuck up and snooty. I simply don't see why other boys get so excited. They tease me too and say I'm gay." Seb was testing the water to see how Arty might react to the G word.

"Yeah, I hate that. I've been teased the same way. I just let it go in one ear and out the other. That's why I punched that boy I told you about back in January. He called me a fairy and a faggot and I got fed up with him. I am who I am and that's all that matters. I'd rather spend a month with you, Walt and Chris than a year with any one of 'em."

"Me too, I'm so glad you're finally here."

Arty said, "I think about you every day. Thanks for the pictures. I have them on my desk at home and I have one by my bed on the nightstand too."

"Which one do you keep by your bed?" asked Sebastian with a grin.

"Uh, one of the last ones you sent. I bought a nice wooden frame for it. It's my favorite."

Sebastian smiled, knowing that the last six photos he'd sent were five by eight prints of him in the Speedo bathing suit. "My favorite picture of you is one of you sitting on the tractor with your shirt off and wearing green gym shorts. You have such an even tan and your hair is so nice looking."

Arthur blushed slightly and smiled.

Soon lunch was served and everyone found a seat around the table. Walt, knowing his aunt's customs, asked her to say grace.

She bowed her head and began, "Dear Lord, bless this food, family, and friends. Help us to be always mindful of Your presence and grace. Guide us in our daily lives that we may continually serve and strive to be more and more like Your Holy Son, Jesus Christ. Amen."

"Amen," everyone replied. Walt was somewhat surprised at the brevity of the blessing as his aunt was typically known for long and involved prayers.

The meal was a complete success. Arthur was amazed at the ravioli as he'd never had it homemade before. Walt explained in detail how it was made from scratch.

Chris said, "This sure is better than that chef boy-are-you-kidding, ravioli that comes in a can." Everyone laughed at Chris's play on words and agreed.

During the meal, Henna asked, "Walt and Chris, may I ask a favor?"

"Certainly," Walt replied and Chris nodded as well.

"As you know we're going to drive on down to De Land later this afternoon. I believe you said it's about a two-hour trip. Walt, I plan to stay with Sis and your dad for a week, but I know Arthur might get bored hanging around with us older folks during that time. Would you mind coming down after a day or two and picking him up so he can spend more time here with you, Chris and Sebastian? I think it would work out better for everyone."

194

"Sure, Mom and Dad already asked us down for dinner on Monday since that's Chris's day off. Arthur can come back with us then. I know he'll fight us every step of the way, but we're going to drag Sebastian along with us too."

Seb grinned and said, "Walt's teasing. I'll be there."

"Wonderful. That works out very well. I need to spend some time with Linda and Steve and do some catching up. Sister talk, family business and what not. I've already asked if Arthur wouldn't mind coming back with you and he's all for it."

Walt said, "That'll be fine, Henna. We'll take good care of him." He gave Arty a hair ruffle as he was sitting beside him.

As soon as the meal was over, Henna said it would be a couple of hours before they would be leaving for De Land, so Seb and Arty took off for Seb's bedroom. Once there, Seb closed the door and said, "Well, we have a couple of hours; what would you like to do? I can take you for a boat ride out to the Saint Johns River, or we could go for a swim in the pool, or just hang out and talk. You're the guest. You choose."

"I'm just glad to be here with you. Sebastian; I've never had a friend like you before. For some reason, you're different than anyone I've ever met. With the boys at my school, it's as though I always have to prove myself. You like me just the way I am and that means a lot to me."

"I'm glad. Like you just said, I like you just as you are. So what should we do?"

"I'd like to swim, but my bathing suits are packed, so the pool might not be the best choice. The boat ride sounds like fun."

"We can still swim. I have extra swimsuits. You could wear one of mine. Tell you what, I'll loan you a suit and we can take a quick swim and then take a short boat ride and we'll still be able to hang out and talk. We'll be able to do everything. How about it?"

"Okay, that sounds good. We're about the same size, so let me borrow a suit."

Sebastian went to a chest of drawers that Walt and Chris had bought for him to keep some clothing here for his frequent visits. He was smiling inwardly as he reached in the drawer and pulled out the light blue Speedo he'd worn in the photograph. He tossed it to Arthur who caught it and looked it over rather wide-eyed.

"Uh, do you have any suits that are like shorts? This one is not the kind I'm used to. It kinda shows everything and I'm a little shy. Is this the one you wore in the photo?"

Sebastian said, "Yeah."

"It looked good on you, but I'd feel funny wearing this around Mom. She's kind of old fashioned. She even said a few things when I got the picture of you in it."

"What did she say?"

"Well, as you know, Mom's pretty religious and she said that you might as well have been wearing your birthday suit. I was afraid she wouldn't let me keep it."

"Wow. Sorry. I had no idea she might be bothered by it. Tell you what. Since she's here today, we'll both wear shorts. I don't want to cause her any reason to not like me. After you come back on Monday night, you can try it on then though. I have the blue one and a green one, so we'll both look like we're wearing our birthday suits."

"That makes sense since we have the same birthday anyway."

"Hey, if you want, once you come back, we can even go swimming in our real birthday suits sometimes. Walt and Chris won't care. I swim in their pool naked every once in a while."

"Really, they don't get mad?"

"No. They're really swell guys. They're like my second set of parents. I love them the same way I love my mom and dad. I'm anxious for you to meet my parents too. They'll be down for a visit just after you come back from De Land. We can go to my house while you're visiting and spend a night there too if you like."

"Cool. I'm anxious to meet your folks and see the museum where you work. Bet it's neat."

"It is. Well, we'd best get changed. Let me get you a pair of shorts. What color, red, blue, green or black?" Seb held up four pairs of gym shorts for Arty to choose from.

"You pick. What color shorts would you like me to wear?"

Seb almost slipped and said what came first to his mind, *clear ones*, but said red and tossed Arty those. He then asked, "What color should I wear? Arthur looked them over and chose the blue ones.

"Where should I go to change?" asked the boy.

"I'm going to change right here. If you're shy, I'll turn my back." Seb was hoping he would say he wasn't.

"I'm a little shy sometimes. I hate changing at school and usually don't play sports so I won't have to shower. I guess we might as well get used to one another though since I'll be staying for a month. Just please, don't make fun of me."

196

"Why would I make fun of you, Arty? I'm your friend and would never do that."

"I didn't think you would. It's just that I'm a little different down below with my blond hair and uh, some other things."

"It's okay. I promise I won't make fun." Seb was thinking, *what other things?* "If you're ashamed because you're a bit skinny, you needn't be. I'm much skinnier than you. You at least have some muscles on your arms. Mine look like sticks. Come on, don't be shy." Seb broke the ice by pulling off his shirt. Arty went to the door and checked to make sure it was locked before pulling off his tee shirt. He unlaced his shoes next, pulled off his socks and looked up toward Sebastian who had already kicked off his shoes and stepped out of his pants leaving only his briefs on.

Seb was grinning and said, "You're falling behind, Arty. I'll wait for you to catch up."

Arthur unfastened his belt, unzipped his jeans and wriggled out of them. He was wearing boxer-style underwear. "I keep asking mom to buy me underwear like you wear, but she always gets me boxers. I think I'm the only boy at school who still wears boxers. It's kind of embarrassing. She says that your kind shows too much, like the swimsuit, I guess."

"Okay, Arty, the moment of truth. We have to get you past the shyness. On the count of three, we'll both put on the clothes we wore on March twenty-sixth, fourteen years ago."

"Please, don't make fun of me. I know you didn't when you saw my stupid blond hair, but there's more. Promise?"

"I promise." *What could be affecting him this much,* thought Sebastian. "Ready? One, two, three." Both boys dropped their underwear. Sebastian saw absolutely nothing wrong with Arty. He was beautiful. Arthur's eyes went right to Sebastian's privates and opened wide in surprise.

"You're just like me. You still got skin too!" Indeed, Arthur was uncircumcised and very well endowed for a fourteen-year-old. He was large and not only that, he was starting to get larger. Arthur scrambled to pull on his shorts as he was getting an erection quite rapidly. Seb was keeping up in that department too and because he knew Arty was shy, he dressed quickly as well.

He's gotta be gay, thought Sebastian as he continued to see the elevation behind the red shorts. Arty went to the desk chair and sat down.

"Why are you so shy about being uncircumcised? It's hardly ever done to boys in England and most of Europe. Aren't there other boys at your school who are the same as you?"

"I've only seen one other at school and he's a Korean kid. I guess they don't do it much in Korea."

"It's that way in a lot of foreign countries."

"Really? I don't know exactly why I never had it done when I was born. Mom said if it had been up to her she would have had it done because the Lord told Abraham to do it to all little boys when they were born. I think Daddy, who was uncircumcised, wanted me left alone down there and made the decision. He wasn't as religious as Mom is. She told me that since God told people to do it, it should be done and since Jesus was a Jew and had it done, even Christians should do it out of respect to Him and God both."

"Well, I don't mean to criticize your religion, but what does a little extra skin on your dick have to do with loving God. If he didn't like the extra skin down there, he should have made us that way in the first place. I saw a painting of Adam and Eve once and Adam had a foreskin just like you and I do. Of course, it was just the way the artist thought he might have looked."

Arty said with a grin, "Uh, sorry I was so shy. If I'd known you were like me, I wouldn't have been so shy. I'm glad we're alike that way too. I hated being different at school since all the other boys had been operated on. With that and my blond hair, I'm kinda shy and ashamed."

"Uh, Arty, You have nothing to be ashamed about. You have a very nice looking body."

"Uh, so do you. I won't be so shy next time."

"Good. Let's go for a swim?".

They did just that and for the next two hours spent most of the time in the pool. They romped and played like nine-year-olds and were exhausted by the time Arty was due to leave. They decided that after Monday they would have more time for boating and other activities so they spent all of their time in the pool. When they changed back into dry clothing, neither experienced uncontrollable reactions although both were doing some quick peeking whenever possible.

By three o'clock it was time for Henna and Arthur to head south to De Land and the Bower home. The goodbyes this time between Sebastian and Arty were not as emotional as the one back in Kentucky, for both knew that they would soon be spending a whole month together. Both could hardly wait to begin.

Chapter 22
Great Expectations

On Sunday, June eleventh, the day before the visit to De Land, Nigel and Libby asked Chris and Walt over for dinner and asked if it would be all right for Sebastian to stay with them while they took a two week trip to England to visit relatives. They knew Sebastian would no doubt be spending much of his time with Arthur during his visit anyway and would be mostly bored seeing English relatives he barely knew or remembered. Walt and Chris assured them he would be more than welcome to stay with them.

That evening Nigel also announced he was putting Walt on the payroll at his firm right away, but for the first month or two, he preferred that Walt work at home on developing the new project. It was Nigel's intention to keep what Walt had been hired to develop a secret from the rest of his staff to make sure his company was the first to explore this new venture. Some employees, if they learned of Nigel's concept, might leave and sell the idea to competitors before it got off the ground.

Nigel explained in part what was about to happen. "Walt, a number of deliveries will soon be arriving at your home. Two gentlemen will be helping you set up the equipment and train you in its use. Plan on working with them for three or four days. Fellows, my firm will be making your house payments this summer for rental of your space."

Chris said, "There's no need for that, Nigel. We're friends. You're welcome to... "

"Won't hear of it, Chris; it's a tax deduction anyway. Good for you, good for my company."

"Uh, any special space requirements we have to consider?" Walt asked.

"If you and Chris have no objection, I believe one corner of your two car garage will suffice; that or a portion of your study. Two desk-like workstations will come along with the equipment."

"The study will be best. Can you at least give me a hint of what this is all about?" asked Walt with a grin. "I'm dying of curiosity and need to start thinking about what you expect of me."

"All right, but everyone here is sworn to secrecy."

"Okay, who do I have to help you murder, Nigel?"

"The competition. Namely, Sunshine State Billboards, Inc." Everyone laughed.

"As you may be aware, more and more businesses are recognizing the mind-boggling value of modern computers. Up until recently, they have been unbelievably expensive, large and difficult to use. Their primary function has been two-fold: number crunching, that is, high-speed mathematical computation and the other has been data processing and information storage. A new field is beginning to unfold." Nigel paused for effect.

"And what is that?" Walt prompted.

"Computer graphics. There are less expensive machines now being offered that have the capability of graphically rendering high-quality artwork in not only two dimensions, but in three. I've seen demonstrations of what is possible and I have decided that our company should branch out into this new frontier."

"Nigel, I have very little experience whatsoever with computers. I have no idea how they work," said Walt with alarm.

"So much the better. You'll start from the ground up without any preconceptions. The beauty of the machines I've ordered for you is that you don't have to know how the bloody things work. You won't have to program them. They already have what's called software installed; that's the programs that make them work. They will be artist-ready. All you have to do is experiment, design and develop ways these machines can render, animate and create artwork that we can sell to our clients. They're made by a company called Apple and the variety I've purchased is called a Macintosh."

"Okay, I've used one of those a little bit at the university. I've seen some of the graphics they're capable of rendering. You're right; they're pretty amazing."

"Up until now, we've concentrated on outdoor advertising and signage. That may soon be a fading field. More and more, people are complaining about billboards cluttering up the environment and frankly, I rather agree with them. They make a lot of money for us, but they're bloody ugly. I want one part of our company to move into television ad creation with cutting edge animation and graphics that grab the attention and basically blow people's minds."

"This is kind of scary, Nigel. I hope I'm up to meeting your expectations. I just thought I was finished school. Looks like it's back to the books. Am I up against any sort of deadline? Will I have others to help me if I need assistance?"

"The answer to your first question is yes, sort of. I'm setting a year as your developmental period. By this time next year, I hope to be able to start offering our customers something unique and visually amazing to help sell their products on television. Currently, graphics animation for television and even for motion pictures has been the old Disney-style of cell-by-cell animation or that horrid, stop-action, modeling clay rubbish. Both are time-consuming to produce and very expensive. A one minute, full-color, cell animation segment for television today can cost a company up to a half million dollars for bare minimum effects and graphics."

"Wow, that much?" asked Chris.

"Indeed. High-end material like Disney Studios might turn out can cost well over one or two million for a one minute spot. Computers can take an artist's basic sketches and generate high-quality animation with very little human intervention. It's top quality animation too, with full color, full texture, 3-D movements; the works. Wait until you see what these machines can do, Walt. Disney isn't the only Walt in the business now."

"You've set some high hurdles for me to jump over, Nigel. I'll do my very best, but if I feel I'm not up to this task, I'll let you know right away. I did take a few courses dealing with animation, so I have the basic concepts to work from."

"I know. I've seen your transcript and your work. You'll do fine and if you need assistance, let me know and I'll make sure you have it. The company is in very good shape, but I see a need to keep up with the future. I don't know if you fellows invest money in stocks or not, but if you do, Apple would be a safe bet. The cost per share is low right now too. In fact, Walt, I'm doing Apple investments for employees now as a benefit, so you'll be banking shares anyway."

"I'm grateful you have enough confidence in me to let me get in on the ground floor of these ideas. Once again, thank you."

"You're family as far as Libby and I, and of course Sebastian, are concerned. Listen, there's another concept in the works at a number of major universities that I want our company to be a part of. A group of computer specialists at several high-tech schools have been developing a way for computers around the world to work directly with one another and connect users through their computers. These developers are saying that within a decade, people will have small computers in their homes that will allow one to share all sorts of information at very high speeds and barely any cost. The whole thing will be funded by *advertising*, my favorite word. Imagine a massive network of home and business computers all across the nation and even the world. I can foresee so many ways that cutting edge advertising could make a fortune using such an interconnected network."

Walt said, "Think I need any classes concerning computers, Nigel?"

"No. Once you see these machines and what they can do, you'll adapt right away. I want you to think like the artist you already are and how these new gadgets can benefit from your artistic eye and mind. We'll hire a computer specialist if you need technical help."

"Wow, I don't know what else to say. It sounds like an exciting challenge. I'll do my best for you."

"I'm counting on it."

After supper that evening, Sebastian went home with Chris and Walt as they would be going to Walt's family home the next morning. Walt's mind was awhirl with all the new ideas Nigel had planted there. Nigel had loaded him down with a number of brochures and manuals about the graphic design computers he would soon be receiving and Walt spent nearly an hour reading through them, becoming more and more amazed and excited about the challenge before him.

As usual, Sebastian snuggled with them before going off to bed in the room he normally used when visiting. Seb would be sharing the room with Arthur during his visit and he'd done a bit of rearranging, with Chris and Walt's permission, moving the twin beds side by side instead of apart. He could hardly contain himself as he imagined all sorts of things that might happen there this summer.

After Seb went off to bed, Chris asked Walt, "Hon, what are we going to do if Arty starts wondering about our sharing a room?"

"Yeah, I've been doing a lot of thinking about that. I plan on having a second bird and bee talk with him right off the bat. I'm nearly certain he's gay and probably scared to death his mom will find out. If he admits it to me, I plan on telling him about us. I'll see how he reacts to that and of course, swear him to secrecy. If he deals well with it, I'm going to bring you into the discussion, if you don't mind. I want him to see how much love there is between us and what might be possible for him."

"What if your aunt ever finds out?"

"Well, she put me in charge of the subject, didn't she. I'm not going to lie to the boy and reinforce some false hope that he'll someday change. Religion or not, he'll eventually have to make his own decisions about sex, faith, and his future. Hell, with Sebastian here, he may have to make some decisions about his sex life this summer. I think he has it just as bad for Seb as our Little Lord Loverboy has for him."

Chris laughed and said, "Yeah, maybe you and I should start a pool to see how long it takes for those two to lose their virginity. I'd give Seb about three days before he's in Arty's pants."

"Remember, Chris, they've already *been* in each other's pants exploring the marvelous wonders of pubic hair."

"Oh yeah," Chris had to laugh. "I'd almost forgotten that; you're right. Seb's a fast worker. You better have that talk with Arthur right away before he has a single night alone with Sebastian. That might help ease the guilt and make things a lot better for him if it does happen. His first experience with love and sex should be special and not fettered by fear and guilt."

On Monday morning, just after breakfast, Walt, Chris, and Sebastian set off south along Interstate 95. The distance to De Land was roughly a hundred fifty miles and they arrived shortly before eleven o'clock in the morning. Walt's folks gave them a warm welcome. Sebastian had visited before and felt very much at home. He and Arty went off together right away to the guest room where Arty was staying. Sebastian gave him a hug as soon as they were in the room. Arty seemed surprised, but responded in kind and hugged him back.

"Hope you don't mind it when I hug you, Arthur. You're my best friend and Chris and Walt, as well as my parents, have taught me that there's nothing wrong with showing another person how you feel. I love you as my best friend and want to let you know."

"It's okay. I like it; just don't do it in front of Mom, or the other adults. They might not understand and think there's something wrong with us."

"What would be wrong with us, Arthur?"

"I don't know. Nothing I guess, but Mom's so --- you know --- so religious. She once said something about two men we saw in Corbin. They were..." He hesitated.

"What, Arty?"

"They were dressed kind of funny and one gave the other a kiss, right there on the street. Mom said they were homos and would end up in hell for kissing each other. I was only about ten then and didn't understand what was really going on."

"How about now, Arty?"

"Yeah, I guess they were queer, you know gay."

"Does it bother you as much now?" asked Sebastian.

"No. I've heard more about gay guys and I feel it's their business who they like and who they want to kiss. I don't think they'll go to hell. I don't think anybody knows for sure about that stuff anyway."

"You mean going to hell for sins and stuff?"

"Yeah. Seb, I'm gonna tell you something real private, because I trust you more than any other person I know."

Seb thought, *Here it comes. He's going to tell me he's gay.*

That wasn't the case however for Arty said, "Sometimes, Sebastian, I hate going to church with Mom. The people at our church are nice in some ways, but in other ways, they're so hateful. Our pastor gets to going sometimes about sinners and it makes me feel funny. He starts naming who *he thinks* is going to end up in hell. He talks about teenagers who have sex before they get married and about gay people and alcoholics, gamblers, prostitutes and just about everybody who isn't a *God-Fearin' Christian,* as he puts it." Arty had put on a television evangelist voice that caused Seb to nearly choke with laughter.

"You sound just like one of those television preachers. How's he know who God will be mad at?"

"That's just it, he don't. But those people at our church listen to him as if *he's* God. Seb, when I turn eighteen, I'm not going to go to church anymore. I hate it there. I suppose I'll be going to hell too for saying that. Sally and I are a lot different when it comes to religion. I sure as hell won't be going to a seminary." Arty had to laugh at his own play on words.

Seb chuckled too before saying, "I understand and I don't think you'll go to hell. I'm not even sure there is a hell. It might just be something people have made up to make kids and even grown-ups scared enough to behave."

"Do you go to church, Seb?"

"We go to church sometimes at the big Episcopal cathedral in Jacksonville, but the priests there talk more about loving and helping people in need and not judging people. The Episcopal Church in America is like the Church of England we went to in Liverpool. They don't ever preach against gay people or any other folks just because they're a little different."

"I wish Mom would take us to a church like that. I get tired of hearing what hell's going to be like if you sin. It's so damned depressing."

About that time the boys heard Walt's mother call them for lunch, so they left the bedroom and joined the others around the table. Walt's mother said the grace this time and it was really short. The meal was roast pork with potatoes, gravy, salad, fresh corn on the cob and cherry pie for dessert.

After the meal, Chris, Walt, and the boys went for a drive to Blue Springs State Park so the boys could enjoy the natural springs there. The water was chilly as always, but not quite as bad as Ichetucknee Springs had been. Being early summer, there were no manatees in the water, but Arty fell in love with the place as he and Sebastian dived with snorkels and face masks trying to find fossils on the bottom of the headspring area. Shark's teeth from long ago, as well as fossil stingray mouth parts, were common and both boys came away with a few examples of each. Arty was thrilled to find one shark's tooth that was nearly an inch long. Walt told him he'd buy a chain to which he could attach it and wear it around his neck.

Upon returning to Walt's family home it was getting late in the afternoon, and they had to return to Jacksonville, so Walt asked Seb to help Arthur gather up his things as he would be going with them. Art was excited and probably glad to leave the older folks behind and join his buddy at last. After a two hour drive north, they finally pulled into Chris and Walt's place and went inside. They'd stopped at a Denny's along the way for supper, so there was no need to fix a meal. Chris and Walt both decided to go for a swim in the pool after the trip and were joined by the boys who spent most of their time teasing, climbing on and aggravating Walt and Chris who both enjoyed the horseplay as much as the boys.

Sebastian noticed that Arty seemed to enjoy close physical contact with him, hanging on his back, grabbing him around the waist from behind and tickling his feet, belly, and sides. Once or twice he felt Arty brush over his front and did nothing to discourage him. In fact, he did it once himself and saw Arty grin as though he knew that Seb had done it intentionally.

Chris and Walt noticed how carefree the boys were in their play and chatted privately about it. Walt said, "I sure wish I'd met you when I was fourteen. We could have had so much fun discovering love then."

"Yeah. I'm just glad we found each other when we did. We were both a couple of lonely screwed-up nerds. I wish I could give you a big kiss right now, but until you have a talk with Arthur and see where his interests are, we have to be on our best, role-model behavior." They were seated on the second concrete step of the pool and the boys were cavorting in the deep end. Chris felt a hand slid over his way and slip beneath his waistband. "Ooo, I think I'm being sexually assaulted."

Walt giggled and said. "Nope. You're being loved undercover, shut up and enjoy. If I can't kiss you above the water, I damn sure can play with your better parts underwater. Ooo, something down here is alive and growing."

"Pervert. I'm going to have to get back at you in bed later," said Chris.

"Can't wait. Let's go to bed now. I'm sure those two would appreciate being alone for a little while anyway."

"Nope, it's only nine o'clock and you need to have a man to man talk with your young cousin before Seb gets a chance to have a boy to boy encounter of the third base kind."

"Oh yeah, I forgot about that. Let's end the fun and I'll have a talk with Arty. Arthur's sure getting over his usual shyness this evening. He can't keep his hands off Seb. Look at the way he's hanging on his back. Bet Sebastian's feeling something hard and pointy against his backside right now."

"Yeah, and enjoying every inch of it. It's fun watching them make their first clumsy moves, isn't it? I'm sure looking forward to going to bed with you this evening. Watching them has me all hot and bothered. Don't talk too long."

Walt called out, "Hey fellows, sorry to break up your fun, but before bedtime, I have to talk with Arthur about something. It won't take long. Chris has to get to bed soon as he has to go to work tomorrow morning. Everybody out of the pool. Tomorrow's another day."

After the expected groans, the boys complied and left the water. Chris and Walt both noticed the boys' shorts were protruding a bit more than usual and gave each other a knowing grin.

Chapter 23
The Liberation of Arthur

Walt asked Arthur to have a seat on a two-person patio glider while Sebastian and Chris went inside to give them some privacy.

"Having fun, Arty?"

"Oh yeah. This is great. I wish I could stay here all summer long. Seb's such a great friend."

"He's a good boy, Arty and I love him a lot. He's like family to Chris and me. I love you too, son and want you again to know that any time you need someone to talk to about anything, no matter how personal, or difficult a subject, I'm here for you. Remember we had a short talk last January along these lines."

"Uh huh."

"I wanted to ask if any other subjects have come up that you might need to talk to me about."

"Uh, nothing I can think of right off hand, Walt." The boy was looking down at the floor with a slight frown on his face. "You have any questions for me?"

"A few. You look like you might have grown an inch or maybe two since January. Any more big changes in your body you need to discuss?"

"I've got more hair under my arms now, see." He raised his right arm and showed his cousin.

"You sure have. Still a natural blond too. Anything else changing?"

Arty grinned and stammered a bit, "Uh, well, my di... uh, penis has grown some. It gets hard a lot more often."

"That's normal at your age. Remember when I asked you before if your body ever reacts when you think of girls? Has that happened much?"

"Uh, no. It just does it for no reason, most of the time."

"How about thinking about other boys?"

Arty looked at Walt with a mixed expression of confusion and maybe a little fear. He then shook his head no.

"Arthur, I'm going to ask you a question now and I want you to know that no matter what you say, I will be supportive. I have a feeling that you may be worried about something and don't know who to go to for advice. I know your mom would be the *last* person you'd want to talk with about this subject, but we need to talk about it tonight. Do you trust me, son?"

"Yeah, sure. I trust you a lot. I guess there are a few things that I can't talk to Mom about."

"Thought so. Remember, I'm on your side. Arthur, are you worried because you like to think about other boys and sex?"

Arthur just stared at Walt, wide-eyed and full of fear.

"It's okay. Talk to me, son. I love you and want to help. I'm pretty sure I know what you're going through. Arty, are you gay?"

Arthur opened his mouth as though to speak, but closed it and sobbed instead. He leaned forward, covered his eyes with both hands and said in a whisper, "I think I am, Walt. Oh God, I'm afraid I'm going to go to hell someday. I have all these thoughts all the time about other boys --- especially about Sebastian --- and I'm so afraid he'll hate me if he finds out I like to think about him that way."

Walt reached over and placed his hand behind Arty's neck and gave it a squeeze. "Son, it's okay. I'm going to tell you a secret or two this evening and I guarantee, after you hear me, you are going to feel a thousand percent better."

Art moved his hands from in front of his eyes, sat up and looked at Walt through his tears. His lips were vibrating and his nose was running. He sobbed again then turned and flung his arms around his cousin and hugged him tightly, crying with abandon against Walt's chest.

Walt stroked the boy's heaving back and said, "Have you ever wondered, since January, why I live here with Chris?"

Arty separated from his cousin and answered, "No, why."

"If you *are* gay, Arty, it will be okay. I'm gay. I fell in love with Chris last year and it was the most wonderful thing that ever happened to both of us."

Arthur was blinking his eyes and wiping his nose as the reality sunk in.

"You and Chris are gay? Really?"

"Yep. He's my full-time life partner and I hope it lasts forever. You're gay too and that's all right with me."

"Oh God, Walt, I love you. I finally have someone to talk to about this. I've felt so damned lost and alone. Please, don't tell Mom. She'll hate me and make me leave home and..."

"Hush, Arty. Your mother could no more stop loving you than she could swim across the Atlantic. She might be disappointed and confused at first, but she would never stop loving you. Her religion gets in the way sometimes when it comes to subjects like this. Anyway, I'm not going to tell her. That's something only you can do whenever you feel it's the best time to do it."

Walt hugged the boy again and went on, "There's something else too. You've fallen in love with Sebastian, haven't you?"

"Uh huh. I can't help it. He's so nice and likes me and doesn't tease me. Please don't tell him how I've been thinking about him. I don't want to lose his friendship. This could ruin everything. Please promise me you won't tell him."

"Okay, I promise. I won't tell him. You will though."

"Noooo! Please, Walt, don't make me do that. He can't find out about me. Please."

"How else are you ever going to be able to love him like I love Chris if you don't tell him?"

Arty was looking very confused until Walt finally put him out of his misery and said, "Arthur, Sebastian's gay and deeply in love with you too. That's all he talks about with Chris and me. He's damn near been driving us crazy, pining away for you since January."

Arty started sobbing, laughing, hiccupping, or something at the same time. "He's uck, he's a... uck, he's gay too?"

"Get hold of yourself, buddy, or you're gonna choke. Yeah, and he's in love with you. I wanted to have this talk so you two can finally get together and end the misery you've both been going through."

Arty clutched at Walt's arm and said, "Walt, you mean you don't care if Sebastian and I, uh, well, we do things?"

"Son, listen to me. No one in this world is going to change the way you and Sebastian are. It's the way you were born. Have you ever had any thoughts at all about a girl or a woman's body?"

"Huh, uh. Never. It's always been boys and men. I even had a few dreams about you after your visit in January. Chris too, but please, don't tell him."

"Why not? He'd be flattered. Remember, he's gay too. He'll understand. I'm sure most of your fantasies have been about Sebastian though, haven't they?"

"Yeah. Uh, Walt?"

"Yeah."

"How am I gonna tell him? I'm not sure how I can tell him how I feel, right to his face. Will you tell him for me?"

"Sorry, no can do. It's something only you can do and it will make Sebastian so happy to hear you say it. All you have to do is say you love him and want to be his companion. After that, you'll both know what to do. Hug him. Kiss him. And later, when the time is right, make love to him and let him love you."

"But, Walt, we're only fourteen. If Mom were to find out, she'd hate me and never trust me ever again."

"Arty, being gay and fourteen is not the same as it is for heterosexual teens. There are all types of dangers if a teenage boy and girl make love. The main problem is the chance for pregnancy and bringing a child into the world when you're too young to properly care for it. That's never a problem for gay kids, boys as well as lesbian girls."

"Yeah, I see what you mean."

"Remember though, even gay sex has a few dangers. Sleeping around with a lot of gay partners can be dangerous because of sexually transmitted diseases. If you pick one partner to stick with, like Sebastian, you don't have to worry about that."

"Yeah, that's true."

"Being able to make love at such an early age makes the misery of being gay a whole lot less hurtful. Most gay teens don't get a chance like you've been given. They don't have nosy, gay cousins who can help them deal with their problems. Sebastian's parents are one hundred percent behind him. They know he's gay and love him very much. They know Chris and I are gay too and that's why they trust us to help him when he needs advice."

"Wow! They know?" asked Arty as Walt nodded and smiled.

"Your mother, on the other hand, is a completely different situation and will have to be considered in a different way. Has she ever said anything about Chris and I to indicate she suspects our true relationship?"

Arty frowned in deep thought for a few seconds before saying, "She might have a few suspicions."

"How's that."

"Well, once, just after you guys wrote and told us you had bought a house, she said something. She said that it seemed unusual for two guys in their twenties to chip in together on a house knowing they might someday get married and have wives. Then she sort of laughed and said that maybe you both weren't the marrying kind."

"She suspects. I kind of thought she might. I think it's a good sign that she laughed it off. She might be more tolerant than we think. If she thought Chris and I were gay and had too great a prejudice against gays, she would never let you spend a month with us. Maybe your mom might be more accepting than either of us think. My Mom and Dad know now and they love Chris and me unconditionally. Chris's folks are the same way. They love me like a member of the family, which I am."

"Wow. Aunt Linda and Uncle Steve know?" Walt nodded yes. "How long have you thought I was gay, Walt?"

"Chris and I had our suspicions since January. Seb has too. That's all he talks about."

"Does he? That's so nice to know. I really love him, Walt. I can't get him out of my mind. When I'm around him I want to hug him, kiss him and do other, private things with him. My, uh, my penis gets hard every time I look at him or touch him. It's hard right now thinking about all of this."

Walt laughed and said, "I thought I saw a bulge in your swim shorts." Both of them shared a laugh. "So, Arthur, my boy, are you ready to confess your love to Sebastian?"

"Tonight?"

"No time like the present. He had a hard-on when you guys left the pool a few minutes ago too. He's ready to hear it."

"Will you and maybe Chris be there when I tell him?"

"If you really want us to be, but wouldn't you rather do it privately? It's a big moment in your life, Son. One you'll remember for a long time."

Arty thought for nearly a half minute gazing off into the night beyond the patio screen. "Maybe it would be better if we were alone, but right after we talk, I want you and Chris to be around, so if we have any questions, we can ask."

"Okay, I can dig that. You want me to go and find Sebastian. I think he went off to change into dry clothing."

"No," laughed Arty. "He's been in the kitchen, peeping out the serving window the whole time we've been talking. Chris is in there with him too. I wonder if they've been talking about the same thing."

"Maybe. Chris knows what we're talking about. Let's call everyone together first and then you and Seb can talk privately."

"Okay, but if I need you, you'll be close, right?"

"Of course. You'll do just fine." Walt motioned to Seb and Chris to join them on the patio and they soon opened the sliding glass door from the dining room and joined Walt and Arty.

"Hey guys," said Walt. "Uh, Arthur has some things to talk over with you, Sebastian. He may ask Chris and I to join you afterward. So, Chris, how about you and I step back inside for a bit and give these boys a little privacy to work out a few things that have been on their minds for a while. Guys, we'll be right inside if you need us."

Arthur was staring directly at Sebastian with his mouth slightly open and Walt noticed his hands shaking just a bit. Seb was smiling and waiting for Arty to begin.

Just after Walt and Chris left the patio, Seb asked, "What was it you needed to talk to me about Arty? It seemed like you were in a pretty deep discussion with Walt just now. I saw you hugging him and it looked like you were feeling bad at first. Is everything okay?"

"Uh, I, uh, yeah. I had a long talk with Walt and got some good advice about something that's been bothering me. He's super you know. I'm lucky to have him as my cousin. Uh, Sebastian? Uh, you know I'm your friend, right?"

"My very best friend and blood brother too."

"Well, I talked with Walt about how much I like you and it turns out I like you in a different way than I like anyone else. Most of my friends are just friends, you know. We play ball together, or go for a hike together and that sort of thing."

"Okay. I'm following you."

"Sebastian, remember how we talked about things like growing up and getting hair and, well, sex and stuff?"

"Yes. I enjoyed that."

"Well, Sebastian. I, uh, uh... Shit, I don't know how to say this. I really like you a lot, in fact, I guess I sort of *love* you in a lot of ways. And I, uh."

Sebastian moved closer to Arty who stopped talking and just stared at his friend. "It's okay, Arty, you can say it. I think I know what you're going to tell me. Please tell me. I want to hear it so much."

"I... I love you, Sebastian. I love you so much. I want to love you forever. I even want to have scx with you. I'm gay, like Walt and Chris and, oh, Sebastian, please love me too."

"I do, Arthur, I do. I'm gay too and I've loved you since the first time I met you. I want to love you tonight. Right now. I can hardly wait." The two boys flung themselves into each other's arms. Sebastian took the initiative and opened his lips slightly, turned his head a bit to the side and met Arty's willing, warm lips in a long and intense first kiss.

Behind them, they heard the patio door sliding open as Walt and Chris joined them. As they finally separated and turned to their adult companions, both had a glow about them of radiant joy, excitement, and fulfillment. Chris invited everyone into a group hug as Walt and he both congratulated them on their budding relationship.

Walt said, "That was beautiful fellows. I'm so glad we could see that and share in the joy you boys are feeling tonight. It makes Chris and me even more aware of the magic we both share to see that now our two favorite young men can take part in the most wonderful thing two people can experience, and that's true love."

Arthur said, "Thanks, Walt. Thanks for talking with me and telling me that it was okay to be who I am. Chris, I love you too for loving my cousin and being his partner. That sort of makes you my cousin too. And Sebastian, you have no idea how happy I am to know that you love me the way I love you."

"Oh, I have a pretty good idea, since I'm the other half of you now. I promise you, Arthur, I will never hurt you nor do you wrong. I hope we can be together forever. Since I met you in January, there's been nobody else on my mind, or in my dreams. Only you."

"Wow. I feel the same way. The only bad part is that at the end of the month, we'll have to be apart again. I don't know how I'm going to handle that. I wish we lived closer together."

"I know," said Sebastian. "Maybe we can find a way to see each other more often during the year like Christmas or other holidays. Once we're sixteen, we'll get cars and can visit each other that way. Maybe meet in the middle and go camping together in Chris's camper, so we don't have so far to travel."

Walt said, "Chris and I will do all we can to help you guys stay close until you're old enough to be together. This will sort of be a test of your love. Right now, both of you are all excited and I'm sure you both can hardly wait to, *ahem*, get even closer." Everyone snickered a bit.

"You both are pretty young and maybe things will change in your lives that affect what you're feeling tonight. Be prepared for that in case it happens. Sometimes love can hurt."

Chris said, "Walt and I are lucky how things worked out for us. I hope it can be as wonderful for you fellows too. I can tell the love you guys are feeling is strong. It's more than just two gay boys having their first experience."

Walt said, "So guys, tonight is going to be one you will both remember for some time to come. You're both about to cross over the line between boyhood and manhood. You'll share things with each other you've been dreaming of doing for some time. Be kind and gentle. Take your time. Savor every moment of your first intimate experience. One of the most precious gifts we can ever give those we truly love in this way is our body and our sexual selves. Off you go now. Make love, make memories and most of all make each other happier than you've ever been before. Go with our love. Chris and I will be there with you in spirit."

Chris added, "Walt and I will be making love tonight too and like he just said our thoughts will be with you as we join and feel each other's love. You're off on a new adventure, guys. The greatest journey human beings can take is that of love. Have fun. Make each other happy."

Walt and Chris left the two alone. Sebastian looked at Arthur who melted into his arms. Each soon felt the other's hardness pressing between their bodies, insistent and anxious for release. All of a sudden, their hands were everywhere.

Chris and Walt had drawn all of the drapes in all of the windows and glass doors looking out on the patio and pool deck. Sebastian gently pulled away from Arty, bent in front of him and pulled down his bathing shorts to expose his beautiful body. He reached out and caressed Art's sex gently and lovingly. Arty gasped from the intensity of Sebastian's first touch. He warned him to be careful as he felt his control slipping. Seb stopped, stood and kissed Arty once more instead.

Arthur then bent and pulled off Sebastian's suit and took his lover's sex in hand for the first time feeling its hardness and the throb of his every heartbeat. He gently pulled down the boy's soft sheath, exposing its smooth and flawless perfection. Using the young man's natural moisture Art kneaded and pulled at him until Seb whispered, "Careful. Oh god, Arty, it's wonderful."

"You're so handsome, Seb. Are you close?"

"Yes, and it feels better than it ever has in my life."

They were both still standing on the patio deck a few feet from the pool steps. They stepped against one another and pressed their bodies close as they kissed deeply and felt the electric energy of love flowing between them.

"My god, Sebastian, it feels so weird and wonderful. I love it. I love

215

you."

Sebastian said, "Before we go much farther, should we go to our bedroom, or do you want to do more right here? Walt and Chris aren't watching. Nobody is. We can even do things in the pool if you want."

"I'm not sure. I'm feeling so many things right now I can hardly think." He grasped Sebastian's penis once more and fondled it tightly and slowly. Seb did the same for him. Before long they both gasped saying, "Stop!" simultaneously while pulling apart with a giggle.

As they separated, Seb asked almost frantically, "The bed or the pool. I can't wait much longer. I want to feel it with you. I want us to come together. We can do it as many times as we want tonight. I want to do it now!"

Sebastian was nearly frantic with desire as he stood in front of Arty and pawed at his chest, shoulders, and genitals. He covered Arthur's face with kisses as they pressed their young, firm bodies against each other again.

He heard Arty mumble, "The bed. Let's go to bed. Let's go now. Quick." They left their wet bathing shorts behind on the deck before entering the house, both naked and aroused as never before. They stumbled toward their room, closed the door and flung themselves on the bed. A soft light was on allowing them to see one another. Neither noticed that the spread was removed and a soft, fluffy, fur-like cover had been placed across the twin beds ready for them. That had been Chris's idea, both for their pleasure and to save the bedclothes from their love-making. Sebastian pressed Arty down on the furry spread and crawled between his thin, warm legs. He could feel the soft down of blond hair that grew along Arthur's legs. It tickled his cheeks as he pushed his way upward to Arty's sexual center.

Over the next few minutes, each discovered the joy of free and complete love as they coupled orally for the first time. Seb led the way, based upon what he had seen in the camper the night Walt and Chris made love in silhouette. Arty was surprised as he realized what Sebastian was doing, but after the most memorable climax of his life, he took Sebastian the same way and brought unbridled joy and fulfillment to his young English lover.

They made love several times after that, more slowly and in various ways. Afterward, they rested side by side, gently kissing and caressing one another without words for some time. Their eyes and smiles said it all.

Finally Arty spoke, "My god, Seb; that was wonderful. The second time was almost as good as the first. Good lord though, I feel guilty. I can just imagine what my mom would say if she knew what we've just done."

"Arty, we're nearly grown up and what we do from now on in our lives is up to us. Walt and Chris will keep our secret. Don't feel guilty. We are who we are and neither one of us will ever change. Maybe someday you'll choose to tell your mom about who you are, maybe not."

"I might, someday, but I think it'll be a while. Maybe once I'm an adult and not living at home."

Seb nodded before saying, "Until then though, what we do is private. As long as we both want to do this together, nothing else matters. This love is ours and no one can ever take away what we just felt. I know we're only fourteen, but I love you so much and want to tell you something important. Arthur, I want to be your partner for as long as we live. Walt and Chris have decided to join together and be a family; I want us to do the same."

Arty said sadly, "I do too, but, what are we gonna do when I have to leave and go back to Kentucky. It's going to be so horrible to have to leave you, Sebastian. It's gonna break my heart."

"Mine too. But we have to pledge that we'll stay in touch and keep loving each other. I only want you, nobody else. We're probably going to meet other boys who might be gay as we grow up and it's going to be hard to resist wanting to be with them. At those times we have to be real strong and maybe call each other and help each other deal with those feelings."

Art replied, "I love you too much to give in to that. I promise I won't."

Chapter 24
Summer Joys and Sorrows

The month of June was a time of magic for Arthur and Sebastian. Their love grew and flourished as they discovered themselves, growing more and more comfortable in their budding relationship. It was a joy for Walt and Chris as they watched the two boys become young men who could feel comfortable and free in their ability to share emotions and new experiences unfettered by societal pressures.

As the month of June drew to a close, the realization that Arthur would soon be forced to return to Kentucky became more and more frightening to both boys. Twice, Walt came upon Arty crying alone silently just after Sebastian went home for several days when Libby and Nigel returned from England. There were also a few occasions when Sebastian had to be with them for family functions. Nigel and Libby met Arthur and soon came to love and welcome him as Sebastian's companion. They too agreed to make arrangements whenever possible for the boys to be together even if it meant a few airplane trips to Kentucky during holidays so Sebastian could pay Arthur a visit.

Just after July fourth, Arthur started to pack for his return home. Walt had agreed to buy him a plane ticket to Lexington where his mother could easily pick him up. But on July fifth, Walt received an unusual call from Henna in which she asked if it would be possible for Arthur to remain with them for several more weeks. Walt assured her that it would be no trouble and that he hadn't yet purchased the plane ticket home.

"Is there something wrong, Aunt Henna? Anything I can help with?" Walt asked.

"No, I have to make a trip to Frankfort for a few days next week and I thought Arty would probably enjoy more time with you than having to go there with me and stay in a hotel for a few days. I'll be in touch right after I get back. Everything's okay. Thanks for your help. If you need some money for him, let me know."

"No, Henna. He's fine. We're fine. As skinny as he is, he barely eats enough to keep a bird alive. I bought him some clothing the other day; underwear and socks, that sort of thing. He's fine."

"Thanks, Walt, for being so good to him. He looks up to you now and that makes me feel very good. When I get back from Frankfort, I may want to talk with you about a few things concerning Arthur's future."

"Sure, Henna. How is Sally doing at the seminary?"

"Oh, just fine. She's met a nice young man there and they've been dating. I've met him and he's a perfect gentleman. I think those two might be getting serious. He's only a year away from graduation and will become a pastor soon."

"That's great. Give her my love and regards. In fact, let me have her phone number and address and I'll call or write a letter. I'll have Arty write her too." Walt scribbled down the address as Henna read it off.

"Thanks again, Walt, for all your help. I'll keep you and Chris in my prayers. I'm glad you have such a good and close friend. You fellows are good for one another. I have to run now, so thanks again. I love you."

"So long, Aunt Henna; I love you too. I'll keep you in my prayers as well. Be careful in Frankfort."

Walt hung up just as Chris walked into the study where Walt had answered the phone. He'd just arrived home from the museum.

He gave Walt a hug as he asked, "Who was that, Hon?"

"Henna. She asked if Arty can stay another two weeks."

"Oh, that'll break his heart, I'm sure," Chris said with a laugh. He saw the thoughtful look on Walt's face and asked, "Everything okay with Henna?"

"Yeah, as far as I know. She has to go to Frankfort for a few days next week. She said something that has me wondering though."

"What's that?"

"She told me to give you her love and regards and that she was glad I have such a good and close friend. She said we were good for one another."

"Huh. Think she has us figured out?" asked Chris.

"Might be. She said she wants to talk with me about something when she returns from Frankfort. Maybe she's going to ask about us. If she does have suspicions, I don't think it will be a problem. She would never have let Arthur stay with us if she thought we might do him harm."

"Maybe she's even figured *him* out. You know how clever moms can be. Both of our families had their suspicions long before we grew enough balls to tell them."

"True," Walt agreed.

Chris said, "I guess we have to go and break the bad news to Arty now. Where are the two lovebirds?"

"They're out in the boat. Took along the fishing gear and said they'd be back with fresh fish for supper by five. It's near that now, so they should be here soon."

Indeed within twenty minutes, they heard the motorboat approaching the dock along the creek. Both boys soon appeared just outside the screened patio grinning. Sebastian was holding up a string of four, nice-sized bass. Arthur was at a nearby wooden picnic table in the back yard preparing to scale and clean the fish for either frying or freezing. Walt and Chris joined them as they set to work.

Walt said, "Arthur, I have some news about sending you home in a few days."

Arty stopped and looked up worried. "I don't have to go early do I?"

"No. As a matter of fact, we're going to be stuck with you for two more weeks."

Arty and Seb's faces lit up as Arthur said, "All right! I was gonna call mom and ask to stay a few days longer anyway but hadn't gotten up the nerve as yet. How come, Walt?"

"Your mom has to make a trip to Frankfort next week and thought you'd be bored going there with her. Asked me if we could put up with you for a few more weeks and I finally gave in and said yes." He was smiling as Arty started to throw his arms around him in a hug.

Walt said, "Whoa, get away. You have fish innards all over your hands and smell like hell. I'll take a rain check on the hug for later though. I'll never turn down a hug from my favorite cousin."

"This is great, Arty," said Sebastian. "Two more weeks. Thanks, Walt and Chris for letting him stay. I was beginning to dread his leaving. I'm going to miss this guy so much when he has to go home."

"Well, you guys have another two weeks, so enjoy yourselves."

They did.

On July twentieth, Walt and Chris celebrated their mutual birthday. Chris was now twenty-three and Walt was twenty-two. The Bowers, the Walkers, Sebastian and Arthur were gathered at the Walker home in Intercross for a celebratory dinner. After a grand, mid-day meal and several hours of family sharing and conversation, Walt's mom and dad left for De Land. Chris and Walt along with Sebastian and Arthur took a walk along the clay roads to the west of Chris's family home. A few blocks along the way, Walt stopped Chris and somewhat to the boys' surprise, hugged his companion warmly and gave him a soulful and long kiss.

"Happy birthday, Chris," he said as they separated.

"Happy birthday, Walt." They heard the boys giggling behind them as they once again kissed. They turned and saw their young buddies doing the same.

"Hey," said Sebastian as he let go of Arty. "You guys aren't the only ones who can do that. What brought that on? Not that we're complaining."

Chris said, "Well fellows, this spot right here is pretty special to Walt and me. It was just about here that we first kissed a few days after we met. It was here that we told each other we were gay and were falling in love. Whenever we're here for a visit and we pass this place, we have to get a booster shot. Matter of fact, I want to include you guys too. Come on over here. Group hug and kiss."

The boys smiled and drew close and one by one gave their adult companions a hug and a real kiss. Not just a peck on the cheek, but a loving kiss on the lips.

Sebastian teased as Walt and Arty shared their love by saying, "Ooo, kissin' cousins. Isn't that against the law?"

"Back in *Kin*tucky," said Arthur, in a slow Kentucky drawl, "it's a family tradition." Everyone laughed.

Walt said, "All kidding aside, fellows. Chris and I love you guys so much and are glad for your happiness. I know that in a few days, Arty's going to have to go back home, but after these past seven weeks, I have little doubt that you two are like some bird species."

"How's that," asked Arty.

"You're mates for life and I speak from experience. What Chris and I have, I see in you two. Thank God we were able to help you two connect. Walt and I don't need children, we have you guys now and boy-o-boy, are we lucky to have such a wonderful family. You help to complete us."

"I miss Daddy so much sometimes," said Arty with a few tears in his beautiful blue eyes. "Now though, I feel like I have two other dads. I love you both just as much as I loved Daddy. Thanks for helping me understand myself and join up with Sebastian. I agree about that mate for life idea. I'm his, and he's mine."

221

"Ditto," said Sebastian as he hugged his partner close and gave him a quick kiss on his cheek. "I'm sure gonna miss you when you leave. I won't know what to do the rest of the summer. I think the four of us are couples for life."

Chris grinned and said, "Well, I have some special news for the two of you. Walt and I have decided to take two weeks off from work in late August. We'll be going camping and caving in the mountains and just might pass through Eastern Kentucky and maybe we'll take along an English boy and pick up a Kentucky boy and..." He never finished before he and Walt were nearly squeezed to death by their younger companions.

After another group hug, the four resumed walking westward, once more talking about all they'd done and enjoyed during the seven weeks of Arty's visit while making plans for the August trip. The two couples held hands and walked slowly, enjoying nature as they strolled along the deserted clay roads. It was a perfect day, warm but not terribly hot as it had been for several days. Cicadas were buzzing in the trees and a few birds warbled from somewhere nearby in a thicket of jack oaks and wild rosemary. Walt called a halt and pointed off in the distance where the road ahead dipped out of sight at the top of a low hill. There they saw two deer standing and watching them. It was a pair of bucks, rather unusual to see, standing side by side maybe five hundred feet ahead of them.

"I'll be darned," joked Chris. "Would you look at that --- gay deer." Everyone laughed, but as they did so, one of the animals lowered its head and nuzzled against the other's side affectionately before walking off into the brush by the side of the road. His companion followed him.

Sebastian whispered, "I think they just might be gay. Those are both males, right? Do female deer have big antlers?"

Walt said in awe, "No, those are two bucks --- two males. That's the oddest thing I've ever seen. Look at my arm. I've got fricken goose bumps." Indeed his arms were covered with bumps as he shivered and smiled at Chris in wonder. "That was... That was kind of spooky."

Chris smiled and said, "Maybe Mother Nature was sending us a message, guys. Maybe she's telling us it's okay to be who and what we are. I wish I'd had a camera. Maybe it's common for deer to do that. I really don't know. Right now, I don't want to know. For us it was special and I'd like to take it as a sign that things are okay for us.

222

It was four days after the visit to Intercross when Walt got a call from his aunt. She said she would be flying down to visit and would be arriving the next day at Jacksonville International Airport.

Walt was surprised and asked her, "Aunt Henna, is everything okay? I thought you wanted us to put Arty on a plane north?"

"Oh, just a little change in plans, Walt, I'll explain more when I get there. I won't be putting you out visiting for a few days will I?"

"Of course not, it's our pleasure. I'll pick you up. Give me your flight number again. I have a pencil handy now." She gave him the airline, arrival time and number and chatted for a few more minutes before hanging up. Walt shared the news with Chris and the boys. Arty was a little surprised that his mom hadn't asked to speak with him.

The next day, at two-thirty, Henna's flight from Lexington via Atlanta arrived only three minutes late. He and Arty met her at the gate. Sebastian had museum duties and was at work with Chris that afternoon. Normally Arty would have been at the museum too but stayed home to greet his mom at the airport.

After a few welcoming hugs, Arty asked, "Is everything okay, Mom? I was surprised you decided to come down for me."

"Just decided I wanted to get away and come see you and Walt. There's some family business I want to discuss with the two of you once we're at your place, Walt."

As they drove south after leaving the airport, she talked about Sally and her new boyfriend at the seminary and other mundane news about what had been going on back home. She asked Arthur a lot of questions about how he had enjoyed his stay with Walt, Chris, and Sebastian.

After arriving at the house, she took some time to change into more comfortable clothing and then asked to take a walk alone with Walt. Walt was curious and apprehensive at her mysterious manner. This was so unlike Henna. He feared she was about to ask about his lifestyle with Chris.

That was not immediately the case as they walked toward the creek and sat down on several lawn chairs near the dock. Walt waited for her to speak.

"It's beautiful here, Walt. I'm glad for you. You and Chris have a nice place."

"Thanks, Aunt Henna. What's on your mind? I can tell something is troubling you."

Henna sniffed and tears appeared at the corners of her eyes. "Oh, Walt, I'm afraid I have some bad news. That trip I made to Frankfort was to visit the university hospital at Kentucky State University." She paused a moment while gazing outward toward the river in the distance. "I have cancer, sweetheart."

"Oh, Henna. How bad is it?"

"Pretty bad. It's my pancreas and it's probably not going to get better. I'm going to try chemotherapy, but the doctors give me pretty slim odds. The best I can hope for if that fails is maybe six to nine months."

"Oh my god, Henna." Walt left his seat and knelt in front of his aunt and took her hands in his. "Do you need me to come back to Kentucky and help you? Whatever you need I'll do it. I bet Nigel, my boss, would even let me work from up there the same way I work from home here. I'll be..."

She interrupted him, "No, Walt. What I need from you is an even bigger favor. It's Arthur. I don't know how he's going to handle this after just losing his daddy. Looks like it's my turn."

"Don't say that, Henna. You have to have faith in God, the doctors, and the therapy. You have to..."

"Hush, Walter. Listen to me. The next few months are going to be bad ones. The chemotherapy is going to make me terribly sick and weak. I'll lose my hair and... Well, you know, I'm going to begin to look really bad. I don't want Arthur to have to see me going downhill that way. I have to tell him I'm sick. I can't hide it from him, but I don't want him to have to be there and see me withering away."

"Henna, he loves you and will want to be by your side. I'll move up there too for a while and help out. We'll find a way to solve this problem."

"Honey, my mind's made up. I'm going to ask you to be Arthur's parent from now on. He's gonna need a daddy and I want it to be you. I know that he loves you and Chris so much. He loves that boy Sebastian too." Henna smiled at Walt as she ran her fingers through his soft hair and caressed his left cheek. "Honey, I know you and Chris are in love. Why I'd have to be blind not to figure it out. I'm pretty sure Arty's the same way too. It's okay. I still love you all. Am I right?"

Walt was crying openly by now and could only nod. He finally said, "You're right about Arty too. He and Sebastian love each other just as much as I love Chris."

"Well then, sweetheart, he's exactly where he needs to be. He's going to need a lot of love from you, Chris *and* Sebastian this year as he deals with losing me. Maybe we'll have a miracle, and I'll get over this, but we can't count on it, can we?"

"You know I'll do whatever needs to be done. I don't even have to discuss this with Chris either. He loves Arty as much as I do. He'll have two dads who love him."

"That's what I'm counting on. I've already set up things with my lawyer. After Arthur senior died, I took out a life insurance policy for five hundred thousand dollars. Four hundred thousand of that will go to Arty and a hundred thousand and the house will go to Sally along with whatever is in my bank account. The hospital bills will all be taken care of too. I want you to make sure Arty goes to college and has everything he needs."

"I will. Oh, Henna, why is this happening? I feel so damned helpless."

"You and me both, Honey. I'm not looking forward to the next few months, but I'll be more at ease if I know Arty is being loved and cared for here."

"We'll make sure he visits as much as possible, Henna. And when the time comes --- and I hope and pray it doesn't --- when he has to say goodbye, we'll all be there with you."

"Thank you, Walter. I knew I could count on you. I bet you've been walking on eggshells wondering if I knew about you and Chris. I had my suspicions, but that was your business. I know a lot of people who go to my church condemn folks who are different. I don't agree with them anymore. I used to be that way too, but thank God, I've changed. I don't think Jesus would hate anyone His daddy made. We're not here to judge each other anyway. That's His job. I'm doing the one thing I know God wants us to do and that's love one another. I love you and Chris and Sebastian and because my Arty is homosexual he'll have a good loving home to grow up in where no one will make fun of him or misunderstand him.

"Oh Henna, you have my word on that. He'll always be loved and cared for. We'll make sure he gets a good education."

"I know you will. Now both of us need to wipe away the tears and go back up to the house. I'll have a talk with Arthur in a little while. Let's wait until after supper, so we don't ruin everyone's meal. It's going to be hard for me and a thousand times harder for that poor boy. Will you be there when I tell him, Walt?"

"Of course, he'll need us both."

Chris had arrived from work earlier than usual due to Henna's visit and supper was nearly ready when they got back. Sebastian had gone home with his mother for some family function and wasn't present. Walt felt that was probably for the best considering what was to come that evening. After supper, Chris pulled Walt to the side as he'd noticed a change in his partner as well as Henna.

"Is everything okay, Hon? You seemed so distant at supper; so did your aunt. Anything I can do?"

"Oh, Chris, let's step in our bedroom for a few minutes. I'm facing something this evening that is going to be so hard for me and for all of us; especially Arthur." Walt was beginning to cry softly as they entered their room. Chris hugged him as they sat on the edge of their bed and Walt began.

After he finished, Chris held him close as Walt let loose completely and cried as he'd never cried before. It was mostly for poor Arty who was about to learn the bad news. Henna and Walt had set eight o'clock for the meeting with the boy.

Chris said after Walt finished and got himself under control, "Walt, you know I'm one thousand percent behind you. I love Arty as much as you do and will do my part to make sure he has a happy home. God, this is going to wreck him."

"I know. I have no idea how to even begin to tell him. I suppose Henna will do that first in her own way. I'd give anything not to have to tell him, but he has to know."

"Yeah, he does. It'll be rough on him, but that too comes with growing up."

"We'll make sure he visits as often as possible while his mom is still alive. It's probably best that he stay with us though as she'll be in and out of the hospital for the next few months."

"Let's just hope and pray the treatment kills the cancer."

"This is going to be hard for Mom to hear too. She's always been very close to her sister."

"You want me to be there when Henna and you speak to Arthur?"

"I'll ask Henna first. I'm so glad she's not holding our lifestyle against us. She had us figured out last January. Arty too. I told him she'd still love him no matter what if she ever found out. Now with the damned cancer..."

Walt lost control again and wept for nearly five minutes before stopping and saying he was going to take a quick shower to help him relax before their talk with Arty. Chris walked him into the bathroom and helped him undress and get started before going back out and rejoining Henna and Arthur in the living room. He looked at Henna and somehow she knew that Walt had told him. She smiled and nodded.

He came over, sat beside her on the sofa and gave her a hug. Arthur was sprawled on the carpet, immersed in a television show and didn't notice Chris was hugging his mom. She whispered, "Thank you, Chris. I love you too and am not disappointed in you or Walter. I'm glad you found your answers and fell in love with my nephew. You'll make such a good daddy for Arthur too."

Chris bit his lip and looked upward at the ceiling trying to hold back the tears, but it was nearly impossible. He had to step away for a few minutes but soon returned to be with Henna until Walt returned from the shower.

"Thank you, Henna, for understanding the way we are. We'll make sure Arty has everything you want for him. He'll be loved so much. I'm still praying the treatment makes this whole thing moot. You have to keep fighting too. Don't give up or give in. We'll be right there for you when you need us too."

"If it doesn't work, I'm making sure Arthur is provided for; has Walt told you?" Chris nodded yes. "I want you to use some of that money to pay off your mortgage so Arthur and all of you will be sure of having a home. This is such a lovely location. How did you ever find such a place for so reasonable a price?"

"We were very lucky. It was a retired couple who kept the price low. I think maybe they didn't have a complete grasp of how much the place was really worth. We've been thinking of buying the parcels of land on the south and west side of the property since they're undeveloped. That will assure continued privacy and increase the land's value."

"Well, use some of the money for that too. Land is always a good investment."

Walt emerged from the bedroom looking somewhat better. His eyes still looked strained from his tears. He smiled at Chris and Henna. Chris told him they had been talking while he was bathing. It was nearly eight o'clock.

As the television program ended, Arthur turned and smiled at his mom, Chris and Walt. It broke their hearts to have to ruin that

227

beautiful smile and burden that innocent young mind, but it had to be done.

Henna said, "Arthur, sweetheart, Walt and I have to talk with you about something very important; Chris will be with us too as it concerns the entire family."

"Mom, you look sad. You've been looking that way all evening. Is everything all right?"

"Not completely, sweetheart; come here and sit between Walt and me. We have a lot to talk about."

"Okay." Art switched off the television and joined his mom and Walt on the sofa.

"First, some good news," Henna said with a smile. I want you to know that I love you so much Arty and I'm so glad you have such good loving friends in Chris and Sebastian and your cousin Walt right now. Honey, I know that Walt and Chris are gay and I don't mind."

Arty's face turned pale as he stared wide-eyed at his mother. He said nothing, but his one hand was beginning to shake a little.

"I know that you're the same way and have fallen in love with that wonderful boy Sebastian. I love him too."

"Oh, Mom, that's great! I've been so worried you'd not love me if you found out. I didn't want to be this way, but I..."

"You don't have to explain. I've sort of known for some time. Even before you met Sebastian, I could tell you weren't interested in girls like your friends. It's okay. I'm not like all of those other people at our church who judge people and condemn anyone who's different. At one time I did, but thank God, I came to my senses. Come here and let me hug you. That's right. You're my boy forever and I'll always love you."

Arty cried in her arms for a while as Walt and Chris too patted him on the back and shared their love with him.

"I'm so relieved, Mom. Wait until I tell Sebastian. We don't have to keep it a secret anymore."

Henna then said, "Honey, there's something else we have to talk about and this time it's bad news. Much as I wish I didn't have to tell you, it's something you have to know and something you'll have to face. It won't be easy for any of us. We're all going to be very sad for a while."

"What's wrong, Mom. Did something bad happen to Sally?"

"No, sweetheart, this is about me. The reason I asked you to stay here a few extra weeks was that I had to go see some doctors at a hospital in Frankfort. Honey, I'm not well. I have a disease that is going to hurt me a whole lot. Arthur, I may not be able to get rid of this disease."

"What's wrong, Mom? Are you gonna have to have an operation?"

"Maybe that will have to happen too, but for a while, I have to take some really strong medicine that will cause me to be very sick, lose weight and have a lot of other side effects. Honey, I have cancer."

"Oh god no, Mom, please tell me you'll be all right. Please!"

"I wish I could, sweetheart, but I can't be sure. There's a chance I might get better, but I won't give you false hope. This is very serious and not too many people get over this kind of cancer. It's in my pancreas, that's an organ in my tummy that makes insulin and cancer there often spreads everywhere. Mine's an especially bad kind of cancer too."

"Oh, Mom, I can't believe this. It hurts too much. You have to get well. Can other hospitals maybe cure you?"

"I doubt it, honey. I've seen four different doctors and all of them have said the same thing. All I can do now is plan for your future in case I can't beat this. I've asked Walt and Chris to be your parents if I pass on. Since I'm going to have to be in the hospital a lot, Sally is coming back from school for a time to take care of the house. I want you to stay here this year and live with Walt and Chris while I'm taking the treatments. They will bring you up to visit me often. I've made arrangements for that."

"No, Mom, I want to go back with you so I can help you get better. I'm still getting over Daddy and now this is happening. Maybe God is punishing me for being gay."

"No!" snapped Henna with righteous anger. "I'll hear nothing of that. Don't you start thinking you're to blame. These things just happen. Maybe God's calling me home early to be with your daddy. I don't know, but I do know you're not to blame. The fact that you're gay is all right with me because it's the way God made you. I'm glad you've found a nice boy to love who loves you right back. God put him in this world the very same day he sent you to Daddy and me; that was meant to be. Like you, he's very special and I think you two were meant to be together. I'm also glad your cousin and Chris are gay and can make sure you have a loving home where you won't be teased or abused because of the way you are. I'm pleased and proud of my boy and always will be. Don't you dare blame yourself; don't ever do that!"

Chapter 25
Endings and Beginnings

Henna spent a few more days with Chris and Walt before her return to Kentucky. Walt's parents came up for a visit and heard the bad news as well. Linda and Steve Bower took the news hard. After discussing things, Chris, Walt, and Arthur decided it was best for him to go home to Kentucky with his mom and spend a few weeks there to gather his belongings and prepare for the changes coming in his life.

Sebastian had been told of the situation and had done what he could to comfort his partner. Sebastian wanted to go along, but Chris and Walt both said that it was a time for the family to be together and adjust to the trials ahead. Sebastian understood and told Arty he would be there for him when he returned.

Walt arranged for a two-week leave of absence from Nigel's firm and drove Henna and Arty to their home in Kentucky. That allowed Henna, Sally, Walt, and Art to prepare for the difficult times they faced. Arty wanted to spend as much time as possible with his mother before she became too ill from the chemotherapy. He also had to pack up his belongings for the move to Jacksonville.

The fun-loving, carefree boy was no more. Childhood's end had arrived abruptly in so many ways. With Walt's love and support, however, the young man was holding up fairly well. Losing his father the year before had been hard and he was just recovering from that when he was stunned by Henna's news. For several nights, after arriving at their home in Kentucky, he was so distraught that he couldn't sleep.

Twice Arty asked Walt if he could sleep with him. It was the only way he could get any rest. Several nights he slept with his mother, but soon the chemotherapy started causing her to be sick in the middle of the night and she discouraged him from the practice. As she told Walt privately; Arthur had to start letting go.

At least the boy was not showing signs of anger and frustration as many boys his age would normally do when confronted with a no-win situation. Arty instead was very depressed needing love and closeness. Walt spent most of his time with the boy talking him through the grief process, helping him prepare for the move away from home and eventual separation from his mother. Walt assured him that they would still visit her often as the fall progressed and her treatments either helped or didn't.

On July twenty-ninth, Arthur said goodbye to his mother as he and Walt left for Jacksonville. It was a difficult parting. Henna's chemotherapy was weakening her so much that she would now require hospitalization for several weeks. At the end of that time assessments would be made as to whether the treatments were effective or not.

Walt assured Art that they would return for a visit at the end of August, just before school started. Henna would be off the chemo by then and would perhaps feel better. Sally had taken a leave from the seminary to care for her mother and would resume her education at another time. Her boyfriend was extremely supportive and helped as much as possible.

The first night they were back in Jacksonville, Walt and Chris allowed Arthur to sleep between them when he asked. The boy was an emotional wreck and could only sleep if he felt close to someone else. Sebastian came over the next night. His love for Arthur helped tremendously. Having Seb to talk to, love and cuddle with, was the best therapy the boy could have.

As the summer drew to a close, Arty began to adjust to the situation and accept what was coming. Sebastian's love made all the difference. In late August, Sebastian was allowed to go along on the visit to Kentucky. Henna's appearance had changed so radically in the intervening month that she was almost unrecognizable. She had lost nearly eighty pounds and was wearing a wig while her hair grew back. Her eyes were sunken and her skin color was pale. Arty spent as much time with her as possible during the five days of the visit.

Fortunately, the news from the doctors was somewhat encouraging. The spread of cancer seemed to be at a standstill. No other organs had become involved and biopsies of her lymph nodes were encouraging. She had required surgery to remove her pancreas and recovered well from the operation. Now began a waiting game to see if her cancer returned, or remained in remission. Her doctors were somewhat surprised she had done so well. Walt and Arty were feeling more optimistic when they left for home.

Throughout the fall of 1981, Henna remained in remission and surprisingly, had gained back a little weight. She was even well enough to fly south with Sally and spend Christmas with Walt, his parents, Chris, Sebastian, and Arthur. Her color had improved and her appetite was nearly back to normal. The family hoped and prayed that she would fully recover.

Her recovery had helped Arthur adjust better to living with his cousin. He had easily qualified for Stanton Prep and was in several classes with Sebastian as they tackled ninth grade together. It was not unusual for them to spend a week at Sebastian's house and then a week at Arthur's, with Chris and Walt.

Henna had decided that it was best for Arthur to continue living in Jacksonville until she got word from her doctors that she was cancer free. He had adjusted well to life with Walt and Chris and, considering their sexual preferences and his relationship with Sebastian, she felt he was better off remaining there.

Sebastian and Arty celebrated their fifteenth birthday on March twenty-sixth of 1982. Sally and Henna had flown down for a week's visit and everyone had a grand time. All was going well until April of 1982. Henna had started having recurring pains in her joints and neck and a biopsy confirmed the worse. Cancer had returned in force throughout her body. There was no treatment possible this time. The doctors gave her a month. She decided not to tell Arthur until the very last minute but asked Walt to be prepared for what was coming. In mid-May, Sally called to tell Walt that Henna was down to a few days. He now had to break the news to Arthur.

After supper that evening, he and Chris called Arthur to the living room and sat on either side of him on the sofa. Walt started. "Arthur, I have some bad news for you, son. Your mom's cancer has returned and she's very sick." Arthur's face grew pale and his eyes filled with fear. "Son, she's not going to make it this time. You have to prepare yourself for what's coming. Come here."

Walt enveloped his cousin in a fierce hug as the boy's resolve collapsed and he cried like a small child for nearly ten minutes. Chris also held him close rubbing his back and petting his soft, golden hair.

"Can we go see her, Dads?" Arthur had been calling both of them dad for the past six months.

Chris said, "We're all booked on a plane tomorrow morning. Sebastian's coming too. Walt's mom and dad will be flying up out of Daytona to join us. We'll all be there with you, your sister and your mom."

Walt added, "Do you have any questions, son?"

"Is she in pain, Dad? Is she hurting real bad?"

Walt assured him, "No. She's on very powerful pain medication and is comfortable, but, son, I want you to be prepared. She will look very sick. She's lost more weight and is extremely weak. Are you going to be able to handle this?"

"I have to, Dad. I have to be strong for her."

"That's our boy," said Walt. "She's so proud of you. Chris and I are too. You've had a lot on your shoulders this past year and have done so well. We all knew this might eventually come. At least she had an extra year and a fairly good one. We all have some great memories of her visit at Christmas and for your birthday."

"I'm going to miss her so much, Dads."

"I know," said Walt. "We all are. Losing a parent is one part of life we all have to face sooner or later. You've had to face it earlier than most and you've had to face it twice in a very short span of time. It's been hard, but it's left you stronger."

Sally picked them up at the Lexington Airport and drove south to Corbin. Henna had chosen to spend her last few days at home and was under the full-time care of a nurse. After their arrival, she lasted only two days. Arthur, Sally, Walt, and Chris were with her at the end as was her sister, Linda, holding her hands and sharing their strength. Sebastian also visited with her briefly but became too emotional to remain long.

After her passage, Sebastian walked with Art through the woods near his home, holding him close and talking with him as he grieved.

"Seb, I'm so glad I have you and your love right now. I feel so empty and numb. Losing Daddy and now Mom has drained me. Being able to hug and kiss you and know that I have someone I can love and who loves me, makes all the difference. Thank you for being my best friend and my other half. I don't ever want to lose you, Seb. I want us to live together for the rest of our lives."

"Me too, I think if something happened to you, I'd want to die too. I feel like your mom is with your dad now and is very happy. She believed in that and something tells me she is at peace after all that pain and suffering. She loved your dad a whole lot, didn't she?"

"Yeah, I never heard them argue or fight the way some folks do. They always held hands and you could see in their eyes how much they really cared for each other. Mom looked at Dad the same way we look at each other. Walt and Chris have both told me they see the love in our eyes as we look at one another."

"Yeah, they've told me the same. It was so wonderful that your mom understood them and us and the way we are. That made me so happy. Remember when she asked to see me alone just after we got here?" Art nodded that he did.

"What did she say, if it's all right for me to ask?"

"She told me that she was so glad to have me as her son too and that she knew that I would take good care of you and that you'd do the same for me. She said..." Seb had to pause while he got his emotions under control. "She said that she gave us her blessing and that she believed that God would never condemn the kind of love we have like some people at her church might do."

"That makes me feel good too. She had a similar talk with me and gave me an order to never let go of you and to always treat you right just like Daddy treated her. I intend to follow her order to the letter. You're stuck with me for life, as far as I'm concerned. We're so lucky to have Walt and Chris now as our parents. I love those guys as much as I love you."

"I know," agreed Sebastian. "Even though my mom and dad are still alive, I still love Walt and Chris as my second set of parents and my very best friends. There's nothing I couldn't go to them with, for advice or help."

"I know. I can't stand teenagers who hate being around their folks. There's one guy at school, Jeffery Thompson, who is always putting down his dad and mom saying awful things about them because they worry about where he is and who he's hanging out with."

"Yeah, I know him; he's in my trig class. He's a blithering idiot. I hope he realizes someday what a treasure he has in loving and caring parents. He won't have them forever."

"That's so true. I'm glad I loved Mom and Daddy while I had them and never got smart and rude to them. If I had, I'd be loaded with guilt now that they're gone. It's too late for regrets then. I can be proud that I never hurt them or gave them any reason to be disappointed in me."

Seb gave Arty a kiss and said, "I know. It's one of the reasons you mean so much to me. You're so filled with love and respect for the people who are a part of our life. I always try to be the same way with my parents. They've been so understanding with me and the way I am. They knew I was gay pretty early, probably even before I figured it out. They had a long talk with me when I was about eleven and was just starting to grow up. That was when Dad told me it was okay if I liked to look at boys and later love them. He told me how he had mixed feelings when he was growing up and tried both types of relationships."

"I bet you were surprised to hear that from your dad," said Art. He gave Seb a side hug as they walked along the woodland path.

"I sure was, but I was relieved too because I was wondering why I was always wanting to get a look inside my friends' pants, or why I was sneaking peeks at them in their bathing suits. Those things were making me get excited while all my friends were talking about girls and their breasts and sexual parts."

"You had it a lot easier than I did. Gees, every Sunday at church I was hearing about sinful thinking and just knew I was going to end up in hell for thinking the things I was thinking. Up until recently, I was still having a lot of problems with guilt until Mom told me she'd figured me out and that it was okay for me to love you. Seb, I would have gladly gone to hell rather than give you up though."

Sebastian smiled at Arty as he said, "Wow. That's something to hear. I'm like your mom. I don't think Jesus or God Himself would make us this way and then blame us for being who we are. It's people --- ignorant people --- who twist religion to help them make excuses for all the hatred in their hearts and minds. It's their way to get away with and cover up the things they do that deep down they're ashamed of."

They'd arrived at Arty's thinking rock in the boulder-strewn meadow at the base of the old mountain. The boy climbed up on it and sat down. He motioned for Sebastian to join him.

As Sebastian scrambled up and rested beside his lover, Arthur slid against him and encircled Seb with his left arm as he looked around at the nearby mountains and woods. From there none of the ugly strip mines were visible and the forest was still old growth hardwoods much the way they might have been when the land was unknown to white settlers. Both boys sat in silence until Arty finally broke the quiet.

"I wish I could take this place along with me back to Florida. I'm going to miss being able to look at the mountains and woods and sit here where Daddy and I used to talk." Arty paused as he gazed at the mountains. "I wish you could have known him, Seb. He would have loved you too. He was a gentle and quiet man a lot like Chris and Walt." Tears were running down Art's cheeks and Seb leaned over and kissed them away.

"Well, Sally now owns the home property, so we can still come up here whenever we visit. Maybe no one will try to ruin this spot for a while. Chris said they've stopped strip mining in this part of the state, so maybe it will last. I like it here too, but we have some special places now in Florida to enjoy and feel sentimental about."

"Yeah, I suppose we do. Any place is special now as long as you're there with me. We'll make some new memories of our own."

As they were about to leave and jumped down off the wide, flat boulder, Seb said, "I have an idea. Maybe it's silly but I'm going to do it anyway." He picked up a one-foot-wide, half-inch-thick slab of the same black slate Art's thinking rock was made of.

"What are you going to do with that?" asked Arthur.

"Take it home with us. You get that one over there. It's about the same size. We'll put these in our back yard so we both have a little bit of your old home at our new home."

"They won't let us take those on the plane, Seb. Remember we flew here."

"Oh yeah, maybe we could mail them home in a box or something. We'll explain our idea to Walt and Chris and I bet they'll help. They'll both understand. Remember how they always kiss when they walk along that one section of road near Chris's home in Intercross?" Arty smiled and nodded.

After returning to the house, their new parents completely understood and helped the boys make a wooden crate to hold the flat rocks so they could be mailed home. Chris told the boys how the U.S. Postal Service had a special rate often used by geologists whenever they needed to mail rock or mineral samples somewhere. You simply had to tell the local postmaster that you were mailing *Country Rock* for scientific purposes and you could get the reduced rate if the destination was a university, mining company, or *museum*. The day before they flew back, Chris addressed the parcel to himself at the Jacksonville Science Museum and sent it ahead. A little bit of Kentucky was on its way to Florida for his loving sons.

Epilog

Henna's funeral was held two days after the boys took their walk. She was laid to rest beside Arthur Senior in a cemetery beside her church in Corbin. Over sixty friends and relatives attended including Sebastian's parents who had flown up to pay their respects. Walt wished Sally well and offered any help she might need in the days to come. Henna had talked with Sally months before and discussed Walt and Chris's relationship. Sally was very accepting of both them and her brother's and Sebastian's orientation and expressed that to all four the evening just before they returned to Florida.

Even with Sebastian, Walt and Chris's help and love, Arthur was emotionally troubled, unable to sleep well until they flew back to Jacksonville. There, with the help of Sebastian and his two dads, he was finally able to work through his grief and accept his loss.

Walt and Chris allowed Arthur to miss only a few days of school after their return; they felt it was best for him to return to the normal routine of life as rapidly as possible. He and Sebastian finished the ninth grade with excellent grades despite all of the stressful days they were forced to cope with that year.

Walt, utilized a small portion of Henna's insurance money to pay off their loan on the house as she had requested, purchased twelve acres beside and behind their existing land. The remainder was placed in a safe investment fund for Arthur's education and future.

The new addition to the museum would soon be opening and Chris was very busy with preparations for the larger Science Theatre. He was able to hire a full-time assistant curator to help with his growing duties. Sebastian and Arthur both were given junior curator jobs for their weekend duties at the Science Theatre. It was minimum wage for limited hours per week but gave them a greater sense of belonging and put a little spending money in their pockets. It was money they had earned on their own for work well done.

Walt, by now, had developed a successful computer graphic and animation division for Nigel Selkirk's company and supervised several other full-time employees as orders began to pour in from future-thinking clients who realized the potential of computer advertising.

Just after their sixteenth birthday, on March twenty-sixth, both Arthur and Sebastian qualified for their driver's licenses and upon completion of tenth grade in June, they jointly received a new Ford Mustang from their collective parents. That summer, 1983, Walt and Chris purchased a new Dodge travel van and a larger camper and took the young men on a three week trip throughout the American West, visiting seven national parks and collecting fossils and minerals in select locations throughout seven states.

The bond between Arthur and Sebastian was stronger than ever, as was that between Chris and Walt. So many factors had come together to form this unusual and loving family. Upon their return to Jacksonville, Sebastian asked his parents if he could permanently move in with Arthur, Chris, and Walt. They thought the idea was fine as they fully understood the deep love their son shared with Arthur.

The day Sebastian made the move, Chris and Walt presented each of their sons with identical rings much like the ones they too wore. Within were inscribed the words that meant so much to their parents and now would mean much to them:

Arthur and Sebastian
Two Souls, Forever One

In a world that still, in 1983, often dealt harshly with people of their nature, Chris and Walt as well as their adopted son, Arthur and his companion, Sebastian, found happiness and contentment. Love, no matter how different it might be, had triumphed. These two couples faced a bright and exciting future together, no longer haunted by the specter of loneliness, but united by the awesome power of love. But that, as they say, is another story.

The End

Afterword

As I complete this story, I reflect on the many changes that have taken place since the early 1980s, the time in which this tale is set. Today, in 2019, even though there are still complications, complaints, and controversy, gay men and women can be legally married and now enjoy the same freedoms afforded all Americans. They can love and be loved without hiding and lying to their communities, friends, and families, thus removing, or at least easing, the painful stigma they have had to contend with over the past centuries. In many states, gay adoption is now sanctioned by law and has been found to be highly successful for both the loving parental couples and their children who now enjoy a home filled with love.

I was a single, gay man in 1986 when I adopted my son. He was eight-years-old then and filled a need in my life to have a son and feel the joy of parenthood. I wasn't a perfect father, however; and in 1989, made several serious mistakes that disrupted our family and brought much hurt and confusion to my son, my mother and my father. My parents have passed on now. I miss them and their constant and steadfast love during the long years of my difficulties.

Over the years, my son and I --- despite my selfish blunders, errors, and transgressions --- have worked things out and I'm happy to say that he has forgiven me and still loves me as he approaches his forty-second birthday and I celebrate my sixty-eighth on March 26th. He has recently married and I am pleased to now have a lovely daughter as well.

I now dedicate this book to him and to the familial love we share. Thank you, Keith, for all the years of steadfast love you've shown me in spite of my foolish and selfish errors. I love you and your dear wife, Carrie with all my heart and am graced by your forgiveness, your love, and your trust.

Note to My Readers

Two Souls, Forever One, for the most part, ends well for my four protagonists, even though death touches young Arthur's life. I'm told I'm a sucker for happy endings, but those are the kind of stories I most enjoy reading myself. I know life isn't always so rosy, but I am who I am and will continue to favor upbeat resolutions for my characters. The world is a dark enough place with entirely too many sad and tragic stories, so I strive to bring a smile, a laugh or a few tears of joy to my readers. I experience all of the above when writing, for I'm a sentimental softie and write with a handkerchief, or box of tissues handy.

I write primarily for nostalgic, gay, male readers, but I sincerely hope others who read my work --- straight men and women --- can learn to better appreciate the experiences of those of us who were born with a different set of sexual interests. I also hope that a number of gay teenagers --- boys and girls alike --- will read this tale for it may help them make the adjustments in their lives necessary for happiness.

I enjoy hearing from my readers and encourage you to send me your comments, compliments, and gripes. They all help me become a better writer who can satisfy the needs of my loyal readers. I cannot answer all of your letters, but I do try and answer the more pertinent and thought-provoking ones. Hey, if I spend all my time writing answers, who's going to write the stories? You can contact me through Goodreads or Amazon Publishing. Visit my blog at:

https://www.goodreads.com/author/show/18473266.Cameron_DeCessna/blog

By the way, De Cessna is a pseudonym. Authors use pseudonyms mainly to separate their works of imagination from their real lives and the lives of their family. Please respect my privacy.

Thank you for purchasing and reading my novel. I hope I have touched your heart, entertained you, and made your world a little brighter. That, more than anything, is my ultimate goal. You keep reading and I'll keep writing.

**Cameron De Cessna,
North Central Florida --- March, 2019**

Manufactured by Amazon.ca
Bolton, ON

25391888R00133